The Secoi__ _____

Alex Gerlis was born in Lincolnshire and worked as a BBC journalist for nearly thirty years. His first novel, *The Best of Our Spies* (2012), has been an Amazon bestseller and optioned for television serialisation.

The Second Traitor is Alex's thirteenth novel and the second in a new series of four books, spanning the mid-1930s to the late 1950s, through Stalin's Great Purge, the rise of the Nazis, the Second World War and the early Cold War.

Previously Alex has written three series of espionage novels all set in Europe during the Second World War and all published by Canelo.

Alex lives in London, is married with two daughters, and is represented by Gordon Wise (books) and Jethro Thompson (film/TV) at the Curtis Brown Group.

alexgerlis.com

Facebook: Alex Gerlis Author

Twitter / X: @alex_gerlis

Blue Sky: @alexgerlis@bsky.social

Also by Alex Gerlis

Spy Masters

The Best of Our Spies
The Swiss Spy
Vienna Spies
The Berlin Spies

The Richard Prince Thrillers

Prince of Spies
Sea of Spies
Ring of Spies
End of Spies

The Wolf Pack Spies

Agent in Berlin
Agent in Peril
Agent in the Shadows

The Double Agent series

Every Spy a Traitor
The Second Traitor

ALEX GERLIS

THE SECOND TRAITOR

CANELO

Penguin Random House

First published in the United Kingdom in 2025 by

Canelo, an imprint of
Canelo Digital Publishing Limited,
20 Vauxhall Bridge Road,
London SW1V 2SA
United Kingdom

A Penguin Random House Company
The authorised representative in the EEA is Dorling Kindersley Verlag GmbH. Arnulfstr. 124, 80636
Munich, Germany

A CIP catalogue record for this book is available from the British Library.

Print ISBN 978 1 80436 378 2
Ebook ISBN 978 1 80436 380 5

Cover design by Blacksheep

Cover images © Alamy, Shutterstock

Printed and bound in Great Britain by Clays Ltd, Elcograf S.p.A.

Look for more great books at
www.canelo.co | www.dk.com

'O, what a fall there was, my countrymen!
Then I, and you, and all of us fell down,
Whilst bloody treason flourish'd over us'

Mark Antony in *Julius Caesar*, Act II, Scene 2, William Shakespeare

Main Characters

BRITISH

Charles Cooper	Also known as: **Christopher Shaw, Malcolm Lyle** Codename: **Bertie**
Archie	Codename of British traitor
Sir Stewart Menzies	Head of MI6
Lieutenant Commander James McConnell	Invasion Warning Sub-Committee member
Pamela Clarke	Invasion Warning Sub-Committee member
Will Drysdale	Invasion Warning Sub-Committee member
Percy Burton	Head of The Annexe
Joan Burton	Wife of Percy Burton
Murray	Annexe assassin
Phillips	Senior MI6 officer
Simpkin	MI5 officer
Ernest Harvey	MI5 officer

Timothy Kerr-Walters	MI6 officer
Anthony Stokes	MI6 officer
Gilbert Cavendish	MI6 officer
Rex Larkin	MI6 officer
Walter Morley	MI6 officer
The Hon. Edward Slater	MI6 officer
Tommy Browning	MI6 officer
Charles Whittaker	MI6 officer
Nicholas Oates	Senior MI6 officer
Piers Devereaux	Senior MI6 officer
Williamson	Moscow desk, MI6
Beatrice Fletcher	Formerly The Annexe
Donald Hatton	Member of The Group
Arthur Kemp	Member of The Group
Bernard Melrose	Member of The Group
Muriel Armstrong	Member of The Group (Colchester)
Lister	Moneylender in Paddington
Martin	Moneylender in Fulham
Superintendent Martin Docherty	Special Branch

Inspector Jack Brown	Special Branch
George Banks	MI6 officer, Moscow
Rice	Naval attaché, British Embassy, Stockholm
Wates	Assistant governor, Pentonville prison
Richard Marsden	Doctor at St Christopher's Hospital

IRISH

Joe Gallagher	Senior IRA member in Hamburg
Sean Maguire	IRA member in Hamburg and London
Bridget McKearney	IRA/The Group, aka Edith Maple
Duffy	IRA Army Council member
MacBride	IRA Army Council member

GERMAN

Manfred Hoffmann	agent, aka Albert Heath
Helmut Schröder	Abwehr Hamburg, aka Herr Hamburg
Günter König	Abwehr Hamburg

Emil	aka Agent Riga
Ernst Schwarz	Klein's KPD contact
Kapitänleutnant Arthur Klein	Kriegsmarine officer & agent
Wilhelm Canaris	Head of the Abwehr
Grand Admiral Erich Raeder	Head of the Kriegsmarine
Vice Admiral Otto Schniewind	Kriegsmarine
Rear Admiral Kurt Fricke	Kriegsmarine
Frieda	Kriegsmarine secretary
Hauptmann Karl	Heinkel crew
Oberleutnant Reinhard	Heinkel crew

RUSSIAN

Ivan Alexandrovich Morozov	NKVD *rezident* in London
Ivan Mikhailovich Maisky	Soviet ambassador to London
Nikolai Vasilyevich Zaslavsky	OMS officer, Moscow
Osip	OMS NKVD *rezident* in London (deceased)

DUTCH

Arnold Visser	aka Gerrit Hendriks, Agent Tallinn

Marcus van Leeuwen (Henk)   Dutch resistance, Rotterdam

Joop Brouwer   Dutchman in London hospital

Jaap Smit   Resistance, Ijmuiden

Father Maes   Priest, Hoogstraten

Henk   Dutch communist in London

OTHERS

Captain Gustaf Lindström   Swedish tanker captain

Prologue

'Have you ever watched a man die, Miss Clarke?'

Pamela Clarke shifted uncomfortably on the back seat of the car and inched closer to the door and away from the young man sitting next to her, who'd edged a bit too close during the short journey. She pulled her raincoat tight over her knees and gazed out of the window. It was a few minutes after ten o'clock and there was something about London in the blackout that she quite liked: the city had an unusually peaceful atmosphere and was far quieter than usual, as if soundproofed. She thought about Will Drysdale's question. No, she hadn't seen a man die as such, but she had seen her grandfather a couple of hours before he died and a few minutes after, and on both occasions it looked as if he was peacefully asleep.

But she didn't think this was the answer her colleague was after, so she said no, she'd never seen a man die.

'It's not a pleasant business; I can assure you, Miss Clarke. Whether we get to witness it depends on how our chat with the poor fellow goes first, eh?'

A few hours earlier Pamela Clarke had been summoned to the office of their boss, Lieutenant Commander James McConnell at the Invasion Warning Sub-Committee in the Old War Office Building in Whitehall. He explained he'd just received a message from the governor of Pentonville prison.

> A German spy – a Dutchman going by the name of Gerrit Hendriks, arrested in Kent in June soon after landing in a dinghy, convicted of espionage under Section 1 of the Treachery Act in a secret trial at the Old Bailey last month

I

and due to hang at eight o'clock tomorrow morning. Now wants us to know that Gerrit Hendriks is not his real name, and his codename is Agent Tallinn, and is imploring us to bring someone from British Intelligence to meet him as he has important information to share about the German invasion.

'You'd better go and see this chap, Pamela,' McConnell suggested as he stood awkwardly by her desk after handing her the message. 'Very much your area. You've investigated all these other spies they've sent over, haven't you?'

'Very well, sir, and—'

'Not that I don't trust you implicitly, but take Drysdale with you, always useful to have another pair of ears there. I know he's not terribly experienced and has rubbed one or two people up the wrong way, but he's a bright enough chap and speaks decent German.'

'As do I, sir. Can you pass me that file behind you, please? The dark green one. Thank you.'

She opened it and leafed through its contents. 'You say his execution is in the morning?'

'Yes, at eight o'clock. Doesn't give one terribly long, does it?'

'No, sir, almost certainly not long enough. Is there any possibility of delaying the execution if we find we need longer with him?'

'Most unlikely, I'm afraid. This has come up before. The Home Office is always most reluctant to postpone an execution, to the point of outright refusal. The imminence of their execution tends to have a dramatic effect on these Nazi spies. They'll do anything to delay their death. Human nature, I suppose. The most we tend to get, though, is second-rate information of which we're already well aware.'

'I have a feeling, sir, that what this man may have to tell us is going to be more than second-rate.'

'How come?'

She tapped the dark green file now open on her desk. 'The codename he uses, sir: Agent Tallinn. I think I can now discern a possible connection between it and the codenames of some of the other Nazi agents, including ones we've picked up in intercepts. I think Mr Drysdale and I need to get down there as soon as possible.'

–

In the event it took far longer than Pamela Clarke would have liked. Will Drysdale was returning from Bletchley and Lieutenant Commander McConnell needed to make the necessary arrangements with the prison and the Home Office, and by the time the car arrived to take them to the prison it was already dark.

They were met at the prison by a nervous-looking man who introduced himself as Walters, one of the assistant governors. He explained the interview with the prisoner would have to be conducted in the condemned cell.

'Our protocol is that once a prisoner enters the condemned cell, they don't leave it.' He coughed and then laughed awkwardly. 'Until they go to the gallows, that is! Please do follow me.'

Gerrit Hendriks was sitting at a rough wooden table in the middle of the cell, alongside a prison warder. Another warder remained by the door.

Pamela told the prisoner that she and her colleague were from British Intelligence, and they understood he'd asked to see them to share information about the German invasion.

The man looked up properly for the first time since they'd entered the room. He looked older than twenty-seven, the age given in his file, and was thin, apparently tall and with a pale complexion. He appeared to have a cold and his eyes were red, as if he'd been crying.

'My real name is Arnold Visser, and I am from Zwolle, though in recent years I've been living in Amsterdam. I went there to find work as a graphic artist but for long periods I was unemployed. I attributed this to the fact that so many Jews had escaped from Germany, meaning there was an oversupply of graphic artists in Amsterdam. Because of this I joined the NSB, the Dutch Nazi Party. I thought it would give me a degree of privilege in the event of the Germans occupying the Netherlands, but then I rather foolishly stole a car, which turned out to have been requisitioned by an SS officer. Unfortunately, there was no immunity for me. My membership of the NSB appeared to make little difference. I was arrested and told that I had a choice: either to be sent to a German work camp or co-operate with the Germans. I chose the latter option. I was then sent to Hamburg and told I would now be assisting German Intelligence.

'I'd made what transpired to be the error of revealing my fluency in English, and was told I was to be one of a number of agents who'd be sent to Britain to help prepare for the German invasion.'

'How come your English is so good?'

'I studied at the Birmingham School of Art for one year. Let me tell you, had I known what they had in mind I'd have happily volunteered to go to the work camp! But now... this...' Arnold Visser dropped his head and bit his lip, pointing to his surroundings.

'I was captured, as you know, soon after I landed and I accept now I should have been more forthcoming when I was questioned, but the Germans had warned me that they'd know what I was up to and if I betrayed them there'd be consequences for my family. I should have tried to do a deal and offered to spy for the British, or at least told the court that I'd been forced to spy for the Germans, but I was foolish and now here I am, a few hours from my death. I bitterly regret everything. If I had my time again, I'd have turned myself in as soon as I saw that policeman.'

'Tell me about your mission.'

Ask your questions in a manner which invites someone to tell you a story, in such a way that they don't have the option of giving a short answer. You'll draw out more information that way...

'After our training in Hamburg – which only lasted a couple of weeks – we were taken to Boulogne in France and embarked on a small fishing boat. About five miles from the English coast, we were put into a small dinghy and then we paddled with the tide until we reached the coast.'

'You say "we", Mr Visser?'

'A Belgian called Emil, from Antwerp. He was a nice guy, actually. Very smart. I don't know his circumstances, but he'd been blackmailed too by the Germans into spying for them. I was a bit puzzled why they'd chosen him because his English wasn't very good.

'We landed near a place called Dungeness and then we split up. My orders were to go to a small town called Lydd and Emil was to head north to a place called Ashford. We were meant to gather as much intelligence as possible about the coastal defences – gun emplacements and suchlike – and what military units there were in the area. I was given brief training in how to recognise military insignia. They were also interested in the state of the roads – how wide they were, for example.

As soon as I had all that information I was to meet up with Emil – we had a series of rendezvous times close to the railway station in Ashford – and from there we were to go to an RAF base in South London called Kenley and get as much information as we could about it. Then we were to travel to the centre of London and make contact with another agent who would pass our intelligence back to Hamburg.'

'Do you know the name of this agent?'

'Only their codename.'

'Go on.'

'Lübeck: Agent Lübeck.'

Pamela Clarke inhaled deeply.

'And how were you meant to contact Lübeck?'

'I was to go to Victoria Station and telephone a number I'd memorised. No one would answer, but I was to let it ring three times and then end the call before repeating that two more times from other phone boxes. An hour later I was to go to the junction of Wilton Road and Gillingham Street, which I was told was close by the station. Agent Lübeck would then find us.'

'But you never got that far, did you?'

'No, I was arrested in Lydd.'

'This Emil – the other agent. What was his codename?'

For the first time, Arnold Visser hesitated and seemed reluctant to answer. He slumped in his chair.

'I don't want to betray Emil. He had a wife and children. He was also forced to spy for the Germans.'

'You need to tell us everything, Mr Visser.'

'What is going to happen to me? Will my life be spared?'

'Everything you tell us will be assessed, but I do need you to give me the codename for Emil.'

'I don't want to betray him. Has he been caught yet?'

Pamela Clarke sat motionless and didn't take her eyes off the Dutchman. She was aware he was desperate, and her silence dared him to betray his friend.

'Riga: he was Agent Riga.'

'And the telephone number you were to call from Victoria Station?'

Visser hesitated momentarily. 'HYD 1130.'

'And can you tell me anything further about Agent Lübeck?'

Visser hesitated and Pamela raised her eyebrows to indicate she was expecting an answer.

'Only that they were local – that was the word used to describe them: "local".'

'And their nationality?'

'I've just told you, "local" was the only description I was given.'

She leant back and glanced at her watch; it was close to midnight, and at that point the assistant governor coughed loudly and said something about it getting late and the prisoner needing some sleep.

Pamela arched her eyebrows as if to say 'Really?' She was tempted to ask quite why he needed his sleep, given he had such a short day ahead of him. 'I have a couple more questions. You say you were trained by German Intelligence in Hamburg. Can you give me more details please?'

Visser sighed. 'It was by the Abwehr, German military intelligence.'

'And where was this in Hamburg?'

'General-Knochenhauer-Strasse. Not far from the Außenalster lake.'

'And who was in charge of you?'

Another sigh, more hesitation before Visser replied in a quiet voice, 'A man we were told to call Herr Hamburg.'

'Mister Hamburg?'

Visser nodded and his face was now flushed, and when he reached out for a mug his hand shook, and his eyes filled with tears.

'I've told you so much, surely you can help me? I beg you! I'm only twenty-seven and I admit I've made mistakes, but nothing that should cost me my life. I had no intention of carrying out my mission, of spying for the Germans – I promise you! Do you think I'm mad? It was a crazy idea, these silly codenames and then wandering around England in such a conspicuous manner and assuming we'd get away with it. This ridiculous notion of going to London and making a telephone call and meeting someone on a street corner, like a plot from a cheap novel. I had every intention of handing myself in and confessing.'

'Yet it's only now that you're telling us everything.'

'I think that when I was arrested, I must have gone into a state of shock. I didn't behave in a rational manner.'

There was a long period of silence broken by a shout from somewhere in the distance. Pamela recalled Lieutenant Commander McConnell telling her that a prison in the hours before an execution could be the quietest place on earth. Visser was breathing heavily now, as if he was about to vomit.

'I need to speak to people, Mr Visser.'

'What is going to happen?'

'That depends on what those people say.'

—

The assistant governor showed Pamela Clarke and Drysdale down to his office and only left it when Pamela asked him to do so.

When he answered the telephone, James McConnell said there was no need to apologise; he'd been waiting for the call and what the prisoner had to say.

She gave him a detailed summary of what Visser had told them.

'Do you think he has any more to tell us?'

'I didn't get that impression, sir,' replied Drysdale, who'd been listening in on the call.

'The one area which I feel we ought to push is regarding the invasion. Did he have anything further to say about it?'

'Such as?'

'Such as where and when it is likely to be.'

'Not as such, sir.'

'Well, either he did or he didn't, Drysdale. May I suggest you go back and push him on this and then call me back.'

'There is one matter, though, sir, which I do think is of importance. You recall that when you came to see me this afternoon with the message from the governor, it said his codename is Tallinn?'

'Yes – and that seemed to draw your attention?'

'It did, sir, because in that file I referred to I was reminded of the codenames for two other agents who've been captured. There was Rostock, who was caught in Scotland, and Visby, a name Bletchley picked up on a decoded intercept. Well, if we consider all these codenames, sir, then we have Rostock and Visby, which I've just mentioned, then Tallinn, which was Visser's codename, Riga, which is that of the Belgian – Emil – and Lübeck, the contact in London.'

'Plus, there's Herr Hamburg,' Drysdale pointed out.

'Do you see the connection, sir?'

McConnell said not quite.

'The Hanseatic League was a highly effective and wealthy trading organisation involving ports in the Baltic and around the North Sea from the twelfth to the sixteenth centuries. These German agents appear to be named after Hanseatic ports, of which Lübeck and Hamburg were arguably the most important. I would say that there's a German spy ring operating in this country ahead of and in preparation for a German invasion.'

'Which means... what precisely?'

'That we should be on alert for the occurrence or use of any of the other Hanseatic ports, particularly if Bletchley pick them up in intercepts. There are dozens and dozens of Hanseatic ports. If we're aware of them, then that should lead us to more agents.

'And of course, we need to check the contact telephone number for Lübeck.'

'Indeed. We do need to think about the best way of going about this, Pamela, but it does sound as if you're on to something there. Just shows the importance of studying history! More than just a list of dates, eh? But in the meantime, go back to the Dutchman and find out what you can about the invasion.'

–

There was an argument with the assistant governor, who explained that as it was now less than seven hours to the execution the prisoner needed to be allowed to sleep. Drysdale said he couldn't imagine the prisoner would be getting much sleep anyway and Pamela insisted this was a matter of national security.

I insist: just ten minutes.

When they returned to the condemned cell, Arnold Visser was less agitated, as if now resigned to his fate.

'There's still a degree of hope, Mr Visser. If you're able to supply us with information about the German invasion.'

'What do you want me to tell you?'

'When the invasion will be and where.'

The Dutchman laughed. 'Do you really think I'd know that? You seem to be under the impression that the Germans are well organised and know what they're doing. Judging by how half-heartedly we were trained and then left in such an exposed state when we landed, I'd say it's the opposite. All I know is that they are planning to invade this country across a wide front on the south and east coasts. We had little contact with other agents, but from what we picked up, they were being sent to different parts of this country to see where the best places to invade would be.'

'You mention the other agents, Visser. What can you tell me about them?'

'Not much, they seemed to be very much like Emil and me. Mostly Dutch or Belgian, one or two French, an Austrian and a Czech as far as I remember. A couple of Poles.'

'All men?'

'No, some women. There were two others who we only saw from a distance. They were evidently being trained as part of the same operation but for some reason were kept separate from us.'

'And where were they from?'

'That's the thing... As far as I understand from what other people were saying, they were English-speaking but not British, if that makes any sense?'

'American, possibly?'

'I don't think so. I'm familiar enough with the American accent from movies and they weren't American. I overheard them once in the corridor. I thought they could be Scottish, but then Scots are British, aren't they?'

'And names?'

'No one ever used their real name, I only found out Emil's when we were on the boat to England. Everyone was referred to by a codename.'

'Can you recall them?'

'I've told you Emil's. As far as I remember, they were all names of ports. There was Rostock, who came over before us, and Gotland, Bergen, Danzig... As I say, all ports. I hope that helps.'

'And when?'

'Pardon?'

'When will the invasion be?'

'All I ever picked up in Hamburg was gossip. At one stage in our training, we were told that once we reached London, we'd probably go to ground for a few weeks because it wouldn't be long until the invasion. One of the officers training us suggested we wouldn't have to wait more than three months for this. Given that we came over in June, that would suggest September.'

'One final question. This Herr Hamburg, you say he was in charge of the Abwehr operation in Hamburg?'

'Yes.'

'Do you have any idea of his real name?'

Visser shook his head. 'All I know is that he is the man who threatened my family in Zwolle. I have to be careful.'

'That suggests you may know his real name? Come on, Mr Visser, this could save your life.'

'I want to rest now. I have nothing further to say to you.'

–

Lieutenant Commander McConnell arrived at the prison just after six in the morning and met with the governor, after which he told Pamela and Drysdale that they were to stay to witness the actual execution.

'According to the governor, it's not unknown for a prisoner to make a last-minute confession when they see the noose or it's wrapped round their neck. It's possible he may well divulge more information then. It's not going to be a pretty sight, though I'm assured it is very quick.'

Outside the condemned cell they met the executioners, introduced to them as Mr Cross and Mr Pierrepoint. They explained that the execution chamber was just twenty feet from the condemned cell.

'We aim to dispatch them in under thirty seconds from our entering the condemned cell,' said Cross.

'Not much time for a confession, then,' muttered Drysdale.

They waited in the narrow corridor between the condemned cell and the execution chamber, a small crowd of them, silent and nervous. Pamela watched as the two executioners studied their watches and then at a minute to eight, they nodded to each other and swiftly entered the cell.

Moments later, Arnold Visser was marched out. He paused briefly when he came face to face with Pamela; he was drained of colour and trembling as he half nodded before he was pushed on his way. They followed them into the execution chamber, and she gripped Drysdale's forearm when the rope came into view. It was such a shock; she couldn't imagine how the Dutchman must have felt.

By now his legs were being strapped as he was positioned under the rope, a hood already over his head, and as the noose was being carefully placed over it there was a pause of just a few seconds, though it felt like an age. They could hear his breathing and what sounded like a gasp before one of the executioners pulled a lever and the trapdoor sprung open.

Arnold Visser disappeared through the floor, the rope taut ahead of them, swaying with the dead weight of the man's body.

–

As they left A Wing, a voice called them back. It was Walters, the nervous assistant governor, clutching a piece of paper.

'The warders tell me the prisoner wrote this just before he was taken from his cell. He said to give it you.'

Pamela opened the folded piece of paper.

Herr Hamburg – Helmut Schröder.

She passed it to McConnell. 'I think we may now know who Herr Hamburg is.'

Chapter 1

Hamburg
May 1937

'And how is your father?'

The two men stared at each other as if they'd each seen a ghost. Manfred was unsure as to who was more shocked, himself or Helmut Schröder, the man sitting opposite him in the interrogation room in Gestapo headquarters on Stadthausbrücke. The man he'd grown up calling *Lieber Onkel* or 'dear uncle'.

'It's some time since we last had any contact.'

'You fled Dresden, too?'

Manfred nodded.

By May 1937 Manfred Hoffmann was a desperate fugitive. Two years previously, at the age of just nineteen, he'd fallen out with his family in Dresden. They'd enthusiastically embraced National Socialism, and he despised everything they stood for. When it became clear the feeling was mutual, he headed to Berlin which, in the circumstances, may have felt like entering the lion's den but he knew enough about the city to sense he could be safer there. He enrolled at Humboldt University to study medicine and was soon regarded as an outstanding student.

But despite being the Nazi capital, Berlin retained a liberal under-current – or underground at least, with plenty of low-key groups of like-minded students and intellectuals. It was in one of these groups, which met in the cellar of a bar on Ackerstrasse, that Manfred met Hannah, a beautiful girl who'd also studied at Humboldt before she was thrown out because her mother was Jewish.

They quickly became very close, but someone informed on him and one day he was summoned to the dean's office, where he was shown photographs of himself and Hannah and given the opportunity to denounce her and deny they were in any kind of relationship.

Manfred refused to do so, insisting he was proud to be in a relationship with her. He was then ordered to hand in his student pass and all his textbooks and told he was no longer on the course.

His life went downhill after that. He spent far too much time in the cellar below the bar on Ackerstrasse and developed a reckless approach to life, not especially caring what happened to him. One evening in April 1937 he was walking through Prenzlauer Berg and saw a man he knew from the bar struggling with an SS officer who was evidently trying to arrest him. Without thinking about the consequences, Manfred went to the man's defence and pulled the SS officer away, causing him to hit his head on the pavement.

Someone had recognised him and informed the police, and a warrant was issued for his arrest and he fled Berlin. That was when he became a wanted man, a fugitive. He knew better than to head back to Dresden. The first place he could think of was Hanover, which he thought of as more civilised, but in fact it felt as menacing as Berlin. One morning, he only just made it through a checkpoint near the station and was convinced he was being followed. After that he jumped on the first bus out of the city, which was how he ended up in Osnabrück. He waited inside the railway station, coming up with a plan of sorts. He'd take a night train to Hamburg and from there try to get a boat to Britain or even Denmark, or maybe even cross the border by foot to the Netherlands; just so long as he got out of Germany. He was unsure what his chances were, but he did know that as Hamburg was such a large port and a city with a left-wing tradition, it was a good place to try. On the train he found a seat in the third-class carriage. Sitting opposite him was a man just slightly older than himself with whom he got talking. The man turned out to be British and very sympathetic, and when Manfred explained his predicament even promised to try and help him and gave him his mother's address in London.

Buoyed up by this meeting, Manfred felt confident when the train arrived in Hamburg. The man – who'd told him his name was Charles Cooper – had kindly offered to go through the Gestapo checkpoint just ahead of him, the idea being that the Gestapo was bound to be more interested in a foreigner. But the man was waved through the checkpoint, and when Manfred showed his pass he was arrested and taken to the Gestapo headquarters, where it was made very clear to him that he was in serious trouble.

Lieber Onkel Helmut – the man sitting opposite him in the Stadthaus, the Gestapo headquarters – had been his father's closest friend in Dresden; they'd been at school together and were more like brothers. Manfred couldn't recall a time when Helmut wasn't a big part of their lives. His father and Helmut were both enthusiastic supporters of Dresdner, the local football team, and some of his happiest memories were of accompanying his father and Helmut to the Stadion am Ostragehege and then walking home after the game along the banks of the Elbe.

But in the autumn of 1936, there'd been a serious falling-out. Manfred's father joined the Nazi Party and threatened to denounce Helmut as a communist after the two men had a dreadful argument one evening.

'It was so bitter, Manfred, I knew I couldn't remain in Dresden.'

'So, what did you do?'

'I went to Berlin, where else?'

'Like me.'

'Except I wasn't so foolish as to attack a member of the SS. I looked up a former comrade from my days in the Reichsmarine. He put me in touch with Admiral Canaris, who'd been our commanding officer at the Baltic Naval Station. By then the Admiral was running the Abwehr – military intelligence – and we had a long chat and… well… he offered me a job! He said he knew I was reliable and professional and I speak good English, and I was just the kind of person he was looking for.'

'So, you've become a Nazi?'

'Not at all. I'm really a civil servant. I work for the German state, I've always been a patriot and remain one. I'm not even a member of the Nazi Party. Very few Abwehr officers are – not even Admiral Canaris, would you believe. You need to listen to me, Manfred. You're in very serious trouble – you attacked an SS officer in Berlin and became a fugitive and I'm sure you realise the consequences of that. My proposal is this… I can help you escape to England. How does that sound?'

'It sounds good but highly unlikely.'

'My job here in Hamburg is to help establish an espionage operation in England. I'm under some pressure to show I've set up such a network, it's proving to be difficult. I can arrange for you to get to England, and once there you'll be my agent. What do you think? Go to England as a

German spy or take your chances with my friends in the Gestapo here? I know what I'd rather do.'

Manfred also knew, which is why later that afternoon he was released from custody and taken by Helmut to the Abwehr building on General-Knochenhauer-Strasse. A few weeks later, after what could only be described as the most basic of basic training, he was at the docks in Hamburg to embark a merchant ship to Southampton on the south coast of England.

He was travelling on his own identity – Manfred Hoffmann – and his cover story was close to his own story: that he was an anti-Nazi who'd fled Germany as a wanted man after assaulting an SS officer in Berlin. Helmut thought it best to stick to this story because it had a plausible ring to it and could be verified if anyone ever bothered to check it out.

His instructions were to travel to London and settle down there and, once he'd done so, to contact the person who was to be his main link with Hamburg.

But Manfred Hoffmann had no intention whatsoever of becoming a German spy, and he wasn't sure how much Helmut Schröder wanted him to be one either. During his long briefing sessions at General-Knochenhauer-Strasse he got the impression that, more than anything else, he just wanted him away from Germany.

Chapter 2

London and Oxfordshire
September 1939

The village of Flockham was to be found in the lowlands south of Oxford, between the Chilterns to the east and the Cotswolds to the west, and when Percy Burton – the former head of The Annexe – and his wife bought the old manor house in the village in 1928 his brother-in-law, never one generous with praise, had described it as being in the middle of nowhere.

But the relative isolation of the village was one of the features which attracted the Burtons. There being so few people around was a good thing. They could get on with their own lives. And the state of the house meant they could renovate it so it was just right for them. It was a reasonable drive from the village to a number of stations from where Burton could catch a train to London, where he kept rooms for the nights when he remained in the capital.

He was very taken with the history of the village. According to the Domesday Book, in 1086 the land around Flockham belonged to Humphrey de Comeilles, who Burton's extensive research established was a Norman knight who'd come over with William the Conqueror. This pleasant fold of land was his reward for services rendered.

Percy Burton was immensely proud of the village's history. He'd commissioned an artist to reproduce the original Domesday Book entry for the village, which was framed and displayed in the library of the manor house. He never missed an opportunity to elaborate on it for any visitor. His retirement, he decided, would be taken up with writing an extensive history of Flockham.

That retirement should have come much earlier than it did: in 1931 he'd been asked to set up The Annexe as a temporary branch of British Intelligence. It was intended to last a few months – a year at the very most – but in the event lasted for eight years. But because The Annexe had only ever been intended as a temporary measure, the vetting of those who worked for it was not nearly as thorough as one would have expected, and certainly not as thorough as would later become the case. This meant that although Percy Burton presented to all intents and purposes as a decent sort – reliable and hard-working, if somewhat dull – in actual fact he had a view of the world and of politics which for very good reasons he kept secret.

Percy Burton was deeply concerned at what he perceived as serious threats to the British way of life and, indeed, to the country's security. Increasingly since the end of the Great War and during the 1920s, and certainly during the 1930s, he was appalled by what he saw as threats to British values. He was deeply worried by the threat of communism and the increasing influence of Jews in positions of power. As far as he was concerned, defending the Christian nature of Great Britain, and defending it from communism, was in the best interests of the country: it was certainly compatible with his role at The Annexe. He considered The Group to be patriots, certainly not traitors. Or collaborators. Fostering closer ties between Britain and Germany was, in his opinion, in the interests of the United Kingdom.

Had anyone bothered to look too closely into his own views and contacts, then naturally that would have been most incriminating. At the very least it would have been the end of his career. But no one did bother and Percy Burton, notwithstanding the strength of his views, did a very good job of keeping them to himself. To all intents and purposes, Percy Burton did his job and gave no cause for concern. It helped that he was very careful in his contacts with The Group: always at arm's length, always presenting as a slightly anonymous figure.

Of course, it caught up with him in the end, as he always feared it would. He'd put young Cooper on a clandestine mission to infiltrate the headquarters of the British Communist Party in the centre of London and Cooper had somehow got his hands on letters which talked about a secret non-aggression pact being drawn up between Germany and the Soviet Union.

The timing had been terrible. Burton hadn't been able to consult anyone about this so he took it on himself to sit on the intelligence for a few days. When he did let the Foreign Office know, he did so in such a half-hearted way it took a few days for it to register with them.

But once they realised what had happened, he was summoned to Downing Street, where it was clear an investigation was underway, and Percy Burton had to think on his feet. The last thing he needed was to be the subject of an investigation, because who knew where that would lead, and he had a sneaking feeling it wouldn't take too long for them to unearth something incriminating, despite having destroyed the letters as a precaution.

So, he decided to take the wind out of their sails by acknowledging his error – he characterised it as an oversight, most probably caused by the pressure of work – and offered to resign there and then. To be honest, that had rather taken them aback, as if the last thing they were expecting was for Burton to make matters quite so easy for them. The idea that they could wrap everything up so quickly was quite appealing. Everyone would be pleased with the outcome: MI6 would achieve a long-held ambition to see the back of The Annexe; Whitehall would be appeased by having someone take responsibility for what had happened; and Percy Burton was happy to go in return for an assurance about his pension.

–

That was how Percy Burton had ended up back in Flockham in early September. His wife Joan had been shocked; she couldn't understand, she said, how in the same week that war had been declared he'd been allowed to retire. Had he done anything wrong?

He assured her that now the war had begun, the government wished to streamline their security and intelligence services, and as he was past retirement age… Well, here he was. And if he'd done anything wrong, he wouldn't have his pension, would he?

He'd set about making himself useful, cracking on with a series of odd jobs that had been mounting up and generally trying to ensure he'd remain in her good books.

And for a couple of weeks during September, Percy Burton felt as if he'd got away with it. The weather was almost perfect and he took the opportunity to go on long walks and feel rather satisfied with himself. At least he'd done the right thing; he'd done his best, his conscience more or less clear. Who knew how this avoidable and most unfortunate war would work out – maybe once the British government saw the full might of Germany, they'd do the sensible thing and sue for peace.

He even began work on his retirement project, writing the history of the village, and he spent some time trying to work out the exact location of the ploughlands and the meadow mentioned in the Domesday Book.

And then came the telephone call.

–

It was a Thursday morning in the middle of September, and Percy Burton was in the garden trimming the hedges when the telephone rang, and his wife leant out of the window to say it was for him.

The caller was Simpkin from MI5, a man whom Burton had had dealings with over the years and whom he'd never particularly liked. It was notable there were no informalities, such as asking him how he was or he'd hoped he'd not disturbed him.

'A colleague and I need to come and see you, Burton. We are proposing Monday morning. I trust you'll be around?'

'May I ask what it is in connection with?'

A slight pause as if Simpkin was hesitating.

'We have a few questions, that's all. Shouldn't take more than an hour or two.'

Burton said very well, did they need directions, and Simpkin said no need, they knew exactly where he was.

Although it was not yet ten o'clock, Percy Burton poured himself a large whisky and sat at his desk to gather his thoughts.

It could be nothing, of course, but nor was it beyond the realms of possibility that they'd stumbled upon something. It had long been on his mind that this was a possibility, and he'd prepared for it. He'd been careful to ensure that any incriminating material was kept to an absolute minimum and anything he did keep was very well concealed. The lists of names, for example. Members of The Group. He'd built a false section of ceiling in the summer house in the garden. Even someone who knew where it was would struggle to find it.

But there were the bank account details; he kept the chequebook and statements for the Lloyds Bank account in his safe. They'd have to go, and one or two other bits of paperwork, too, and of course anything relating to Murray.

He did his best to remain calm over the Friday and Saturday. He gathered everything to be destroyed and put it in a bundle in the boot room, and then went to work to hack away a rhododendron bush which his wife had always disliked but of which he was rather fond. It gave him an excuse to start a bonfire, onto which he added the bundle of papers.

The more he thought about matters, the more he convinced himself that if they really did suspect him of anything, then the last thing Simpkin would have done was alert him in the way he had. It was almost certainly nothing to worry about; it probably was just what he'd said – the odd discrepancy and one or two other matters arising from the merger of The Annexe into other intelligence agencies. By the Saturday evening, he wondered if he'd perhaps been too rash in destroying everything. He hoped he wouldn't come to regret it.

On the Sunday morning Joan left early for church, as she was helping with the flowers or something like that. He announced he was giving it a miss this week and settled in his armchair in his study with views over the garden and the field beyond the hedgerow, which he was convinced was one of the ploughlands mentioned in the Domesday Book.

When Burton was a young officer in the Royal Navy, he undertook more than his fair share of keeping watch from the bridge and became experienced at surveying the horizon.

The trick was to observe what was there but which then disappeared. You only tend to spot something when it's gone, he'd been told early in his career. Like the space suddenly appearing on the horizon where a ship was when you last scanned it.

And that's what happened. He'd been looking at the apple tree and wondering why the crop had been so poor, yet when he returned his gaze to the hedgerow, he realised it was not as it had been when he'd last looked at it.

Something had been there, but was there no longer.

A shape, a shadow maybe.

Something, or someone.

And it was then that Murray appeared silently beside him.

–

Burton couldn't recall exactly who it was who'd recommended Murray to him. It was almost certainly someone in The Group, because Murray was definitely linked with it and was sympathetic to its aims, but as with everything connected with Murray it was unclear and hard to pin down.

He was quite the most enigmatic person Burton had ever come across. Almost impossible to describe because each time he met him, Murray always looked different – not just in dress but in every other aspect of his appearance, ranging from height to the way he held himself. Sometimes he was a well-spoken Englishman, other times Scottish or Welsh.

Burton doubted Murray was his real name and he had no idea where he lived, but what was not in doubt was that Murray was a very dangerous man. If anyone was proving to be especially bothersome then the word would come to Burton to sort it out – that was one of the useful functions of The Annexe – and the person he'd get to sort it out was Murray.

Murray had killed ten people on his behalf, but Burton was sure the real figure was higher than that.

The Murray who appeared alongside him in his study that Sunday morning was tall and speaking with an English accent, but looked a bit of a mess, most probably because he'd been concealed in the hedgerow for heaven knows how long.

He'd have seen his wife leave for church and would have rightly assumed he had a clear couple of hours.

'What the hell do you want, Murray?'

'You know they're on to you, don't you?'

'Who?'

'I heard that someone called Simpkin from MI5 is carrying out an investigation. By the sounds of it, you must have been careless. You always assured me that you were so careful, that you minimised any risk, that I wasn't to worry... and now, look what's happened. Has this Simpkin been in touch with you?'

'Yes, he rang me on Thursday to say he's coming to see me tomorrow. He said he had some questions.'

'On what?'

'He said something about wanting to pick my brains. But you don't need to worry, Murray. I've always been careful. They can't possibly have any evidence against me. I did have one or two things dotted around here which one would rather they didn't come across, but they all ended up in a bonfire, so you have no cause to be concerned. But thank you for coming to warn me.'

There was an edge to Burton's voice as he spoke because he knew enough about Murray to know just how ruthless he was, and in truth, he doubted he'd risked coming to Flockham just to warn him.

'Is there anything you want, Murray? Are you short of money?'

'Who else knows about me?'

'Hardly anyone, I've always been most cautious regarding you. I suppose the person who knows the most is Cooper. I've no idea what's happened to him.'

'Nor do I. I've been trying to find him but he seems to have disappeared. I hoped you could tell me if you had any idea where he is.'

Burton shook his head. 'And if you find him?'

'As long as he's alive he's a risk to me. I need to eliminate him.'

Percy Burton suddenly felt enveloped by cold and fear. He could feel his body trembling and he had to clutch his hands to hide his shaking. If Murray perceived Cooper as a risk, then he must view him in the same light.

He knew he was no physical match for Murray and he had nowhere to go. His old service revolver was locked away in the boot room. He was trapped in his comfortable armchair.

'Cooper's mother lives in Belsize Park. I can get her address for you if that's any help?'

'Don't bother, I've already looked there. You say you have nothing here on me?'

'Nothing whatsoever, I absolutely assure you.'

'And to do with The Group?'

Burton shook his head and as he did so he glimpsed the summer house out of the corner of his eye. If he thought for a moment that it would save his life, he'd have happily told Murray to look in the false ceiling, but he said nothing.

'My wife will be home soon and she'll be bringing another couple with her back for lunch. Can we agree we'll both keep all of this under our hats and work out a way of keeping in touch, eh?'

He looked desperately at Murray, who shook his head before reaching into a bag he'd placed on the floor and from it produced a pair of gloves and a cloth, which he soaked in chloroform. Percy Burton tried to get up but Murray pushed him down and held the cloth over the older man's face. Burton struggled for a few moments, but Murray was far too strong for him.

–

Murray moved quickly after that. He was exhausted from having watched the house for the past twenty-four hours and it had been surprisingly chilly the previous night, but luck had been on his side when Burton's wife had gone to church on her own.

He closed the curtain, throwing the room into shade, and in the dim light rearranged Burton's body so that it was in a less sprawled position. He opened Burton's jacket, loosened his tie and unbuttoned his shirt. He could hear the man's short breaths, now slightly laboured. From his bag he produced a syringe and removed a vial of liquid from the sock it had been wrapped in. He carefully drew three hundred milligrams of pethidine hydrochloride into the syringe.

The elderly chemist in Antwerp who'd supplied it to him had assured him that dose should be more than enough.

'One hundred and fifty milligrams would be regarded as the maximum dose for an adult. Three hundred milligrams should be more than enough to induce a heart attack. Make sure it's an intramuscular injection. The deltoid muscle would be ideal.'

'And where do I find that?'

'It's the muscle around the top of the arm. Over the shoulder.'

Murray unbuttoned Burton's shirt and pulled it away from his shoulder and injected him in what the chemist had assured him was the deltoid muscle. Hopefully, this would now present as a natural death. An old man dying from a heart attack.

He'd not even finished the injection when Burton's breaths became even shorter, and he groaned as his face became flushed. By the time he'd finished the injection Percy Burton had stopped breathing. Murray checked for a pulse and nodded in satisfaction when he couldn't find it.

He buttoned up the dead man's shirt and straightened his tie and rearranged his jacket. He took out a flannel from his bag and went into the kitchen to dampen it. When he returned, he wiped around Burton's nose and mouth to remove any trace of the chloroform. He stood up straight and carefully observed the scene in front of him with a degree of professional satisfaction. Nothing appeared out of the ordinary. It would be hard to imagine how anyone could be suspicious.

Murray opened the curtains and slipped out of the rear of the house, past the summer house and through the hedgerow where he'd been in hiding for so long, and into a ploughed field towards the small wood beyond that. The countryside was deserted as he carried on, pausing every so often to check he'd not been followed and to take his bearings. At one point he climbed a hill and as he looked toward Flockham he could see the rooftops of the village. In the distance on the other side of the hill he spotted his car, carefully concealed behind the first line of trees. All being well, he'd be back in London for lunchtime.

All he had to do now was find Cooper.

Chapter 3

England
October 1939

Charles Cooper had fled London in a state of shock on Sunday, 3 September.

He was certain he was about to be exposed as a British Intelligence agent inside the headquarters of the Communist Party in Covent Garden, and when he returned to his apartment in Dorset Square he was horrified to discover that Murray, The Annexe's enigmatic and ruthless assassin, was hunting him.

He managed to leave his flat without being seen and ended up at a hotel in Primrose Hill, where he'd booked himself in under the name Percy Dickens. That was on the Friday; he remained in the room, terrified, leaving it only for meals.

On the Sunday morning, he'd come down for breakfast when Pamela suddenly appeared at his table as if she was expected. Now this senior intelligence officer from The Annexe, who always looked so impeccable and so assured, looked anything but. She chain-smoked and the hand which held her cigarette trembled and her hair was unkempt and it seemed she'd not slept in days, and when she spoke, she couldn't have sounded more ominous.

Don't ring the Pimlico number ever again. Under no circumstances are you to go anywhere near Bryanston Square or your apartment or the house in Willesden. You must not visit or telephone your mother. Do not return to King Street. Do not have any contact with anyone from the Communist Party.

And then he'd asked about Murray, and Pamela said to forget about Murray and about Burton – their boss at The Annexe.

'The Annexe no longer exists. For the time being you are in great danger. That applies to a number of us, myself included.'

And although Cooper was shocked to hear this, it somehow confirmed his sense of dread, that something was terribly wrong and it wasn't a case of him being paranoid. This was compounded when Pamela handed him an envelope which she told him contained cash and a new identity.

'Check out of this hotel after breakfast and leave London, and then disappear for a few weeks. There's a telephone number in the envelope. You're to ring that number in the first week of October, not before then. You're to say you have a violin to be repaired, and the person who answers will ask you what the problem is and you're to say the bridge is broken. They'll then give you instructions.'

Before she left, she'd asked him if the name 'Archie' meant anything to him. Cooper had lied and said it didn't.

And then she'd left the room, and Cooper had watched as she disappeared, wondering whether he'd ever see her again. Then he'd gone up to his room, packed and come down to check out, which was when the receptionist told him that other guests were in the lounge listening to a broadcast by the Prime Minister. Cooper had joined them and listened in shock along with the other guests as Neville Chamberlain solemnly announced that as Germany had refused to withdraw its troops from Poland, '…this country is at war with Germany.'

—

When he left the hotel in Primrose Hill, he paused outside for a minute or two to check he wasn't being watched. He then walked down to Chalk Farm Road to catch the 639 bus to King's Cross, because if he was to leave London and disappear for a few weeks that seemed as good a place as any to start.

The station was crowded, which Cooper found reassuring because the chances of anyone finding him were low, given the thousands of people milling around the concourse. It was notable that men in uniform were now evident and families seemed to be waiting to leave the city as trainloads of people arrived in it.

He looked up at the departure board and at all the destinations served by the London and North Eastern Railway, and he couldn't decide where to go. He could head for one of the big cities, like Leeds or Newcastle or Edinburgh, or a smaller town. He was unsure which would be the safest kind of place to go to, because a city would be big enough to hide in but there was also the danger of bombing now the war had begun.

He realised he really ought to get a move on and saw a train for Lincoln was departing in twenty minutes, which gave him enough time to purchase a single ticket and buy a ham roll and a newspaper.

He arrived in Lincoln at 3:30 that afternoon. It was his first time in the city, and as he emerged from the station he was reluctant to draw attention to himself by asking people where he should go. But the cathedral dominated the skyline and so, like a medieval pilgrim, he found himself drawn in that direction, trudging slowly up Steep Hill with the cathedral on his right and into Bailgate. After a hundred yards or so he spotted a rusty sign for a guest house swinging from the front wall of a house, except that the 'H' had faded away, giving the establishment decidedly cockney overtones.

The owner seemed to be put out that he hadn't booked, and as she fussed behind her little desk told him it was most unusual for people to turn up like this – especially on a Sunday – and she had no idea if this was going to be a more regular occurrence now the war had started and she wasn't sure what she thought about that and she'd heard rumours about rationing and what did Mr Lyle think about that. It took Cooper a moment or two to realise that he was the Mr Lyle she was addressing, this being the new identity given to him earlier that day by Pamela and which he'd spent the train journey going over and over in his mind.

Malcolm Lyle... Born 16 August 1910 – same day of the month and a year earlier than his own birthday in October 1911... *Address in Croydon, Surrey... Occupation: accounts clerk* – which Cooper thought was really rather clever, because who'd ever want to have a conversation about accounts?

Mr Lyle agreed with the owner that who knew what this war was going to bring, and she said what a shame, the last war was meant to be the war to end all wars and now here we are, just twenty years later and we don't learn, do we?

The small dusty room at the top of the house was to be his home for the next week and a bit. The sheets weren't changed in the whole time he was there and had a slightly greasy feel to them, and the towels – one small and one not quite so small – were rough and frayed. The room had a fug of old tobacco, and it had been a while since the windows had been cleaned but despite all this, it felt safe. From the window he could observe the street below and the garden to the rear, and there was nowhere someone watching the place could hide unobserved. More by luck than anything else he'd found somewhere secure.

He developed a routine of sorts: in the morning he'd leave the guest house around nine o'clock and head to Eastgate to the north of the cathedral, where he had breakfast at a cafe where the proprietor seemed only too happy to let him stay for as long as he wished. He'd read a newspaper he'd bought along the way before heading off around ten o'clock, and the rest of the morning would be spent visiting the cathedral or the castle or some of the other sights in the historic centre of the town. He'd head back to the guest house in the early afternoon and have a rest. He'd found a large second-hand bookshop near the cathedral, which meant he was never short of reading material.

In the evening, he had his main meal in the guest house. It was usually a stodgy affair, but at least there was plenty of it. And back in his room, he'd think about where to go next and when. Pamela's envelope contained twenty one-pound notes, which along with the ten pounds he already had meant that money was the least of his problems.

As far as he could tell, the war was something of a non-event so far as Britain was concerned: a naval blockade here, an air raid there, talk about rationing. There was certainly a war going on in Poland, though, no question of that. He read in horror about the country being carved up between the Germans and the Soviets, and prayed that the Soviets would never track him down again. The thought that he could in some way – however indirect or unintended – be complicit in all this horrified him.

By 14 September he'd been in Lincoln for eleven days and his instinct told him it was time to move on. The question was where to go next... He thought about Sheffield, but there'd been an article in the *Daily Telegraph* about the big industrial towns being the targets for German bombing raids. That seemed to rule out Leeds, too, so early on the Thursday morning he settled his bill with the owner and headed down Steep Hill to the station, and from there took a train to York.

He booked into a commercial travellers' hotel between the station and the river Ouse. It was an unpleasant place: noisy, smelly, and with the breakfast included in the price of the room served in a canteen in the basement where his fellow guests pushed and shoved to be first to the greasy fare on offer.

York had at least as much history as Lincoln, but Cooper had reached the point where he had no desire to see another medieval castle or one more church. The saving grace was that the weather was decent, which meant he could sit on a bench in the gardens by the river and read his books. This took up much of his time until on the Monday afternoon he noticed a man watching him from maybe fifty yards away. He couldn't be sure this wasn't the same man whom he thought had been following him as he walked by the minster that morning. Although he concluded it was most probably nothing to worry about, he did wonder if he was being a bit rash, exposing himself like this for so much of the time, and it was probably time to move on.

The previous day he'd found a discarded copy of *Country Woman* magazine and in it read an article about Harrogate. It was hard, the article gushed, to think of a more peaceful and discreet town in the north of England, 'where those of a certain class and standing could be assured of being among their own'. That suited Cooper fine, because discretion sounded like just what he needed and he was perfectly capable of meeting the class and standing criteria which seemed to govern who was allowed into the town.

Tuesday, 19 September was a fine day with more than a distant feel of late summer about it, and the bus journey from York to Harrogate was a pleasant one across north Yorkshire.

There was no shortage of places to stay in Harrogate, and he found a pleasant hotel on the quixotically named Cold Bath Road. It was more expensive than he'd budgeted for at one pound a night, though he did get a pleasant room overlooking the gardens at the rear of the hotel with its own toilet and breakfast and dinner included.

Harrogate was the perfect place for someone in his position, and he decided to extend his stay there until Friday the 29th, which he knew was stretching it – both in terms of his luck and his budget – but darting around the country like a hunted animal was tiring, and emotionally draining too.

Pamela had given him the telephone number to call 'in the first week of October' and for some reason he'd decided that he should wait until the Thursday of that week, 5 October; not too early in the week seemed about right.

The question was where to head next. The telephone number Pamela had given him was a London one so it made sense to head in that direction. He departed Harrogate with a real sense of regret and decided to risk heading to Manchester, where he remained for a desolate weekend, and then south to Stoke-on-Trent for no reason other than that it was in the right direction, but after a bleak two nights there he headed south again on the Wednesday to Birmingham.

The last time Cooper had been in Birmingham was four years previously, when he'd been summoned there by a solicitor who informed him that he'd inherited a large sum of money from a paternal aunt.

The money he inherited – £357 – was more than four times his annual salary as a magazine reporter. It enabled him to resign from his job and travel throughout Europe and also begin to write a novel. He left London in February 1937.

On his travels he met an older couple in Switzerland. The Maurers invited him to stay with them in Berlin, which he did in the summer of 1937. At their apartment he was introduced to a man called Eduard, who invited Cooper to Moscow.

This was how Cooper found himself in Moscow in July 1937. It was how Cooper found himself staying at the Lux Hotel on Gorky Street, and this was how he was introduced to a chain of people, each one drawing him further into a web he was unaware of, until he finally met Nikolai Vasilyevich Zaslavsky, who informed him that he worked for the OMS, the secret arm of the Comintern, and now so did Cooper – who was given his very own codename.

Bertie.

He was a very half-hearted Soviet spy, so much so that on his return to London he assumed another identity, that of Christopher Shaw, a name he had thanks to his stepfather. He hoped this would mean the Soviets would not be able to trace him.

And then he was recruited by The Annexe, a branch of British Intelligence so secret that few were aware of its existence.

Cooper had found it hard to come to terms with the fact that he'd managed to end up as a spy for both Britain and the Soviet Union. He wasn't sure if he was a double agent because he thought that involved one of his two masters being aware of his position and exploiting it for their advantage. He wasn't sure what he was any more.

But then, he'd foolishly approached a publisher in London whose name he'd been given in Moscow as someone who may be interested in the kind of novel he was writing. When he went back to see him, Osip – his Soviet handler in London – was waiting for him.

For a crazy few months in early 1939 he found himself working for both the British and the Soviets. For The Annexe, he infiltrated King Street, the headquarters of the British Communist Party. Fortunately, this was something the OMS was also interested in. Cooper got used to writing two different versions of the same report.

In March, a desperate Osip approached him; the OMS was being closed down and all its work taken over by the NKVD, which included Osip's operation in London. This meant Cooper would now be working for the NKVD. It also meant Osip was being recalled to Moscow. He knew that meant only one of two things: a bullet in the back of his head, or Siberia.

Osip was beside himself with worry. He was convinced he'd be killed as soon as he arrived back in Moscow, if not before. He knew the NKVD in London was hunting him.

So, Cooper fixed Osip up in a bedsit in Acton. And then with a ruthlessness which shocked him, he calmly informed Morozov, the NKVD station chief in London, of Osip's whereabouts. This was how Osip ended his days in West London rather than Moscow.

Cooper deployed this ruthless trait again in June when a man called Douglas Marsh approached him in King Street. He recognised Marsh from Moscow and suspected he was a spy, though he wasn't sure who for. Cooper called in his favour with Murray, who disposed of Marsh.

–

On the morning of Thursday, 5 October Cooper woke up early and went for a stroll around the centre of Birmingham, undecided as to when – or indeed whether – he should make the telephone call.

He realised once he rang the number, he'd be pulled back into a world which frankly he'd been relieved to get away from. What was to stop him disappearing and starting a new life? He still had fifteen pounds in cash and access to his two bank accounts.

But the more he thought about it, the more he realised he'd be sentencing himself to a life of fear. British Intelligence was now involved in a war and the whereabouts of Cooper may not be a priority, but he knew that at some point they'd start looking for him. They'd want to know why he'd disappeared. They'd start digging into his background, and who knew what they'd find?

So, he went down to the reception area to use the telephone.

The voice that answered carefully enunciated, 'Thames Musical Instruments and Supplies,' in a very well-spoken voice which for some reason slightly confused Cooper because he'd not been expecting that. He didn't say anything for a moment and the voice said, 'Hello?' Cooper said, 'Hello,' and then, 'Good morning… I have a… um, a violin which needs to be repaired, please.'

'And may I ask what is the problem with the violin?'

'I'm afraid the bridge is broken.'

A pause. 'Very well, then. Please telephone us back in exactly one hour from another telephone box and I will give you the address. Do you understand?'

Cooper replied that yes, he did, though in truth he was confused because his understanding was that he'd be given an address to go to there and then, but he thought better than to query it.

He rang back an hour later, this time from a call box outside the hotel. The same voice answered – 'Thames Musical Instruments and Supplies'– and when Cooper said he was calling about his broken violin, the voice asked how soon he could be in London. Cooper said it rather depended on trains but hopefully by early afternoon

'Very good… When you arrive in London go to Sloane Square and telephone this number to say you've arrived. Do not take a taxi. Please ensure you are not followed. After you've telephoned us, head south down Sloane Street and then turn left into Turk's Row and head towards Burton Court.'

'And then where do I go?'

'You're not to worry about that.'

Chapter 4

London
October 1939

There was a moment's quiet in the office masquerading as the premises of 'Thames Musical Instruments and Supplies' as the second telephone call with Cooper ended. The person who'd been speaking with him nodded at Pamela Clarke, who nodded back and mouthed 'Well done' before turning to a man sitting opposite her as he removed his headphones.

'We could have done with slightly longer on the last call, but given the information I was able to glean from the two calls, I'd say he's in Birmingham.'

'Are you sure of that?'

The man nodded and said he was sure. Pamela turned to two men sitting at the back of the room.

'Let's have a team at Euston Station from noon onwards. It's most important to see if anyone follows him from the train. You've got that photograph of Murray? Remember, he's more than capable of leaving the train much after Cooper does and still catching up with him, despite the crowds. If you can follow Cooper on the journey to Sloane Square, all well and good, but we'll pick him up there anyway when he telephones us. We'll be able to watch him very carefully after that as he makes his way to Burton Court.'

She stood up and said, 'Right then, let's get to it,' and smiled at everyone and thanked them and said, 'Good work,' and the tension in the room lifted. She walked into the corridor in the basement of the Old War Office Building in Whitehall and headed towards her office, stopping on the way to knock on the door of Lieutenant Commander McConnell.

'Cooper made contact today, sir.'

'Oh, good – just as you said he would. You should have had a wager on it!'

'As you suggested, sir. I'm not a gambling woman, though, apart from the occasional tombola.'

'And nor should you be, Miss Clarke, it's not a suitable pursuit for ladies. And you have your plans to meet him in place, I take it?'

'Indeed, sir. We'll be watching him from the moment he arrives in London.'

'And the business with the telephone number… Did that all work out?'

'Yes, thank you, sir, it was just a matter of switching things around at the exchanges. He was calling a Bayswater number, but it came straight through here.'

'Excellent – what they can do nowadays, eh? You'd better get ready to meet Cooper.'

'I'm rather looking forward to catching up with him, sir.'

–

Birmingham New Street Station was so busy it seemed as if half the population of the city were on the move. The irritable man crouching behind the ticket office window told him the 11:00 service was sold out. There were a few tickets remaining for the midday train to London, but there was no guarantee of a seat unless he booked first class, which Cooper did. There was enough of Pamela's cash remaining.

He had a sense of foreboding as the stretch of England between the West Midlands and London flashed past him. Euston Station was as busy as Birmingham and he decided to travel the next leg of his journey by bus, so he walked round the corner to Hampstead Road, where he caught the 137 which took him straight to Sloane Square.

He found a pair of telephone boxes outside the Royal Court cinema and the same voice answered the phone.

'I'm calling you from Sloane Square, about the violin which we talked about this morning.'

'Very good… and you know where to go?'

Cooper said he did. There wasn't a plethora of telephone boxes around Sloane Square and it occurred to him that the purpose of this phone call was so that they could watch him. He peered through the filthy small glass squares of the phone box: a man in a bowler hat sitting on a bench opposite; a man in the distance walking a shade too slowly towards the Peter Jones department store, but Cooper had to acknowledge that was stretching the imagination. It was more likely to be someone far more innocuous-looking, like the lady in the fur coat being pulled along by a poodle. Hadn't he once been told on his training – funnily enough, he couldn't remember if it was by the Russians or the British – that using a dog was a favourite ploy when following someone because somehow people tended to be so well disposed towards dogs that they didn't associate them with anything suspicious.

As it happened, there was another woman with a dog following him as he headed south down Sloane Street in the direction of Chelsea.

This woman was far younger than the fur-coated lady and walked briskly, eventually overtaking him, briefly glancing at him as she walked past. He caught the scent of her perfume as she did so and was convinced he saw her look across the road at a short man in a trench coat walking more or less in parallel with him. It seemed to him that they exchanged looks, perhaps the briefest of nods.

Who knew?

He'd not been sure exactly where Turk's Row was until he'd consulted a helpful map outside Sloane Square Station, but it soon appeared on his right and he turned into it and spotted the open green space of Burton Court behind iron railings ahead of him. He carried on walking, idly wondering whether there may be any connection between Burton Court and Percy Burton. The short man with the trench coat whom he'd earlier spotted walking on the other side of the road appeared alongside him and spoke in a firm voice.

'The house over there on your left, the one with the green awning. You're to go in there.'

'Do I need to knock?'

'Please do as I say.'

It was clearly well planned. He hurried up the steps to the house with the green awning and as he did so the door opened. Once inside a carpeted hallway, a man said to please follow him and I'll take your bag, sir, if you please.

Behind a locked door in the basement was a low-ceilinged room and although it was dimly lit Cooper could tell it was well furnished, with a thick carpet and an expensive-looking rug and a series of armchairs. On one of them sat the unmistakable figure of Pamela, her long legs neatly folded and a smile on her face, which even in the low light Cooper could tell was a warm one. She was genuinely pleased to see him.

She apologised for not getting up but said the chair was far too comfortable for that and please sit here, and pointed to a chair opposite her. A cup of tea appeared on the side table and then whoever else was in the room left, and Cooper heard the door being locked behind them.

'My apologies if the security seems excessive,' said Pamela. 'You'll appreciate that we need to be sure. Let me say at the outset how good it is to see you. I personally never doubted you'd return to us. Tell me where you went when you left London? We know you headed to King's Cross Station.'

'I took a train to Lincoln, where I stayed for around ten days, and then travelled to York and from there to Harrogate. After that... Manchester, followed by Stoke and I arrived in Birmingham... yesterday, it must have been – days and places have become a bit blurred, you understand – and that's where I called you from this morning. I thought as the telephone number you gave me is a London one, that is where I'd be heading.'

'So, something of a circular tour of England, then?'

'Yes, I suppose it was. It wasn't intended like that, I just wanted to keep moving. To be honest, it was quite... tedious, I think is the word.'

'Did you have any difficulties with your new identity?'

'No, Malcolm Lyle turned out to be an agreeable travelling companion. I hope you don't think I'm being out of order if I ask what all of this is about, Pamela?'

'All of what, Cooper?'

'You know, the security here, sending me off round the country like a fugitive, all the precautions to travel here from King's Cross... the questions... locked doors, and that's on top of what happened in London the weekend war broke out: Murray appearing outside my apartment, no one responding to the telephone call I made to the emergency number, the safe house in Willesden being empty, and then you tracing me to that hotel in Primrose Hill and giving me all those warnings about who I was not to contact and pretty much bundling me out of town. I'd appreciate knowing what this is all about.'

'When was it we first met, Cooper? February 1938?'

'Yes, outside Aldgate Station, where you were handing out Communist Party leaflets. I realise now that was the start of my recruitment to The Annexe.'

'It was indeed... and you officially joined The Annexe that May or June. Percy Burton would have told you something of the history of the organisation you'd been recruited to?'

'Briefly, yes... He told me that The Annexe had been formed a few years previously to act as a point of liaison for MI5 and MI6. He explained that the name came from the fact that the building where they were based in Bryanston Square was an annexe of the Ministry of Transport, and also because it was an adjunct – or an annexe – to the world of British Intelligence.'

'And did he explain that it had only ever been intended that The Annexe would last for a year or two?'

'Yes, he said The Annexe had evolved into carrying out jobs considered too sensitive for MI6 and MI5, not least because it came under no official scrutiny.'

Pamela nodded and then leant back in the armchair. 'If anyone were to ever write an official history of The Annexe – which I very much doubt would be permitted, but for purely argument's sake let's say they did – then they'd inevitably observe that it grew in a manner which no one had ever expected or indeed intended. It evolved both in terms of its size and its remit.

'The Annexe was formed in 1931 and it was thought its work would be done within a year, perhaps two at the most. But Percy Burton was a remarkable man in many ways. People thought he was very amenable and efficient enough, but not much more than that. In fact, he was most assiduous and ambitious. He was determined to make The Annexe indispensable and in so doing, serve his own purposes.'

'What purposes?'

'Purposes may not be quite the right word... What I'm getting at is that no one really looked too closely at Burton's background, which may well seem remarkable in hindsight, but do remember, he was originally brought in for perhaps a year at the most. A thorough vetting would have seemed excessive in those circumstances. In any case, Burton was always regarded as very loyal and proper. It has, however, become apparent that he was using The Annexe to further his own political interests.'

'Which are?'

'It now turns out he was most sympathetic to what one would call the pro-German right. There's evidence which seems to support the case that he was gathering intelligence on their behalf. Such intelligence operations as we were involved with all seemed to be aimed against organisations and individuals on the left, hence your clandestine role inside the Communist Party. We've been especially concerned at how he deployed Murray, the assassin. He seems to have used him for his own purposes. What little we know of Murray suggests that he is a man with dangerous pro-German views, which he managed to keep hidden. Once war between this country and Germany became inevitable, he either took it on himself, or acted under the direction of Percy Burton, to start disposing of agents of The Annexe. We know of two who were killed – presumably by Murray – and one other who disappeared. We know you were a target, which is why we wanted to get you away from London in some haste.

'Burton was forced into retirement because of the way he handled the intelligence you obtained in August which so accurately predicted the Nazi–Soviet Pact. With the benefit of hindsight, it's clear Burton tried to conceal it for as long as he could. We only discovered what he was up to when The Annexe was wound up in that last week of August, which is why you were rather left in no man's land, for which we are most sorry.

'We took the view that with Murray hunting you and others – myself included – it would be best for you to get out of London and have no contact with anyone who could reveal – however inadvertently – your whereabouts. I'm sorry we couldn't tell you more at the time, but I hope you understand why. We've used the month or so in which you've been away to regroup and to try and remedy the damage done by The Annexe.

'There are concerns that the Nazis could launch an invasion of the British Isles. In some quarters this is regarded as highly unlikely, that invading this country is too enormous and dangerous an undertaking. Others see it as a very genuine and likely threat, and believe it could happen within the space of a few short months. The more we've dug into Burton's involvement with the pro-German far right in this country the more we've begun to realise that many of these people are what one would call a Fifth Column: collaborators so sympathetic to the Nazi cause that they are willing to facilitate a German invasion. They see themselves as having an important role to play in providing the Germans with intelligence to assist an invasion – the state of our coastal defences, troop movements, location of airfields and anti-aircraft units – that kind of thing.

'Following the closure of The Annexe, I and a number of other former colleagues have joined a new intelligence organisation based in the Old War Office Building in Whitehall. It's called the Invasion Warning Sub-Committee, to address the concerns of which I've been speaking regarding a possible German invasion. And that is where you come in, Cooper. You, too, will work for the Invasion Warning Sub-Committee. You are to find out who these people – the collaborators – are, where they are, what their lines of communication are, how they contact Germany and who they contact there.'

'And do I have a say in all this?'

'In all what, Cooper?'

'Well… in sending me away from London like that and then telling me – not asking me – that I'm joining this new organisation. You make it sound like a *fait accompli* with me having no say in what I'd like to do.'

'What would you like to do, Cooper?'

'I don't know, Pamela. Maybe have a think about things. I could volunteer for the armed forces and do my bit.'

'You're already doing your bit, as you put it. The problem with working in Intelligence, Cooper, is that one inevitably operates in the shadows and so by definition people don't see what you do. They don't recognise one's contribution to this country's security. I'm afraid we cannot willingly permit someone with your experience and skills to wander away from our world and become a soldier.'

Cooper reached over for his cup of tea, which was now cold, with an unpleasant scum forming on the surface, and obviously winced as he sipped at it because Pamela asked him if he was all right and he replied that he wasn't sure.

'And in any case, now that we've got conscription, it will seem odd, won't it, a man aged between eighteen and forty-one, I think it is, not being in uniform? I'd appreciate some time to have a think about things and take stock. I resent being told what I'm doing, as if I'm a child.'

'I'm afraid, Cooper, that time is something we cannot afford at the moment. I appreciate this is all rather rushed and an awful lot to take in, but if you were to refuse to join the Invasion Warning Sub-Committee it would be exceptionally difficult.'

'In what way?'

'One would have to see.'

Pamela made this sound somewhat menacing, and Cooper wondered if he'd reached the point where he was pushing matters a bit too far.

'Perhaps if I see what this new organisation is like?'

'That isn't how it works, Cooper. Is that a yes or a no?'

'I think it is probably a yes, in that case.'

'Very well, then. If I may say, I think you have made the right decision. Over the next few days you'll be fully briefed. This whole building is a safe house which we use. You'll stay here until we deem it safe to go elsewhere. That will only be after Murray has been caught.'

'And may I ask you a question?'

'Of course.'

'All these allegations – I suppose that's what they are if he's not been convicted of anything – against Percy Burton. They're terribly serious, aren't they? I mean, it's tantamount to treason, surely, collaborating with the enemy like that. Has he been arrested and interrogated? Wouldn't that be the best way to find out what he knows and get some inkling as to who all these collaborators are?'

Pamela Clarke shifted uncomfortably in her chair, uncrossing her legs and then crossing them again. From the floor above them came the sound of furniture being moved and she glanced up at the ceiling in an annoyed manner.

'I'm afraid that we never had the opportunity to question Burton.'

Chapter 5

London
November 1939

The rumours began surfacing in the corridors of MI6 Head Office around the middle of November – that the new Chief had decided to promote some of the younger, junior officers, and that poor old Phillips, the chap who'd been driven to a nervous breakdown by the Archie case, was going to be in charge of that: demoted to Personnel, a consequence of what happens when you fail to catch a traitor.

But there was another set of rumours – far more pernicious ones – that in fact Phillips was getting closer to discovering the identity of Archie, who may well be based inside 54 Broadway itself. The so-called promotion exercise for the younger officers was no more than a front, a cover for Phillips and a man called Harvey from MI5 to investigate people's backgrounds in detail.

Archie didn't know what rumour to believe, though he knew which one he preferred. He worried he couldn't rule out not having made a mistake or two along the way. There was no denying he'd allowed himself to be spotted by that Branstone character in the Kremlin, and then almost fallen into Phillips' trap and turned up outside the theatre.

And the life of a traitor was such a vulnerable one that it depended not just on him not making a mistake; there was Osip, his OMS case officer in London, who'd disappeared earlier in the year, but the last time he saw him it was obvious Osip was a worried and frightened man. A worried and frightened man is prone to making mistakes; had Osip been so distracted that his usual precautions hadn't been good enough? Might he even have been followed?

He decided it was safest to believe the rumour that the promotion process Phillips was overseeing was just a cover for the hunt for the traitor. It was such a sensitive case – the notion of a Soviet agent inside

41

54 Broadway – that this was perhaps the best way of their going about it. It's what he would have done.

He'd bumped into one of the first to be interviewed that evening in the Naval and Military club in Piccadilly. Archie had to admit that this normally likeable man, with an equable temperament, looked quite shaken, as if he'd just finished a particularly brutal rugby match and then been given some unsettling personal news.

He looked grey and drank two large gin and tonics before he spoke.

'I don't know how to put it... It's as if they didn't believe anything I said. I even began to wonder if they thought I was a spy!'

He'd laughed at the very thought and Archie joined in, and then he told Archie at some length about how they'd picked up on the fact that his aunt Elspeth had been a suffragette and even imprisoned at one stage, and in later life had been known to be a radical and possibly even a communist, and was he aware of that? He'd replied that of course he was aware of that but calling her a communist was going a bit far, wasn't it?

And then they'd asked him whether it was true that he'd gone to his aunt's funeral and he'd replied she was his mother's sister, what on earth did they expect? He very much regretted that he'd rather lost his temper at this stage and raised his voice, and then they'd asked him to account for how soon after he'd joined the Service a bank account had been opened in his name and one thousand guineas had been deposited in it.

'I told them it was a legacy from Aunt Elspeth and had they bothered to check, that could have been easily ascertained... They seemed to accept that, but even so... I'll tell you what, I got the impression that they were trying to rattle me and they very nearly succeeded. It was an unnerving experience. You'll be fine, though. No skeletons in your cupboard, eh?'

Archie's summons came a couple of weeks later, in the second week of December: a note from Phillips asking him if he'd be so good as to come to his office at ten o'clock on the Tuesday morning and it would be advisable not to make any other appointments for that day.

It didn't help that they had guests in the country that weekend – his wife's brother, whom he couldn't abide, and his wife – and what most annoyed him about them was that neither of them had any respect for the fact they were guests in his house and therefore ought to respect his privacy. His brother-in-law, for example, had the infuriating habit of wandering uninvited into his study and making himself at home, pulling up a chair and helping himself to one of his cigars and giving him the benefit of his opinion that he really ought to get himself a better paid job and had he ever thought of the City?

So, by the time they drove back to London on the Sunday night he was quite agitated, and it didn't help that his wife was with him, because since the war had begun, she'd been avoiding London, terrified at the prospect of bombing.

That night he'd drunk far too much, which was the cause of an argument that was patched up somewhat on the Monday night when she made a very agreeable dinner of pheasant and apologised and said she realised she ought to be more understanding about the pressures he must be under now there was a war on.

He woke up in the early hours of the Tuesday morning in such a state that he threw up in the bathroom. When this happened for the third time his wife was waiting anxiously in the corridor when he emerged from the bathroom, and asked whatever was the matter, and he said he wondered whether the pheasant may have been off and that led to another argument.

He left home just after eight o'clock and decided that a walk across Hampstead Heath would be the best way to calm his nerves, and it ended up being an especially long walk: starting around the Spaniards Inn and emerging at Parliament Hill, from where he walked towards Kentish Town and caught a taxi to work, arriving in good time for his ten o'clock interview.

It had all started rather well and was far more agreeable than he'd feared. Phillips had assured him that he was to see this as no more than a chat, really; they were talking to all the officers on his grade to assess which ones would be recommended for promotion. Then the man called Harvey had asked whether he'd been out in the country and pointed at his shoes, and Archie noticed they were muddy. He said he'd taken a short cut across the heath to get to work and Harvey had nodded. This had unsettled Archie, because firstly it showed that Harvey was observant, if nothing else, and secondly, because if they bothered to check – by looking at a map, for instance – then it was clear that going across the heath wasn't any kind of a short cut.

He was more uptight after that, unnecessarily defensive, and he was convinced that Harvey noticed this. Much of the interview was a review of his work and reflected the opinion of the senior desk officers that his reports and analysis were spot-on and most prescient – a word which Phillips used on more than one occasion. At one point he did ask what Archie attributed this to, and Archie asked what he meant.

'Your prescience... You seem to have an unerring ability to get it right, that's what I mean.'

Archie did what he'd been told to do in Moscow, and coughed and shifted position in the chair and allowed himself a few seconds to consider his response. He couldn't very well say that he was being fed intelligence from the Soviets, hence the 'unerring ability to get it right'.

'I like to think that I've developed the ability to be truly objective in my analysis. I think it's important to avoid telling the recipient of a report what you think they want to hear because you think that may make them well disposed towards you. I do see why people do that, but I think it only works in the short term.'

'You must have some particularly good sources?' Harvey sounded sceptical as he asked the question.

'Are you asking me to reveal my sources? Is this the proper forum to do that?'

'Of course not,' said Phillips, who then said he wanted to turn to his lifestyle and wanted some clarification on how he was able to afford a town house in Hampstead, along with a decent-sized place in the country and school fees.

Archie allowed himself a few more seconds' thought. There was no doubt that the money the Soviets gave him from time to time certainly helped, no question about that. He needed to be careful, because money was something they could easily check out.

'My wife's family is very comfortable, fortunately; they help out with school fees and the running costs of our place in the country – it was originally on her side of the family anyway.'

Phillips nodded, as if that was the answer he was expecting, but as he did so he leafed through some papers in front of him. As far as Archie could tell from where he was sitting, they looked as if they could be copies of his bank statement; he certainly spotted the Coutts Bank's distinctive three crowns logo.

'There doesn't appear to be much in the way of a record of transactions from her family to you?'

Archie said this was because his wife's family had a preference for cash and sometimes paid bills directly themselves. 'May I ask if you're trying to imply something? Because I have to tell you that I've nothing whatsoever to hide, unless you've spotted my occasional bet on the horses. I can supply you with the details of my bookmaker if you wish.'

Phillips said no not at all and Archie was quite pleased with the tone he'd struck, slightly offended but not too angry, and the interview ended soon after that.

Later that evening, after his wife had gone to bed and he was relaxing with a large Cognac by the fire, he was able to reflect on how the interview had gone and he allowed himself to acknowledge that, all things considered, it hadn't gone too badly. They certainly appeared to have nothing on him; the question of his loyalty or his political views had never come up, and if he was honest, then the questions about his finances were fairly standard stuff. He felt he'd answered the question about how well informed he was reasonably well.

His only concern was Harvey, who had said little but seemed like a particularly wise old owl, and on more than one occasion had looked at him in an unsettling manner, as if he didn't quite believe everything he was being told.

But Archie put this down to his anxiety – an inevitable aspect, it seemed to him, of living as a double agent.

He did reflect, though, on how much longer he could sustain this life. The Nazi–Soviet Pact had quite unsettled him. It was one thing working for the Soviets – he could justify that in his mind because he saw that as working towards world peace, and that was surely in the interests of the United Kingdom – but now the Soviets were allied with the Nazis, that was an altogether different matter.

The Germans were unequivocally the enemy and that meant he was unequivocally a traitor. If he was caught it would be punishable by death, the thought of which caused him to shudder and pour another large measure of Cognac.

He'd speak to the Soviets, that's what he'd do, he decided. Explain the situation to them, tell them there'd been a close shave at work and he thought it best if he kept his head down for a while as far as supplying them with intelligence was concerned.

Surely, they'd understand.

–

November had been a truly wretched month for the Service.

In the first week the head of MI6, Admiral Sir Hugh Sinclair, had died following an operation for cancer. The following week there'd been a disaster in the Netherlands when two MI6 officers had been tricked into going to a meeting on the German border, apparently with a Wehrmacht general.

It turned out to be an ambush: the two British agents were arrested and a Dutch Intelligence officer was killed. It was a serious embarrassment for the Service, and as a consequence all their intelligence network in the Netherlands was compromised. They had no agents left there to speak of, certainly none they could be certain the Germans weren't on to. Whitehall had made their displeasure very clear and used it as a further opportunity to express their disappointment at having discovered the Service's paucity of spies in Germany. It was made abundantly clear that, given the considerable sums being spent on the Service, they'd expected to find some kind of an intelligence operation in the Reich.

Sinclair's deputy, Sir Stewart Menzies, replaced him as head of the Service and quickly decided there needed to be a shake-up at Head Office, as the Service's headquarters at 54 Broadway in St James's was known. As he was heard to comment on more than one occasion, either they shook themselves up or someone in Whitehall would do it for them.

He decided one of his priorities had to be what to do with what Sinclair had called his high-flyers, the fifteen or so younger officers recruited by the Service in recent years and who were all seen as being terribly bright and evidently marked out for preferment. Menzies recognised that now there was a war on, there'd be ample opportunities in the armed forces and elsewhere for these younger officers to realise their ambitions. He knew that if he didn't do something about it, then many of them would simply go elsewhere, which was the last thing the Service needed.

So, on a bitterly cold and wet weekend in the middle of the month, Menzies had skipped church on the Sunday morning and gone on a longer than usual walk in the countryside, and by the time he returned home, he'd developed a plan. On the Monday morning, he wrote a brief note to one of his senior officers, Phillips, and asked to meet him in The Caxton after lunch.

The note worried Phillips; he was one of the most senior officers in the Service, and before that an officer in the Royal Navy. Since 1937 he'd been rather sidetracked by the hunt for a Soviet agent, a British traitor. All the evidence pointed to the fact that this man – who went under the codename Archie – worked somewhere at the heart of the British state, quite possibly for one of the intelligence agencies, quite probably within MI6 itself.

It was something which really didn't bear thinking about, and at first Phillips had made some headway in the hunt for the traitor. But a series of setbacks – including the unexpected and inopportune deaths of people who may have been able to help identify him – had led to all those involved admitting they'd reached a dead end. Archie the traitor had an unerring ability to stay one step ahead of them. They had no clue as to his identity.

The hunt had rather taken over poor Phillips' life. He took the failure to identify Archie quite personally, so much so that earlier in the year he'd had what the doctors told him was a nervous breakdown. The Service had arranged for him to be admitted to a clinic in Surrey and he feared his career was over.

But by August he had recovered and the outbreak of war in September meant he wasn't as disposable as he'd feared. Nonetheless, he'd been at something of a loose end on his return. The Service's medical officer had told him he should work shorter hours, and he devoted most of his time to reviewing the case of Archie, but even then, it was clear he was nowhere nearer finding him. He did wonder whether the war meant Archie had gone to ground.

But the ominous note from the Chief asking to meet him at the Caxton Bar in St Ermin's Hotel, a few doors along from Head Office, sounded like this may be it. He could imagine how the Chief would put it: ...*many years' loyal service... putting country first... much appreciated... opportunity to leave with your head held high... chance to concentrate on your health... who knows what opportunities the future may bring?*

But this was a very good example of what the doctors at the clinic in Surrey had described as his anxiety and his all too vivid imagination, which had a habit of leading him down a dangerous path.

Don't always imagine the worst!

The Chief was friendly from the outset and seemed to be genuinely pleased to see him and insisted he had a proper drink, as he put it. That was a bit awkward as Phillips was still on medication, which meant that he had to be careful about mixing it with alcohol, but nonetheless he allowed himself a single malt, with plenty of water, hoping that would dilute any harm it may do.

'How are you getting on, Phillips? Managed to put all that... business behind you?'

'I hope so, sir. They told me to take it slowly, but I must say, coming back to work has been a boost. There's only so many walks in the country one can cope with!'

'I read the file on that traitor Archie. We still seem to be none the wiser, do we?'

'I'm afraid so, sir. I fear we may have missed him. I've been reviewing the case and I feel that we had two unfortunate blows in the summer of last year. In the June we were approached in Moscow by a man we believe was a Comintern official, who said he'd provide us with the identity of this Archie in return for us organising his escape from Moscow. This chap disappeared; we suspect he was arrested. And then in August, Branstone was murdered in his rooms in Cambridge. He was the man who—'

'Yes, I've read the file in some detail, Phillips, thank you. And this Archie didn't fall into that trap you set for him at the Phoenix Theatre last October?'

'Not as such, sir, by which I mean that I do believe he may have turned up outside the theatre but then spotted my people there and made off. It may well be that the suggestion that I was going to meet an informer from the Soviet Embassy in the foyer of the theatre was too enticing for him. I fear that we may have frightened him off altogether now and I blame myself. But I do suspect he may well be one of us.'

'One of us?'

'Inside the Service, sir.'

'Don't beat yourself up over this, Phillips. We're obviously dealing with a very clever chap, as despicable as he is. I can't abide the thought of a traitor among us, but I think the way one will catch him is by being patient and measured and cunning about it. Sooner or later, he'll make a mistake, his luck cannot last forever.

'I want you to continue trying to find him, Phillips, but in the meantime, I have another job for you. I'm somewhat concerned about all those young chaps Sir Hugh recruited. It seems to me that, not through any fault of their own, too many of them haven't flown quite as high as they'd have liked. My worry, for want of a better word, is that now there's a war on there'll be ample opportunities for them to go elsewhere. The intelligence branches of all three armed forces are recruiting like mad, for a start.'

The Chief pushed his empty glass across the counter and the barman poured more whisky. The Chief gestured with his hand to keep going until it was a large double. Phillips shook his head and said, 'No thank you,' and was unsure whether he was meant to say something.

'You were saying, sir, about there being a lot of opportunities elsewhere for our younger officers?'

'Indeed, which is where you come in, Phillips. What I want you to do is gather up all their files, check what they've been up to, talk to the senior desk officers and the heads of station – find out what they make of Sir Hugh's young chaps – by which I mean, which ones they really rate, what their skills are, which ones we should consider to be indispensable.'

The Chief had uttered the word 'indispensable' with something of a flourish, as if particularly pleased to have chosen it, and knocked back the remains of his glass.

'And trustworthy, sir?'

'That's a given. One expects they wouldn't be here if they weren't, would they?'

'You are right, of course, sir, though I do fear I have become somewhat cynical with all this Archie business. I'm no longer sure who to trust.'

'Well, Archie won't be one of these chaps, will he?'

Phillips said he very much hoped not.

'And interview each of them, Phillips. Once you've done all this, I want you to come up with the names of half a dozen of them who I can promote to a new grade I intend to create. They'll recognise it's a promotion, with more money and more status. Hopefully that will ensure none of them jumps ship, eh? And when I announce it, I can assure the others this process will be repeated annually, so the ones who miss out won't feel too miffed, eh?'

–

It took Phillips until the first week of the new year to complete his task. It was a lengthy process, involving reviewing the files for each of the fifteen junior officers and then compiling reports on them. He could only do that after he'd interviewed all the desk officers in the Service and as many of the station heads as he was able to – a less laborious task than it would have been had not so many of them been forced to return to London after the outbreak of war.

There'd been extensive background checks, too. Phillips had been surprised at how casually so many of them had been recruited in the first place, which appeared to have been largely based on who they knew and which senior officers in the Service their fathers or uncles had been at school with. As part of this he'd checked them all out with MI5 and with Special Branch, and this unearthed more than a few question marks… unwise or undeclared friendships and political allegiances.

He'd made a note of all these 'discrepancies', as he termed them, and kept them up his sleeve for interviews with each of the fifteen men.

Phillips was not a trained interrogator, and he'd told the Chief that, although none of the fifteen were suspects as such, it may nevertheless be an idea to have someone skilled in counter-espionage sitting in on the interviews as a precaution and to assist with the final decision.

Which was how Ernest Harvey came to be involved. Harvey was an experienced MI5 interrogator, past retirement age but who'd returned to the Security Service at the outbreak of war. Phillips trusted Harvey's experience and judgement. It was agreed he'd sit in on the interviews and his primary role would be to observe and then advise.

Harvey turned out to be a cautious man, meticulous and at times over-deliberate in his approach, but Phillips came to realise that masked a sharp and incisive mind. He was very good at spotting apparent flaws or discrepancies and suggesting the most fruitful areas of questioning.

Charles Whittaker was a good example of this. In many ways Whittaker was the smartest of the fifteen being interviewed: a first from Oxford, followed by Sandhurst and a short-service commission in the Coldstream Guards, where he was very highly regarded; fluent in Italian, French and German, and generally very well liked, with a number of clandestine pre-war missions into Germany to his name, all of which had been viewed as successful.

But it transpired that Whittaker had been having an affair over a number of years with an older woman, one who was involved in the Liberal Party, and he'd failed to declare it, although there was some dispute about that as he claimed he had mentioned it to his line manager, albeit in passing.

By the first week of January, Phillips had his list of recommendations for promotion. There were six names on the list he submitted to the Chief, who then consulted with his heads of department, which he assured Phillips was just a formality.

It turned out to be anything but. One of those heads of department was Nicholas Oates, who ran the Americas – North, South and those awkward bits in between – and he asked to see the Chief.

'I see that Tommy Browning's name isn't on the list of six for promotion, sir...'

The Chief scanned the list to confirm that this was indeed the case. 'That would be because he didn't make Phillips' final half dozen. He and the chap from MI5 were most thorough, I can assure you, Oates.'

'I'm sure they were, sir, but Tommy Browning is terribly good, he's done some solid work for me. He's Andrew Browning's boy, you know.'

'Twentieth Hussars?'

'Yes, sir. I was at school with Andrew, year below me, decent tennis player. Killed at Cambrai in 1917. Took a week to die, I was told, awake the whole time.'

The Chief said perhaps they ought to call Phillips in.

Phillips was clearly put out when asked why Tommy Browning was omitted from the list.

'Not the best of the interviews, sir, and I have to say that a question mark or two came up.'

'Can you elaborate please, Phillips?'

Phillips shifted awkwardly in his chair and coughed. 'Some suggestion he may have batted for the other side in the past, sir, some mention of younger boys at school. That can make one vulnerable to blackmail, as you know, sir.'

'Nonsense, Phillips,' said Oates, looking quite offended. 'I've known the family for years and have never heard any suggestion of that. Browning's married with children, for heaven's sake, so he's hardly likely to be… inclined in the way you're suggesting, is he? What is your source for this slander, Phillips.'

'A colleague of Harvey's at MI5. Someone who was at the same college as Browning.'

'There we are, sir… Damaging a chap's career and reputation on the say-so of anonymous tittle-tattle. I'll tell you what, sir, I'll personally vouch for Tommy Browning. I'd trust him with my life.'

'That's very commendable, Mr Oates, but surely we have to be absolutely certain of the integrity of who we appoint to a senior position in the Service?'

'That is true, Phillips,' said the Chief, 'but that would apply to who we appoint to any position in the Service. I'm happy to take Nicholas's word, though. Let's add Browning to the list, please.'

'But you said you wanted us to appoint six, sir. Browning would make it seven.'

'Thank you, Phillips. What I actually said was half a dozen. I think seven counts as half a dozen.'

The following day Menzies announced the promotions. His memo to staff said he was delighted to announce the promotion to a new grade of the following officers:

Thomas Browning

Gilbert Cavendish

Timothy Kerr-Walters

Rex Larkin

Walter Morley

The Hon. Edward Slater

Anthony Stokes

–

Archie's relief was short-lived; he did worry this promotion could be another trap, one designed to lull him into a false sense of security. But he decided that, on balance, it was better than not getting the promotion, though it caused him to think again about his relationship with the Soviets.

It was a matter which had preoccupied him over the all-too-brief Christmas break, and in a drunken moment on New Year's Eve he had made a resolution – something he normally avoided doing – to contact the Soviets. It had been a while since he'd heard from them anyway.

Chapter 6

England
November 1939

For the next few months, the safe house with the green awning in Turk's Row in Chelsea was home to Charles Cooper, although he now went by the identity Pamela had given him when he left London the previous September: Malcolm Lyle, the accounts clerk from Croydon.

Special Branch had made some enquiries and were confident the Malcolm Lyle identity hadn't been compromised. They arranged for any record of that name in the various places he'd stayed on his travels to be removed.

On his second day in the safe house a car arrived just after nine in the morning to take him to Whitehall and to the Old War Office Building, opposite Horse Guards Parade. This, he soon gathered, was his new place of work.

He was met in the ornate entrance by a man who introduced himself as Will and shook hands a little too vigorously, and guided Cooper away from the wide staircase which he'd begun to ascend and pointed to a narrower, descending staircase. They reached the second basement level and then paused in a lobby area where Will showed his pass and signed Cooper in. The guard took a while to inscribe his name in a ledger and check the time against that on his wristwatch and a large clock on the wall before handing Cooper a piece of card with a number on it to pin to his lapel.

Only then did he press a buzzer and almost immediately a large door behind them clicked open. Cooper followed Will into a long, low corridor, dimly lit and with prominent piping running along the ceiling, giving it the feel of a lower deck of a large ship.

'We're along here,' said Will, who looked like the kind of person who was naturally chatty but was uncharacteristically avoiding small talk on this occasion. 'It's quite a walk; these corridors don't half keep you fit. No need for cross-country! Ah, here we are.'

Will pressed a buzzer to the side of a door with frosted glass panels and when it opened, they were in a narrow lobby area with what was obviously a two-way mirror, because Will stood facing it and nodded. Moments later another door was unlocked and opened, and Pamela was waiting for them on the other side and wished him a good morning and said she hoped he'd slept well and to please come this way.

The room she led him to was small with a low ceiling, oak-panelled with a thick carpet and dominated by a large table. Sitting at the head of it was an older man, who half rose as Cooper came in and who then pointed to one of the spare chairs, so now Pamela and Cooper were sitting either side of him and Will was next to him. For a moment no one said anything and there was much low-level coughing, which in Cooper's experience was the traditional start to meetings in England.

Eventually the older man spoke. 'The return of the prodigal son! I'm delighted to see you returned safely, Mr Cooper. When Pamela told me about your leaving London and the arrangements for your return, I did wonder whether you'd come back... Not that I doubted your loyalty, but then you did leave London in what I understand were somewhat rushed and possibly mysterious circumstances, and no one would have blamed you had you taken your time to see how the land lay. Did it ever occur to you not to return to us?'

'Only in an abstract sense, sir.'

'We'd have caught up with you sooner or later, Mr Cooper. You did the right thing to come back.

'Pamela tells me you expressed some concern at being asked to continue your Intelligence career?'

'It was more that I was told rather than asked, sir.'

'I see... What we all need to understand is that the war requires each of us to serve our country to the best of our abilities, Mr Cooper. You're an experienced Intelligence officer. That is how you'll serve your country.'

Cooper felt himself half-nodding; this was more of an order from McConnell than an explanation. Now was not the time to question an order. The silence continued, filled with coughing, and Cooper said, 'Thank you,' and the man at the top of the table said it had been most remiss of him not to introduce himself.

'My name is McConnell, Lieutenant Commander James McConnell, Royal Navy, seconded to head up the Invasion Warning Sub-Committee. I understand Pamela may have mentioned it to you yesterday. In short, the role of this committee is rather as its name suggests, to prepare this country for a possible enemy invasion. We do this by co-ordinating the work of all three armed forces and gathering all the intelligence in one place so that we can analyse it and plan accordingly. Some of our staff here are from the forces, others like Pamela – and indeed you – have come from the world of intelligence and security. Some, like Will here, have been specially recruited.

'We do know that the Germans are considering, if not actually planning, an invasion and have set up an espionage operation based in Hamburg to provide them with the intelligence they need. Their intelligence gathering in this country is two-pronged: on the one hand, sending over agents to operate clandestinely in this country. The second prong is what one might call the Fifth Column in this country, by which I mean those people – of whom we estimate there may be quite a few hundred – who hold what can be termed extremist political views sympathetic to the Nazi cause.

'We think that the two prongs are not separate, in that the Nazi agents who are sent over here will often make contact with the British collaborators, who they will look upon to assist them. Additionally, the collaborators will also be very well placed to help gather intelligence for the Nazi spies.

'We need to infiltrate this Fifth Column. We don't know nearly enough about it. We do have some intelligence on them which our colleagues in the MI5 and the police Special Branch have gathered, but it's not enough. Part of your job, Mr Cooper, will be to infiltrate these collaborators.

'I'm giving you one of these, Mr Cooper.' McConnell passed an envelope across the table. 'It's a warrant card, issued by the City of London Police. All my officers have one. Makes life much easier when it comes to having to identify yourself – we can hardly have you announcing you're working for the Invasion Warning Sub-Committee, can we? The presentation of this card ought to be enough to ensure people co-operate with you, but don't abuse it. The City of London Police have been very decent to let us have these cards, but clearly, they don't want us to go around arresting all and sundry. The Metropolitan

Police refused to let us have warrant cards issued by them. Let's move on to the next matter: this chap Murray.

'As far as one gathers, Percy Burton recruited him to act for The Annexe in what might be termed a freelance capacity. I shouldn't need to emphasise in the strongest possible terms that carrying out assassinations on behalf of what I understand Burton called the British state is completely unacceptable. It has never been the official or unofficial policy of any British government. There's no such thing as a nod and a wink in that respect. Since Burton retired in August we've unearthed all kind of things about him, most downright unpleasant. I think Pamela told you yesterday that we believe he was mixed up with Nazi collaborators, and we think that Murray may come from that world too. He's now hunting down the various people who knew what he was up to, and I'm afraid you're one of those people, Mr Cooper.

'This will be handled terribly carefully, but we need to keep a very careful eye on you, Mr Cooper, because that way we may be able to find Murray. Once we get our hands on him, then we believe that he could well lead us to these collaborators.'

'When you say keep a very careful eye on me... it sounds as if I'm being set up as a decoy.'

More silence. More coughing and Lieutenant Commander McConnell looked at Pamela, prompting her to answer, which she eventually did.

'"Decoy" may be slightly over-dramatising it. I think what we mean to say is if we watch you all the time, then sooner or later we may catch sight of Murray before he gets close to you. To that end, you'll remain in the safe house in Chelsea, which is very secure. I know you'll understand when I say that we have ended the lease on your flat in Dorset Square and put all your possessions into safe storage. Anything you need can be brought to you. You will have no contact with your mother. She's been told you're safe and abroad and she's not to worry. You will not use public transport or walk around. You will only travel in one of our cars and—'

'Then how will Murray ever have the opportunity to spot me if I'm going to be wrapped in cotton wool all the time?'

'Because in a number of very controlled circumstances you will be seen in public places, where we think Murray may be looking for you, places where we know he's been seen before. On those occasions, you will be very closely watched. He won't be able to get anywhere near you. Hopefully, we'll be able to spot him and then arrest him.'

'I'm not too sure how I feel about being made a target for a field sport... but I have another question. Yesterday I asked Pamela why Burton wasn't able to be more helpful in this regard – finding out about these collaborators and their whereabouts. I'm not sure you fully answered that, Pamela.'

This time it was Pamela who glanced at Lieutenant Commander McConnell, as if imploring him to answer. He cleared his throat before doing so.

'Percy Burton is dead, I'm sorry to tell you, Mr Cooper. He died of a heart attack in September at his home in Oxfordshire. It was a Sunday, and his wife Joan had gone to church. When she returned home she found him dead in his armchair. He was getting on, but even so, it must have been a dreadful shock for her.'

'The thing is, though, Cooper, by coincidence, Simpkin from MI5 had arranged to travel down to talk with him the following day. Told him he wanted to pick his brain; he was careful not to alert him, but actually Simpkin was planning to arrest him and search the house.'

'And nothing incriminating was found?'

Pamela shook her head. 'But that's not to say that there are no clues to be found there. I think you ought to go down there and meet with his wife. We're satisfied that she knew nothing about his work or what we'd describe as his extracurricular activities – his politics, if you like. You're a charming young chap, Cooper. You go down there. We'll sort out a car for you and you can take a nice bunch of flowers and say you heard the dreadful news, very fond of Percy, come to offer your condolences – see how that goes. You never know what she may tell you.'

Lieutenant Commander McConnell said that sounded like a very good idea. When Cooper asked when they wanted him to go, Pamela said there was no need to hang around and this Saturday seemed to be as good a day as any, and she looked at Will and asked him to sort it.

'And make sure you buy some nice flowers. I'm sure you have impeccable taste.'

–

That first Saturday of November was one of those early English winter days that come as a shock to the system, where there's a sharpness and bitterness in the air meaning that the no man's land of autumn has been replaced by the harshness of winter.

Will had turned up a bit before ten in the morning in a light green Rover Speed, with a dark-suited driver who kept glancing at them in the back through his rear-view mirror.

In no time London was behind them and the English countryside began to roll past. As they sped through the Chilterns, Cooper noticed a sheen of bright hoar frost glinting on the slopes of the hills. Soon after that they turned off the main road, came to a crossroads and the driver halted in the middle of the road, apparently unsure which way to turn before Will suggested he turn right.

Fifteen minutes later they turned onto a smaller road, this one with a more uneven surface and houses appearing on either side. Soon they came to the centre of a village and Cooper saw a sign above a shop for 'Flockham General Stores'.

They drove through the village and turned into a lane, and from that into the driveway of the house where Percy Burton had met his death.

Will had explained it would be best if he didn't come in, and he'd spend the time walking round the area keeping an eye on things.

'Good luck... and don't forget these. You may want to offer to put them into water for her.'

Cooper rang the bell and when there was no response knocked on the door, and soon after he heard a voice on the other side asking who it was.

'My name is Charles Cooper, Mrs Burton. I'm a former colleague of your husband and I...'

The door swung open and a short but smartly dressed lady with immaculate white hair was peering at him. She wore a pearl necklace and what seemed to be a cashmere cardigan and exuded elegance.

Joan Burton smiled and said he should come in.

'Remind me of your name?'

'Cooper, Charles Cooper.' Joan Burton had an assured and confident poise and an accent sharp enough to open a bottle of dry sherry, yet refined enough to open a garden party.

'Please do excuse the mess, Mr Cooper. I'm afraid that since Percy died, I've rather let things go.'

Cooper said he understood and shook his head sympathetically. By now they were in the lounge, and he handed the flowers to Mrs Burton and asked her if she'd like him to put them in water, and she said not for the time being, thank you and please do sit.

'You say you worked with Percy?'

'I did, yes.'

'And where was that?'

Cooper wasn't sure how he was meant to reply. He had no idea whether she even knew of The Annexe.

'It was at the last place he was at.'

'Ah, I see... and what brings you here?'

'I was always terribly fond of Mr Burton. He treated me very decently and I was so sorry to hear of his death. I'd mentioned to him that I've family nearby in Abingdon and he said to pop in when I was next in the area, and I thought I'd drop by to pay my respects and pass on my sincere condolences.'

Mrs Burton said, 'I see,' and how nice the flowers were, and then she was silent and Cooper was unsure what to say. The only sounds were the kitchen clock and the wind whistling through the house.

'I understand that his passing was sudden.'

'Very sudden. I went to church one Sunday morning and he was dead when I got back, still sitting in the armchair he'd been in when I left. Heart attack, apparently. Percy wasn't terribly fit, slightly over-weight and he smoked and drank, which my sister says could be connected to a heart attack, but who knows? Everyone has their own theory, of course. I suppose one just has to be grateful that it was quick.'

'Had there been any signs of illness?'

'You sound rather like a detective, Mr Cooper! No, not really. I mean, he'd slowed down somewhat, but then, haven't we all? Our family doctor did mention that he'd had a touch of angina a couple of years ago, but the last time he saw him, around two months before he died, he thought he was doing well.'

'And there were no suspicious circumstances?'

Joan Burton narrowed her eyes and looked purposefully at Cooper. 'I'm not sure what point you're endeavouring to make, Mr Cooper. It was a heart attack. What could possibly be suspicious about that?'

'I was just wondering whether... Well... it was so sudden. Maybe suspicious wasn't the right word. Unusual, maybe.'

'Well, seeing as you mention it... One of the local farmers – Mr Hartley – helps me out with the grounds, and only last week he told me that on the day Percy died one of his men was poaching rabbits in the field behind the house. Last week he admitted to Mr Hartley what he'd been up to and said on the morning Percy died, he'd noticed a man hurrying across the field from the direction of this house towards the woods. He didn't say anything at the time because one doesn't own up to poaching, but I think it must have rather been on his conscience.'

'Did he give a description of the man?'

'Tall, hat and trench coat, possibly in his forties, carrying a bag.'

'And has anyone told the police?'

'I thought about it, but I'm not sure I see the point. As far as they're concerned the death is not suspicious. Percy died of natural causes. The coroner didn't even hold an inquest. But who knows...? After all, the world he – you – worked in...'

'Did he ever talk about his work?'

'Good Lord, no!'

'But you know what he did.'

'More or less, yes. One didn't want to know the details and, in any case, he wouldn't have given them. Over the years I learnt not to ask, and Percy certainly didn't tell.'

'And his political views, did he ever express them to you?'

'Most certainly not. We never discussed such matters. This is beginning to sound like an interrogation, Mr Cooper!'

'Not at all, Mrs Burton. It's just that I was so shocked by Mr Burton's death, and especially the suddenness of it. Was there anything suspicious about his behaviour?'

'When?'

'Well, since his retirement?'

'Only the bonfire.'

'I beg your pardon?'

'I think it was on the Friday before he died. He told me he'd had a telephone call and some men from London were going to visit on the Monday to pick his brains – that's how he put it – and I do have to say that he seemed a bit distracted by that, if that's the right word. That afternoon he dug up the rhododendron bush I'd been on to him about for years. I couldn't abide it, but Percy rather liked it and he was a terrible procrastinator. I had to pester him constantly. But that Friday he dug it up, said he didn't want it to hang around, so he set a bonfire, which all seemed rather out of character for Percy. Later that afternoon I was upstairs having my afternoon nap and was awoken by the strong smell of smoke, and when I looked out of the window the bonfire was still going and Percy was putting armfuls of papers on it, documents and the like. There was a large pile and he was checking them as he put them on the fire.

'I thought it odd because he'd never done anything like that before… quite out of character. When I checked the bonfire after he died it was, of course, just a pile of ashes… Who knows…?'

'Who knows what, Mrs Burton?'

'Who knows what he was burning. Maybe nothing of any consequence. I did ask him what he was up to, and he said he'd been meaning to clear out his study for ages and the bonfire had spurred him into action.'

Mrs Burton looked a bit strained now and Pamela had told Cooper to be careful not to push his luck, so he said he really ought to be on his way and he was sure she had plenty to do.

He was in the hall putting on his coat when she asked him if he had a minute and disappeared into the dining room.

'There is one thing, Mr Cooper. I wasn't sure whether to mention it to anyone, but seeing as you're here and worked with Percy I may as well. A few years ago, he insisted on having a summer house built. I was never terribly keen on it. After all, one doesn't want to spend what one gets of summer in a hut full of spiders, but he had it built nonetheless, and I particularly resented how it hid the view of my lovely rose bushes. I decided to have it taken down and last week Mr Hartley brought his men along to do it. Well, would you believe it, they came to me and said when they removed the roof, they came across what they described as a gap in the ceiling and in it was an envelope wrapped in oilskin. When I opened it, it was a list of names and addresses which meant nothing to me, and I wondered whether it may be connected with his work. Perhaps you'd like to take it, Mr Cooper?'

Cooper said he was most grateful, and he wished her well and when he was in the back of the Rover, he told Will it had gone very well and told him about the list and took it out of the envelope.

It was a dozen sheets of cream-coloured foolscap paper, stapled together in the top corner and, apart from the top sheet, the others were typed lists of names and addresses. The top sheet had just two words typed on it:

THE GROUP

Chapter 7

Germany
November 1939

By the November of 1939 a communist in Berlin was as rare a sight as a pink elephant at the zoo, although no communist in their right mind would have gone anywhere in plain sight.

For a start, the KPD – the German communist party – had been driven underground in March 1933 when the Nazis had come to power and the Reichstag had obligingly passed the Enabling Act, which effectively banned opposition and concentrated political power in the hands of Hitler. Although eighty-one communist deputies had been elected, they never took up their seats. Leaders of the KPD, including Walter Ulbricht and Wilhelm Pieck, fled to Moscow.

Quite a number of KPD members had come to the view that survival outweighed ideology and had joined the Nazi Party. 'If you can't beat them, join them' was a phrase often used to justify their actions. Others said it was a perfect example of taking the short journey from one extreme to another. For the thousands who had remained communists and gone underground, the Nazi–Soviet non-aggression pact of August 1939 had proven to be extremely awkward, if not downright confusing.

Having understood that the Nazis were their sworn enemy, they now found that they were apparently on the same side. But few people were fooled by this, least of all the Nazis who continued to oppress those communists they came across, throwing thousands of them into concentration camps such as Dachau and Sachsenhausen. In the traditional communist areas of Berlin – Wedding, Moabit, Kreuzberg and Prenzlauer Berg – the communists who'd gone underground went even deeper. It was rare for them to gather, maybe two or three meeting in an apartment just so long as they trusted the others there. And there were still some bars where a sympathetic owner would allow comrades to meet in upstairs rooms or the cellars.

But if a communist in Berlin was a rare sight, then a communist in the Kriegsmarine was even rarer, and one who was an officer was so rare as to be more or less extinct.

But one or two did exist. Take Kapitänleutnant Arthur Klein.

Klein was born in Aachen in 1908 to a respectable middle-class family. His father was an optician, and his mother taught science at a girls' school, and her father – to whom the young Arthur had been especially close – was an engineer who instilled in his grandson a respect for science, emphasising that through science one would discover objective truth.

Perhaps in tribute to his grandfather – who died when Arthur was fifteen – Klein decided to study engineering at Aachen University, which was regarded as one of the top universities in Germany for technology. He was, in many ways, a model student: hard-working and clearly very intelligent, and with his friendly disposition he was popular among fellow students and his lecturers.

And it was one of those lecturers – a man called Krüger – who asked to see him one day towards the start of the final year of his course, which was 1929. Krüger asked if he could come to his office at the end of the day, and when Klein did so he was surprised to find that Krüger unlocked his door before opening it and then locked it again once he was inside.

And Krüger was not alone. Sitting alongside Krüger's desk was a slightly built man with a weathered face, who stood up when Klein entered and shook his hand warmly and said he was delighted to meet him and he'd heard so much about him, and then Krüger said he'd better explain.

This is Erich Neumann, he said: Fregattenkapitän Erich Neumann – a senior officer in the Kriegsmarine – and at that point Neumann had helpfully taken out an identity card, which he showed to the young student. Krüger said he'd been approached in absolute confidence – this meeting was also taking place in conditions of confidence, he should understand – to see if he could recommend any outstanding students who may be suitable for a project Fregattenkapitän Neumann was running for the navy, and Klein was the first student he'd thought of.

Klein – no wiser at this point but slightly flattered nonetheless – said thank you very much and at this point the navy man took over.

Herr Klein may well be aware, he said, that under the terms of the Treaty of Versailles, the Kriegsmarine was only permitted to have 15,000 sailors and a limited number of ships – thirty-six, in fact, including a dozen torpedo boats, which as far as he was concerned, barely counted.

'And no submarines. It's a ridiculous situation, quite improper. The Kriegsmarine has recently begun to take clandestine steps to remedy this. We will rebuild our navy by whatever means necessary. We have established a front operation in the Netherlands to build new vessels, particularly submarines. This expansion of our navy is a priority... and we are looking to recruit smart young men to assist us in this. We are especially keen to recruit men with a background in engineering and someone like you would be very well qualified. I presume you're interested?'

'It would be a great honour for the university,' said Krüger. 'And of course, for you. I've no doubt you're perfectly suited for this role.'

'Let me assure you,' said Neumann, 'that you will receive proper training. There's no question of throwing you in at the deep end. You will join as an officer cadet with the rank of Fähnrich and once you complete your training you can apply for promotion. Let me tell you, too, the salary is a very good one and a life in the navy is hard to beat... the camaraderie, the excitement, being at sea... the women!'

Klein asked if it was possible to think about it, maybe to discuss it with his family, but Neumann said that was out of the question. 'You must understand that this issue of re-arming and re-equipping our armed forces is a very sensitive one. I would need you to agree now.'

'And as I said, Klein – this is a great honour for the university.'

At that point Arthur Klein couldn't really have cared less about the university, but as it happened, he had recently been thinking about what to do when he graduated and hadn't been able to make up his mind, but he did want to do something interesting – exciting, even – and this proposal from the navy sounded like it was worth looking into. He said, 'Very well,' and Neumann clapped his hands and said he was delighted to welcome him on board and all he needed to do was sign this document... here and once again on the next page, and before he knew it, Arthur Klein was an officer cadet in the Kriegsmarine.

–

That had, of course, been ten years earlier and Arthur Klein had to admit it was a decision he'd never regretted. His work in the Kriegsmarine had been interesting and not without excitement. After his training he'd been based in Bremerhaven and then Kiel, and for a while in The Hague where the front organisation overseeing the expansion of the navy was based, and that had gone especially well. He'd learnt Dutch and found putting his engineering skills to the test to be most satisfying.

He'd been promoted to Lieutenant and was on course to reach Kapitän zur See rank very soon.

But that was not to say that his life had not been without complications. In fact, there was one rather significant complication and it was entirely of Klein's own making. After he signed up to join the Kriegsmarine in 1929, Krüger had told him not to worry about his degree; there was no question he'd pass his exams. And although he didn't stop studying, Klein was able to indulge other interests. One of these was swimming – which as a man of six feet three inches tall was a source of wry amusement when people discovered he was called Klein – and the other was attending lectures on current affairs, which had always fascinated him.

His interest in politics had become more acute as the political situation in Germany became more charged. Even in the comparative calm of Aachen – a traditionally wealthy spa town dominated by its university – the poverty and economic problems were obvious, and one evening Klein found himself at a lecture which claimed it had the answer to this. It was given by a lecturer from the university, a man who described himself as a Marxist and who explained in the clear and logical language of a scientist how the ills of society and the solutions to those could be explained by a clear understanding of Marxism–Leninism.

It all felt very logical to Klein and he began to attend meetings of the Communist Party in Aachen, which it had to be said was not exactly a communist stronghold. He did wonder if this interest in communism may be a problem, given that he was about to join the Kriegsmarine. He was sure that if the navy found out about his political interests, they'd take a dim view of it, so he was very careful when attending these meetings.

In fact, for a couple of years, he did very little about it, other than attend the occasional meeting and read widely on the subject, and everything he read only served to reinforce his views.

But once he was posted in The Hague it was easier to be active. By 1933 many German communists had fled to Dutch cities; there was a group based in The Hague and Arthur Klein took to attending their meetings. He was always very careful about not revealing who he was or what he did, but one evening, as he was walking back to his lodgings after a meeting, an older man caught up with him as he was about to cross a road.

'I've seen you in our meetings recently, haven't I?'

He was considerably shorter than Klein, perhaps by as much as one foot, and was craning his neck as he peered up at him.

'Quite possibly, yes.'

'Ernst Schwarz,' the man said, having now gripped Klein's hand and shaking it vigorously, seemingly reluctant to let go. 'From Berlin.'

Klein had never given his name to anyone at the KPD meetings – which was not in itself unusual. Instead, he simply said, 'Arthur.'

The man crossed the road with him and carried on in the same direction. When Klein came to his turning, he stopped and wished Herr Schwarz a good evening and said who knows, we may meet again soon.

'I have no doubt at all that we will meet again soon. In fact, I have every expectation that we will do so, Lieutenant Arthur Klein.' His eyes sparkled as he looked up at him with a self-satisfied grin on his face, as if to say, 'See, I know your name and rank!'

Klein had no idea how to respond, but didn't need to because Schwarz spoke first.

'You'll be surprised how much we know about you. You are from Aachen and joined the Kriegsmarine when you left university in 1930. You joined the Kriegsmarine as an officer cadet and are now involved in their clandestine operation based here in The Hague to secretly re-equip the navy, in violation of the Treaty of Versailles. You work for the NV Ingenieurskantoor voor Scheepsbouw, which we know is a front for the Kriegsmarine. And somehow, you've managed to keep your interest in communism from your employers, which is quite impressive. What more would you like to know?'

Klein said that was more than enough, thank you, and he really ought to...

'You really ought to find time to have a proper chat with me, Arthur, we have so much to discuss. We couldn't quite believe our luck, finding a communist serving as an officer in the Kriegsmarine.'

–

That was Arthur Klein's first encounter with Ernst Schwarz. The two met again at the weekend at a farmhouse near Leiden lent to them by a Dutch communist, where he was introduced to two others, one German and the other Russian. And by the end of that weekend Arthur Klein was, to all intents and purposes, a spy for the KPD, promising to pass on intelligence from inside the heart of the Kriegsmarine.

A very small part of him felt conflicted – more fearful, actually, because at the end of the day espionage was espionage – but above all else, he'd been persuaded that this was how a true Marxist–Leninist should behave. He'd be doing what he could to undermine the Nazis and to further the cause of communism.

A few months later he was posted to Berlin, to the Kriegsmarine headquarters in the Shell-Haus near the Bendlerblock. And he was promoted; he was now Kapitänleutnant Arthur Klein, with a very pleasant apartment in Charlottenburg and an agreeable lifestyle, even if it was all lived against the backdrop of the Nazi regime.

But at least the Kriegsmarine felt less affected by National Socialism than did many other parts of the state. Very few of his close colleagues were Nazis. For much of the time he could convince himself he was working for the navy and for Germany rather than the Third Reich.

Ernst Schwarz turned out to be less demanding of Klein than he'd feared may be the case. Certainly, he passed on the occasional document and wrote the odd report, but by and large Schwarz was quite easy-going.

'It's important you concentrate on establishing yourself and concentrating on your career – avoiding any suspicious activities. But don't worry, Arthur, there'll be a time when we'll want much more from you.'

And then that time came.

–

By November 1939 the war was in its third month and there was plenty of activity around the Kriegsmarine headquarters, all to do with blockades and protecting shipping and ensuring the fleet was ready for combat.

In the middle of the month, Klein was called into a meeting in a large room in the basement, one usually reserved for meetings that required a highly secure environment.

There were perhaps thirty of them in the room, and they all fell silent and rose to attention as Grand Admiral Erich Raeder – the head of the Kriegsmarine – marched in, closely followed by his chief of staff, Vice Admiral Otto Schniewind and a couple of other lower-ranking admirals.

Raeder stood in front of a large map showing the northern coast of Europe, the English Channel and the North Sea, and the south and east coasts of England. He spoke in a confident manner in his native Hanoverian accent and explained that part of his role as the head of the Kriegsmarine was to plan well ahead, to anticipate the plans of the Führer and ensure that the Kriegsmarine was ready to play their part. He picked up a rod from the table in front of him and tapped it sharply, and at that point a spotlight came on to illuminate the map behind him.

'I have no doubt that at some point in the next twelve months the Führer will turn his attention to Great Britain.' He tapped the map, hitting a point just north of London. 'I anticipate that once we have taken care of other countries in Europe, he will expect us to have a plan to undertake a large-scale landing in England. Most probably here… and here.' He'd pointed to the south-east corner of England. 'Now I know if I were to ask any one of you what you think of that, you'd come up with a series of perfectly valid reservations. You'd point out how strong the Royal Navy is and that any sea crossing by an invasion force would be very vulnerable to attacks by the RAF. Maybe you'd also question where we would land and wonder how feasible those locations are, because we know little about the state of the English beaches and their coastal defences, and no doubt, you'd mention the tides and unpredictability of the weather.

'I accept all that.' He paused and stared up at the North Sea for a few moments. 'But that isn't the point. If the Führer requires us to be responsible for planning a seaborne invasion of Great Britain, then we have to do that. We simply cannot say "yes, but" or "we're not quite ready for it". We start planning now. Each and every one of you in this room will have a role to play. If I'm to advise the Führer that such an invasion is unfeasible, I need to have the facts at my fingertips.

'Your work will be co-ordinated by Vice Admiral Schniewind and Rear Admiral Fricke. In the next days you will have meetings with them to discuss your specific roles. Are there any questions?'

Ernst Schwarz had returned to Berlin soon after Arthur Klein was posted there. Klein had no doubt that Schwarz's job was to keep an eye on him and to be the conduit for the intelligence he passed on; he was, in other words, his controller.

Klein lived in an apartment on Bach Strasse, just off Charlottenburger, close to a gentle tree-lined bend in the Spree. He always met Schwarz somewhere in or near Moabit, a bit further north, usually in the cellar of a bar or a warehouse around Westhafen, Berlin's large inland port connecting the Spree and the Havel to the Berlin canal system. Traditionally the area had been a stronghold of the KPD, and it seemed that Schwarz had enough contacts remaining in the area to feel safer in it.

Klein's route home every day after work took him through the Tiergarten, and just before he emerged from the park to cross Charlottenburger he'd pass a row of three benches on his left; if Schwarz wanted to meet him there'd be a chalk mark on the base of one of the legs of the bench. If he wanted to meet with Schwarz then on his lunch break, he'd take a stroll down Bendlerstrasse into Lützowstrasse. On the junction with Woyrschstrasse he'd go into a grocery shop, where the woman behind the counter had an exhausted and put-upon air that was so common in Berlin, and Klein would ask whether she had any honey in stock and she would ask whether he wanted clear honey or set, and he'd reply that it didn't matter so long as it came from bees, and as a consequence, he had a dozen jars in his kitchen, which would take some explaining if anyone ever asked.

The day following Raeder's briefing Klein was summoned to the office of Rear Admiral Kurt Fricke, a severe-looking man with a strong Berlin accent which sounded uncannily similar to Schwarz's.

'You will have paid attention to the grand admiral's briefing yesterday, Klein. I am sure you have many questions arising from it. I'd be surprised if an intelligent man like you didn't. What the grand admiral needs is a series of options to decide whether a seaborne landing is feasible. His approach is to ask a series of questions and base his conclusion upon the answers he receives. For example, some other officers are looking at the English coast and suggesting where would be the ideal place – or, more likely, places – to land. Others will look at ports of embarkation, while there are issues like the effectiveness of the Royal Air Force and tidal conditions to be addressed. It is highly unlikely that an invasion will be contemplated before we have extended our control over other parts of Europe. My feeling, and I know it is that of the grand admiral, too, is that at the very least we would have to have control of the Dutch, Belgian and northern French coasts.

'There is another very important area, Klein, which we would like you to work on. How do we transport perhaps one hundred thousand men – it could well be more – along with artillery, tanks and other armoured vehicles, plus supplies to the English coast?'

The rear admiral leant back in his chair and kept his gaze fixed on Klein, who wondered if he was expecting an answer there and then.

'In steamers and similar ships, maybe, sir?'

The rear admiral shook his head. 'To transport an invasion force such as described we would require more than fifteen hundred such ships. We doubt we can access more than three hundred steamers at the moment. But there is an answer, though, Klein: barges.'

'Barges?'

'The canals and rivers of Europe are full of them, Klein. Within a few short months we hope – and expect – to have control of most, if not all, of these waterways and therefore of the barges on them. The types of barges vary, and your job will be to carry out a detailed assessment of these different types, a stock-taking, if you like. Barges are capable of carrying very heavy loads and can be towed across by larger ships. What we want from you, Klein, is an inventory of the different types of barges, how much each can carry, how seaworthy they are, the mechanics and other considerations involved in towing them. As an engineer, you're the ideal man to undertake this. Do you have any questions?'

'You want me to look at barges throughout the Reich?'

'Your survey should also include Poland and the Protectorate of Bohemia and Moravia now that those countries are under our control. The latter is especially important because of the significance of the Danube as a trade route. You should also undertake clandestine surveys. The Netherlands is, of course, a country you're familiar with. The Dutch canals and ports are very important for us. Belgium, too. We will work out cover for you when you visit these countries.'

'And when do you want my report by, sir?'

'As soon as possible, Klein.'

–

That lunchtime he visited the grocery store on the corner of Lützowstrasse and Woyrschstrasse and bought yet another jar of honey. At least he didn't need to worry about Christmas gifts this year. The protocol for meeting with Schwarz was that each time they met they'd agree the venue of the next meeting, whoever called it. When they'd met a fortnight before, Schwarz had said their next meeting would be at a workshop on Saatwinkler Damm, a charmless road running along the edge of the canal and in the unnerving shadow of Plötzensee Prison.

As far as Klein could tell, the road mainly comprised industrial premises and warehouses and the workshop was where vans and lorries were repaired. It locked up at six in the evening, but Schwarz had a key to a gate down a narrow alley.

Klein found Schwarz in a partitioned office off the main workshop. He was sitting in the dark and gestured for Klein to sit down too.

'What do you have to report? Get on with it. We don't have too much time.'

Schwarz was wearing the blue uniform of Deutsche Reichsbahn; he'd got a job with them when he followed Klein back to Berlin. Now he was some kind of official at Friedrichstrasse Station. Klein didn't ask too many questions.

'Very well, then, I'll come straight to the point. They're planning a seaborne invasion of Great Britain. Grand Admiral Raeder wants the Kriegsmarine to prepare for it and has set us to work on planning various aspects of the invasion. My job is to conduct a survey of barges from across—'

'Barges…? Seriously?'

'They're talking about sending more than one hundred thousand men across the sea, along with all their vehicles and equipment. You clearly can't just commandeer a few dozen merchant vessels and passenger ships for that. They think that barges may be the best way of getting so many people across the sea. I'm reporting to Rear Admiral Kurt Fricke. According to him, the waterways of Europe are full of these barges.'

'I'm finding this all rather hard to believe. Are they going to travel across under their own steam, if that's the right word?'

'I think the plan is to tow them across, but it's all in its very early stages. I must carry out my work as soon as possible.'

'And when will this invasion take place?'

'I don't know – I get the impression that Raeder doesn't know either. I think the point is that he is expecting Hitler to order an invasion, and when he does that he wants to be as well prepared and as well informed as possible.'

Schwarz let out a long, low whistle and said this was extraordinary and obviously as soon as he had any firmer intelligence, Klein was to share it and meanwhile, he'd pass this on.

'Pass this on to who?'

There was a long pause and from not too far away came the sound of a ship's siren and in the distance shouting, quite possibly from the prison.

'I think I have the right to know. I'm risking my life every day doing this. All I need is to bump into someone on the way back from this meeting or for your woman in the grocery shop to be arrested – or you to come under suspicion – and then I'll end up across the road from here in Plötzensee. I understand their guillotine is very sharp.'

Schwarz spread out his hands in a 'What can I say?' gesture.

'I want you to be honest with me. I suspect you're more than a mere comrade from the KPD. I believe you have links with the Soviets, and that worries me because now the Soviet Union is in an alliance of some sort with the Reich. If the Soviets are given whatever intelligence I come up with and the Germans find out about it because of this alliance, then I'm in trouble, aren't I?'

Schwarz shook his head vigorously. 'That's not going to happen, Arthur. Let me be honest with you. Yes, I am a member of the KPD and yes, I also work for the NKVD, the Soviet Intelligence service. But just because there is a non-aggression pact between the Reich and the Soviet Union doesn't mean the two countries are allies. I can tell you that the NKVD certainly does not trust the Nazis. They believe it is only a matter of time before Hitler turns his attention to the Soviet Union, though Comrade Stalin refuses to countenance that. The NKVD see their role as building up as much intelligence as possible about the Nazis' intentions and war plans. Intelligence from sources such as yourself is invaluable, and I can absolutely assure you that it will not be shared with anyone else.

'And as far as your safety is concerned, yes... Well – espionage is a very dangerous game. But the NKVD isn't aware of your identity. They only know you as one of my sources. I hope that helps reassure you.'

Klein said actually it did. He couldn't promise when he'd have more for him because, apart from anything else, he had to travel around to conduct his survey of barges and suitable embarkation ports.

'Hopefully you'll be able to update me in the new year, Arthur?'

'Hopefully, yes.'

Chapter 8

London
November 1939

They gathered in the lounge of the safe house on Turk's Row soon after they returned from visiting Mrs Burton in Oxfordshire.

Will and Cooper sat next to each other at the dining table opposite Pamela and Lieutenant Commander James McConnell as they studied the document.

'This is excellent, Cooper. Well done – well done indeed!'

'Thank you, sir.'

Pamela and the lieutenant commander both treated the document as if it were a gold nugget and Cooper the lucky prospector. There were ten sheets of typed names and addresses, with around twenty-five names and addresses per sheet. The list appeared to be grouped into geographic regions – LONDON, SCOT, E. MIDS, WEST & S. WEST, and so on. Ten regions in total, with varying numbers of names and addresses: London had eighty, for instance, whereas East just twenty.

As far as the names were concerned, there was little notable about them. Page two, under EAST, for example:

Ronald W. White	7 Common Road	Norwich
Capt. (Rtd) G. R. Herbert	17 West Road	Dereham
Revd. A. W. Tarry	The Vicarage, Terrington Rd	Ipswich

Mrs Susan Falkener	4 The Risings	Litcham
Mr Nigel Duke	The Lower Lake House	Swaffham
Irene Barton (Miss)	1 Brooks Close	Thetford

And so on: a list of more than two hundred names and addresses, no telephone numbers; none of the names particularly stood out other than a reverend here and a retired military officer there, but they all agreed that this was undoubtedly valuable. If the Invasion Warning Sub-Committee wanted to find collaborators, The Group would appear to be a very handy list of them and a good place to start.

'I hope you chaps didn't have any plans for tomorrow… I want you to go through every name on the list. As you know, we have twelve Regional Commissioners responsible for monitoring threats to public security in their area. They include those who've previously expressed support for the Nazis or espoused views in common with theirs – Mosley's lot and suchlike. I'd be surprised if this list doesn't have something of an overlap with their lists. You'll need to check with Special Branch and MI5 to see what they know about any of these people. My sense is that this Group will have some kind of structure, possibly even an organised network of collaborators which will assist German agents in this country. Up until now, we've just had the names of individuals whose importance or significance we have little idea of. We've not known who's a crank or who represents a real threat. I cannot overstate quite how important this list is. I will speak to each Regional Commissioner tomorrow, and also the heads of MI5 and Special Branch, to ensure you receive maximum co-operation. I'd like to think that by the middle of next week we'll have made significant progress.'

It was mid-afternoon on the Saturday, although the light had faded quickly, and it had already the feel of night about it. Will and Cooper said it may be best if they went in the office there and then, and perhaps called a few of the secretaries in to help them compile copies of the list.

'I think you're right to make a start now,' said McConnell. 'This is a big job. And as far as the matter with Murray goes, I think that will have to wait a few days.'

–

Will Drysdale and Charles Cooper worked ten long days in a row, starting at seven o'clock every morning and rarely leaving the Old War Office Building before ten and sometimes even eleven at night.

By the following Monday copies of the lists had been sent to Special Branch and MI5 and the Regional Commissioners were each sent the lists of the names of people in their areas. They organised a card index system for every person and opened a file for each one. Three new filing cabinets had been requested and arrived the following day, to everyone's surprise.

By the end of the week, they began to hear back from those they'd sent the lists to. Many of the names had been members of Mosley's British Union of Fascists and were already on the Regional Commissioners' lists. Some were unknown and would be of particular interest. Others had hitherto been thought to be of minor importance, but their presence on this list would elevate the interest in them. Four of them were dead.

A debate followed about what to do with the names: should all the people be pulled in for questioning – or watched, or their houses searched? No one could quite decide; as McConnell said, while they needed to find out as much as possible about The Group, they had to be very careful about alerting its members.

They needed to find a more discreet way of investigating it, perhaps of infiltrating it.

'There's something else we need to be mindful of… As matters stand, they aren't guilty of any criminal offence. They're simply names on a list, which only makes them suspects. To build a case against them that merits their arrest and interrogation, we need evidence of them committing a criminal offence such as being involved with Nazi agents. If we turn up at these addresses and start searching their properties and questioning them, well – we're going to frighten the horses, aren't we? Give the whole game away. They'll realise we're on to them. We need to catch people in the act. We must be careful about how we approach them.'

And then a man from Special Branch turned up on the Friday morning and said he'd had an idea to cross-reference the names with those of people currently detained under Defence Regulation 18B, the emergency legislation passed in August to detain those with particularly strong Nazi views. He'd found that nine of the named people were currently detained under 18B and one of them was of particular interest.

'Donald Hatton is a businessman from Bedford, owns several garages in the area and is quite well off. Formerly a Conservative councillor in the town and since 1936 very active in the British Union of Fascists. We understand he was a donor to the BUF, and we know that he visited Germany in 1937 and 1939, the last visit a month before war was declared. On that basis he was arrested and has been detained under 18B since mid-September. Mr Hatton has not taken this very well. He retained solicitors and counsel to apply for a writ of *habeas corpus*, which is about the only way to be released under 18B, though very, very few people manage it. Mr Hatton was unsuccessful in his court action and is currently a very bitter man in Wandsworth prison. He blames us for losing his business and his reputation in the town. His wife, we are told, has left him. He claims he's an unimportant figure in the fascist movement and ought to be released. My feeling is that he could be co-operative if he's questioned about The Group, especially if he believes he could be released as a result of his co-operation.'

–

The governor of Wandsworth prison was particularly helpful. 'Of course you can come and interview Mr Hatton,' he said. 'Any time you wish. Would you like us to ensure he's in a co-operative mood?'

'What do you mean?' said Cooper.

'On occasion, we've been asked to put a prisoner in a particularly uncomfortable cell the night before they're interrogated, one with a broken window pane, perhaps, or somewhere very noisy and then maybe forget to give them their supper. Softens them up, I'm told. May I suggest you come and visit him on Sunday? Prisoners seem to be particularly miserable on Sundays. Perhaps that's the day when they think of their families and of relaxing and Sunday roasts and what have you. The place is usually quieter than on other days and my officers say the prisoners tend to be more compliant. Also, because of staffing, they spend more time in their cells, so he may well welcome a chance to get out of it.'

So, on the Sunday morning a car collected Cooper from the safe house on Turk's Row, stopped to pick up Will near Battersea Bridge and fifteen minutes later they were inside Wandsworth prison.

Donald Hatton was a tall man, younger looking than Cooper had expected, with a suspicious look on his face, a nasty shaving rash on his neck and signs of an even nastier cold. He was pushed into a chair opposite Will and Cooper.

Will avoided introducing themselves and explained they were here to ask some questions and if Mr Hatton was as co-operative as they hoped he would be, then that would very much count in his favour.

'In what way?'

'If and when your detention under 18B is reviewed.'

'At my court case I was told there was little to no prospect of that happening. I'm being treated like a common criminal, as opposed to a man of some standing. It's quite appalling that we have gone to war apparently to defend democracy and what have you, yet the British government acts like some cheap dictatorship and yet is so ready to criticise Herr Hitler and his government. I'm a respectable businessman, a person of some standing in my community, and yet here I am among common criminals. There's a man on my landing who sexually assaulted young children – and I'm expected to mix with people like that! Am I really to believe that by helping you I may be released early? You can't guarantee that, can you? Why, you've not even given me the courtesy of introducing yourselves.'

He folded his arms in the manner of a child indicating they weren't playing this particular game and threw his head back as if to say, 'So there.'

'What can you tell us about The Group?'

This had been Pamela's suggestion. She said he was bound to complain and moan at first but if he was asked that question straight out, without any warning or preamble, then he may be caught unawares.

Hatton looked shocked, gripping the table with both hands, and quickly lowered his head. He frowned and narrowed his eyes and asked Will to repeat the question.

'What can you tell us about The Group?'

'I'm afraid I've no idea what you're talking about.'

'Really, Mr Hatton?' said Cooper. 'I've been watching you. At the mention of the words "The Group" your demeanour switched in an instant from what I'd have described as combative to frightened.'

'I'm not frightened, I can assure you.'

'Then what can you tell us about The Group?'

'As I've just told you, I've no idea what on earth you're talking about.'

'We have reliable information, Mr Hatton, that there is an organisation of pro-Nazi sympathisers in this country whose role is to assist the Germans. We have evidence that you are a member of this group. Anything you can tell us about it will count in your favour.'

Hatton shook his head but now he was looking quite flustered; perspiration had appeared on his brow and he was running his hands through his hair in an agitated manner, and they could hear the nervous tapping of his feet from under the table.

Cooper opened his notebook and Hatton's eyes followed him turning the pages.

'Does the name Richard Vennell mean anything to you, Mr Hatton? Address in Biddenham in Bedford, lives in the appealingly named Lavender Cottage. Or how about a retired army major called Maxwell Hoare with an address in the Shortstown area of Bedford? And for good measure, two more residents of Bedford... Doreen and Martyn Johnstone – that's Martyn with a "y". They're all on our list, Mr Hatton, as being people from Bedford who are members of The Group. Along with you. So perhaps if you'd be so good as to tell us what you know about it.'

Hatton inhaled slowly and noisily through his nostrils and exhaled equally noisily and slowly through his mouth.

'Despite my being detained – quite improperly, I may add – under 18B, I can assure you that my involvement with the fascist movement is no more than marginal. I know very little, other than the odd item of gossip one hears.'

'What kind of gossip?'

'Rumours – unsubstantiated ones at that. Maybe that The Group is some kind of self-help organisation, that kind of rumour. A charity as much as anything else: standing bail for someone, giving them a lift to hospital if required. That's all I've ever heard. I've no idea how or why my name has appeared on that list. I've nothing further to add. I fear I'm wasting your time – and indeed, mine – although my time is wasted every minute that I'm illegally held in this cursed place.'

'We do have the option, Mr Hatton, of letting it be known in the right circles that you've been most helpful to us. I imagine the personal repercussions for you and your family could be quite serious if that becomes known?'

'But I'm not being helpful, though, am I? I just mentioned I'd heard rumours... I shouldn't even have told you that.'

'That's the point, though, Mr Hatton.' For someone who was normally so amenable and quietly spoken, Will could at times sound menacing. Threatening, even, which was the tone he struck now. It seemed to have the desired effect on Donald Hatton, who looked flushed and frightened and shifted in his chair as if he was trying to get up.

'I'll deny it. Everyone will know you're lying.'

'Big risk to take, Mr Hatton. I'm told Wandsworth is full of people detained under 18B. Some very unpleasant types here. Are you really prepared to let them think you're being helpful to the authorities? And word is bound to reach The Group, isn't it? I'm not sure what they'll think of that, but I can't imagine they'll be terribly happy with you.'

Hatton pushed his chair back and leant forward so his hands were straight and gripping the table once more. 'I don't think you have any idea whatsoever what you're doing or who you're doing it with. If you knew anything about The Group, then you'd drop this. It's too dangerous. I beg you to leave me out of this.'

'You seem to know a lot more about The Group than you've been letting on, Mr Hatton.' Cooper fixed his gaze on the prisoner, who now looked terrified.

'I've told you enough. These people will kill you without a second thought!'

–

The ever-accommodating prison governor was waiting in the corridor when Donald Hatton was led out of the room where he'd been with Charles Cooper and Will Drysdale.

'I hope that was satisfactory from your point of view?' He asked the question in the manner of someone who, while not exactly prying, wouldn't have been offended if they'd taken him into their confidence.

Cooper said they needed to let Hatton have a while to reflect on matters.

'With some luck he may decide to be of more assistance than he was just now.'

'I could help you in that respect,' said the governor.

'In what way?'

'A week or two in solitary confinement can certainly concentrate the mind.'

'Are you able to put in him in solitary confinement for no reason?'

'From the sounds of it, gentlemen, the national interest is a good enough reason.'

Chapter 9

It had never occurred to Archie that life as a double agent was ever going to be a smooth one. He'd been recruited as an MI6 agent in 1931 while still at Oxford, and started work with the Service that September. That same month he'd been on holiday in France when he encountered a man called Emil in Paris, bumped into him again in Lyons, and then at a fateful encounter in Cannes a few days later it emerged that these encounters had been anything but coincidental.

Emil was fully aware of Archie's sympathies at Oxford for the Soviet Union and the Communist Party, of his recruitment by a tutor called Maurice Gilbert and his espionage efforts on his behalf, notably photographing secret documents which his father brought home from his work in Whitehall.

Maurice Gilbert had died of natural causes, but that hadn't let Archie off the hook, as he'd hoped at the time. Gilbert had been astute enough to provide his Soviet masters with all the evidence they needed to prove that Archie had been working for him – and them – and they were delighted he'd secured a position with the Service. From now on, it was explained to him in the South of France, he'd also be working for Soviet Intelligence, and he even had a codename: Archie.

At the time Archie had tried to dismiss his involvement with communism as a youthful indiscretion, insisting that he'd not been serious. But he'd quickly realised it was hopeless to pretend that he was anything other than trapped. He was a Soviet agent – and a British one.

He was told by Emil that it may be a while before he was contacted and that in the meantime, he should concentrate on establishing himself at MI6 and doing his very best to avoid arousing suspicion.

He'd been summoned to Moscow in 1937 – a risky detour while on a solo holiday in Austria – after which his career as a Soviet agent began properly. In April 1939 he met his contact in London, Osip, for the last time and was told soon after that Osip was dead, and from now on, he'd be handled by the NKVD *rezident* in London, Ivan Alexandrovich Morozov. He'd been passed from one Soviet Intelligence agency to another, it seemed. Traded, like some common or garden commodity.

At MI6 he'd quickly acquired a reputation of being bright and hard-working. He married Alice in 1934. She came from a wealthy family, which was very much part of her attraction. Their first child was born the following year, the second one the year after, and most people would look at him and think his life was fine, even an enviable one: a good career, a wife and two children, with places secured at the best boarding schools, homes in London and the country. It was not unusual for people to tell Archie how lucky he was. If only they knew, he thought – if only they knew. It was rare for him to encounter tradesmen or manual workers or pass people queuing outside the cheap shops in the poorer parts of town or observe the infirm and those clearly experiencing hard times without envying their uncomplicated lives.

What did they have to worry about apart from their obvious ill fortune? How many of these people – who'd never had much expect-ation from life in the first place – spent every waking hour and quite a few of their non-waking ones waiting for a summons or a telephone call which would be the first sign of their being unmasked as a traitor? What did they know of the constant fear, the strain of having to live an apparently normal life while carrying out this duplicity, the enduring sense of anxiety, the inability to relax for even one moment?

And since August, this was compounded by the fact that the Soviet Union was now in a non-aggression pact with Nazi Germany. Whichever way Archie looked at it – and heaven knows he'd tried – that meant he was now unequivocally on the wrong side, with all the unthinkable implications such an act of treason brought with it.

In recent weeks he'd been experiencing a recurring nightmare, where he was arrested and tried in a medieval court, standing shackled and barefoot on a rough stone floor before being sentenced to death, and when asked if he had anything to say, was unable to speak before he was then marched into a courtyard, where the flimsy robe he'd been wearing since his arrest was ripped from him. He was dragged naked in front of his family and everyone he knew to be hanged, drawn and quartered, conscious until the very end.

–

He'd only met Ivan Alexandrovich Morozov three times: first at an initial meeting in May, where the Russian had said they should treat it as an opportunity to get to know each other.

'More a social occasion than anything else!'

Archie couldn't think of any circumstances in which he'd mix socially with Morozov, a gruff-sounding man with passable enough English but an accent that at times rendered it incomprehensible. He was notably large: six feet tall certainly, and thickset in a way that his clothes always sat badly on him. And he was forever perspiring, as if he'd hurried to wherever he was. He had a habit of pulling a large handkerchief from his jacket pocket, like a magician, and using it to wipe his face and the back of his neck, all the time accompanied by the odour of cheap Russian tobacco and sweat.

It struck Archie that the Service took so much care with ensuring that the agents they had operating abroad did their best to blend in. The worst thing for an agent was for them to stand out, but then it was quite possible he was being sensitive about it. He was surprised that whenever he saw Morozov in public more people didn't pay him attention.

Not that he saw him in public much. When Morozov wanted to meet him, Archie would find a chalk mark on the inside of the gatepost at his Hampstead home. The mark would be a circle, roughly shaded in, and then Archie would know to look behind the ornamental stone lion by his front door. There'd be either one, two or three pebbles neatly placed there. Depending on how many pebbles, he'd know which one of three safe houses to go to after work the following day. And this method of communication wasn't as rash as may have seemed; the front of the house was shielded by a high hedge.

He'd last seen Morozov at the end of August, a few days after the Ribbentrop–Molotov pact between the Soviet Union and Nazi Germany had been announced. This time it was Archie who'd requested the meeting, telephoning a tobacconist's shop in Hackney and asking if they had any Dutch cigars in stock and if so, would he be able to pick them up that evening? That meant he wanted to meet

Morozov, but it was not an emergency. A request to collect the cigars as soon as possible would have signified it was.

He'd phoned the tobacconist's and, sure enough, the following day there was a disc chalked on the inside of his gatepost and two pebbles behind the stone lion. That meant they'd meet in the safe house in Earls Court, which suited him fine as it wasn't too far away. Morozov appeared put out, as if he had somewhere better to be. He was sitting at a kitchen table covered with a dirty oilcloth, smoking and tipping the ash onto a plate of biscuits, which he then pushed towards Archie.

'What do you have to tell me?'

'It's more that I have something to ask you, Ivan.'

'You've brought me here to ask me a question? It had better be important!'

'I'm concerned about this pact with Germany... Does this mean that if I supply you with intelligence, it will be shared with the Germans? In which case, I'm really not sure—'

'Not sure about what?' The Russian's eyes narrowed, and he ran a hand across his forehead before wiping it on his sleeve.

'Not sure it's worth the risk. I mean... with the Germans?'

Morozov said nothing for a while, taking the time to light another foul-smelling cigarette. 'You should understand that as Marxist–Leninists, it is not our place to question decisions made by our leaders. They see the whole picture; we are only able to see part of it. You can be assured that any decision Comrade Stalin has made, will have been made in the best interests of the Soviet Union.'

The meeting wrapped up soon after that, Archie promising to gather what he could on the British war effort and Ivan undertaking to tell Moscow that it was not to be shared with the Germans. When Archie left, he wasn't sure he believed Ivan when he said he'd ask Moscow not to share his intelligence with the Germans.

He didn't feel any easier.

–

'Yes, Dutch cigars, and I'd like to collect them as soon as possible.' There was silence on the other end of the line and Archie asked if they'd like him to repeat it, but the man said there was no need, he understood.

This time the meeting with Morozov was in Stepney, in a room above a fruit shop on Salmon Lane. The long walk from Burdett Road Station allowed him enough time to check he wasn't being followed.

Morozov was notably friendlier, even going to the not inconsiderable effort of getting up to greet him with a warm handshake, the kind where he used both hands to shake his. Archie always felt this seemed a bit too Masonic, which was really not his cup of tea, even if most of his wife's male relatives were all for hitching up their trouser legs and whatever else it was the Masons got up to behind closed doors.

'Please sit down, Archie, make yourself at home,' which was of course a ridiculous thing to say as this hovel was totally unlike his notion of home. Morozov sank into a low sofa and wiped his forehead.

'We'd hoped to have heard from you before now,' the Russian said. 'Moscow doesn't like it when an important source goes dry.'

'You could have contacted me.'

'We agreed at our last meeting, Archie, that the situation is delicate. I didn't want you to feel under too much pressure. What do you have for me?'

'I don't have anything as such, Ivan – I've not brought anything with me, if that's what you mean.'

'So, you've come empty-handed, even though you called this meeting?'

'I'm happy to answer any questions you may have.'

Morozov shook his head and said he was disappointed. It seemed to Archie that his handler didn't have the intellect to know what questions he should ask. He realised he only did what Moscow told him.

'I've been promoted at work, Ivan.'

'Congratulations, Archie! That's wonderful news. I hope it means you will be able to provide us with even better intelligence?'

'I'm not sure it's necessarily quite as straightforward as that.'

'What do you mean?'

'A number of colleagues on my grade were promoted at the same time, but they looked very closely into our backgrounds and then subjected us to particularly rigorous interviews. At my interview it felt at times as if I was being interrogated, and I do know that they'd been looking at my bank accounts.'

'Are you saying they suspected you?'

'I did wonder about that, but I don't think so, although of course they are still looking for a Soviet spy codenamed Archie and—'

'Hang on, Archie, slow down… This is the first I've heard that they know there's a Soviet spy called Archie! You'd not told us this? Surely informing us of something so vital was a priority? It's inexplicable that you didn't tell us. Moscow will be—'

'I did inform you.' Archie made an effort to appear as calm and as confident as possible. Telling a blatant lie came naturally to him.

'When? This is the first I've heard of this, and I'm sure no one in Moscow was aware of it because if they were, then I'd have known too and—'

'Osip knew. I told him.'

'When, exactly?'

Archie shrugged, now almost enjoying the fabrication. 'I don't know the exact date, Ivan. It wasn't something I noted in my diary, if that's what you mean. But it would have been some time in late 1938. My guess is around November because the theatre incident happened in the October.'

'I've seen all your files and all of Osip's notes and there is no mention of this, not a word. Are you sure?'

'Of course I'm sure! I informed Osip about everything. It's hardly my fault if he failed to pass the information on to Moscow.' Archie knew full well the NKVD had disposed of Osip. It was very easy to blame a dead man.

'You said something about a theatre?'

'I'd better start at the beginning, Ivan, though I have to say I'm surprised you knew nothing of this. And you're not going to like what I'm going to tell you, though. When I was brought to Moscow in May 1937, I was in the Kremlin one day and went for a walk on my own at lunchtime. I ended up in the Taynitskaya Tower where a man spoke to me in English. I cannot remember exactly what he said, I think he was asking me for directions. But unfortunately, I made the error of replying in English, and to make matters worse, there was something familiar about him – I was sure I'd met him some years previously.'

'Where?'

'It was only after the encounter that I recalled where we'd met. It was when I was at Oxford, in a chess tournament. I didn't mention it at the time, and I doubt he remembered who I was because nothing came of it, but the following August, I saw him again in London, near an underground station. He saw me and tried to follow me, but I didn't let on. To cut a very long story short, I found out where he lived – which was at a college in Cambridge – and went there and disposed of him.'

'You mean you… killed him?'

Morozov sounded incredulous. Archie nodded.

'So, no harm came of this. Had he known who I was I'd have been arrested long before then. There was another incident, though, last summer. A British diplomat in Moscow was approached by a man who said he worked for the OMS, and he wanted help in escaping the Soviet Union to Britain. In return, he was willing to give the British the identity of a Soviet agent called Archie who was operating in London. As far as I understand it, this man never turned up for his next meeting and the British assumed he'd been caught. But he'd given them enough… and for some reason London linked this with the man – me – being spotted in the Kremlin. The man I'd met was called Branstone and it turned out he was working for British Intelligence. So that's how they know about Archie.'

'How did he get into the Kremlin?'

'He was looking at icons, I believe.'

Morozov shook his head and let out a long whistle. 'I simply cannot believe that Osip failed to pass this on. It was absolutely essential Moscow should have been informed. This account you're giving me is rather garbled, Archie. We will need to sit down and compose a much more detailed and coherent version, you understand?'

'Of course, I'm sorry, I'm just surprised you didn't know this.'

'And you said something about a theatre, after which was when you say you told Osip?'

'Oh, yes… The man the Service put in charge of the hunt for me is called Phillips, and for some reason he seems to have suspected that the Soviet agent he was hunting was an MI6 officer. I'm not too sure why he thought this, but then he called a meeting for all the officers based at Broadway and said that evening he was due to meet an informer from the Soviet embassy who may have information about the identity of Archie. He was meeting the informer in the foyer of the Phoenix Theatre on Charing Cross Road. I decided to go along and watch from a discreet distance, but once I was there, I realised it was a trap…

there were watchers all over the place. I only just managed to get away without being spotted.

'This Phillips was also the man who interviewed me for this promotion, but you don't need to worry, I'm not a suspect. I think it is best to see this as a warning and it's why I've asked to see you... I'm concerned at the risk I'm taking. Even coming here for a meeting is full of danger. I spotted a civil servant I know from the War Office at Fenchurch Street Station. I don't think he saw me, and even if he did, he wouldn't necessarily think anything of it... but do you see what I mean?'

'I'm not sure I do. What is it you're suggesting, Archie?'

'I'm suggesting it may be for the best if I lie low for a while.'

'How long is "a while"?'

'Possibly a few months?'

'Months! Moscow won't accept that.'

'Well, at the very least, Ivan, I need to be clearer about what it is I'm meant to be doing. I told you the last time we met, I was recruited to work for the Soviet Union, not for Nazi Germany. They're the enemy.'

Morozov nodded and fumbled in his jacket pocket to find his cigarettes and took a while to light one. 'Leave it with me, Archie. I doubt Moscow will agree to what you propose, but I can get some clarification on exactly what it is they want from you. Can we meet here again next Monday – at the same time?'

'I thought you never use the same safe house twice in succession?'

'It will be easier than me arranging another one in such a short space of time.'

–

When they met again the following Monday, Morozov looked like a man who'd just returned from a funeral. No effusive greetings this time; instead he looked tense and worried. No sooner had they sat down than he began to tell Archie how Moscow had insisted that Osip had never said a thing to them about what he described as Archie's 'mistakes', and in any case, even if he had told Osip, he should also have told Morozov the first time they'd met.

'And were Moscow able to give you any clarification on what my role is now? Exactly what it is that you're looking for from me?'

Morozov appeared distracted, hauling himself up from the sofa and pulling the blackout blinds back just far enough so he could observe the city below him. It had been snowing when Archie walked from the station and now Morozov commented that the snow was heavier.

'It's probably what you'd call a blizzard. In Moscow we'd call this a pleasant spring day! Does the name Maisky mean anything to you?'

'Your ambassador here in London?'

Morozov nodded. Archie actually knew an awful lot about Ivan Mikhailovich Maisky; he'd written a detailed intelligence report on him for the Service, which ran to some twelve thousand words and had been widely praised around Whitehall. He'd interviewed dozens of people who'd come across Maisky and he felt there was little he didn't know about the man.

Mid-fifties, father a Polish Jew, mother Russian Orthodox, brought up in Omsk, studied at St Petersburg University, regarded as an intellectual and a Menshevik rather than a Bolshevik, but clever enough to get on with the right people and also clever enough to see which way the wind was blowing, so he allied himself with the Bolsheviks and ended up working for the People's Commissariat for Foreign Affairs, then a diplomat in London, Helsinki and Tokyo before being appointed ambassador to London in 1932 and he'd been there ever since. He'd acquired a reputation as a tough negotiator who mixed in left-wing intellectual circles.

Archie had been especially interested in Maisky's early history of being anti-Bolshevik, and wondered whether this may suggest an opening for British Intelligence. He'd identified some of the people he mixed with who may be helpful in this respect, and as far as he was aware, this was something that was yet to be followed up.

'Although I don't answer to him directly, he takes an interest in intelligence matters and he's obviously trusted by Moscow. He is aware of your case, Archie. He wants to meet you.'

'When?'

'As soon as possible?'

'And where do we meet?'

'You still have that lock-up near Kentish Town Station, is that right?'

'Yes.'

'When you leave work on Wednesday – that's the day after tomorrow – go to Kentish Town and to the corner of Lady Margaret Road and Countess Road. Do you know where I mean?'

'It's near my lock-up.'

'Exactly. You'll see a small blue Fordson van waiting there with the name of a bakery on the side. Someone will open the rear doors as you approach. The van will bring you to the embassy in Kensington Palace Gardens. There's nothing the police can do about the van; they're not allowed to stop it. It's a van we regularly use to deliver bread – and other things.'

–

Archie left 54 Broadway soon after 4:30 on the Wednesday afternoon, explaining that he was meeting someone at the Foreign Office, but instead headed straight to Kentish Town and from there to the lock-up he rented in a quiet alley behind a parade of shops.

Once he was sure no one was around, he retrieved the key from its hiding place in the gutter and once inside, opened one of the suitcases he kept there and removed a long trench coat, slightly shabby, and then put on a pair of well-worn boots and a cloth cap which he felt went with the coat. Thus disguised, he headed for the corner of Lady Margaret Road and Countess Road. He was obviously expected because as he approached the van one of the rear doors opened and a man helped him in.

It was an uncomfortable ride, lying down on the rough metal floor of the van between trays of bread and being bumped around. The van slowed down and the man crouched in the back with him gave him a blanket to cover himself and said it wasn't long now.

–

Ivan Mikhailovich Maisky was a short man, little more than five feet five, with a few strands of greying hair swept optimistically over his bald head and a prominent moustache which appeared to weigh down his face, an effect which was compensated for by a friendly smile. He looked more like a family doctor than a Soviet diplomat and he greeted Archie in what seemed to be a curious manner, as if he was finally meeting one of his agents, especially one who also worked for the British Secret Service.

They were in the rear entrance of the embassy on Kensington Palace Gardens, close to where the bread van had parked, and Archie was still stiff from his journey among the loaves of bread. Morozov was there, too, and said they were going to the ambassador's residence next door, and Archie would understand if he was searched, which of course was just a formality. One of the security men hovering around the ambassador searched Archie more roughly than he thought appropriate and then they headed to the residence.

Once inside they stopped at an open door behind which was a flight of stairs going down to what was clearly a basement. Maisky gestured towards it and said, 'Please,' making it clear Archie should go first.

Archie hesitated and said, 'No, please after you,' to the ambassador and then there was an awkward moment as he gestured to Maisky by placing a hand on his elbow. One of the security men stepped forward as if Archie was about to assault him, and all the time Archie was thinking that this was not right, because to the best of his knowledge basements and the Soviets tended to mean one thing. This could all be a trap to dispose of him; after all, Moscow had made it clear that as far as they were concerned, he'd made a number of mistakes. Archie worried he was now seen as disposable, and he feared he could be about to be disposed of in the basement and no one would have the faintest idea he was here.

He left work at 4:30… said he was going to meet someone at the Foreign Office… last anyone saw of him… disappeared into thin air…

From the basement came the sound of metal scraping on a stone floor and Archie wondered if this was something to do with what they were planning to do to him. He took one step back and at that point Morozov must have realised what was going on and said he wasn't to worry, what did he think was going to happen down there, and then laughed out loud and the ambassador joined in and Morozov said to follow him.

The basement was enormous, running under the whole of the ground floor, and from the sound and smell, it was where the kitchens were. It also had a much higher ceiling than he'd expected. They entered a small room next to a pantry, just the three of them, with the security guards waiting outside the closed door. As far as Archie could tell, this was a secure room, with the walls cladded with what appeared to be a soundproofing material.

Ambassador Maisky started to speak as he took his seat. His English was good – far better than Morozov's – and with a type of almost faux upper-class accent Archie had noticed in the English spoken by some foreigners. Maybe it was the circles he mixed in.

'I want you to understand something, my friend.' He paused and leant back in his chair, and Archie was disconcerted at being addressed as 'my friend' because that was how some of the teachers at school would address a pupil before punishing them: English public-school-speak to indicate that the person being addressed thus was anything but their friend.

'I hope you appreciate quite how unprecedented this meeting is. The protocol in our overseas missions is to maintain a separation between our diplomatic functions and our intelligence operations. For me to meet one of our agents in person is most unusual and not without risks, even more so when that agent is a national of the country where I represent the Soviet Union, and especially considering the work that you do.

'The decision for me to meet with you in person has not been taken lightly but we –' he pointed to Morozov and then to himself to emphasise who was meant by the 'we' – 'we felt it was an important opportunity to make it clear to you how much you are valued, and also to clarify the nature of your work for us.

'On that point, let me say this... I know that since the Soviet Union entered into an arrangement with Germany you have expressed some unease, which I understand. Working for communism and for peace is a different proposition from working – as you may see it – for a country at war with yours. But let me say this... The Soviet Union is neither an ally nor a friend of Germany. They are our ideological enemy. But Comrade Stalin is a shrewd man. The non-aggression pact is simply a way of us buying time. We don't doubt that Hitler wishes to eventually invade the Soviet Union. We are a country replete with natural resources which he needs. The Ukraine is Europe's greatest source of wheat. We have ample supplies of coal and oil, and our Black Sea ports are of enormous strategic importance.

'But while he sets about conquering northern and western Europe, it suits him not to have to worry about the Red Army. And the truth is, our defences are such that we would struggle to withstand a Nazi invasion of the type we are currently witnessing elsewhere in Europe. As long as we have a non-aggression pact with them, we can concentrate on strengthening our military.

'So, that is why you need to understand that our temporary arrangement with Germany doesn't mean that you are working for them. Is that clear, my friend?'

Archie realised he'd just been given an extraordinary insight into the thinking of the Soviet leadership. He'd have to incorporate this into a report, though in a way which would conceal the source. It would have to come across as his opinion. He told Maisky he appreciated the clarification, and the Soviet ambassador nodded in acknowledgement before continuing.

'Which brings me to the question of what intelligence we expect from you. Of course, we're interested in anything important that you can let us have, but I appreciate you'd like us to be more specific, my friend. As I've already intimated, our main worry is that Hitler will at some point turn his attention eastwards and attack the Soviet Union. I cannot state strongly enough how imperative it is for that to be delayed as long as possible. And this is where your country comes into it. Our intelligence suggests that Hitler's next objective is the United Kingdom. His intelligence services and armed forces have been told to prepare for an invasion of this country. It's vital to us that Germany exerts considerable time and effort to planning and preparing to invade this country. As long as they're doing that, then we're not under threat. Your country needs to be seen to be preparing for this, and should an invasion take place – our assessment is that this is a strong possibility later this year, possibly around September – then you must be strong enough to resist it, to drive the Nazis back, and in so doing deliver a body blow to them. We are not convinced that your government is taking this threat nearly as seriously as it should. Chamberlain is, after all, the man who advocated appeasement. We'd like to see you provide intelligence to your masters which helps to underline this threat.'

'And how do you suggest I go about this? Intelligence is based upon analysis and sources—'

'Don't worry, my friend, we intend to provide you with intelligence to use in this respect. An excellent source of ours in Germany is providing us with first-class intelligence. We're looking for ways of getting this intelligence to you to use in such a way that the source is protected but that the information they provide is credible. I need to add something else... We are deeply concerned about the prospect of your country and Germany coming to an agreement, an end to hostilities, if you like. There is nothing more that Hitler would like. He never expected this country to declare war on him. He knows that your navy is vastly superior to his. They are constantly putting out feelers for peace and our assessment is that your government under Mr Chamberlain may be open to the idea, in the right circumstances. This would obviously be a disaster for the Soviet Union, because were he to conclude a treaty with your government then that would be one enemy he'd no longer need to worry about.

'We want to see you providing intelligence to your government which will help convince them that not only is Germany planning to invade your country, but also that all this talk of peace is a trick – a ruse for them to lull you into a sense of false security.'

Archie nodded and said this was quite a lot to take in and, of course, there'd need to be a credible way of him presenting the information. 'If you don't mind my saying, we're going to need to come up with a bloody clever way of me passing on the intelligence you provide me with in a way which won't in itself arouse suspicion. I can hardly come up with a report and plonk it on a desk at work and not expect to be asked where it's come from.'

Maisky nodded and said something in Russian to Morozov, who replied, and then a brief conversation took place between the two Russians. Eventually Maisky stood up and held his hand out to Archie and gave him another Masonic-style handshake.

'Don't worry, we'll sort something out. I said earlier in our conversation how much you are valued. Let me assure you, my friend, that you are our most important agent in this country. We will do everything we can to protect you and to help you. I hope you understand that.'

By now the ambassador had released his grip on Archie's hand and was clutching him by the shoulders, and Archie tensed up as he thought Maisky was about to hug him.

'May I ask a question, please?'

'Go ahead, my friend.'

'When I met with Emil in Paris last April and he told me Osip was… no longer… and that from then on, I'd be working for the NKVD and for Mr Morozov here, I also asked him about another agent working for you who Moscow had told me was in a position to help. I wondered what had happened to him. I could certainly do with some help.'

Maisky turned to Morozov and the quick conversation which followed became quite animated, with much shrugging on the part of Morozov, who eventually replied.

'The truth is, Archie, we're not sure about this other agent. We also wonder what happened to him.'

Chapter 10

Beatrice Fletcher was obliged to retire from public service, as she liked to call it, at the end of August when The Annexe was shut down.

It had all come as something of a shock, to be perfectly honest. She'd been working for The Annexe ever since its inception in 1931, having previously been a secretary in the personnel department of the War Office, where one morning she was called into her boss's office to be told she was being transferred to work for a gentleman called Percy Burton.

She very much took to Percy Burton; he was polite and considerate, and very soon she was what he liked to call his right-hand woman. The Annexe was a top-secret organisation, and Beatrice was a model of discretion. It was not a large organisation, and she looked after a number of matters, including personnel. The work suited her, and the move had come at the right time: she was fifty and unmarried and she was happy to devote herself to her work.

It was a considerable shock when she turned up for work on the last Monday of August 1939 to be met at the entrance by a gentleman in an ill-fitting brown suit who told her that, for reasons that need not concern her, The Annexe no longer existed and she was no longer required. When she asked him what she was meant to do, he said that as she was past her retirement age she would receive her pension, and in addition she was being paid three months' salary to tide her over, plus a further month to cover any leave owing.

Beatrice was so shocked that to her embarrassment she began to cry – not hysterically, of course, but her eyes did fill with tears, and they trickled down her face – and the man in the brown suit clearly didn't know what to do. He told her that at least the four months' salary would be net of tax and she should enjoy her retirement.

Beatrice Fletcher had considered her retirement, of course. She'd planned to sell the small terraced home in Chiswick that she'd inherited from her parents and move to somewhere further up the Thames; she loved to take day trips to the small, pretty towns tucked into turns on the river. But she hadn't expected this to happen quite so soon.

Nonetheless, she soon pulled herself together. She managed to sell her house in Chiswick – admittedly for less than she'd hoped, but the estate agent told her that the war had had an adverse effect on prices, which she could quite understand. She found a small cottage in Marlow, a pleasant town with plenty of what were described by the estate agent who sold it to her as 'amenities'.

The cottage was a bit isolated at the end of a lane that was prone to flooding, but on the plus side it was just a couple of hundred yards from the river, which she happily spent two or three hours a day walking alongside.

She was returning from one such walk in early January when she saw the man. It was a sunny afternoon, which had lifted her mood after a lonely and bleak Christmas and New Year. As she entered the lane, she noticed the figure of a man darting from her front gate towards the tall hedge. She thought that it must be the man from the farm, which was responsible for the lane, as he had promised to come and sort out some drainage. She called out, 'Good afternoon,' but there was no response and she imagined he was just getting on with it because it was a miserable job, all that water and mud.

When she entered the cottage, she removed her boots and put on the kettle, as was her habit these days: a nice cup of tea after her walk, two digestive biscuits and the *Daily Telegraph* crossword. That could occupy a good hour. She was getting used to finding ways of passing the endless time.

She must have dozed off because she was woken by the sound of a floorboard creaking in her hall and the door behind her opening. She was sitting in a high-backed armchair, so it was something of a struggle to turn round to see who it was. By the time she did, a tall man dressed in a dark raincoat and with a trilby hat pulled low over his face had appeared alongside her. She managed to ask him if there was anything she could do to help, but he didn't say a word, and the last thing Beatrice

Fletcher was aware of was a pair of black leather-gloved hands holding her mother's embroidered cushion in front of her and then pushing it very tightly into her face.

—

A fortnight later, Pamela pulled Cooper aside in the offices of the Invasion Warning Sub-Committee.

'Do you remember Beatrice Fletcher – Percy's assistant from The Annexe? You may have known her as Trixie. This may jog your memory.' She showed him a photograph.

'Ah, yes – made me sign a pile of forms when I joined. Rather strict, I seem to recall. Efficient, though. Is she joining us here?'

'She died maybe two weeks ago, so in the circumstances, most probably not.'

'What happened?'

'She'd moved to Marlow after she retired in August. Her body was discovered at the weekend.'

'And the cause of death?'

'At first it was believed to be non-suspicious. The milkman noticed her milk hadn't been taken in for a few days and couldn't get any response when he rang the bell, so he contacted the police who broke in and found her dead, slumped in her armchair. The coroner ordered a post-mortem as her doctor said she'd been in good health. The pathologist's report indicated that she'd been dead for up to a fortnight and gave the cause of death as asphyxiation. The discolouration of the lips and cheeks are apparently a sign, along with evidence of burst blood vessels in the eyes.'

'Do they have any idea of who could be responsible?'

'Murray would have known of Beatrice, and he would most probably have known quite how much she knew – she was Percy's confidante, after all. Despite there being no witnesses or evidence, he must be considered a suspect. The indications are that he's looking to eliminate anyone who may know what he was up to... first Percy and now Beatrice. You and I are also under threat, though we're taking precautions. As you know, we've moved your mother and stepfather to a nursing home in Lincolnshire so he can't get at you through them. They're there under a false name.'

'My mother will be hating it.'

'Apparently, she does. From now on, finding Murray is a priority, Cooper. You're to start walking around the areas where you used to live and work, in the hope that he may be watching for you there. Don't worry, we'll be watching you very closely. We may flush him out this way. Our absolute priority will be to catch him alive and question him. Hopefully he'll lead us to The Group.'

In truth, the very last thing Cooper wanted was for Murray to be caught alive, because he had no doubt whatsoever that if questioned, Murray would reveal how Cooper had asked him to kill a man called Douglas Marsh. Then they'd look into who Douglas Marsh was and discover he was a Soviet agent based in the Communist Party headquarters in Covent Garden, and start putting two and two together and asking what it was that a Soviet agent had on Cooper that meant he wanted him killed.

But Cooper knew that for the time being he had to go along with this plan. Over the next week he visited Dorset Square, where he used to live, and walked from there down Baker Street and then to Bryanston Square, where The Annexe had been based. For good measure he walked up and down Oxford Street and along Bond Street and through Mayfair to Hyde Park, all the time aware he was being carefully monitored, but it was unnerving nonetheless and not a little disappointing when at the end of these walks there was a debrief and he was told there'd been no sign of Murray.

During these 'excursions', as Pamela liked to term them, Cooper walked in fear that the capture of Murray and his exposure was imminent. But then he began to come up with a plan.

He'd last seen Murray in June the previous year. Murray had found him in Regent's Park and told him that he owed him a debt for getting him out of trouble in Brussels. He said if he ever needed his help, he could contact him through a barman called Bernard at the Seven Stars pub in Carey Street in Holborn.

'...ask him if they have any Island malts. He'll ask which one you prefer and you're to say a Talisker.'

And it had worked, so that when it looked like Douglas Marsh had discovered his identity, Cooper had contacted Murray through Bernard. The two men had met at the Seven Stars and walked from there to Lincoln's Inn, where Cooper told him about Douglas Marsh and Murray said he needed a few more details, which Cooper duly provided.

A week later, Douglas Marsh was dead.

Now, Cooper realised he had a possible way of finding Murray, but it was an outside chance at best – and an enormous risk.

He knew he'd need help. As it happened, he and Will Drysdale had become good friends. Drysdale had come to stay at the safe house in Turk's Row over Christmas as the security officers there were on leave. Cooper learnt Drysdale's parents had both died when he was young and he had little in the way of family – one or two distant cousins, but no one who really cared. Cooper told him that his own father had been killed in the Great War and he was to all intents and purposes estranged from his mother, and it was clear they had much in common. What would have otherwise been a rather dull festive season turned out to be anything but, and as 1939 turned into 1940 Will and Cooper enjoyed a warm friendship.

One evening he and Will were relaxing after dinner at the safe house. There'd been a long walk that day, all the way from Dorset Square into Oxford Street and then down Park Lane and around Hyde Park, and there'd been no sign of Murray, despite the number of people watching being doubled.

'Either he's around or he's not taking the bait,' said Will.

'He's very clever, Will. He's probably realised I'm being watched.'

'I do wonder what the point of all this walking around London is,' said Will. 'It's like playing Monopoly, visiting all those places.'

'I do have a possible lead to Murray, from my days with The Annexe,' said Cooper. 'I only remembered it today and it's a long shot, and to be honest, I don't want to tell Pamela because then she'll alert all those other chaps and go in heavy-handed, and Murray will know what's going on. Do you trust me?'

'Of course.'

'Tomorrow night, we're going to the pub. We'll need to take our guns, though.'

The following evening, he and Will put their Enfield revolvers in their jacket holsters and left Chelsea, heading for Holborn. As agreed, they entered the Seven Stars pub separately.

But there was no sign of Bernard, so Cooper asked one of the other barmen.

The man looked around and leant conspiratorially towards Cooper, looking up at him with rheumy eyes. 'Did you know Bernard well?'

'Well, we met a few times. I always enjoyed my chats with him when I popped in.'

The barman gazed down at the surface of the bar. 'I'm sorry to tell you, sir, that dear old Bernard passed away just after Christmas. It came as a terrible shock to all of us. He was a good man, Bernard – and a patriot too, sir, if you get my meaning. The Seven Stars opened in 1602 and it felt as if Bernard had been around since then!'

Cooper said he was most terribly sorry and if it wasn't an intrusive question, had Bernard been unwell?

The barman looked up at him, a mournful expression on his face. 'Christmas and the New Year is a hard time for many of us, sir. What with the loneliness and the war... It must have been too much for poor Bernard.'

'When I came in previously, I always made a point of asking Bernard for a Talisker and he always obliged, so I'll have a Talisker, please, and raise a toast to him. I'm sorry, I didn't catch your name?'

'It's Arthur, sir, and I shall get you a Talisker.' And then he leant even closer, his manner even more conspiratorial. 'And may I ask your name, sir?'

Cooper sat down and pondered what had just happened: the shocking news of Bernard's death, apparently a suicide, but another person connected with Murray dead. And then Arthur's reference to Bernard being a patriot and understanding when he'd ordered a Talisker.

But he felt he'd pushed it as far as he dared. Arthur seemed to understand when he referred to the Talisker. Maybe he was a link to Murray after all.

From the outset Cooper had appreciated what a dangerous game he was playing. It was vital that Murray would think that he had been indiscreet, that he'd made a mistake. He'd explained to Will how he was going to play the decoy.

'When I leave the Seven Stars I'll head towards Lincoln's Inn. If he's going to take the bait – if he even knows about it – then my guess is that he'll head there, too. You go there first, Will, and wait for me to arrive. If I'm right, then Murray will follow me. Make sure your Enfield is ready.'

–

Cooper walked down Carey Street and then Serle Street, the metal taps on the soles of his shoes clattering on the cobblestones.

At the end of Serle Street, he paused before turning into Lincoln's Inn Fields, past the library and the gatehouse and into the elegant and silent world inhabited by barristers and judges – where they had their chambers, and which was home to many of them. He'd already transferred his revolver from the holster to his coat pocket and now he quickened his pace, eager to get it over and done with.

But Lincoln's Inn appeared to be deserted, dark and still, no sign of life anywhere. Cooper walked past the church and towards a large arch, his eyes slowly adjusting to the gloom. He wondered why on earth he'd come up with such a perilous and frankly foolish idea in the first place; maybe the best thing would be to turn around and head home and hope that Will would do likewise.

This was the moment when he felt a presence behind him, a breath on the nape of his neck and something sticking into the back of his coat.

'Keep walking, Cooper.'

There was no question it was Murray. Cooper paused and whatever it was in the back of his coat prodded him and Murray said, 'Over there,' and all Cooper could hope was that was where Will was waiting, so he headed in that direction.

They walked further into the complex and ahead of them there was a light in the porch of one of the buildings, its door open. Cooper must have spotted the figure crouching inside it at the same time as Murray did, because Murray muttered 'bastard,' and then possibly the word 'trap,' but Cooper couldn't be sure because this was the moment that Will chose to dash out of the porch, his revolver held high above his head for some reason. Murray pushed Cooper to the ground and took aim at Will, who was now less than a hundred yards away, and as he did so, Will crashed to the ground.

Cooper had already drawn his own revolver and aimed it at Murray as he swivelled towards him. There was a split-second pause as each man tried to make out the other in the dark, but Cooper fired twice, hitting Murray somewhere on his torso.

Cooper's ears were buzzing from the gunfire and now he could hear people shouting from the windows of the barristers' quarters above them. He stood over Murray's body, sprawled awkwardly against a bench. A large patch of blood was spreading across his chest and a small trickle of it running from his mouth. But Murray was still alive, his eyes half open and his mouth trying to speak. Still alive and still able to ruin Cooper, even with what may be his dying breath.

By now people were in the courtyard and approaching them. Cooper noticed Murray's gun, just out of the dying man's reach, but nevertheless he shouted out, 'Be careful, he's got a gun!' and fired point-blank into the side of Murray's head.

–

Cooper didn't think his bosses or for that matter the police were going to believe his story, but he was so devastated – so truly upset that Will had been killed – that he told his version in a genuinely shocked manner which they seemed to accept.

'We decided to go for a walk and then for a drink and found ourselves strolling along the river for ages, and before we knew it, we were by Temple.'

Pamela had interrupted at this point and said that was a very long walk indeed, and Cooper said maybe an hour, but it didn't feel like it.

'When we reached Temple, I remembered the Seven Stars and told Will it's the oldest pub in London. He said in that case we had to go there, which we did. We had a drink or two and then walked through Lincoln's Inn on the way back. We were heading for High Holborn to catch a bus and we thought that could be a short cut. The next thing I know is Murray appears out of nowhere. All three of us drew our guns, more or less at the same time, and opened fire simultaneously, or so it seemed. I saw him hit Will as I shot Murray and... Poor, poor Will... He didn't deserve that.'

He spread his hands as if to say, 'There we are…' and Pamela asked him to explain why he shot Murray twice. 'One of the barristers who came down told us Murray looked to be conscious, if wounded, when you shot him in the head. You know we wanted him alive, Cooper.'

'I'm aware of that and I'm bitterly disappointed we didn't get him alive, but I fear it was a case of him or me. His gun was by his hand, and he was reaching for it. I simply couldn't take the risk.'

Everyone else in the room nodded and Pamela said she could see what he meant, but Cooper thought to himself: You don't really, Pamela. You really don't appreciate the extent of the risk I was taking.

Chapter 11

London
February 1940

Cooper had always found February to be the most miserable month of the year, and in London that first February of the war it seemed to be especially depressing. The days were short, the skies unremittingly grey with a hint of menace, the weather cold and damp.

This February had been especially miserable for Cooper. It started with Will Drysdale's funeral, which was only allowed to go ahead after an inquiry concluded that he'd been shot dead by Murray and that Cooper's actions that night were considered not to have contributed to his death. The inquiry did wonder why the two men had taken it on themselves to go for such a long walk when they knew Cooper was in danger, but they appeared to accept Cooper's explanation.

There had been questions about why Cooper had administered the *coup de grâce* when it was apparent Murray was still conscious, but it was agreed that on balance he was right, given that Murray could still have reached for his own gun.

The man from Special Branch brought in to assist in the inquiry had questioned why Cooper hadn't simply kicked Murray's revolver away, but Lieutenant Commander McConnell said he ought to be more understanding and, in any case, couldn't he see how terribly upset Cooper was?

Will Drysdale was buried in a bleak churchyard in a seemingly abandoned village south of Cambridge. He was interred next to his parents, whose gravestones recounted a sad story: Will had been ten when his mother died, thirteen when his father passed away, and he'd outlived his father by just fifteen years. Cooper felt overwhelmed with guilt and remorse: if only he'd not set the whole thing up. He'd regret that for ever.

There were a dozen of them at the funeral: Cooper, Pamela, Lieutenant Commander McConnell and a couple of others from the office, and some of Will's distant cousins who were overheard wondering who'd inherit whatever money he'd left. The vicar who carried out the ceremony was accompanied by a couple of churchwardens and the ceremony concluded with a sparse rendering of Psalm 23, much of it drowned out by the whistling wind from across the Fens. At the mention of walking through the valley of the shadow of death, Cooper felt his eyes fill with tears.

It really couldn't have been a more miserable morning, and after the ceremony they headed back to London. No time for a farewell drink.

The whole incident had been hushed up, of course, in the way that these matters were now there was a war on. The police said this was an attempted robbery gone badly wrong; the robber apparently unaware that his intended victim was armed. No mention was made of Cooper or of anyone else being involved, and the silence of the barristers and other witnesses was ensured by the invocation of 'national security'.

The coroner agreed to hold a paper inquest and soon the whole unfortunate business was quickly swept under the carpet.

'It is most unfortunate that we never got the opportunity to question Murray. We don't even know where he lived so we can't search his premises. He could have led us into the heart of The Group.' Pamela shook her head and looked at Cooper in a manner suggesting he was partly to blame for this. It was the day after Will Drysdale's funeral, and they were in her office in the lower basement of the Old War Office Building.

'All the more reason, then, to double our efforts to discover more about The Group.' She tapped the copy of the list of its members on the desk in front of her.

'Will and I spent considerable time and effort, as you know, working on that list, Pamela. We've researched every name on it and cross-checked them with Special Branch, MI5 and the relevant Regional Commissioner. We checked names against addresses and wrote up what we could find about each person. I think I could recite every name on the list off by heart.'

'There's really no need to bother, thank you, Cooper. The question now is what to do with all these names.'

'While being mindful not to alert them.'

'Exactly, and remembering that Lieutenant Commander McConnell says that as matters stand, their only offence is being on a list, which is not actually an offence – but it's all we have on them. I daresay if we raided all their houses, we'd unearth a few incriminating documents – pro-Nazis leaflets, the odd swastika flag, maybe a copy or two of *Mein Kampf*, but that will hardly break the spy ring. We need to catch them red-handed.'

'To do that we need to have them approached by German spies, don't we?'

Pamela nodded. 'Ideally, but that is easier said than done. First, find a spy!'

Cooper said of course he understood that.

'I was rereading the notes poor Will took when we interviewed Arnold Visser just prior to his execution. He told us their instructions were to contact an Agent Lübeck from a telephone box at Victoria Station, and when we asked him what more he could tell us about Agent Lübeck he said he'd been told they were "local". We pushed him a bit on that, but he either couldn't or wouldn't elaborate.

'"Local" could mean any number of things, but I think we have to consider the possibility that Agent Lübeck is British.'

'Or it could mean they live in London.'

'Indeed, it would. And there's something else, Cooper. Given that we believe there's a connection between the Nazi spy ring and The Group, Agent Lübeck is likely to be on this list.' She held up the document.

'All we need to do is find out who they are.'

Although he obviously didn't say so at the time, it suddenly occurred to Cooper that another lead was staring him in the face. He resolved to follow it up as soon as possible.

–

'Sometimes, one's arrangements actually work out in the manner one had envisaged: most satisfactory.'

Pamela had a habit of opening conversations in something of an obtuse manner, as if she was playing a game and Cooper was expected to guess what she was talking about.

'Any arrangements in particular?'

She leant back in her chair, allowing the light to catch her smile. Not for the first time, he noticed how white her teeth were, contrasting with her pale skin and her dark eyes.

'As you know, we moved your mother and your stepfather from their flat in Belsize Park to Lincolnshire out of concern for their safety and yours. Their flat has been left vacant, but we did take the precaution of advising the porter in their block that should anyone enquire after either them or you, then he was to inform the police. We gave him a telephone number to use, which was to Special Branch.

'We were informed by Special Branch yesterday afternoon that a foreign gentleman arrived at your mother's block that morning, enquiring after you. The porter had instructions that in such circumstances he was to say that you were away and ask the person to return the following day. He also asked the gentleman for his details, as he'd also been instructed. The gentleman declined to leave his details but did promise to return the following day, which he did, this morning.

'When he returned the porter asked him to wait and said you'd be coming down, and then he telephoned the police. Soon after that the police arrived and arrested him.'

'And do we know who this foreign gentleman is?'

'He says his name is Manfred Hoffmann, though he also has a British identity card in the name of Martin Heal, and he claims to have met you in Germany. He's currently at Hampstead Police Station on Rosslyn Hill. I suggest we go up there to meet him, and on the way there perhaps you can tell me who on earth this chap is.'

–

In May 1937 Cooper had taken the night train from Düsseldorf to Hamburg. When it stopped at Osnabrück a man in his early twenties joined the train and sat opposite him.

They got speaking and in the way these conversations go on trains, they were bound by a kind of confidentiality afforded by the dark and the transient circumstances of the journey. Once he realised Cooper was English, the man confided in him. Manfred Hoffmann told him he was from Dresden and had been studying medicine in Berlin before he was thrown out of university for refusing to denounce his Jewish girlfriend. Soon after that he got into a fight with an SS officer and was now a fugitive. He was heading for Hamburg, hoping to catch a boat out of Germany.

Cooper had said he'd do what he could to help: he'd given him his mother's address in London and said he could contact him through her. And when the train pulled into Hamburg Cooper said he'd go through the Gestapo checkpoint first, hoping that as a foreigner he'd divert attention away from the young German.

But it hadn't worked out like that. Cooper got through the checkpoint easily enough but when he turned round, he saw Manfred being arrested and watched hopelessly as the young man was marched away.

He'd never expected to see him again.

And now he was in Hampstead Police Station.

When he and Pamela arrived, they were taken to an interview room, where Manfred was waiting for him.

Cooper reckoned that Manfred would now be in his mid-twenties, but he looked as young as when they'd first met. He had a slightly dishevelled and bemused air about him, as if he was unsure where he was and what was going on.

They greeted each other warmly, not quite an embrace but a hand on the shoulders type of greeting.

'Have I been arrested?'

'I don't think so, no. This is my friend Pamela, by the way.'

Pamela shook his hand and said she was very pleased to meet him.

'What on earth happened to you, Manfred?' ·

'I'm here in London!'

'As I can see, but the last time I saw you was at Hamburg Station when you were arrested by the Gestapo. I didn't think I'd see you ever again.'

Manfred said it was a very long story.

'As you know, when we arrived at Hamburg Hauptbahnhof I was arrested by the Gestapo. They took me to their building in the Stadthaus and I was thrown into a cell. I thought that was the end for me. I have never known such despair. I sat on the cold floor in that wretched cell and tried to pray, even though I have never been religious. But then a miracle really did occur. Later on that afternoon a man called Helmut Schröder turned up at the Stadthaus. He was one of my father's oldest friends from Dresden until they fell out a few years previously over politics and money. Helmut told me he was now a senior officer for the

Abwehr – German military intelligence – in Hamburg. He said he'd spotted my name on the daily arrest sheet and had come straight to the Stadthaus.

'You must understand that, growing up, we were very close to Helmut. He was like one of the family. I think he felt obliged to help me, but he also saw a way he could help himself, if you see what I mean. Helmut's job was to train agents to be sent to Britain and he saw me as a potential agent – he knew I spoke good English. So, I was released by the Gestapo and trained to be an agent for the Abwehr. I arrived by boat in Southampton from France and was questioned by the port police, who said I wasn't allowed to travel to London, so I ended up in Newcastle.'

'As an Abwehr agent?' Pamela sounded as if she were interrogating him.

Manfred laughed, probably not the response she was expecting.

'Good Lord, no! Do you think I'm mad? I was a fugitive from the Nazis, a sworn enemy of them. Do you really think I was going to spy for them? I just wanted a quiet life. I was happy enough to remain in Newcastle where I had a job as a porter in the hospital and that was that. I was even able to get a British identity. I'm now Martin Heal. I can assure you I never did anything remotely connected with espionage.'

'How come you've waited until now to contact Mr Cooper?'

'I was restricted in terms of where I was permitted to travel. I had to remain in the Newcastle area and report to the local police station once a fortnight. But then there was talk of sending me to an aliens' camp on the Isle of Man, and at the same time I'd applied to resume my medical studies and was granted an interview at St Mary's Hospital here in London. That interview didn't go very well because they insisted I needed the papers from the medical school in Berlin, and of course how was I going to get those? This was the point when I decided to contact you, Charles. When we met on the train you gave me your mother's address in Belsize Park. And – here I am! I don't understand why I've been arrested. It makes no sense.'

He spread out his arms and smiled. 'Perhaps if you have any contacts who can help me get a place in medical school, that would be appreciated. And in London would be good. As long as it's somewhere warmer than Newcastle!'

'Hang on, Mr Hoffmann, I fear you're rather getting ahead of yourself.' Pamela straightened herself, adopting the posture of a school-teacher ticking off a mischievous pupil. 'Before we start planning your medical career, we need you to answer a few questions. You arrived in this country three years ago, you say?'

'I arrived in this country in July 1937, I think it was.'

'And in that time, you've had no contact with the Abwehr?'

'I've told you that.'

'Tell me, when you were briefed before you left, what instructions were you given about making contact with Hamburg?'

'I was told that when I landed at Southampton, I was to travel to London, find somewhere to stay and go to Stepney Green Station. From there it would be a very short walk to a shop selling kitchen items on Nicholas Road, just on the corner with Globe Road. The shop was called "McGregor's", and I was to ask for Mr McGregor and then enquire if they sold a pan large enough to roast a goose. They'd ask how I'd managed to get hold of a goose and I'd reply that it had flown from the Continent.'

'Seriously?'

'Yes. I know it sounds odd saying it like that, but that was what I was told to say. Then I'd be given my instructions by Mr McGregor. Of course I had no intention of going there, but when I finally came to London a couple of days ago, I decided to see if the shop was there, more out of curiosity than for any other reason. I had no intention of going in. In fact, as a precaution I didn't get off at Stepney Green but at the stop after that, Mile End, and then I walked back. I found the shop on Nicholas Road but it was all boarded up, like it had been abandoned.'

'Bombed?'

'No. I saw plenty of buildings around there which had been bombed, some of them destroyed – even whole blocks – but this one was intact, if you see what I mean. It looked like it hadn't been occupied for some time: abandoned.'

–

'And you trust him, Cooper – believe all of his story?'

Cooper looked Lieutenant Commander McConnell in the eye. 'Absolutely, sir, no question about it. It was impossible that our meeting on the train and his arrest at Hamburg Station could have been staged. I would say his story is totally genuine. He went along with his recruitment as a German agent purely as a way of escaping to this country. He's been minding his own business in Newcastle until he arrived in London a day or so ago. Not once has he undertaken any kind of activity which could be construed as espionage.'

'And this shop in Stepney Green?'

'We've checked it out, sir,' said Pamela. 'It does appear to have been abandoned. What records we've been able to check show the shop was run by a Mr McGregor, and a Mr and Mrs McGregor occupied the flat above the shop. We have no details, though, of when they left the premises. We've been unable to find any trace of them. We have no idea where they are now.'

'Nonetheless,' said Lieutenant Commander McConnell, 'this Hoffmann could just be creating a cover story to fool us, couldn't he? Take himself off to a place like Stepney Green and find an abandoned shop or house or whatever and then claim that was his contact. Makes it hard for us to check out but sounds feasible enough.'

'Except, sir, we have this.' Cooper stood up and passed a document to McConnell. 'It's The Group directory I got from Percy Burton's widow. It's open at a page showing members in the London area. And there'll you'll see a Leonard McGregor of Nicholas Road, Stepney E1. Which would appear to verify Mr Hoffmann's story, sir, don't you think? How would he have known of any connection with The Group?'

McConnell kept his eyes on The Group membership list and nodded his head slowly and told Pamela she may well be right. He finally looked up from the document and addressed Cooper and Pamela.

'I have an idea. Give me a day or two.'

–

When they reconvened, Lieutenant Commander McConnell appeared to be particularly energised.

'I asked our colleagues in MI6 to see what parts of Mr Hoffmann's story they could verify. They were able to confirm they're aware of an Abwehr officer called Helmut Schröder who's based at General-Knochenhauer-Strasse in Hamburg. So that part of his story would appear to be correct.

'I have what you may consider to be a rather radical idea. We train Mr Hoffmann as a British agent and send him back to Hamburg, along with a story as to why he's been inactive as an Abwehr agent thus far but is now keen to start.'

Pamela frowned. 'You don't think it may seem odd, him somehow getting himself over from this country back to Hamburg and what...? Turn up at the Abwehr offices and announce he's "reporting for duty"?'

'I take your point, Pamela, but he can quite reasonably tell them in Hamburg that when he visited this contact in London they weren't there, and he had no other way of getting in touch with them. It wasn't as if they gave him a fall-back plan. Returning to Germany would be his only option.'

'But... sending him back to Germany?'

'We send agents back into Occupied Europe all the time, particularly if they're nationals of the countries they're being sent to. It's not nearly as odd as you think and, in any case, in the business of espionage, Pamela, everything is odd, nothing is ordinary. We can slip him over through the Netherlands and see how we go. If we're lucky, they'll send him back with a new set of instructions and that will give us a first-class lead into the German network here and to The Group. I think it's an opportunity we must take. Do you think he'll be open to this, Cooper?'

'He's an anti-Nazi, sir, so I'd hope so. Nonetheless, what we're asking him to do is very dangerous indeed and he'll be more than aware of that. Maybe if we were to promise him that if all this works out then we'll do our level best to get him into medical school, he may be agreeable.'

'We need to get this Manfred chap to a safe house, put the fear of God into him that if he betrays us our reach is long, and then train him. Can you sort out the safe house and the training, Pamela? Cooper, you'll be the point man for our German friend.'

—

By the end of February Manfred had sailed through all the rigorous checks that were required before he could be recruited as an agent. Pamela found a safe house in west London and Manfred moved in to start his training. It would take a few weeks, they were told... perhaps even a couple of months, which Cooper thought was excessive. When he was recruited as a Soviet agent in Moscow, he'd had far less training than that, but he thought better than to point that out.

And once that was sorted, Cooper could turn his attention to the lead that had been staring him in the face.

He did wonder whether it was worth what would be a considerable risk. Now that Bernard and Murray were both dead, and so, too, Douglas Marsh, he could be forgiven for thinking that there was no one else around aware of his links with Soviet Intelligence.

But there was someone. He'd need to play it very carefully, but it could lead him into The Group.

He began with a telephone call to the Seven Stars in Carey Street, the pub through which he'd previously contacted Murray. He made the call from a telephone box on Cheyne Walk, just past Battersea Bridge.

'The Seven Stars, can I help you?' The woman's voice sounded rushed and the background noisy.

'Good evening, yes... I was wondering if Arthur Baxter's on duty tonight?'

'The only Arthur working here is Arthur Kemp. He's on tomorrow night. Can I take a message for him?'

Cooper said there was no need and when the woman asked if he wanted to leave his name, he said not to bother, but thank you very much.

Now he knew Arthur's surname, the following morning, he was in the office early and the first thing he did was check The Group's membership list. And sure enough, there he was:

Arthur Kemp	17 Mafeking Court, Trundleys Road	Rotherhithe, London SE

There was also a Bernard on the list – surname Melrose, with an address in Bermondsey – whom he believed was the same Bernard who'd worked at the Seven Stars.

Cooper then waited a week. During that time, he'd had to move out of the safe house on Turk's Row as his life was deemed to be no longer in danger. By a happy coincidence another flat was available for rent in the building where he'd lived in Dorset Square, and his former landlord was delighted to welcome him back as he'd been such a good tenant.

It took him a day or two to organise the move, and then he decided it would be a good idea to leave a bit of a gap between his telephone call to the Seven Stars and returning there.

He went back on a Thursday night, wearing a cloth cap pulled low over his face, a pair of spectacles, and with a scarf covering much of the lower part of his face; even he'd had trouble recognising himself in the mirror. He spotted Arthur Kemp behind the bar.

Last orders were called at a quarter past ten and Cooper left the pub ten minutes later and positioned himself in the deep recess of a doorway diagonally opposite on Carey Street, with a good view of the pub. At ten past eleven he watched as Kemp left, turning left towards Chancery Lane. Cooper dropped in behind him. Kemp was walking slowly, no doubt tired from his evening's work. He turned left into Fleet Street and waited by a bus shelter.

Cooper sidled up to him. He'd removed his cap and glasses, and Kemp certainly recognised him because there was a look of surprise on his face, which quickly turned to one of shock.

'Could we have a chat please, Mr Kemp? I think you may have an idea what it's about.' Cooper then took out his warrant card from his coat pocket and held it in front of the other man.

'You're a copper, then?' Kemp looked stunned.

Cooper nodded.

'Who'd have…? I…'

'Can we walk this way please, Mr Kemp?'

Cooper steered him away from the bus stop and into the next turning on the left, which was Fetter Lane, and thanks to the blackout was pitch dark, with only a few shafts of moonlight providing any way of seeing ahead of them. There was a narrow alleyway on the right, its entrance barely visible in the dark, but Cooper had taken the precaution of visiting the area at the weekend, so he'd know his way around. So far, all had gone according to plan.

Halfway down the alley was the overhang behind a tall building and Cooper guided Kemp into it.

'Do you realise, Mr Kemp, that you are an accessory to murder?'

'What on earth are you talking about?'

'Last month I visited the Seven Stars and inquired after Bernard. You told me he'd died. I told you how I'd ordered Talisker from him, and after I left the Seven Stars I was followed into Lincoln's Inn by Murray. It was too much of a coincidence. You must have told him about me. Murray threatened me and then killed a fellow police officer, before he himself was killed.

'Our best legal advice, Mr Kemp, is that makes you an accessory to the crime, which in this case is murder, and that is punishable by the death penalty. Are you following me?'

Cooper couldn't see Kemp's face very well in the dark, but he could hear his heavy breathing and could smell the fear on him.

'How could I possibly have known what was going to happen, sir? All I did was oblige a gentleman and pass on a message. I didn't even know this man, Murray. When Bernard was alive, I'd occasionally help him out if he wasn't around and pass on a message for him, but no more than that. You have to believe me, sir.'

'I don't believe your innocent messenger story, I'm afraid, Mr Kemp. You are a member of The Group, after all. Is that correct?'

Kemp's breathing quickened and he made a sound best described as a whimper and then said he had no idea what Cooper was talking about. It had begun to rain – a few drops at first, but it quite quickly turned heavy and noisy, too – so Cooper had to raise his voice.

'Come on, Kemp, I've seen the bloody list! Arthur Kemp, of 17 Mafeking Court, Trundleys Road, Rotherhithe. You're a member of a clandestine organisation of Nazi sympathisers called The Group that helps German spies in this country. Don't treat me as a fool! I can arrest you now and by the morning you'll be up before the magistrates on a murder charge.'

Kemp said nothing; he was panting now and Cooper wondered whether he was prepared to bargain.

'You don't need to worry about the consequences, Kemp. Murray's dead.'

'If I were to tell you what I know, would that help me, sir?'

'It would indeed, but I'd want to know quite a lot.'

'In return for what?'

'In return for accepting that all you did was innocently pass on a message.'

'And I'd be let go?'

'With a warning as to your future conduct, of course.'

'Very well then, sir. The Group is a… group of like-minded people. It started out as being supportive of the new Germany and admiring the progress being made there, but gradually – over the last year or so – it became more pro-Nazi and developed into a network to help Germans who may be working undercover in this country. I was very much on its margins, sir, you have to believe that. Bernard was more involved and he was the one who recruited me – he knew what I thought of Jews and communists and I was happy to help in a small way. But I'm most certainly not a traitor, sir – I'm a patriot!'

'I need more substance than that, I'm afraid, Kemp.'

'What would you mean by "substance", sir?'

'I mean that names would be a good start.'

'Names of who?'

'Stop messing me around, Kemp. The names of other people associated with The Group.'

'I never met anyone else, apart from Bernard. And the Irish woman.'

'What Irish woman?'

'She seems to run The Group in London, as far as I can tell. Bernard said that she's a German agent herself and she's so important she has a German codename.'

'What is it?'

'Bernard did tell me, but I can't quite recall—'

There was a gasp of shock and pain from Kemp as Cooper grabbed him by the throat and slammed him hard against a wall, knocking the back of his head on the brick.

'Give me the name, Kemp, or I arrest you.'

'Now I think about it, sir, I do recall it was the name of a German port: Lübeck, if I remember correctly. But I can't remember her real name, only that it wasn't an Irish one, even though she was Irish, if you follow me. And that's it, I don't know anyone else. After Bernard died the only contact I had with The Group was through Murray.'

'And presumably you contacted him by telephone?'

'Yes, sir.'

'And Murray's number, please?'

'I can't remember it, sir…'

Cooper pushed Kemp's head back hard against the wall. Kemp squealed in pain as his head scraped along the rough brick.

'MIN 8460.'

It was Cooper's turn to breathe heavily. He reckoned he'd got as much as he was going to get out of Arthur Kemp.

Whatever Kemp knew, it was too much. He was clearly a danger to him.

'Have I been helpful, sir?'

Cooper said he had, and he was going to give him a caution as to his future conduct, and he could hear Kemp breathe more slowly. There was a little chuckle of relief and Kemp said, 'No hard feelings, sir.'

Cooper said, 'Indeed, no hard feelings.' He reached out to shake the other man's hand; he grabbed the outstretched right hand and plunged the knife deep into Kemp's stomach and then again, higher up, into his chest.

Arthur Kemp slumped to the ground, dropping into a pool of his own blood, which Cooper couldn't see, but he could hear the splashes as he stepped in it. He checked his pulse and when he was satisfied Kemp was dead he hauled the corpse behind a large bin. He covered the pool of blood with some old newspapers and used a couple of the sheets to wipe his own shoes. The rain was now torrential, which Cooper hoped meant the blood would be washed away. He was about to hurry away when it occurred to him that Kemp could be identified by whatever he had on him. In the man's jacket pocket, he found a wallet and as far as he could tell, there was no other paperwork. Cooper took the wallet and Kemp's wristwatch and disposed of them and the knife he'd used down a drain off Baker Street, where he'd stopped on his way home. He knew the police made a point of inspecting drains close to the scene of a crime.

He'd gathered important information on The Group and on Agent Lübeck, and he had Murray's phone number, though he'd need to think carefully about how he'd pass on this information without arousing any suspicion.

Arthur Kemp had now been taken care of.

No hard feelings.

Chapter 12

England
March 1940

When his wife was pregnant, she had an annoying habit of getting up during the night and early in the morning to throw up noisily in the bathroom adjacent to their bedroom.

Timothy Kerr-Walters found this not only unpleasant but also annoying, as he found it difficult to get back to sleep. He'd insisted she go and see the doctor about it, but she came back saying she'd been assured it was natural and maybe he should be more sympathetic.

His lack of sympathy was ironic because now it was his turn. He was finding it increasingly hard to get to sleep and when he did finally doze off, he'd wake up in the early hours of the morning, wide awake in bed, propped up on the pillows and staring at the strange shapes formed on the ceiling by the moonlight falling through the gaps in the curtains. He'd doze off for another hour or two, but he'd then wake at six – always six o'clock, even at the weekends and even when they were in the country – but this time it was not to gaze at the ceiling but to hurry into the bathroom and throw up, much like she'd done years before.

She was such a heavy sleeper she hardly noticed all this. She did once or twice and admonished him for drinking too much, and he'd laugh it off and say he must be pregnant and then add bitterly, 'Chance would be a fine thing,' and there'd be another argument.

Of course, the amount he was drinking was quite possibly a contributory factor to his insomnia and his early morning visits to the bathroom, but Timothy Kerr-Walters knew it was more complicated than that. No one could quite appreciate the pressure he was under. It was hard to know where to begin. Money, of course, was a problem. Working for the Service was not like working in the City or in business or for a law firm, as so many of his contemporaries had done after university. He realised that now that the war had begun, he could well have been called up, but from what he understood there were many perks – if that was the right word – enjoyed by officers, especially in Guards regiments, which compensated significantly for their lower salaries.

And of course they were in uniform, always looking smart and impressive, and people clearly admired them, whereas Timothy Kerr-Walters had to shuffle around in his suit. He didn't know if it was his imagination, but people would look at him as if wondering why he wasn't in one of the armed forces.

He was ashamed to say he'd found a moneylender. He'd heard about him from Archer, an acquaintance of his brother-in-law, with whom they were staying for a shooting weekend. Archer was one of those very attractive and terribly confident fellows, the type who never seemed to encounter any of life's problems and worries. He and Timothy Kerr-Walters were walking to a clearing in the woods for lunch, and Archer was telling him how he was building a new house in Hampshire and Kerr-Walters asked why they were selling Oxfordshire, and he replied they weren't.

'Don't need to, old chap. I've been doing some wheeling and dealing, not quite above board but not too far below it. Broke a few rules by buying gold and diamonds. Whole thing would have been scuppered if I was called up but I've managed to postpone that for a year.'

'How?'

'Paid the rather excessive fees charged by a doctor on Harley Street to diagnose me with some nasty chest condition: quite rare, I'm told. Keeps me away from danger for a while.'

'All this comes at a price, surely?'

Archer paused and beckoned Kerr-Walters to come closer. Shots were echoing around the wood, followed by the desperate flapping of a bird plummeting to earth close to them. 'I found a moneylender. I was expecting a bearded Jew in the East End but this chap turns out to be one of us, more or less. He even has an office in Paddington. Do you want his number?'

The moneylender's office was above a menswear shop on Praed Street, opposite St Mary's Hospital. The man was called Lister and ran a property advice consultancy as a front for his other activities. Kerr-Walters had telephoned to make an appointment and then climbed the narrow staircase to the top of the building, where Lister turned out to be not quite 'one of us', as Archer had described him. He was more grammar school.

There was no small talk. Behind his desk was a partially open safe, in which Kerr-Walters could see piles of banknotes. Lister got straight down to business.

'I don't ask too many questions. The less I know, the better. Obviously, I need to know names, addresses, occupation, bank et cetera, et cetera, but what you want the money for is none of my business.'

Kerr-Walters said he understood, and Lister passed him a sheet of paper to fill in. He did wonder if this was a breach of protocol – he doubted the Service would approve, exposing himself like this. Under 'occupation' he wrote 'civil servant' and Lister seemed satisfied with that.

'How much do you want to borrow, Mr Kerr-Walters?'

He hesitated. 'I'm not terribly sure, I...'

Lister tapped his fingers on the desk in a frustrated manner. 'Most people who come to see me have a pretty good idea of what they want to borrow, otherwise, they wouldn't be here, would they?'

Kerr-Walters said he could see that, and then he started to mentally calculate how much he'd need: the school fees; the cost of the new maid his wife had insisted on hiring; the car; the place in the country; replacing the kitchen in their town house, which was apparently urgent, although the existing one seemed perfectly adequate to him...

'How about one hundred pounds?'

Lister said nothing, but lit a cigarette and then started writing on a pad of paper.

'And when would you be able to pay me back?'

'I'd not really thought about that.'

'About paying me back?' Lister looked concerned.

'Obviously I know I have to pay you back. I meant when...'

'I charge a fee of five per cent of the total borrowed plus interest at half of one per cent per month, with a minimum of three months' interest. Maybe that helps, Mr Kerr-Walters.'

'Hang on. Half a per cent a month is what...? Six per cent per annum! The banks charge two per cent.'

Lister pushed the pad away from him and leant back in his chair. 'Go to the bank, then, Mr Kerr-Walters.'

He'd considered that, of course, but he'd already reached his over-draft limit. So, he told Lister that he'd go ahead, and Lister said to wait a few minutes and he'd draw up the agreement, and did Mr Kerr-Walters have the proofs of identity on him he'd asked him to bring along and if he could see them, please?

Fifteen minutes later Kerr-Walters emerged into Praed Street with twenty five-pound notes in his wallet and a strange sense of both relief and regret. He walked round to the Barclays branch on Edgware Road, where he deposited nineteen of those notes in his current account, and used the remaining one to stock up on decent Scotch.

–

But his nights remained sleepless, and mornings still began early with the trips to the toilet. Kerr-Walters had a constant sense of being overwhelmed, of having allowed himself to be drawn into situations which he then felt trapped by. His predicament reminded him of when he was young and he'd accompany the woodsman at his grandparents' place in the country who'd set traps for the vermin: clever devices with large and inviting openings, but once inside there was no way out.

He was in one of those traps, quite unable to extricate himself.

The pressure at work was enormous. He'd been pleased to be promoted in January, but if Kerr-Walters thought that was going to make life easier, he was mistaken. He soon reached the point where he wondered if it would have been better if he'd failed the interview, but it was quite typical of him to have sailed through it in the manner in which he did. He was good at that – persuasive, skilled at charming people and talking himself out of trouble – and he knew he'd impressed Phillips. He was less sure about Harvey from MI5, who had looked at him suspiciously and who reminded him of one of those annoying spinners, always threatening to bowl you out with the next ball. In truth, he wasn't sure Harvey had bought everything he'd said, but on reflection, he realised he'd obviously not done too badly. It just went to show that one can worry too much, and just because one may be guilty it didn't mean that was obvious to others.

Once promoted, Kerr-Walters was put in charge of establishing and running espionage rings in the south-east of France, including the border areas with Italy and Switzerland. The job also included responsibility for analysing the intelligence which came in and writing reports on it. He quickly realised, though, that he'd probably oversold his fluency in French. In truth, he was competent rather than fluent, and this caused him no end of trouble. Part of his job was to analyse French Intelligence reports, and he struggled so much with them that he got in the habit of taking them home and working on them at night and at the weekend, consulting his dictionary like a schoolboy cramming for an exam. All this was, it went without saying, in clear breach of protocol. One did not take work home. It was rule number one, though it had to be said that there were quite a number of rule number ones.

And then there was his opposite number with the Free French, a disagreeable and corpulent chap from Bourges called Moreau, who spotted early on his difficulty with French and insisted on using it with him, preferably at speed. He dreaded his twice-weekly meetings with Moreau.

Now there was talk of a trip to Switzerland and maybe even going over the border, and it wasn't that Kerr-Walters was frightened – far from it – but nonetheless, it wasn't going to be easy and the very thought of being captured and no doubt tortured… Not that he was a coward, but…

There'd even been some talk of being sent for parachute training somewhere near Manchester. The thought of that terrified him – jumping out of a plane, that was, not Manchester, though he'd never been that far north. He wasn't sure whether to mention his fear of heights.

It all added to his considerable worries.

–

But the pressures of work and his money worries – plus the state of his marriage, crumbling like the place in the country he'd been persuaded into buying against his better judgement – were as nothing compared to the visits to Earls Court.

Funnily enough, the grandfather of one of his school friends was an actual earl who lived in Earls Court – the part which is more Chelsea

— and Kerr-Walters had been to visit him once, and for this reason the area always held a certain cachet. But in recent times he'd been drawn to the area for altogether less wholesome reasons. His visits there were now of a clandestine nature.

He dreaded going, but not quite as much as he dreaded not going.

Kerr-Walters knew what he was doing was regarded by most people as immoral, but that was none of their business.

He knew that all his other problems would be as nothing compared to the consequences of being caught as a result of these visits. He did his best to keep them as few and far between as possible, but in truth they were more frequent than that.

Afterwards, his anxiety was fuelled even further, the sleepless nights even harder. He imagined that the lines of shadows thrown across the ceiling by the moonlight were prison bars. He'd sometimes tremble with fear, so much so that, once, his wife woke up and asked whatever was the matter with him. When she turned on the bedside light, she asked him if he'd been crying and he told her not to be so ridiculous.

But the truth was that Kerr-Walters was often on the verge of tears these days, sometimes tipping over that verge, and the vision of prison bars on the ceiling felt not so much like a product of his imagination as a real possibility.

The sense of having lost control of his life, and his destiny being in the hands of others — including those who may not have his best interests at heart — was very profound.

He wondered how much longer he could carry on.

Chapter 13

London

April 1940

Edith Maple from Edmonton in north London had actually been Bridget McKearney for the first forty years of her life. That was until two men who said they'd just arrived from Dublin appeared in her fruit shop in Islington one sunny afternoon in September 1938 and said they needed to speak with her, and it would be helpful if she closed the shop so they'd be uninterrupted. She didn't need telling twice, and nor did she need telling who they were because she already had a very good idea, and she certainly didn't need telling not to argue with the IRA.

They'd locked the door and turned the sign to 'closed' and then pulled down the blinds and walked into the windowless storeroom at the back of the shop. The shelves were stacked with boxes of fruit and one of the men – who sounded as if he was from Derry – helped himself to an orange and slipped another one into his coat pocket.

Her help for the cause was very much appreciated, the man with a Dublin accent assured her. She knew better than to ask what that work was, even though she hadn't done that much other than attend meetings, deliver the odd parcel and go on errands, and allow the fruit shop to be used as somewhere messages could be received and passed on – a kind of Republican post office, if you like. But there they were praising her commitment and her trustworthiness, and she muttered something about her absolute belief in a united Ireland and how it would only come about through armed struggle. The man from Dublin and his friend from Derry nodded, the latter helping himself to yet another orange.

'We need to do everything we can to defeat the enemy,' said Derry, the juice of his orange running down the side of his mouth before he wiped it with his sleeve. 'Do you not agree?'

128

Bridget McKearney said she couldn't agree more.

'We've checked you out very thoroughly, Bridget McKearney. We know people who know your folks in Letterkenny, and we know we can trust you and we think you're the right person.'

Bridget was unsure if it was in order to ask what she was the right person for, but Dublin explained.

'Are you familiar with the saying, "The enemy of my enemy is my friend"? I believe it was something an Indian philosopher said hundreds of years ago. I don't recall his name.'

'It sounds familiar.'

'So, who is our enemy, Bridget?'

'The Brits, obviously.'

'And who's their enemy, Bridget?'

'Apart from us? Germany, I'd guess.'

'You'd guess right. I mean, they're not at war yet but I'd be surprised if they're not by this time next year. Would you agree, Bridget?'

'I would, yes.'

'So, although there are aspects of Germany which may not be quite to our liking, Bridget, we recognise that we share a common enemy. So the Army Council has decided it is imperative we should seek to co-operate with them, which they recognise may be slightly... distasteful. I think that's the word, but needs must. So, we have a mission for you, Bridget McKearney. Are you prepared to volunteer for this mission?'

'Well, I'd be wanting to know a bit more about this mission, wouldn't I?'

The man from Dublin helped himself to a pear and leant towards her.

'The thing is...' He paused as he bit off the top half of the pear, stalk and all, and spat it on the floor. 'The thing is, Bridget, this is what you could call a top-secret mission. I know that sounds like a scene from an American spy movie, but there we are. And given it's top secret, as I say, if we tell you all about it and then you have a think and say, "No thank you, it's not for me, I'd rather stay here and sell apples all day and not worry about the Brits oppressing us," then we'd have let you into our secret, wouldn't we? So, the way it works is that you either say yes now and we tell you what it's about, or you say no and we leave here and you're none the wiser.'

'And the Brits continue to oppress us,' added Derry. She noticed he'd slipped another orange into his pocket.

Bridget McKearney said she understood.

'And what would be your answer?'

She thought about her life: to make any kind of living with the fruit shop she had to work six long days a week, starting at six in the mornings when the fruit was delivered and shutting up shop twelve hours later. The rent was about to go up again. Her tiny flat above the shop was damp and mouldy. Life wasn't easy.

'My answer is yes.'

The two men nodded to each other and Derry shook her hand. Dublin did likewise and said she was to listen very carefully.

'We need you to give up this shop and your little flat upstairs, and we want you to change your name and appear to be a Brit and move somewhere else in London. There's an organisation we want you to be involved with which helps the German cause in this country – secretly, of course – and if there's a war then it will be especially important. We want you to play a key role in this organisation, which is called The Group. It's been around for a year or two now but is not very well run. In fact, it's crying out for someone to take it over and run it properly and turn it to our advantage. That's where you come in, Bridget.'

It was an awful lot for Bridget McKearney to take in. She couldn't understand why they couldn't find anyone better. She wasn't sure how she felt at first about being asked, in effect, to be a German spy, but the more she thought about it the more she saw the logic: realistically, the IRA on its own had little – if any – chance of defeating the British state. But the Germans did, and if that happened then they'd certainly reward the IRA, so helping the Germans was certainly justified.

Things moved very fast after that. She gave up the shop and moved to Luton while they established her new identity as Edith Maple. Her beautiful long hair was cut brutally short, into the severe, unbecoming style worn by so many English women of her age, and her talent for mimicry came in handy as she perfected her English accent.

And then she moved to the house they'd got her in Edmonton, opposite Pymmes Park and just round the corner from Silver Street Station and everything was paid for; she no longer had any bills to worry about. It was a lovely house, not small and not overlooked, either, which was important as it would be a safe house, too. There was a generous allowance deposited in her Post Office account every week, which was ironic, because there'd been a series of raids at post offices in London recently. It wouldn't have surprised her to find out they had been the source of the money.

Helping to run The Group was a full-time job. Joining had been easier than she'd imagined and it didn't take her long to get stuck in. It was the kind of organisation where people were happy to make plenty of noise but reluctant to do the hard work, and she was prepared to do all that.

It wasn't easy, though, not least because most of the English folk in it were crazy, wide-eyed idiots, as she called them; fully committed Nazis and trying to be more German than the Germans. Of course, they had no idea about her background, which was a good job as most of them put the Irish quite high up on their hate list, though lower than Jews and communists. But she had to bite her tongue: 'The enemy of my enemy is my friend.'

And then the man from Derry turned up to tell her to be prepared for the arrival of visitors 'from abroad', as he put it.

'You mean from Ireland?'

'No, from somewhere on the Continent. But there will be a visitor from Ireland soon. A very important man.'

She was to provide a safe house for them and do all she could to assist.

She'd understand that he couldn't go into detail and she said of course, but this very important man had been in a foreign country – he'd paused and looked at her in a way to indicate yes... *that* foreign country – where he'd been trained in the business of espionage. When he arrived in London, he'd be organising an espionage ring, and with some luck it would work so much to Germany's advantage that the war could end soon, and before we'd know it the Germans would be here in Britain and the Brits would be beaten and Ireland would be united.

In truth, the man from Derry was clearly fond of his drink and was given to hyperbole at times, but notwithstanding that, this was clearly an exciting development. When he asked her if she wanted to know who the man was and she said, 'Yes, of course,' he led her into the kitchen and turned on the taps and whispered into her ear, his breath hot and heavily alcoholic.

Of course she'd heard of him; you didn't get much more important than that. A hero of the Rising. She was amazed that a man so important would be filling this role.

What an honour for her.

And he'd be here in just a couple of weeks now.

All being well.

Chapter 14

There weren't many people whom Helmut Schröder disliked as intensely as Günter König, which was exacerbated by the fact that the feeling was clearly mutual.

Helmut Schröder generally tried to get on with people in Hamburg, and especially his colleagues in the Abwehr headquarters on General-Knochenhauer-Strasse.

That wasn't difficult. They were an agreeable bunch, by and large. Most of them lived, as he did, around one of the two man-made lakes in the city, the Außenalster and the Binnenalster. But there was little socialising; people tended to keep to themselves after work and this suited Schröder fine. He realised he was fortunate to have this job. It was interesting and it kept him well away from conscription, and the fact that Nazi party members were in such a minority in the Abwehr was not to be underestimated.

But Günter König was one of that minority. He cut an odd figure – not unlike the Führer in many ways: slight and below average height, with greasy brown hair which flopped onto his forehead, and the moustache, seemingly especially cultivated in admiration of the Führer. König's wife Dorothea was an enormous woman whom Schröder would often see – in truth, it was hard to miss her – walking by the Alster, pushing a large pram and with other children following behind. Whenever he encountered Schröder at work, König would bellow out 'Heil Hitler!' before waiting expectantly for the appropriate response. Like Schröder, König was responsible for the recruitment, training and running of secret agents.

As far as Schröder could ascertain, none of König's agents were destined for Britain. Of course, he quite understood the need for secrecy and that there had to be a limit about how much information was shared, but even so… It seemed wrong that while he was required to brief König about his agents and their missions – so as to avoid confusion and overlaps, he was told, whatever that meant – there didn't seem to be the same requirement for König to inform Schröder about *his* agents.

Günter König was rarely seen around General-Knochenhauer-Strasse. The Abwehr had a smaller facility in the grounds of the Polizeigefängnis Fuhlsbüttel, the police prison to the north of the city, by the airport, and that was where he preferred to train his agents.

Helmut Schröder rarely visited Fuhlsbüttel; the prison there was gaining a particularly unpleasant reputation, and he preferred the more civilised atmosphere of General-Knochenhauer-Strasse. But one afternoon in March he had to travel up there for a demonstration of some new radio equipment. He found himself in a room with König and a nervous radio technician from Berlin with shaking hands, which Schröder thought must be a singular handicap for a radio technician.

At the end of the presentation König suggested Schröder join him in his office for schnapps.

'And how is life treating you, Helmut?'

Schröder said he mustn't complain. He sipped his schnapps, not a drink he was terribly fond of. He was finding König's unaccustomed friendliness quite disconcerting.

'You are still single?'

Schröder nodded in reply. This really wasn't any of König's business. He'd finish his schnapps and leave.

'Dorothea has a cousin, Hertha, who is moving to the city. Perhaps you'd like to…'

Rather too quickly, Schröder said no thank you, he was fine. The thought of a relative of Dorothea made him shudder.

'And tell me, Helmut, which agents are you sending over next?'

Schröder mentioned the names of a couple of agents he knew König was already aware of.

'And you, Günter, I hear you have two agents here?'

König shifted uncomfortably and shrugged. 'I always have agents here, Schröder. That's why I'm so well regarded by our superiors!'

It was Schröder's turn now to shift uncomfortably because he noticed König had dropped the 'Helmut' and was addressing him by his surname, and he'd also dropped the uncharacteristic bonhomie.

'So much so,' said König, 'that I am now working on a most important mission – and also to Britain. A mission that could very well affect the outcome of the war!'

'Well, Günter, we all hope our missions will have a positive impact on the outcome of the war, don't we?'

König waved his colleague's response away in a dismissive manner, his arm sweeping in front of him. 'I don't mean minor missions like sending people over hoping they'll let us know what a particular beach is like or the state of the roads. I'm talking about helping to construct alliances against the enemy, Schröder, the kind of strategic activity that wins wars.'

König sat back, his chest puffed out like a proud Prussian general, his Führer moustache twitching with excitement. 'But maybe I've already told you more than I should have done, Schröder.'

'Alliances? That sounds impressive, Günter. My congratulations.'

König nodded, accepting the praise in as humble a manner as he could manage, clearly a bit disappointed his colleague hadn't pushed him more.

'By alliances, Schröder, I mean with other… countries, or at least with representatives of them.'

Schröder said that sounded very important, and would König mind if they refilled their schnapps glasses? Loosening the other man's tongue would be worth the headache he'd get later. König filled up both their glasses and drank his in one go, pausing to refill it.

'It is important that we exploit the neutral countries in Europe, Schröder. Portugal, Spain, Switzerland, Sweden… We do our best to exploit them, if that's the right word, to our advantage. There's another country I've not mentioned, Schröder.'

König looked at him quizzically, expecting an answer.

'Turkey?'

'Apart from Turkey.'

Schröder said he really wasn't sure, at which point König slammed his hand down on his desk and his moustache twitched rapidly.

'Ireland, Schröder! Have you heard of it?'

'Of course I've heard of it.'

'Although it is a neutral state, they have no love for Great Britain. Within Ireland there's a very important organisation called the Irish Republican Army, which fought a war against Britain after the Great

War. This led to the partition of the island of Ireland, but the IRA still regard Britain as their enemy, and they're keen to fight them to unite the whole of Ireland.

'And we – the Reich – are now working with the IRA, Schröder. If we can tap into their undoubted expertise and their knowledge, and also their resources, then we can infiltrate a hidden army onto the British mainland! As I understand it, Irish people blend in naturally in Britain. It's a perfect scheme.'

From what Schröder knew about the Irish situation, he understood it was a lot more complicated than that, and König had failed to mention that the IRA was not part of the Irish government, but he wasn't minded to point this out. He was doing what he could to encourage König to talk.

'And I am the man in charge of this, would you believe, Helmut! I currently have two very important members of the IRA with me here in Hamburg. Soon, when their training is complete, they'll return to Ireland and from there to Britain, and the effect on the war will be… Well, just you wait and see!'

'This sounds like a very important mission, Günter. May I ask who these men are?'

König now looked like a man who realised he'd perhaps said too much; who knew he'd been indiscreet. He said that was enough for today and Schröder would be wanting to get back to General-Knochenhauer-Strasse.

Schröder got up to leave, pausing in the doorway when König called him back.

'Have you not forgotten something, Schröder?'

'I don't think so, I—'

'Heil Hitler!'

–

Joey Gallagher was beginning to regret ever coming to Hamburg.

It had seemed like a good idea when it had been discussed at the meeting of the Army Council a couple of months back and, in fact, he'd been one of those voting in favour of the proposal, but he'd been taken aback – to put it mildly – when Duffy turned to him after the vote and smiled as he spoke.

'We're pleased to see you voted in favour of the proposal, Joe. So, you'll be happy to know that you'll be our man going out there.' Duffy leant back and folded his arms across his chest and smiled again, and at that point MacBride – who'd been writing furiously – put on his spectacles and read out from his notebook.

'The Army Council endorses the proposal to explore and develop links with German Military Intelligence with a view to the Irish Republican Army undertaking and expanding our espionage operations on the British mainland, supported by said German Military Intelligence. The purpose of the operation will be to undermine the British state by facilitating the interests of Germany. To that end, the Army Council agrees to send Deputy Chief of Staff and acting Head of Intelligence Joseph Gallagher to Hamburg.'

MacBride gave the same knowing smile as Duffy, and as a sea of hands shot up to show all in favour, Joe Gallagher knew he'd been set up. The resolution would have been sorted before the meeting started. It was a stitch-up. That's how it worked. Heaven knows, he'd organised enough of them himself.

The day before he set sail from Rosslare on a dirty Dutch steamer, he was told he'd have a companion on the trip. He had no doubt that Sean Maguire, a hardline IRA member from County Wexford, was there to keep an eye on him.

Joe Gallagher hadn't been feeling on top of the world for a few weeks before the trip, and the four-day voyage to Hamburg only made him feel worse. He shared a cramped cabin in the bowels of the ship with Maguire, and the rough sea and the incessant noise of the engine on the other side of the bulkhead made the voyage near intolerable. There was little to do other than lie on their bunks, clutching the metal rails as the ship tossed and dropped, and listen to Maguire heaving and complaining. Twice a day a crew member would bring them bowls of something barely edible, which would have been an issue if he had anything approaching an appetite.

When they docked in Hamburg, they were driven to the north of the city, to what looked to all intents and purposes like a prison camp. At first Gallagher wondered whether this really had been a stitch-up by the Army Council, and why they had gone to such lengths to get rid of him when a bullet would have sufficed.

But then they were introduced to Günter König, who was the man who'd be looking after them, and who explained he'd be preparing them for their mission. Herr König seemed pleasant enough even though he was clearly a Nazi – not that that should have come as a big surprise, given where they were.

But the longer Gallagher remained in Hamburg, the more he regretted being there. It soon became clear quite what the mission entailed: that after his training was completed, he and Maguire would return to Ireland by submarine – which sounded like a truly dreadful prospect – and from there travel to the British mainland, where they'd be based in London and work with other German agents as they gathered intelligence in preparation for a German invasion.

He couldn't help wondering that almost everything he was being asked to do was more to the advantage of Germany, with any benefits to the IRA somewhat limited. He did ask Herr König one day quite how this would all lead to a united Ireland, and was told, 'We'll see.' When he asked for an assurance that if Germany successfully invaded Great Britain, Germany would actively bring about a united Ireland, the response was that this was something which could happen 'in the long term'.

And what made matters worse was that Sean Maguire was quite intolerable, forever chatting away with König as if they were great mates and laughing at his jokes, and then telling Gallagher how he shouldn't be so dismissive of National Socialism because there was certainly something to be said for it.

Occasionally their training took them to the main Abwehr offices in Hamburg on General-Knochenhauer-Strasse, which was by the Alster. There were others being trained there – also people being sent to Britain – but the Irishmen were discouraged from having any contact with them, and that suited Joey Gallagher fine.

Frankly, he just wanted to go home. He was still feeling unwell, even though the German doctor he finally got to see told him he was fine, but he wasn't sure how true that was.

Then Herr König called Gallagher and Maguire into his office and said they were as ready as they'd ever be, and they'd be returning to Ireland.

Chapter 15

London
April 1940

The letter was addressed to 'Special Branch' and sent to 'Scotland Yard, SW1', with 'PRIVATE & CONFIDENTIAL' typed in the top left corner of the envelope. It was written on a plain sheet of pale blue paper – the same colour as the envelope – and was dated '26th February 1940', followed by:

TO WHOM IT MAY CONCERN

IN THE NATIONAL INTEREST

Cooper had wondered whether the reference to 'the national interest' was going a bit far – over-icing the cake, as his mother would have put it – but he retained it, nevertheless.

> Dear Sirs
>
> To my shame and regret, a year ago I was persuaded against my better judgement to become involved with a group of what I thought at the time were like-minded patriots but who I now realise are ENEMIES OF THE STATE. It transpired that they sympathize with and do their best to assist Nazi Germany. Once I discovered this, I ceased all contact with the group.
>
> I read in the newspaper last week that the body of a man called Arthur KEMP was discovered in central London and that he had been murdered.

I am writing to inform you that I came across Mr Kemp in this group. I knew the names of very few people in the group, but I did know Mr Kemp and a friend of his called Bernard MELROSE. There was also an Irish woman there who seemed to be in charge. I never found out her name, but I was told by Mr Kemp that she was very important and in charge of all their activities in London and had links with Germany, and I believe she was also known as Lubeck or something to that effect.

The one other person I came across was a Mr George THOMSON, who I happen to know lived in the basement at 7 Love Lane, London EC3, which is off Eastcheap. I know his address because Mr Kemp once asked me to deliver a package there.

Yours faithfully

A PATRIOT

This was the version which Charles Cooper finally sent, and it was probably the seventh iteration of the letter. He typed it on a second-hand typewriter he'd bought at a shop in Queen's Park and which he disposed of after he'd sent the letter. He'd worked hard to get the tone right; he imagined it coming from an apparently respectable but shaken middle-class woman who'd found herself drawn into matters which terrified her, and which she was now trying to extricate herself from.

He hoped the random use of capitals was an authentic touch and the language just about right.

For Cooper, the purpose of the letter was to let the Invasion Warning Sub-Committee know about the Irish woman whom Arthur Kemp had told him was Agent Lübeck.

As for coming up with an address – and indeed, identity – for Murray, that had been much more complicated.

His starting point was the telephone number Kemp had given him – MIN 8460. Had he contacted the Post Office through the Invasion Warning Sub-Committee, then he'd have been given the address associated with that number quickly and without hesitation. But he couldn't risk alerting anyone to the fact that he knew the number. Questions would be asked, and he couldn't be sure he'd be able to answer them.

MIN 8460 was a number on the Mincing Lane exchange, which covered the area around Bishopsgate and Fenchurch Street in the City of London. He'd killed Kemp on a Wednesday night and, as far as he could gather, his body wasn't discovered until the Friday morning. Fortunately, it had rained throughout the night of the killing and well into the following day, so no blood had been visible from the alley, and the body was only found when someone went to move the bin it had been hidden behind.

Cooper found a report of the murder in the *Evening News* on the Monday.

Brutal Slaying in the City

There were no other useful details in the story. The police evidently had no clues and were appealing for witnesses. They were still trying to ascertain the identity of the victim.

Cooper waited until the Wednesday – exactly one week after he'd killed Kemp – before calling MIN 8460, but no one answered, which meant that at least the number was still in service. The following day he called the operator from a telephone box inside Baker Street Station and explained he was trying to contact a Mr Keith Redpath, telephone number MIN 8460.

'A Mr Redpath, you say, sir?'

'That's it, yes.' Redpath had been the name of a much-disliked maths teacher.

'And a telephone number of MIN 8460?'

'Correct.'

A long pause and the sound of pages being turned.

'There's no Mr Redpath on that number, sir.'

'Are you absolutely sure?'

The operator said she was, and Cooper said if that was the case then could she tell him who was on that number, because it really was most important.

'I'm afraid I'm not allowed to give you the name of the subscriber, sir. I would need to check with my supervisor but he's at lunch.' There was another pause. 'I'll tell you what, because I finish early today and I'm in a good mood, I'll give you the name. It's a Mr George Thomson – Thomson without a "p".' She giggled briefly, clearly at the use of the 'p'. Cooper laughed, too, and said she'd been terribly helpful, and decided not to push his luck and ask for the address.

No George Thomson was listed in the telephone directory, so on the Saturday he visited the public library close to Liverpool Street Station. It took him a few hours, ploughing through volumes of the electoral roll for the area covered by the Mincing Lane exchange. Eventually he came across the only George Thomson listed in that area:

George D. Thomson   Basement, 7 Love   London EC3
                        Lane

Cooper waited until the weekend to travel to Love Lane. It was hard to imagine a street less appropriately named: narrow and dirty, the walls of the houses blackened by years of soot and grime, the houses run-down and shabby, their windows filthy and the smells of every kind of household waste permeating the air. The basement of number 7 was reached from a narrow set of precarious-looking metal steps leading to a tiny paved area in front of the window and front door. The paved area was covered in litter and the remains of a rat. He spotted another one scurrying around. He noticed that behind the greying net curtains was a set of window bars – the only ones visible in the street – and the door had three keyholes, which suggested the owner was exercising a high degree of security.

He carefully descended the metal steps and stepped gingerly over the dead rat before knocking on the door with his gloved hand. There was no reply. He knocked again and then tapped on the window, and from the floor above him, which was one above street level, a voice called out.

'I don't think you'll have any joy there, darling.' It was a woman's voice, hoarse and with a strong cockney accent. Cooper said thank you and could he come up and maybe ask her a question or two.

'The gentleman who lived below you?'

'George?'

'Yes.'

'What about him?'

'When did you last see him?'

She frowned as if trying to recall when she'd last seen George. 'Not for weeks, darling, maybe back in January. Must have been, because my

Bert joined up in the first week of February and we'd not seen him for a bit by then.' She spoke as if she was permanently suppressing a cough, her voice rasping.

'Do you have any idea where he is?'

'No, darling, he must be on one of his trips. Always going off, George was, sometimes for weeks on end.'

'What did he do?'

'No idea, darling. I never asked and he never told me – he wasn't that type: very quiet and very private. Never had any visitors, no lady friends. What you want him for anyway?'

'I'm... uh, from his bank... Martins... and we'd been awaiting a reply from him to some correspondence from us. I was in the area so thought I'd pop by.'

The lady nodded as if impressed, her arms folded across her ample breasts. She had a cigarette wedged in her mouth and some of the ash had gathered on her bosom. 'Must be nice having a bank, personal service and all that. Can anyone join a bank?'

'It depends on a level of income, I'm afraid.'

She let out a throaty laugh and said, well, that ruled her out, then, and did the gentleman want to come in for a cup of tea, but Cooper said he really must get going, but many thanks anyway.

–

'When did you say Special Branch received this letter, sir?'

'Two, three days ago, Pamela... Took them another day or two for someone to twig that this may be of some interest to us. Hodges had it biked round here this morning, which is good of him because the Branch tend to be quite possessive these days when they get their hands on something, especially as there's some link with a current murder case.'

'May I see the letter, sir?' Cooper reached out for it. Lieutenant Commander McConnell had already said they'd found no fingerprints on it, and Cooper had been tempted to say they needn't have bothered. Of course it had no fingerprints on it.

'You checked the names against The Group list, Cooper?'

'Yes, sir. Both Arthur Kemp and Bernard Melrose are on it. But George Thomson isn't. In fact, from what I was able to ascertain since you gave me the names this morning, we can find no records of George Thomson. He has no criminal record and hasn't served in any of the armed forces.'

'We may need to go and have a look around his property. Same applies to the other two. Pamela, can you sort out the search warrants, please?'

'Yes, sir. But don't you think there's a danger we could alert people if we search these addresses?'

'I take your point, but we need to take that risk, I'm afraid. And the woman referred to in the letter: Irish. Are there any Irish names on the list?'

'No, sir. Of course, she doesn't have to have an Irish name to be Irish.'

'The letter says she's in charge of The Group in London.'

'It does refer to her as Lübeck, so you're probably correct.'

'We clearly do need to find her.'

'I have an idea, sir.'

'Go on, Cooper.'

'If we were to try and visit all the women on the list with an address in London – there are just over sixty of them, we can come up with credible pretexts for visiting them – then we can see who's Irish.'

'I'd need to be convinced that wouldn't alert them, and in any case, it could take forever. I still think we need the German spies. How's Manfred's training going, Pamela?'

'Very well, sir. He'll be ready next month.'

'Can we bring it forward?'

'I can ask, sir.'

—

Over the next week they checked all three properties – those of Kemp, Melrose and Thomson – but found little of any interest. Cooper was surprised how spartan and sparse was Murray's property, the basement in Love Lane. Compared to the filthy exterior, it was clean and tidy inside, with little of note and hardly any personal possessions: no photographs, no letters, just a few bills and a small collection of history books. They'd even taken up the floorboards, but there was nothing there apart from a colony of rats, put out at being disturbed.

They found some political literature at Bernard Melrose's property in Bermondsey, but it was of no great consequence: old copies of *Action*, Mosley's newspaper. Arthur Kemp's apartment in Rotherhithe was a hoarder's den which took days to search properly, but again, nothing of any interest.

Cooper had a close shave when he left Murray's place in Love Lane and heard the voice of the lady he'd spoken to, asking a policeman what was going on.

She told him a gentleman from George's bank had been round only a week or so ago, and when the policeman asked if he'd given a name, she said no.

'Can you describe him, by any chance?'

'Not really, darling. He looked like any gentleman, really. I could pass him in the street now and not recognise him!'

Chapter 16

Archie arrived at his Hampstead home shortly after six on Wednesday, 8 May. It was a warm evening: the trees were in late blossom and the gardens bursting into colour, and he was in an uncharacteristically good mood.

His wife was in the country and the housekeeper had left a cold supper in the fridge. The previous evening he'd opened a bottle of 1930 Château Cheval Blanc, which he'd found at his in-laws', and it really was a most sensational St-Émilion, unquestionably one of the best he'd ever had; almost half of the bottle remained.

He'd been dreaming about it all day.

His good mood vanished within moments of arriving home. As always, he checked the inside of the gatepost and there was a circle chalked on to the post. His shoulders sagged and he swore beneath his breath and then looked behind the ornamental stone lion by the front door and sure enough, there were two pebbles, which meant he was to meet his Soviet contact the next day at the second safe house they'd agreed when they last met.

It was the one in Earls Court and his heart sank because it was one he'd used a few times before. Oddly enough, Osip had also used it before he was disposed of, and Archie thought it strange Soviet Intelligence appeared to rely on such a relatively small number of safe houses.

Notwithstanding his reservations about going back there, Earls Court did have the advantage of being somewhere he could walk to from work and the distance was just right for him to ensure he wasn't being followed.

He headed west through Sloane Square and across Chelsea and then along Old Brompton Road, constantly pausing to check he wasn't being followed, frequently crossing the road, glancing into shop windows and going into a tobacconist's.

When he was satisfied no one had been watching him, he turned off Old Brompton Road and within minutes was inside a small mews house off Wetherby Road. He'd often wondered about this safe house: perfectly pleasant and very quiet, but the dozen houses gathered around the cobbled courtyard were very close to one another and it was, he had to say, the kind of place where he could well bump into someone he knew.

There'd been two bodyguards in the hall and one of them had searched him. When he was finally taken into the upstairs room where Ivan Alexandrovich Morozov was waiting for him, Archie asked the NKVD man if that had really been necessary. Morozov said it was, and at that moment Archie heard a toilet flush. Seconds later a short man with a bald head and a large moustache, which seemed to be there to compensate for the lack of hair elsewhere on his head, entered.

Ivan Mikhailovich Maisky: the Soviet ambassador. *What on earth,* thought Archie, *is he doing here? How did he get here? Isn't he always followed?*

'You're probably wondering why I'm here, Archie,' said the ambassador.

'It had crossed my mind, yes.'

'It is urgent that I see you.' Until then Maisky had been smiling, but now he looked very serious. 'It seemed more feasible that this time I come to you.'

'Did you travel here by bus?'

Morozov looked shocked that Archie had said that; at first the ambassador looked confused, and then laughed. 'Of course – your English sense of humour! Very good, very good... No, I use a disguise. Perhaps not the most sophisticated act of subterfuge, but it seems to work. And there's no need to worry. We have plenty of people in the area on lookout. Anything suspicious and we'll hear about it right away. Tell me, Comrade Archie, how is the war going?'

Archie shrugged. 'Hard to know quite what to say really. Looks like the Netherlands and Belgium may be about to fall and France is clearly in Hitler's sights, and meanwhile there's even concern here about the possibility of a German invasion. In fact, I'd like to think I may have been in some way responsible for this. After we last met, I wrote a report based on interviews with various contacts, including some Belgians and French recently arrived in this country. I was able to raise the prospect of a German invasion – I think I said we ought to treat it as a probability rather than a possibility. I suggested that Hitler was bound to continue his offensive campaign in Europe, that it was against his nature to consolidate his gains, and that from a strategic point of view, it made sense for him to head west rather than attack an ally to the east. I hope that has helped alert London to the Nazi threat. But I'm not a military man, Your Excellency. Surely you ought to be well informed about what the Germans are up to, they're your allies, after all.'

'I've told you before… We're not allies, we are partners in a non-aggression pact. There's a big difference. One of the paramount differences is that we don't trust them, and this is why I needed to see you so urgently today, Archie. Tell me, what is going on in this country?'

'In what sense, Your Excellency?'

'All the rumours about a change of prime minister. It is alien to us that something like this is discussed so openly in public. In the Soviet Union, there are gatherings in corridors and then a meeting of the Politburo and that's it. Someone goes, and if they're lucky it will be to their *dacha* rather than to a prison camp. But here… I don't understand. Why is Mr Chamberlain being sacked?'

'It's a complicated business, Your Excellency. There's a feeling that for this country to fight the war most effectively, there needs to be a coalition government – that is, to bring the Labour Party into government. But while the Labour Party have agreed in principle, it appears they will only join a coalition if Mr Chamberlain is replaced as prime minister. They are actually deciding on this tonight.'

'And who will be the new prime minister?'

'That is a good question. The person preferred by the Conservative members of Parliament and their peers in the House of Lords is Lord Halifax.'

'The Foreign Secretary?'

'Correct. It is believed that His Majesty the King would also prefer Lord Halifax, and Mr Chamberlain has let it be known he wishes to see him as his successor. But the Labour Party see Halifax as an appeaser. They'd prefer Mr Churchill.'

'Who would you prefer, Archie?'

'It's really not up to me, Your Excellency. My personal view is that I would have concerns if someone who seems intent on reaching a peace agreement with Germany were made prime minister.'

'So, you'd prefer Mr Churchill?'

'Absolutely.'

'I don't understand democracy, Archie. If your king wants something, surely he gets what he wants, no?'

'Not really. It's complicated, but some people would say that a king is not strictly part of the democratic system.'

Maisky frowned and smiled as if confused. 'You see, Archie, what concerns me, and what certainly concerns Moscow, is that if Lord Halifax became prime minister, it would be only a matter of time – weeks, maybe – before the British government sat down with the German government and reached some kind of peace deal, one most likely allowing Germany a free run in Europe and keeping what territories they've taken control of in return for promising not to invade this country. And if that happens, Archie, then I think I told you last time we met, we believe it is inevitable that Germany will then turn its attention to us. They'll tear up their non-aggression pact and invade the Soviet Union. In short, Archie, peace between Great Britain and Nazi Germany will be a disaster for the Soviet Union. And Mr Churchill?'

'What about him?'

'What about his attitude to the Germans? Would he sit down and talk peace with them?'

'I very much doubt it. He's been warning about the Nazi threat for years. He's an outspoken opponent of appeasement. He's hardly likely to change his tune now.'

'So, we need to hope for Mr Churchill to become prime minister. When will we know, Archie?'

'Certainly by the weekend.'

'Is there anything you can do to influence matters?'

'Me? I sometimes wonder if you think I'm more important than I am!'

'Do you know the Duke of Windsor?'

'No, I've never met the man. My brother shot with him once.'

'Shot what?'

'Pheasants, I believe, Your Excellency.'

'But don't you mix in the same social circles?'

'Not quite.'

'But you're all aristocrats, surely!'

'There are clearly gaps in your knowledge and understanding of the British class system, Your Excellency, which is quite understandable. I mean, there are aristocrats and aristocrats. And you shouldn't make the mistake of confusing the Royal Family with the aristocracy. They aren't aristocrats.'

'What are they, then?'

'They're Germans, Your Excellency. They only changed their name from Saxe-Coburg and Gotha because of the Great War.'

'That would make sense, then.'

'What would?'

'You recall that before you gave me an interesting lesson on the British class system, I asked if you knew the Duke of Windsor. As you may be aware, the duke has been dividing his time between the British military mission to France and this country, where the duchess resides. We have very strong intelligence that there has been contact between the duke and representatives of the German government. The duke has always been sympathetic to Germany and to the Nazi ideology. We believe he resents the way he and his wife are treated by the King and the British government. He feels they ought to be treated with more respect and be accorded higher status.'

'It's not exactly news, though, that the duke is sympathetic to Nazi Germany. After all, he and his wife went to visit Hitler at his place in Bavaria a couple of years ago. I'm not sure what your point is.'

'We have intelligence that the duke is passing on top-secret intelligence about British military plans to the Germans. We know he is doing this through a French-American businessman called Charles Bedaux. We have reason to believe that Bedaux is an Abwehr agent.'

'You're saying that the brother of the King is a German spy?'

The ambassador nodded. 'And we are worried that if the duke is allowed to continue in this fashion, a momentum for peace could build up around him. And that represents a serious threat to the Soviet Union.'

'And you want me to…? I'm not sure what I'm meant to do with this intelligence, Your Excellency.'

'I want you to be aware of it. Maybe incorporate it in your reports. I'd be surprised if that doesn't corroborate existing intelligence on the duke. It will all help to underline the dangers of seeking peace with the Germans.'

'I take your point, Your Excellency.'

'And you're doing well in your Intelligence Service, Archie?'

'Yes, thank you. Since I was promoted in January, I think it was, yes… It's been fine.'

'"Fine"? I've come to realise that the English use certain words that they render devoid of real meaning. In my experience, "fine" can mean anything from excellent to terrible.'

'In this case, it would be somewhere in between. I wouldn't call my job exciting but my role is as a senior analyst, which means I have to write reports based on intelligence from our agents and other sources, such as diplomats and informers, and I interview refugees to this country from Europe, emigrés and the like. I write cogently, and some of the help you've given me has enabled my reports to come across as being particularly prescient.'

'So, these reports can influence British policy?'

'One would hope so, yes… to an extent.'

'And in respect of what you mentioned earlier – worries about a German invasion. Would that be something you'd be expected to write a report on?'

Archie made a face to suggest the answer wasn't quite so straight-forward. 'Yes and no. I mean, it would seem odd if I were to write a report on the invasion for no apparent reason, such as being asked to do so by someone at Broadway. What is it you're getting at?'

'Has there ever been any talk of you being sent into the field?'

'They're beginning to talk about it – funnily enough, one of my chums mentioned it to me today. There's a course they send you on. A month at a cold house surrounded by fields, where you get shouted at and roughed up from time to time. Sounds very much like boarding school, in fact.'

'If you were to apply, would you have any say in where you'd be sent?'

'I doubt it.'

'But if you had an agent, Archie – a source in another country – would you be able to be sent there?'

'I think that would certainly help.'

'Let me be frank with you, Archie... We have an excellent source in Germany. He's as good as you get and very closely involved in planning the invasion of this country. If we can find a way of establishing this source for you – by which I mean you can start to refer to them and their material – then maybe you can find a way of getting yourself out there to meet him.'

'To Germany?'

'That's unclear at the moment. We'll let you know.'

'I have one more question?' It was Morozov, awkwardly shifting his large frame in the deep sofa, digging his elbow into the armrest to move. 'You may recall that Osip was running an agent codenamed Bertie, another Englishman. We have lost all contact with Bertie. Because he was recruited as an OMS agent and run by Osip we know very little about him, other than that his real name is Charles Cooper. He also used the name Christopher Shaw, according to a note from Osip in the files. With the benefit of hindsight, it may have been better if we'd brought Osip back to Moscow and forced the information out of him rather than disposing of him here in London. But we cannot trace this Cooper and would very much like to do so. We found out all this information on him when we looked through Osip's files again, when you were telling us about him and what had happened to you in Moscow. I don't suppose you have any idea as to the whereabouts of this Bertie?'

'I've never met him, don't know anything about him, I'm afraid. I assume you've had a proper look for him?'

'Of course, Archie, we're not amateurs. It is difficult for someone to just disappear, but we have so little information... We assume he's using another name. All we have is a photograph we found in the OMS files in Moscow. Here... Do you recognise him?'

Archie held it to the light, slightly angling it to get a clearer view. 'To be honest, it's such poor quality that I'm not sure I'd recognise him even if he was sitting next to you now.'

'Very well, but may I ask you to look out for him nonetheless?'

Archie promised that if he ever came across a blurred man, he'd let them know. Morozov said it would be helpful if he took matters more seriously.

'And you're going to look into volunteering to be sent into Europe?'
'I said I would.'
'And you'll let us know what happens?'
'Yes, through the tobacconist's in Hackney as usual.'
'As usual.'

Chapter 17

England
May 1940

'You'd better come in, Phillips. You sounded rather excited on the telephone.'

Phillips apologised and said he was most sorry if that was the case, but actually it was a matter of some urgency, and he was grateful the Chief could see him at such short notice. He took a moment or two to catch his breath and compose himself.

'I have to tell you, sir, that I think there's a distinct possibility we may have found our traitor.'

'Archie?'

Phillips nodded, wondering quite how many other traitors the Chief had in his in-tray.

'Yes, sir.'

The Chief sat very still and fixed his gaze on Phillips as he took in what he'd just said. 'One of us?'

'I'm afraid so, sir, as we've long feared.'

'You'd better get on with it and tell me, then, hadn't you?'

Phillips drew a deep breath, because once he'd said the name there was no way of ever unsaying it.

'Timothy Kerr-Walters, sir.'

The Chief stared intently at him, gripping his fountain pen tightly between the fingers of both hands and raising his eyebrows as if to say 'Really?'

'Kerr-Walters, eh? Promoted him in January, didn't we?'

'One of the seven high-flyers, sir, indeed.'

'Never been under any suspicion before?'

'No, sir: impeccable background.'

154

'Fully vetted, I presume?'

'Of course, sir.'

'And how have you come to this conclusion, Phillips?'

'In the manner one always suspected may be the case, sir. He made a mistake – or more to the point, a series of them.'

–

For a brief time, Timothy Kerr-Walters had enjoyed a period of relative calm. For a few days after borrowing one hundred pounds from the moneylender in Paddington, he actually slept well at night and wasn't sick in the morning.

But it was only ever going to be a passing respite; his worries ran far too deep.

The money he deposited in his Barclays Bank account didn't last nearly as long as he'd hoped, and he was quickly back in overdraft. The main culprit was the new kitchen: his wife had decided she had to have one like her sister. He'd pointed out that the difference was that her sister's husband worked in the City, and she'd replied that was hardly her fault and why should she live in straitened circumstances, and he'd shouted that not having a new kitchen like her sister's hardly amounted to straitened circumstances... Naturally, a full-blown row had ensued.

So, he went back to see Lister on Praed Street, who thought he'd come to make his first repayments, but Kerr-Walters said, 'Actually, would it be possible to extend the loan?'

'By how long?'

'Actually, I was going to ask by how much. I'd like to borrow an extra one hundred pounds, please.'

Lister reacted in the manner of someone who'd heard this all before.

'That would be the five per cent fee of five pounds, plus an interest rate of three quarters of one per cent per month.'

'But I thought I was paying half a per cent per month?'

'That was on the original loan of one hundred pounds, Mr Kerr-Walters, and you've not paid any of that back... yet. Those are my terms.'

He folded his arms and allowed himself the faintest of smiles.

So there.

At least that paid for the kitchen and the next term's school fees for the two children. What Kerr-Walters had not realised was that his wife was so thrilled with the new kitchen that no sooner had it been completed, she engaged the same company to install a downstairs toilet, complete with a sink and an adjoining laundry room with all the accompanying machinery. The cost was eye-watering: almost as much as the kitchen.

His insomnia started again, as did his early morning visits to the bathroom. He received a letter from his bank manager informing him that his overdraft had exceeded agreed levels, and unless he could arrange a hasty injection of funds, please could he make an appointment to discuss his financial affairs.

He could hardly go back to Lister in Praed Street to ask for more money when he'd not paid off any of the first two loans. He found what he hoped was the solution in the most improbable of places: a poster pasted on a wall close to Euston Station:

WANT THE MAXIMUM AMOUNT OF CASH WITH THE MINIMUM AMOUNT OF QUES-TIONS?

FUL 4881

That sounded exactly what he was after: plenty of money, few questions. And although a notice on a wall in Euston was not his preferred method of seeking finance, beggars can't be choosers, and it was a Fulham number and he'd always thought of Fulham as being semi-respectable, between Chelsea and the river.

It turned out to be a pleasant white-stuccoed terraced house in Mimosa Street, off the Fulham Road and reassuringly close to King's Road: the right side of the tracks. The front door was opened by Martin, the man he'd spoken to when he'd rung FUL 4881, and Martin seemed to be very friendly... *Please come in... I hope you don't mind cats... Through here... Can I get you a cup of tea, maybe?*

It was a sun-filled sitting room overlooking a neat garden, and couldn't have been more different from Lister's office above the menswear shop on Praed Street.

Martin carefully placed Kerr-Walters' cup of tea on the side table next to his armchair and sat down opposite him, notebook and pen in hand. An elderly black cat stirred on a chair by the window.

This all felt terribly civilised. Quite the opposite of what he'd been expecting.

'May I ask how much money you wish to borrow, Mr Kerr-Walters?'

'I'm looking for one hundred and fifty pounds, please, but obviously would need to know your terms.'

'You seem to be a very respectable gentleman, sir, but you'll understand that I will need to be satisfied as to the security of my loan, if you follow me. I'll need to check out your identity, et cetera. May I ask when you have in mind to pay that back?'

'I would hope within... six months, if that sounds reasonable?'

'I don't see a problem with that, sir, depending of course on my checks being satisfactory. May I ask your occupation?'

'I'm a civil servant.'

Martin nodded. 'If we were to say ten per cent for repayment in six months... In other words, you will repay a total of one hundred and sixty-five pounds.'

Kerr-Walters did some quick mental arithmetic. That made it a bit pricier than the first Lister loan, but cheaper than the second one, and Martin seemed pleasant enough – certainly friendlier than Lister – so he said yes, that was fine.

'Very good... and have you brought with you all the paperwork I requested?'

Kerr-Walters passed the envelope to Martin, who said he'd check him against the electoral roll and his bank details, too, and when Kerr-Walters asked him how on earth he'd be able to do that, Martin winked.

'May I ask where you work in Whitehall?'

'Oh, it's terribly tedious... the Ministry of Supply. I'm just a pen-pusher really.'

This was his standard response, a well-rehearsed one, designed to sound as uninteresting as possible and bring any conversation to a swift end.

'Very well, Mr Kerr-Walters.' Martin pronounced his name carefully with three syllables, each one spoken as if it was a separate name. 'Give me two days to get the money. Can you return here on Thursday?'

–

Kerr-Walters returned to the house in Mimosa Street on the Thursday. He'd telephoned beforehand and Martin assured him everything was in order. He still worried he was being rash, but he couldn't think what else to do. He planned to use one hundred pounds to begin paying off Lister's loans and the remaining fifty to pay the builder and the school fees. He ought to be on the road to recovery now.

When he entered the sunny back room, he spotted three bundles of five-pound notes on the small table between him and Martin. Each one had a wrapper showing the figure £50.

'May I make a proposal, Mr Kerr-Walters? When we discussed the terms of this loan, I said that in return for a loan of one hundred and fifty pounds for six months, you'd repay a total of one hundred and sixty-five pounds.'

'That's right.'

'My proposal is that I will still lend you one hundred and fifty pounds, but rather than repaying me one hundred and sixty-five pounds, I shall only expect a repayment of just one hundred pounds.'

Kerr-Walters had been brought up to believe that if something sounded too good to be true, then it probably was, and this seemed to be a case in point.

'How on earth will that work?'

'I'd like you to do me a favour, Mr Kerr-Walters. I have a friend – a Dutch gentleman called Henk, who arrived in this country a few weeks ago. Henk was an active member of the CPN, the Dutch Communist Party, and as such was fleeing the Netherlands, where he was a wanted man in his own country. He also feared a Nazi invasion, which is indeed now underway. Henk managed to jump ship when it arrived in Harwich and is therefore in this country illegally. He is not registered and has no identity. There's a limit as to how long he can remain like this.

'I would like you to obtain a National Registration Identity Card for Henk. In this envelope here, I have photographs of him for you to use for the card, along with details of his date of birth and address and a suggested name: Harold Eric Jackson. Henk's English is excellent and his accent flawless. The risk is minimal. All we need is the card, and I'd hope that as a civil servant—'

'Even if I had the ability to do as you ask, it would be quite improper for me to do so. Indeed, were I caught, the implications would be most severe – not just for me but for you, too. And for your friend.'

Martin shrugged and said nothing, but he did smile, and in the silence Kerr-Walters had time to consider the proposal. As it happened, what he was being asked to do was not nearly as unfeasible as it seemed. Senior MI6 officers, of which he was now one, did have the authority to create false identities for operational purposes. Their agents and sources and contacts often needed documentation, and senior officers could request such paperwork, including the National Registration Identity Card. In his experience it had always been quite straightforward. And in return for this favour, he'd save sixty-five pounds, which would make an enormous difference. He'd be able to pay off Lister entirely, which would be one less worry.

'Very well... and I'd get all the cash now?'

'Yes.'

'And when would you want the identity card by?'

'The end of next week would be very much appreciated.'

–

Elsie was based in a stuffy cubbyhole of an office in Registry, and she responded well to flattery. When Kerr-Walters asked her if she'd had her hair done differently, she smiled and patted her hair and said as it happened she had and how nice of him to notice, and asked how she could help.

He handed her the photograph and the details she needed – name, date of birth, address – and Elsie said, 'If only all the officers were so efficient. Give me two days, Mr Kerr-Walters, sir, and it will be ready.'

Martin was thrilled when Kerr-Walters turned up at the house in Fulham with the identity card (AITK/137:9) for Jackson, Harold E., of 7 Rhodes Court, Hurlingham Road, SW6. The photograph had been affixed and was stamped. All it required was a signature.

Martin handed Kerr-Walters the contract for the loan of one hundred pounds, repayable in six months.

The money lender had been as good as his word.

Life was looking decidedly rosier, less overwhelming.

And apart from the matter he needed to deal with the following day, all was good.

–

For early May, the weather was absolutely dreadful; with the storm-like winds and heavy rain, anyone entering the building did so completely drenched. There was a damp atmosphere about the place, along with the unpleasant odour associated with wet clothing.

Phillips had suffered from a nasty cough for the past few days, and felt so dreadful as he settled at his desk that he wondered whether he should head home. He probably would have done if it wasn't for the weather.

And then his day got worse.

His secretary put her head round the door. A gentleman from MI5 was waiting for him downstairs. Should she bring him up?

It turned out to be not one but two MI5 officers who'd come to see him: the disobliging Simpkin and Harvey, the man who'd assisted him with the promotion interviews.

Simpkin spoke first, in the manner of a somewhat put-upon barrister opening a routine prosecution at a provincial assizes.

'Last Wednesday, officers from the Metropolitan Police arrested a Dutch communist called Henk Bakker. They'd been searching for him since he jumped ship in Harwich some months ago. Henk is considered to be a threat to national security, and quite possibly a Communist agent. He was spotted on the King's Road in Chelsea and taken into custody. On his person he had a National Registration Identity Card in the name of Harold E. Jackson, with his photograph on it. The card appeared to be genuine – that is, not a forgery. On further examination it was ascertained that the card was issued from your Registry here… in this building. When approached, the lady who'd issued the card…'

'Elsie?'

'Elsie told us the card had been requested by Timothy Kerr-Walters. He'd supplied all the details, including the photograph. So, we looked further into Mr Kerr-Walters. We checked his bank account at Barclays and discovered that in recent weeks unusually large sums of money have been going in and out of his account. Something in the region of three hundred pounds in cash have been deposited on three separate occasions.'

'Shouldn't I have been informed of this?'

'You're being informed now, Phillips.' Simpkin was enjoying this. 'I shouldn't need to tell you, Phillips, that this is most serious. Firstly, facilitating the issue of a National Registration Identity Card to a foreign fugitive, and a communist to boot, and the evidence of suspicious transactions on his bank account.'

He stopped speaking and Phillips could have been excused for thinking he'd noticed a hint of a smile on Simpkin's face and a look of 'What are you going to do about it?'

'Well, those are clearly serious concerns, Simpkin. I think I'd better go to see the Chief.'

–

After he explained everything to him, Phillips was surprised at the Chief's reaction. Menzies appeared calm and almost nonplussed.

'They looked at his bank details before consulting us, did they?'

'It would appear so, sir, yes.'

The Chief shook his head.

'And no one's spoken to Kerr-Walters about this?'

'Not yet, sir.'

'Well, we better had, don't you think, Phillips?'

'Absolutely, sir. Simpkin has made Harvey available to assist us.'

'I bet he has. I imagine he's enjoying this. But I advise caution, Phillips. None of this is evidence that Timothy Kerr-Walters is Archie. I think we're still a long way from that. I agree it's all very suspicious, but at the moment it's what our learned friends would call circumstantial evidence. We need to bring Kerr-Walters in, certainly, and question him very closely, which needs to be handled sensitively. It's Friday morning. Wait until this afternoon and then approach him in a friendly and informal manner and say you'd like a chat Monday morning. Get Harvey to have him watched until then.'

–

Timothy Kerr-Walters knew the game was up.

For a start, Phillips appeared to be making too obvious an effort to be very casual when he stopped by and asked if he minded putting aside some time on Monday morning for a chat, nothing of great importance.

But he'd already spotted Simpkin and Harvey from MI5 leaving Phillips' office, and Phillips going into the Chief's soon after.

And then when he left Broadway and headed home, he could have sworn he was being tailed as he headed to the station. He'd decided to hail a taxi, but when he got home he suspected the house was being watched, and when they set off for the country in the morning there was no doubt they were being followed.

He made up his mind on the Saturday afternoon.

Life had become intolerable, and he was no longer in control of it. He'd been an utter fool to borrow the money, and to get that identity card had been an act of madness.

Kerr-Walters spent a few hours in his study, sorting out his affairs, such as they were, and then he wrote a few letters, all rather awkward and difficult. He told his wife to confirm with her brother they'd be going shooting the following day.

He was remarkably calm that night, sleeping straight through it and waking up late. It was as if he'd reached the end of a journey.

At the shoot he bumped into his brother-in-law's friend Archer – the man who'd recommended Lister and got him into all this trouble – and Archer lent him a Purdey because he had a spare one. Kerr-Walters thought if he'd had a Purdey hunting rifle, let alone a spare one, then all his money worries wouldn't have started in the first place.

He waited until they stopped for a break and then slipped behind some trees as the shoot resumed. He knew he needed to act quickly because any minute now the beaters would appear. Once he heard the first shots, that was his cue. He held Archer's beautiful Purdey under his chin, his hands trembling but his mind resolved.

All in all, it was quite some price to pay.

Chapter 18

London and the Netherlands
May 1940

In the very early hours of Friday, 10 May 1940, a dark blue Wolseley pulled up outside the dark form of a large detached house in West London.

Much of the ground floor, and certainly its entrance, was concealed behind a high privet hedge, which was one of the reasons why, six months earlier, the property had been requisitioned by British Intelligence. For the past few weeks it had been used as a safe house and training base for a very special agent.

That night, the senses of this very special agent were highly primed, alert to every sound. He listened carefully as the car stopped outside, and as its doors slammed shut and footsteps approached the house. He listened as the front door opened and quiet words were exchanged, and soon after that Cooper knocked gently on his door.

'Manfred, it's time.'

'I know, I'm ready.'

The German had been resting on his bed – sleep being out of the question – and he stood up and put on his jacket before washing his face and combing his hair and picking up his rucksack and coat, checking once more that the papers were safely concealed in its carefully tailored lining. He followed Cooper downstairs to the small dining room next to the kitchen. The gas fire was on, as it had been throughout his time there; his abiding memory of the house would be of a place that was safe and cosy but far too warm.

There was a pot of coffee on the table, along with a rack of toast with butter and jam and a boiled egg next to it, which they knew he was partial to, but in the early hours of that particular morning Manfred Hoffmann didn't have much of an appetite.

Next to the toast rack, somewhat incongruously, lay an Enfield Mark 2 service revolver and a box of ammunition. He'd been trained on it at a nearby firing range and had been assured he was a good shot. Pamela was sitting at the top of the table, directly opposite him. As ever, she looked immaculate, as if she'd spent some time preparing to go out for dinner.

'Did you get any rest?'

He picked up the scent of her perfume, which always reminded him of a summer evening. 'Not really.'

'I didn't think you would. Nervous?'

Manfred nodded as he slowly chewed a piece of toast.

'And you remember how to contact us when the time comes?'

'Yes'. Manfred sounded annoyed. He'd been through this so many times.

'Just tell me the telephone number, please.'

'WHI 7492.'

'Very good. Cooper, be so good as to check everything, please.'

Cooper duly emptied the contents of the bag onto the sofa. There was little more than a change of clothes, and extra pairs of socks and underwear and a pair of boots. The boots were of excellent quality, but had been made to look worn and scuffed. There were three different hats because, as had been explained to Manfred in his training, people tended to notice headwear, and if you were being followed and had the opportunity to change it, that could be an enormous help. He spotted Cooper checking the labels. It was essential that everything was German-made; nothing could be allowed to arouse suspicion.

Cooper then opened the hidden pocket inside the coat and removed its contents.

His identity card and Nazi party *Mitgliedskarte* were all in the name of Ernst Werner, with an address in Eilbeck in the east of Hamburg. The other papers all told Ernst Werner's story, should anyone be interested, which he had to assume they would be, though he very much hoped they weren't. Most important of all was a letter from Hamburg's oldest hospital, the Asklepios in Altona, stating he was being discharged after an eight-week stay for typhoid fever. According to the letter – in what Manfred considered to be a touch of genius – he was still considered to be infectious and should avoid close contact with people, and should in no circumstances be involved in the preparation of food. There was also a letter from the Oberkommando der Wehrmacht armed forces recruitment office in Hamburg, acknowledging that Ernst Werner was exempt from military service on account of his ill health and that this exemption was to be reviewed at a further medical examination in January 1941.

And finally, a letter from his employer in Bremerhaven saying they expected him to return to work as planned in the autumn, and in the meantime, pleased find enclosed your renewed travel permit authorising journeys from Hamburg to Bremerhaven.

None of the documents would have withstood serious scrutiny, but as Manfred had been told, that wasn't really the point. The point was for these documents to be good enough to get him through basic checks.

There was also a faded black leather wallet with a few photographs inside, one of a pretty girl with a message on the back (*with much love, Eva xxx*), crumpled cinema and bus tickets, and ten ten-Reichsmark notes, far more money than he was used to having in his wallet.

Cooper had taken out a small bottle of quinine tablets, prescribed for the treatment of typhoid fever, and a smaller bottle of tablets labelled 'aspirin'. He'd received them from a doctor who'd come to the safe house the previous week and explained that these tablets mimicked some of the symptoms of typhoid fever, such as a pallid complexion and a raised temperature.

And finally, four packets of Sturm Neue Front cigarettes. Manfred had no idea where they'd got them from; they weren't exactly a popular brand in British tobacconists'. He recognised his own lighter, which had come with him when he'd escaped from Germany.

'Everything's in order.'

'And the pistol?' Manfred asked Pamela.

'There's a false bottom to the rucksack. Look...'

It was designed to take the shape of the Enfield revolver, with plenty of clever padding to conceal its presence.

'This is Curtis. He'll be driving you to Dover.' She nodded towards a thickset man in his forties wearing a Royal Navy uniform. 'He knows his way around. He'll take you straight to the ship.'

'There's not likely to be any traffic on the way, and I'm allowing two and a half hours for the journey,' said Curtis. 'Captain wants to sail at six. He doesn't like to be kept waiting. We'd better get a move on.'

'Hang on... What time do you make it?'

Manfred glanced at his watch. 'Five past one.'

Pamela shook her head. 'This is a good example of what we told you about avoiding silly mistakes. Your watch is on English time. You need to put it forward an hour to Middle European Time. A basic error like that is easily made, but could cost your life.'

They moved slowly towards the hall, their footsteps echoing on the parquet flooring, and they paused by the porch. Pamela held out her hand for Manfred and as he took it, she leant forward, awkwardly angling her head towards his.

He moved forward and kissed her right cheek, and then she turned to offer her left cheek, in the Continental manner. She now clasped his hand with both of hers.

'*Viel gluck, Manfred. Sich vorsehen.*'

It sounded as if she'd rehearsed wishing him luck and telling him to take care, but he'd always wondered whether she spoke better German than she gave the impression of doing. She patted his hand and briefly placed one hand on his shoulder, the smell of the summer's evening enveloping him.

And with that, Cooper guided him by his elbow out of the door and they followed Curtis to the car. Manfred glanced at his wristwatch. It was ten past one on a still, dark and silent morning – ten past two in Germany – and he was terrified.

–

He wasn't quite sure why Cooper accompanied him on the drive down to Dover. In truth, as much as he liked Cooper, he'd rather have been alone with his thoughts in the back of the car. He felt somewhat nostalgic as he watched the darkened forms of urban and rural England, his home and refuge for the past three years, flash past as the Wolseley hurried down to the south coast.

Occasionally Cooper patted him on the thigh in an apparently reassuring manner and asked him if he was all right before sighing and saying he was a 'good chap'.

Once Manfred had bumped into Cooper and it became apparent that he worked for one of the British Intelligence agencies, Manfred had told him all about how he'd been recruited by the Abwehr but had done nothing about it. Manfred was closely questioned and then someone had the bright idea to hire him as a British agent.

Manfred was unsure how he felt about this. He had the sense of being swept along, with little opportunity to express his opinion. Although he was an avowed anti-Nazi and this was an opportunity to help undermine the Nazi regime, there was no disguising how dangerous this mission was.

He'd been turned into a double agent, and being sent back to Hamburg felt so – he struggled to express even to himself quite how he felt – 'compromised' was probably the best word.

Most of the journey was along the A2 but the road signs had been removed in case of a German invasion. Just after Curtis told him they were about half an hour from their destination they were stopped at a roadblock but were soon waved through. He heard Curtis tell them they were on 'Royal Navy business'.

Events moved quickly after that. They arrived in Dover and Curtis drove through a series of checkpoints and security gates, and then too fast along narrow dock roads and eventually along a wide quay with Royal Navy vessels docked either side, before braking sharply by a large crane. Alongside them were two enormous Royal Navy destroyers, HMS *Codrington* and HMS *Hereward*.

Curtis got out and came and held Manfred's door open. At the bottom of the gangplank for the *Codrington*, he pointed to Manfred.

'Just you. *You* wait in the car. Best to say goodbye now.'

Cooper stepped forward and awkwardly embraced Manfred.

'Until we bump into each other again, my friend! Take care...'

Manfred said, 'Indeed,' which he'd learnt was a very useful English response, conveniently covering – or masking – a range of emotions and circumstances, both positive and negative. He turned quickly and trudged up the gangplank, which felt like a sheer rock face.

Curtis escorted him into the captain's cabin.

The captain pushed a whisky towards him. It was a drink he normally despised but, in the circumstances, he thought it best to tackle it slowly.

'We set sail at six, just under two hours' time. If we can keep up seventeen knots per hour, then I hope we'll reach our destination in three days. I understand you've been told that our mission is to evacuate the Dutch royal family and bring them back to this country. Our understanding is that the Germans are about to invade the Netherlands, and the expectation is that they won't be able to hold out for more than a day or two... a week at the most. When we get there, you're to leave the ship, and I'm told you know what to do?'

'Yes, sir – I'm to meet a man at a particular location near where you'll dock, and he'll look after me from there.'

'Jolly good. It could well be a bumpy crossing, always is to the Hook of Holland, and the Luftwaffe may well take an interest in us en route, but I'm promised plenty of air cover. My instructions are that no one else on board is to know you're here, so my advice is to stay in here and get some rest. By the sounds of it, you're going to need it.'

–

Early on the morning of Friday, 10 May, the two Royal Navy destroyers docked at IJmuiden, the deep-water port on the North Holland coast and the place where the North Sea Canal to Amsterdam started. Manfred gazed through the porthole at the crowds milling on the quays; there were thousands of people, many with cases, whole families. The captain came down to check he was ready.

'You'll not have terribly long. You have everything?'

'Yes, sir.'

'My advice is not to speak unless you can avoid it, and if you do, do so in English. My understanding is that the German invasion of this country began this morning. You may find you're not too popular given the current circumstances.'

–

Manfred's instructions had been to head to a ship's chandler's called Van Heel, at the end of the main quay and close to the start of the North Sea Canal. At the counter at the rear of the store he was to ask for a dozen candles and a large box of matches. The man he wanted was called Jaap, according to Pamela.

'Jaap Smit. He's a very tall man and will be wearing brown overalls. Once you identify yourself to his satisfaction, then he'll take care of you.'

Jaap Smit had nodded at Manfred, who was clutching his box of candles and matches.

'And I understand you're looking to continue your journey?'

Manfred replied, as instructed, that it depended on the weather.

'Come this way.'

Smit led him to a room which opened onto a loading bay.

'There's a bathroom there and some food on the table. Help yourself, it will be a long journey. In normal circumstances it would take around three and a half hours, but these are anything but normal circumstances. The German invasion has started, and the roads are crammed with people moving in every direction.'

The van they were travelling in headed south from the port, through the northern and eastern outskirts of Amsterdam, and then east through the province of Overijssel, keeping south of Groningen, and towards the German border.

The roads were so crowded they kept having to slow down, and on at least two occasions they had to pull off the road when German war planes appeared overhead. Just after midday they pulled into the village of Bourtange in Westerwolde.

Outside a deserted bar Jaap pointed to the east. 'The German border's just over there. You could walk there in five minutes, but it's going to be safer with him.' He nodded towards an older man, ambling slowly towards them followed closely by an Alsatian, in the manner of a dog unwilling to leave its master's side.

He introduced the man as Pieter, and Pieter turned out to speak even better German than Jaap. Manfred watched as Pieter accepted an envelope from Smit.

Manfred took his boots from the rucksack and put them on, then followed Pieter and his dog along a path that circled the village and across a stretch of well-tended fields until they came to a pleasant avenue of gently swaying trees alongside a stream. Pieter pointed to the other side. '*Duitsland*,' he said. They were just metres from Germany. A bit further on they were able to ford the stream. Once on the other side, in Germany now, they carried on as before until they came to the brow of a hill with a village in the distance. Pieter pointed to a bus stop.

'A bus should arrive in an hour. It will take an hour and a half to get to Oldenburg, and you know what to do from there?'

Manfred nodded.

'I'll keep an eye on you from a distance. If you hear me whistle like this –' he let out a piercing whistle and the dog barked loudly – 'then don't get on the bus, and head back to the stream, where I'll find you. But you ought to be all right. The Germans are more bothered about people trying to get out. There's not exactly a queue of people trying to get in!'

For the first half-hour Manfred was the only person on the bus to Oldenburg, but as they headed east through Lower Saxony it gradually filled up and he became aware of hushed conversations; the war had given normally reserved people something to talk about. Frequently on the journey military convoys passed them, heading west towards the Netherlands. Not for the first time, Manfred wondered if he was mad for having agreed to return to Germany, which he'd been so lucky to escape from three years previously and where he was still most probably a wanted man. He hung on desperately to the hope that after all this time away, and with Germany now at war, maybe the authorities had forgotten about him; that they had more important matters on their mind than a fugitive from the past.

The bus pulled up in a square outside Oldenburg's rather beautiful Art Nouveau station. The whole area was teeming with troops forming up into units or queuing up to climb into lorries.

It was an hour to Bremen, where Manfred changed and then bought a return ticket to Bremerhaven, for which he had a travel permit. If questioned, he'd say he'd been to visit his employer there. The British had told him it was always better to be in possession of a return ticket. It was another two hours to Hamburg: plenty of time to reflect on the last occasion he'd taken the train into this city, and when he'd met the friendly Englishman – an encounter that was the reason he was back here now.

This time, it was much smoother. When he showed his pass at the barrier, he made sure Ernst Werner's Nazi party *Mitgliedskarte* was visible, too, and he was waved through, not forgetting to give the 'Heil Hitler!' greeting.

Manfred headed out of the station onto Steintorplatz and then east towards the centre of the city, across Adolf-Hitler-Platz and past the Rathaus. Close to the canal, backing on to Alter Wall, he found a cheap guest house. He was relieved when the receptionist assured him all his papers were in order, and was then somewhat thrown when she asked how come he was staying in the centre of the city when he was registered as living in Eilbeck.

'I have some important meetings in the centre over the next few days and prefer not to have to rely on the trams – you know how it is these days.'

She nodded as if she quite understood.

–

There'd been a lot of discussion in London about just what the nature of Manfred's mission in Hamburg was, and how he was to contact Helmut Schröder.

Eventually an older man had come to visit him in the safe house. It seemed he was the man in charge of Pamela and Cooper, and he was very proper and spoke in that clear and sparse manner that Manfred associated with military people.

'We do know that Helmut Schröder is a senior officer with the Abwehr in Hamburg. You've helped corroborate intelligence we already had that he is running the operation to infiltrate Nazi agents into this country. You would appear to have been a very early recruit, and thankfully you were inactive. You are going to need to give him a satisfactory explanation as to why this was the case. You are also going to have to explain how you got back to Germany and why you're there. It's not going to be straightforward, but we'll work out a story together.

'How you approach Schröder is another matter. You can hardly turn up at General-Knochenhauer-Strasse and ask to see him, can you? We'll work that out, too. And then there's the purpose of your visit. I want to know as much detail as you can lay your hands on about his operation: names of agents, where they're being sent, who their contacts are here… It is important to remember that no detail is too minor.

'Hopefully, Manfred, if you keep your nerve, he'll believe you and they'll find a way of getting you back to Britain. I hope that's all reasonably clear?'

–

Manfred spent his first day back in Hamburg doing as he'd been advised in London: walking round the city, getting the feel of it and acclimatising himself. He headed down to the port and through the network of canals around the docks and the Speicherstadt, which comprised the largest warehouse complex in the world. The truth was that the port area was more than a city within a city; it was another world.

He got used to the constant refrain of *moin* – the generic Hamburg greeting, as in *moin, moin*, to which the reply was invariably *moin, moin*. He had forgotten what a friendly city this could be, so different from Berlin. From the port he headed up to St Pauli, and by the landing bridges he joined a long queue to buy a *Matjes*, the salted herring in a crispy roll with a few slices of onion. Then he headed up to the Reeperbahn – not quite as seedy as it had been before the war, but still with a decided edge to it – and he kept walking because he didn't want to return to the guest house too early.

When he'd been in Hamburg in 1937, Helmut Schröder had lived in a very handsome apartment on Fehlandstrasse in the theatre district, between the Staatsoper and the Binnenalster, the smaller of Hamburg's two artificial lakes. Manfred left the guest house at seven the following morning and headed in that direction.

He knew Schröder was a man of habit and that he usually left his apartment around 7:30, walking down Theaterstrasse and then catching a tram on Jungfernstieg to take him up to General-Knochenhauer-Strasse.

Manfred lay in wait for him at the end of Theaterstrasse, watching the street with his back to the Binnenalster, and sure enough, at around 7:35 the unmistakable figure of the man he'd known all his life as *Lieber Onkel* – 'dear uncle' – appeared, walking briskly, pausing briefly to greet someone and doff his Homburg hat at them. Then he turned into Neuer Jungfernstieg, and at that moment Manfred slipped in behind him. It was only when they were outside the Vier Jahreszeiten, the city's smartest hotel, that he came alongside Helmut Schröder and wished him a very good morning, and added, '*Lieber Onkel*,' just for good measure.

Manfred was amazed at how admirably Schröder kept his composure. He didn't pause or alter his step or reply straight away; instead he nodded, and then after a moment or two said they'd go round the block to a cafe he knew by the Staatsoper. Manfred thought it was odd, because would you really take someone like him to a place where you were known?

But he didn't argue, and five minutes later they were alone in the tiny upstairs room of the cafe, the view from the small window dominated by the opera house.

'You'd better tell me exactly what the hell this is all about.'

'I'm not sure where you want me to start?'

'How about what happened when you left Hamburg in April, I think it was, three years ago, and we hear nothing from you since? That would be a good start. And then if you're still in a mood to be helpful, you could perhaps explain why you've turned up in Hamburg now – and how you got here would be a welcome additional detail.'

'It was very difficult, *Lieber Onkel*, because as soon as I arrived in England I was interviewed by the police in Southampton. As I was a German national, I was told I was only allowed to go to certain places and that didn't include London, so I had no way of contacting the person you'd given me the details of. They said I had to go to Newcastle, which is a city in the north of England where I could hardly understand what they were saying at first, but that's where I stayed and—'

'I thought restrictions on German nationals began after the war started?'

'Don't you believe me? All I wanted to do was get to London, but there were all kinds of restrictions. I had to report to the local police station every week. Eventually they said I could travel to London to look for work there – this was a few weeks ago, in February. The first thing I did was go straight to the shop in Stepney, the one where I was to give my coded message. But when I got there, it was boarded up.

'I had no idea what to do. The shop was my only way of contacting you. I felt... stranded. But I also felt an obligation to you, *Lieber Onkel*, because if you hadn't helped me when I was arrested here by the Gestapo, then... I don't like to think what would have happened to me. I know this sounds a bit crazy, but I decided to see if there was a way I could return here.'

Schröder looked as if he was carefully weighing up in his mind what Manfred had just told him. Pamela had told Manfred to keep it simple, and he wasn't sure whether the detail of the policeman was a complication, but Schröder nodded.

'I find the idea that you've come here to find out what is going on scarcely credible, Manfred. If I didn't know you, I'd find it impossible to believe. Tell me, how on earth did you get here?'

'It wasn't difficult, *Lieber Onkel* – there are ships crossing from England all the time to pick up refugees and troops and one thing and another. I got on a steamer at Dover that was sailing to Rotterdam and travelled across the Netherlands by train. I saw plenty of our troops on the journey. It's amazing, *Lieber Onkel*, we now control half of Europe – the Netherlands, Belgium, Poland, Czechoslovakia, Denmark and Norway. It will be France next, and then Great Britain!'

Schröder said, 'Yes, indeed,' and half smiled, and said it had been a remarkable few months. 'Who would have believed that events would have moved so fast, but the battle for France will not be so easy, and as for invading Great Britain… Well, it is opportune, to say the least, that you are here now.'

Chapter 19

Arthur Klein had been asked to present himself at two o'clock on the afternoon of Monday, 10 June, and as it didn't do to be late, he'd turned up at 1:45. The admiral's secretary had said Klein should wait in her outer office, and then it transpired the admiral himself was running late, and now it was approaching 2:30 and Klein was distinctly uncomfortable.

For a start, the office was far too hot, and he was nervous enough as it was, and every time the admiral's secretary glanced up at him, she caught him staring at her, which was hard to avoid. He'd seen her before around the building, and she was quite the most beautiful woman in the Kriegsmarine headquarters, her long dark hair falling naturally across her slim shoulders, and with piercing green eyes that made her look as if she were about to ask him a question.

It was all most disconcerting, and even more so when she paused from her typewriter to carefully apply some dark red lipstick and spray a little cologne around her neck. When their eyes met, she smiled.

'The admiral shouldn't be too long, Kapitänleutnant.'

Her accent sounded familiar; that could be an opening.

'Are you from Aachen by any chance, Fräulein?'

She smiled again and shook her head. 'I'm from Koblenz – not too far away! You may call me Frieda, rather than Fräulein.'

He laughed and said in that case he was 'Arthur', and she said she knew, and he was pondering how to phrase an invitation – maybe a coffee one lunchtime... or perhaps a drink after work, if that didn't sound too... well, presumptuous – but at that moment the door to the inner office swung open and Rear Admiral Kurt Fricke beckoned him in.

Fricke was not alone. Joining him at a long, polished table was Vice Admiral Otto Schniewind, Grand Admiral Raeder's chief of staff and the key man in the navy's planning of the invasion of Britain. He sat as if to attention, his Iron Cross prominent.

'Sit down, Klein. Please put down all those papers you're carrying – are you writing a book, eh? Please don't look so flustered!'

'He's bound to look flustered, Otto. He's been sitting with Frieda while we've been chatting away!'

'Who can blame him for being so flustered, then? She's not spoken for, I believe, Klein. A good-looking young man like you...'

'Don't put ideas into his head, Otto. Once we've finished with him today, Klein's going to be too busy for that kind of distraction.'

The two admirals laughed, and Schniewind opened a packet of cigarettes and passed them round.

'Enough of that. To business! I need to tell you, Kapitänleutnant Klein, that in the past fortnight, Grand Admiral Erich Raeder has been summoned to meet the Führer on no fewer than three occasions to discuss the plans to invade Great Britain.'

There was a pause as both the admirals opposite Klein drew on their cigarettes at the same time and exhaled simultaneously.

Schniewind hesitated and gestured with the hand holding his cigarette to help him find the right words. Trails of smoke drifted over the table. 'Now that we have occupied the Netherlands, Belgium and France, along with the countries in the east and Norway and Denmark in the north, the Führer is determined we should plan an invasion of Great Britain. After they somehow managed to evacuate so many of their troops from Dunkirk, they represent a threat to us and our ambitions – that is how the Führer sees it, Klein.'

'The Führer,' said Fricke, 'is on the verge of making an invasion of Great Britain the subject of one of his orders, and we are not in a position to argue.'

Schniewind opened a folder in front of him.

'You're thirty-two, Klein, still a young man. And a smart one, too: you have a degree in engineering. Very few of our officers have degrees. There was a time when you had to be at sea by the age of fifteen to be considered a sailor, and someone with a degree would be distrusted, but times have changed, maybe for the better. Who knows?'

'It goes without saying, Klein, that what we are about to tell you is in utmost confidence. I cannot stress how sensitive this information is.'

'I understand, sir.'

'Because of this,' said Schniewind, 'as of today, you are being promoted from Kapitänleutnant to Korvettenkapitän.'

Klein wasn't sure how to react. It was almost unheard of for a staff officer – as opposed to someone in command of a vessel – to reach that rank at such a young age.

'I am very honoured, sir, thank you.'

'If that doesn't impress Frieda, then I'm not sure what will! Kurt…?'

Fricke reached behind him, picked a long roll of canvas and stood up to unfurl it with Schniewind's help and attach it to the wall behind him. It was a large map showing the northern coast of Europe, from Brest in the north-west corner of France to Hamburg in the east, and the southern and eastern parts of England. The Channel and the North Sea – *Nordsee* – were shown in dark blue, in contrast to the different shades of green chosen for the countries.

'We are, of course, not the only people working on plans for an invasion of the British Isles. The Luftwaffe is about to launch a major assault on Great Britain with the aim of eliminating the aerial threat from the RAF to any invasion. Does the name Franz Halder mean anything to you?'

'Army, sir?'

'General Halder is the Army High Command's Chief of Staff. He has responsibility for the army's invasion plans. His plan is to invade along a front from here –' Fricke reached up and indicated a point in the south-east of England – 'which is a town called Ramsgate in the county of Kent, to here – another town called Weymouth in an area called Dorset. That's a front of some two hundred miles. His plan envisages an initial wave of some thirty divisions – infantry and armoured – totalling around half a million men. Of course, that's a very wide front, but from what we know, the British coastal defences, and especially the reserves they hold behind the first line of defence, are not very strong. According to their intelligence, the Army High Command believe that even after Dunkirk, the British Army is still weak within its own borders. Although they have somewhere in the region of thirty-five divisions, only a dozen infantry divisions and perhaps one armoured division are what we could call fully operational. Halder is of the view that a two-hundred-mile front would stretch them, and be a significant advantage to us.'

'But surely a—'

'Hang on, Klein. Please let me finish. I imagine you were going to point out what should have been obvious to any Kriegsmarine officer, namely that facilitating and defending such a long front would make our navy extremely vulnerable to the Royal Navy, which as we know is numerically stronger than us. We have proposed a more concentrated front, from here – a town called Deal, which is close to the easternmost point of Halder's planned front – to here… Dungeness. That's a front of just thirty-five miles, and would, of course, be far more concentrated. Far easier for us to ensure a secure passage, but Halder believes it is too narrow, and no doubt if the British get their reserves there in good time, then it will be very difficult, but the truth is that any invasion is going to be difficult.

'The Führer now has all this information. He knows what we think and what the Army High Command's plans are. He will make the decision. What I will say is that I think we're still some time away from an invasion.'

'Do we have any idea when it will be?'

'I would say that we will need a minimum of two months to organise everything – not just us but the army, too. And the Luftwaffe will need time to weaken the British air force. My estimate would be some time in September. If we were to leave it any later than that, then the weather conditions and the tide will make an invasion out of the question, at least until next year.'

As the three men studied the map, the silence was broken only by the rhythmic sound of Frieda's typing on the other side of the wall.

'The Kriegsmarine's responsibility is to organise the transport of troops and equipment and to protect them while en route. Your task, Klein, is related to the invasion proper. At the end of last year, you did excellent preparatory work on the landing craft we'd need, and especially the barges. Grand Admiral Raeder was most impressed. We are now putting you in charge of procuring all the barges we'll need, and overseeing their conversion and the arrangements for where they'll be docked in preparation for the invasion.'

Vice Admiral Schniewind stood up and turned to the map. 'The main assembly and embarkation ports will be from here… Emden in the east, Rotterdam, Antwerp, Ostend, Dunkirk, Calais, Boulogne, Le Havre and Cherbourg – here in the west. You speak Dutch, I understand, Klein?'

'I do, sir. Not fluently, but—'

'You'll be based in Rotterdam. Because of its facilities, its size and location, it makes sense for that port to be the centre of the Kriegsmarine barge operations. We've already established a significant presence in the city. We have our headquarters on Heemraadssingel, and we've taken over the Veerhaven to establish our naval base.'

'And when would you like me to start in Rotterdam, sir?'

'Tomorrow, if that's not leaving it too late, Korvettenkapitän Klein.'

–

Klein realised he couldn't possibly leave Berlin without telling Ernst Schwarz, so he'd told Fricke that he had an urgent dental appointment the following day. As it made little sense to travel on a Friday, how about if he went to Rotterdam on the Sunday so he could start work on the Monday morning?

Fricke reluctantly agreed and called in Frieda. He informed her that Kapitänleutnant Klein was now Korvettenkapitän Klein and would be moving to Rotterdam, and please could she assist with the necessary arrangements?

'Congratulations, Korvettenkapitän. I am very impressed,' she'd said when they were alone in her office.

'Impressed enough to join me for a celebratory meal this evening?'

Frieda looked up, surprised, but she smiled and said she'd need to change some arrangements.

'Do you already have a date?' Klein immediately regretted saying that, but she laughed.

'So, this is a date, is it?'

'I hope you don't think I was being too presumptuous.'

'Not at all. In fact, I'll only agree to dinner if it is indeed a date. How about that – not too presumptuous, I hope?'

Klein said that sounded fine – quickly realising that 'fine' didn't sound fine – and Frieda said in that case it was a date, and she'd meet him at seven o'clock at Café Kanzler on Kurfürstendamm, and with some luck they'd get a table outside.

Klein left work at five o'clock, hoping to get to the grocery shop on the corner of Lutzowstrasse and Woyrschstrasse before it closed. The unsmiling woman behind the counter was alone in the shop.

'I need a jar of honey very urgently.' She'd understand that he needed to meet Schwarz the following day.

'Tomorrow lunchtime.' He said it as urgently as possible. He was breaking protocol, but he had to be sure she understood the urgency of what he was saying. 'Make sure you tell him that.'

Her raised eyebrows remained there for a while, and she replied, 'Very well,' in her coarse Berlin accent.

–

'I bought you a jar of honey, Frieda.'

'That's very... sweet of you, Arthur, what an... original gift. Kriegsmarine officers usually bring flowers on a date.'

'You must have received a lot of flowers in your time, Frieda.'

'And what are you suggesting, Arthur?' She threw her head back and laughed and then straightened her hair, her long fingers playing with it as she spoke. 'I think we ought to order.'

They chatted easily until the food arrived: how she lived on Budapester Strasse in a flat overlooking Zoologischer Garten, which she shared with two girls, one of whom worked at the Air Ministry on Wilhelmstrasse and the other in the army headquarters in the Bendlerblock. 'So, we cover the armed forces between us!'

'But no one who works at Prinz-Albrecht-Strasse?'

Frieda went quiet and looked around in case anyone had overheard them. Arthur immediately regretted what had clearly been an indiscretion. He'd been foolhardy, and the fact that he was nervous was no excuse. He'd made the mistake of assuming this pretty and friendly girl was unlikely to be a Nazi. Frieda sipped at her glass of white wine and leant forward, speaking softly.

'I don't think someone who worked for the SS or the Gestapo would fit in with us. Let's leave it at that. Are you looking forward to moving to Rotterdam, Arthur?'

Klein replied that he was and that he liked the Netherlands, though he wasn't sure how much time he'd have to enjoy the country.

'Maybe I should come and visit you?'

'That would be very nice, Frieda.'

–

The next venue for Klein and Schwarz to meet was in a furniture work-shop on Triftstrasse in Wedding, close to the junction with Antwer-pener Strasse.

Klein had left the Shell-Haus late in the morning, explaining he had his dental appointment and had to attend to other matters before his departure for Rotterdam. He took three trams to ensure he wasn't being followed.

He found Ernst Schwarz at the rear of the workshop, indicating he should follow him. In an upstairs room Schwarz drew the curtains and told Klein to sit down.

'Why is this so urgent?'

'I'm being sent to Rotterdam.'

'When?'

'At the weekend.'

'When did you find this out?'

'Yesterday. And I've been promoted, by the way – to Korvetten-kapitän, would you believe?'

'Congratulations. How long will you be in Rotterdam?'

'However long it takes.'

'However long what takes? Come on, stop playing games with me!'

'However long it takes to invade Great Britain.'

Schwarz's eyes narrowed. 'I think you'd better tell me everything, comrade.'

Which Arthur Klein did: everything he could recall about the plans for the invasion, and the meetings with Hitler, and his role with the barges. Schwarz had sat with his eyes closed as Klein talked, taking it all in, occasionally asking a question.

'I know Rotterdam quite well from my time in The Hague. We had a very active branch of the CPN there. From what I understand, most of them went underground when the Nazis invaded. They're still very strong around the docks.'

'I wasn't planning on joining the Communist Party in Rotterdam, thank you.'

'No, but we're going to need to find a way of keeping our lines of communication with you open. Did you say you have somewhere to live?'

'Apparently the Kriegsmarine has officers' quarters on Heemraadssingel, close to the headquarters.'

'I know the area well, it's very pleasant – overlooks a very pretty canal. Look, I need to get a message to Moscow and then find out who we trust in Rotterdam. I imagine that will take at least a week or two, but in the meantime, you should get your bearings. But one day you'll be approached by someone asking you if you know someone called Shark, and you're to ask if he's from Dordrecht and the man will say... Hang on, let me think, this is important... If the man says no, he's from Breda, then you know he's our emissary, your contact, and you're to trust him.'

Chapter 20

England
July 1940

'We've put him in a room on his own at the end of the ward, and frankly, it's quite beyond me why anyone gave you the impression that this poor man is in any state to be interrogated. And which organisation did you say you were from?'

Archie had a dislike of doctors – not because he was afraid of needles or being prodded about, or anything as petty as that – but he didn't like their attitude, which tended to invite or expect deference, and even obedience: the sense that they always knew better.

'First of all, Doctor Marston, I never said which organisation I'm from. I said it is a matter of national security and that should suffice, surely? And secondly, it is absolutely essential I see him. Not, I stress, to interrogate him, but simply to ask him a few questions. Again, for reasons of national security.'

'Very well, then, for no more than ten minutes. We'll give him something to take the edge off his pain and I'll ask one of my nurses to be in there with you in case he has a relapse. And, by the way, it's Marsden.'

'I beg your pardon?'

'I'm Richard Marsden. You called me Marston.'

Archie had deliberately got the man's name wrong because he found it was a useful way of regaining control of a conversation.

'I'm afraid that is quite out of the question, doctor.'

'What is?'

'Having anyone else in the room. National security.'

The doctor nodded and his shoulders sagged as he realised he was having to give way to this rude and insistent man, whom the hospital manager had told him that according to the local chief of police was very important.

National security.

'And may I ask, how long does Mr Brouwer have left?'

'That is a question one is always reluctant to answer because it is very difficult to be precise, and depends on how he responds to the medication and other treatment we give him. The gentleman arrived in this country at the end of May, I believe it was. His cancer must have been very advanced even then, but he says that while he'd experienced severe stomach pains and discomfort for quite a while before leaving Holland, he only saw a doctor when he reached this country and by then it was too late. It's, what…? Tuesday today. I'd be most surprised if Mr Brouwer lived much beyond the weekend.'

'In that case,' said Archie, standing up, 'I'd better get a move on, hadn't I?'

The doctor looked quite appalled.

—

The previous Monday, Archie had returned to his Hampstead home to find a chalk circle on the inside of the gatepost and four pebbles behind the stone lion, which meant that the following evening he left work as early as was feasible. He made his way to a once elegant house close to Wandsworth Common and entered it through a side gate and under a canopy of overgrown shrubbery to find the back door unlocked and the bitter aroma of Russian tobacco inside.

Despite it being a warm – even humid – evening, Ivan Alexandrovich Morozov was sitting at the kitchen table wrapped in a raincoat, his wide-brimmed hat and a neatly folded scarf on the table in front of him next to a large ashtray. He gestured for his visitor to sit down opposite him.

'We never hear from you, Archie.'

'I don't know what you mean. It's not as if you don't know how to contact me. And in any case, we met in Earls Court not that long ago, on the ninth of May, I think it was.'

'We did indeed, and today is the twentieth of June: exactly six weeks ago.'

'When your ambassador told me you have an excellent source in Germany – I think his actual words were "he's as good as you get". He then said something about finding a way of establishing this source for me, whatever that meant, and then my finding a way of getting to meet him. I have to say, though, that the notion of my going to Germany is ridiculous.'

'And you were going to look into offering yourself for work in the field?'

'I was waiting to hear back from you.'

Morozov sighed and gave the impression of being annoyed and exasperated. Archie recognised there was clearly a tension between the two of them, which he found hard to believe was helpful. It was odd being on the same side as someone you didn't get on with.

'Well, you're hearing back from us now. Comrade Maisky never intended you to go to Germany. That is obviously out of the question. The source we described as being "as good as it gets" is now based in Rotterdam. He's an officer in the German navy – the Kriegsmarine – but he's also a loyal comrade and a long-established agent of ours. He moved to Rotterdam to co-ordinate the Kriegsmarine's operation to get hold of as many barges as possible and convert them to carry troops and equipment to Great Britain. He will be a valuable source of information.

'If you can establish a pretext for getting into Rotterdam and meeting him in person, then the report you'll compile will be very powerful indeed: a detailed account from an excellent source of how the German threat to this country is a very real one. It will force your government to take it seriously, and remember... If they take it seriously, then that will help reinforce their opposition to Nazi Germany and keep the attention of the Germans away from the Soviet Union. Moscow considers it imperative that you undertake this mission.'

'But surely, wouldn't it be in the Soviet Union's interests for Germany to attempt an invasion of this country? If that happened, then it would tie up the Germans in the west for months, perhaps years. I'm not sure what benefit it is to you for the British government to be aware of the invasion threat.'

'Our biggest worry, Archie, is that even with Mr Churchill now your prime minister, the possibility of a peace deal between Britain and Germany remains. There is no doubt that is the intention of Hitler.

They remain hopeful that there are enough people in this country – in prominent positions – who wish to stop the war. If they see that Germany is planning to invade Great Britain, then hopefully they'll be less well disposed to seeking peace with them.'

'You're talking about the appeasers, and I can assure you that Mr Churchill is most certainly not one of those.'

'But he may have trouble resisting them. Were he to receive intelligence which shows how advanced are the German plans, then that will strengthen his resolve and his position – and relieve the pressure on the Soviet Union. You need to find a way to get to Rotterdam, Archie. Then you will meet with our agent. When you return, you'll be a hero!'

Archie drummed his fingers on the oilskin tablecloth; he realised he'd been given an order from Moscow. And he could see the point Morozov was making. A mission into enemy territory would be an enormous risk, but would elevate him in the Service, from someone who wrote considered and well-received reports to a proper secret agent.

'If I return.'

–

Archie had been told that Joop Brouwer was fifty-two, but the man in the hospital bed looked considerably older, propped up on a small mountain of pillows, the skin on his face tight and with a yellow hue, and bloodshot eyes which swivelled around the room.

Archie was relieved to have found someone who met his requirements so perfectly. After the last meeting with Morozov, it had seemed that what the Soviet agent was after was so specific as to be almost impossible. Archie needed to find someone who'd arrived relatively recently from the Netherlands, with some link to Rotterdam, and whom he could use as an apparent source of intelligence with this person being in no position to subsequently contradict him. And he needed to find them quickly.

At first, he'd toyed with the idea of completely fabricating a source, which was not a totally ridiculous notion, but it did rather rely on his superiors not bothering to check, and that was asking a lot. Then Archie thought he could find someone who fitted the bill, and whom he could question in such a way that he could insert the relevant intelligence into his report. Indeed, it was while exploring this option that he obtained a list of recent arrivals from the Netherlands supplied to him by Special Branch. One name had jumped out.

> BROUWER, JOOP:
> age 52.
> From BREDA.
> Occupation: lawyer
>
> BROUWER a prominent member of the Social Democratic Workers' Party. He was informed soon after the Nazi occupation of THE NETHERLANDS that he was on a GESTAPO Wanted List and sought to escape from THE NETHERLANDS. He was part of a small group which departed the HOOK OF HOLLAND by boat on 25th May, arriving HARWICH on 28th May. Brouwer was vouched for by the Dutch government-in-exile and cleared by SPECIAL BRANCH on 30th May. He was given temporary accommodation in London, but collapsed on 10th June with serious internal bleeding and was taken to hospital, where he was diagnosed with terminal stomach cancer.

Archie had found it difficult to believe his luck. It had taken a fortnight to track down which hospital Joop Brouwer was in and then arrange a visit, and now he was pulling up a chair next to the poor man's bed and very gently shaking him by the shoulder, because he wanted to be sure he had his attention. The man had an unpleasant smell, and Archie held a handkerchief close to his nose.

'Mr Brouwer, it's very good of you to see me. I realise this is a very difficult time for you.'

Archie knew that sounded too crass, so he patted Brouwer reassuringly on the shoulder and asked if there was anything he wanted – some water, perhaps? – and then wondered if it was the done thing to smoke and if so, should he offer a cigarette to the Dutchman?

The Dying Dutchman. Rather good, that. He should use it in his report. Or perhaps not.

Joop Brouwer turned his head very slowly towards Archie but didn't reply, instead raising his eyebrows.

'I mean, if there's anything you need me to get you, or anything else which could help?'

The Dutchman shook his head.

'Are you being well cared for here? I can help on that front if you're having any problems.'

'I am being very well cared for, thank you very much.'

Archie recoiled, as the Dutchman's breath was foul. He was craving a cigarette.

'Did they explain to you why I was coming to see you?'

'Something about security. Have I done something wrong? As you can see, I'm already being punished.' He smiled, displaying a crooked set of yellow teeth in his shrunken mouth.

'I appreciate you seeing me because I do understand how... unwell you are. I work for British Intelligence, Mr Brouwer, and I'd like to ask you some questions about the Netherlands.'

Joop Brouwer nodded.

'I understand you left around the twenty-fifth of May?'

'Correct.'

'About a fortnight after the German occupation?'

'Also correct. It would seem you know the answers to your questions already.'

'Why did you leave, Mr Brouwer?'

'The Gestapo were beginning to round up socialists, communists, Jews, liberals... anyone they decided was the enemy. I was told I was on their list. I left Breda and hid at a friend's house nearby in Rotterdam.'

'And in Rotterdam... did you have an opportunity to visit the docks?'

Joop Brouwer shook his head and winced in pain. He was trying to reposition himself, but was struggling. Archie awkwardly helped to rearrange his pillows.

'No. I remained in the attic of my friend's house, which is in Diergaarde, some way from the docks. It was too dangerous to go out. There are German patrols and checkpoints all over the city, and especially around the port.'

'Why is that?'

'I'd have thought it's obvious! The port was quickly taken over by the Germans. Their navy occupied Veerhaven and the whole docks area became subject to martial law. It would have been suicide to go anywhere near there.'

Archie nodded. Brouwer clearly had little in the way of specific information, but that really didn't matter. Archie would make up what he needed and attribute it to him. The most important thing was that he was speaking with the man.

'And tell me about your escape?'

Joop Brouwer winced once more as he struggled to get into a comfortable position.

'My friend contacted people he knew who'd already arranged for people to leave the Netherlands by boat. I was taken to the Hook of Holland and from there four of us boarded a fishing boat – we were concealed in the hold. We were told that the Germans don't bother too much with single ships. They're not worth running the risk of attracting the attention of your navy. And here I am. I'm really of very little help, I'm afraid.'

'Please don't worry, Mr Brouwer, you've been of more help than you can imagine. I do appreciate your time.'

'It's not like I was doing anything else.'

Archie patted him gingerly on the shoulder once more, and then stood up and wondered what on earth he should say. The doctor had told him he doubted Brouwer would last beyond the weekend, and he could see what he meant. The Dutchman looked dreadful.

But he'd served his purpose.

–

'I'm sorry, sir, but this is simply not on.'

Lieutenant Commander McConnell had never seen Pamela Clarke quite so angry. A few minutes earlier she'd demanded – that was the only word for it – to see him, and now she was standing in his office in the basement of the Old War Office Building with Cooper standing next to her, looking slightly sheepish, as was his way, clutching some papers.

'Perhaps you'd better tell me what is not on, Pamela.'

'This, sir.' She snatched the papers from Cooper's hand and dropped them onto McConnell's desk. '*We*, sir, are the Invasion Warning Sub-Committee, and while I'm fully aware that the Service believes they're the most important intelligence agency and that the world ought to revolve around them, that doesn't mean they have a right to trample all over what is meant to be *our* work.'

'Perhaps you could explain – and maybe sit down, both of you?'

'If perhaps I may explain, sir, because I was the one who obtained this report.' Pamela shot a disapproving glance at Cooper, who appeared oblivious to it.

'Yesterday I was speaking with a chap I know at MI5 about some of these Nazi sympathisers we're interested in and he asked what we at the Invasion Warning Sub-Committee made of this MI6 report about Rotterdam and I said "what report" and he passed it on to me. It was written on the second of July – Tuesday – and today's the fifth so *if* we were meant to be getting a copy which we certainly ought to be doing then it would appear to be lost in the post.'

'Let me read it, Cooper.'

SUBJECT: ROTTERDAM
FROM: D4, North Europe Desk 2
Date: 2nd July 1940

Acting on information received, I attended St Christopher's Hospital in London on 25th June to interview Dutch national JOOP BROUWER, who had been a patient at the hospital since being admitted as an emergency on 10th June. MR BROUWER was diagnosed with advanced stomach cancer, for which he was given a terminal diagnosis. MR BROUWER escaped from the Netherlands by boat from the Hook of Holland on 25th May, arriving in Harwich on 28th May. He was security cleared by Special Branch on 30th May, and was living in London prior to his hospital admission.

I had been informed that MR BROUWER had information he wished to pass on to British Intelligence. I was able to interview MR BROUWER over the period of an hour in his room at the hospital. The intelligence MR BROUWER provided can be summarised thus:

• He escaped from BREDA to ROTTERDAM after the Nazi invasion.

• In ROTTERDAM he was able to spend a considerable amount of time in the port area thanks to extensive contacts there.

• BROUWER reports that detailed preparations are underway to use ROTTERDAM as the main base from which to launch the German invasion of this country. BROUWER says these preparations are quite advanced.

• According to BROUWER, all the main docks in the central section of the port are being used for the conversion and storage of barges, which are currently in the process of being requisitioned.

Sadly, I have to report that JOOP BROUWER died on Sunday 30th June, so it is not possible to obtain further information from him. However, I believe this intelligence is credible and requires further investigation. I believe this is important and urgent enough to merit a covert mission to visit ROTTERDAM to assess the current situation there and corroborate BROUWER's intelligence. He supplied me in absolute confidence with the name of a contact in the ROTTERDAM docks who would be willing to assist us.

I am, of course, willing to undertake this mission myself.

D4

When McConnell finished reading, he said he could quite appreciate why they were so annoyed that his organisation had been kept in the dark, but well done indeed to Cooper for getting his hands on it.

'Thank you, sir. As you can see, the report is not only clearly our territory, but it actually uses the word "invasion". Did it not occur to anyone at Broadway that this may be of some interest to us? After all, we may well be able to assess the information contained in the report.'

'And what is this nonsense about "D4" – whoever that is – authoring the report. Since when did the Service resort to anonymity?'

'I have seen them do this increasingly, Pamela, and indeed I raised it with Menzies. As far as I can gather, they've become much more secretive recently because he's so concerned about this traitor they're convinced is in their organisation – at the very least, if not actually in it, then close enough to it. Hence the anonymising of their reports. However, I'm bound to say that in the case of this report, if the person behind it is suggesting that they themselves go on a mission to Holland, then I don't blame them for keeping their name off the record.'

'He says he was acting on "information received". Difficult to check that out.'

'Indeed.'

'I did check this patient, sir, and a Joop Brouwer, if that is how one pronounces it, did indeed die at St Christopher's Hospital in east London on Sunday. I spoke with a Dr Marsden, who confirms that last Tuesday – the twenty-fifth of June – a gentleman referred to him by the police did visit Mr Brouwer. He said it was a brief visit.'

'Says in this report it was for an hour.'

'Well, there we are then. Memories invariably differ,' said McConnell. 'Look, for what it's worth, I do agree that this would appear to be out of order, and at the very least it's queering our pitch. I'll have a word with Menzies. I'm sure he'll be decent about it.' He reached and placed his hand on the telephone. 'Give me a few minutes.'

–

Pamela and Cooper were called back in ten minutes later.

'Menzies absolutely dug his heels in, I'm afraid,' McConnell said, looking like someone who'd been on the wrong end of an argument. 'Gave me a lecture on the need for security and refused to tell me who this "D4" is, other than that he's one of their best chaps. He wouldn't accept that we have first rights over anything to do with any invasion. Sounded as if he'd like to get his hands on us, to be honest.'

'In what sense, sir?'

'In the sense of taking us over. He's an empire-builder.'

'And this D4 – offering to go to Rotterdam?'

'Visiting Cook's Tours to book his ticket and hotel as we speak. Menzies says it normally takes a minimum of a month to get one of their officers ready to operate behind enemy lines. They see this case as so urgent, and D4 as being so uniquely placed, that they've cut it down to two weeks.'

'So, when will that be, sir?'

'A week on Monday, and the most I could get out of Menzies was a vague promise that we'll get some kind of report once he's back. I'm holding out for us getting to meet him on his return, and he didn't say no.'

'That's if he makes it back, sir.'

'Indeed, Pamela, indeed.'

Chapter 21

The rendezvous with the Belgian fishing vessel had taken place as planned just after midnight. When the two boats gently came together like familiar lovers, Archie scrambled from the British boat which had brought him from Harwich onto the Belgian one. Once he'd picked himself up from the deck and looked round, the British boat had already slipped away and was now no more than a hint of a shadow disappearing into the pitch dark.

The skipper took Archie down to the hold and to a coffin-sized cupboard which was to be his hiding place until they reached Zeebrugge. He'd been told they'd have to speak in French, although – as with most Flemish speakers – the skipper would only do so with great reluctance. And so it had proved: it was a tense atmosphere, only slightly lifted when Archie handed over the carefully wrapped package.

…to help with your costs.

Archie had been briefed by Piers Devereaux, a senior MI6 officer who'd insisted that Archie would have to enter the Netherlands through Belgium. He wasn't prepared to risk any contact with anyone in the Netherlands, so it was to Belgium that his journey in Occupied Europe was to begin.

They docked at Zeebrugge on the early morning tide, and from what Archie could hear, the Germans seemed to only have a passing interest in the boat. No one was watching as he hurried from the deck into the rear of the lorry filled with crates of fish that was parked alongside.

He'd hidden behind the crates during the two-hour journey to Ghent, and when they stopped in an alley by Gent-Sint-Pieters railway station he climbed out and waited until the lorry disappeared before removing a jacket from his knapsack. He knew he'd still smell of fish, and the only consolation was that it may keep people away from him.

According to his papers he was Luc Dubois, a vet from Liège, and he'd not worked out why they thought it was a good idea for him to be a vet. He just hoped that no German checkpoints had a sickly Alsatian guard dog with them.

The journey across East Flanders to Antwerp took just over ninety minutes and saw Archie's first encounter with the Germans. It was a bored-looking Belgian ticket inspector with an improbably young German soldier behind him. The Belgian checked the ticket and nodded, and the German asked for papers, which Archie handed over.

'I'm travelling to Antwerp – *Anvers*,' he said in German.

The soldier smiled very briefly at the sound of his own language and reached out for the *Carte Nationale d'identité* in the name of Luc Dubois.

'You've travelled from… where?'

'Ghent.'

'So a vet from Liège is travelling from Ghent to Antwerp. Are you a tourist?'

Archie had an answer ready, about having been summoned to Ghent and then instructed to go to Antwerp and from there to somewhere else, and if it helped, he had a letter to this effect in his pocket, but the soldier laughed at his own little joke about being a tourist and handed back his identity card. He said it was pleasing that someone in Belgium had made the effort to speak German.

'If only more people could be so co-operative!'

It was only when they disappeared down the carriage that Archie realised how nervous he was. His hands were shaking as he put his papers back in his pocket, and he gratefully accepted the cigarette offered by an old man sitting opposite.

Once in Antwerp he took a coach to Hoogstraten. The journey was through various villages and then the larger town of Brecht, where all the passengers had to leave the bus to present themselves to a German checkpoint, where Archie was saved by a Flemish woman who had the wrong papers and was intent on arguing with the guards. By the time they'd finished with her they hurried the rest of the passengers through, barely looking at their papers.

When they arrived in Hoogstraten he headed for the church – Sint-Katharinakerk.

Head to the rear of the church, the right-hand side. Sooner or later, someone will ask you if they can help. Tell them you are waiting for Father Maes.

'And then what?'

'You wait for Father Maes.'

–

Father Maes looked far too young. He was nervous, which was obviously not a good sign, and spoke in a disconcertingly high-pitched voice. He told Archie in not very good French to follow him. Five minutes later they were in the priest's house, a dark building which didn't feel much like a home.

'We are maybe one mile from the Dutch border, but we will take a longer route to avoid the river and the canals. The Germans patrol those areas more. At the moment they're quiet around here. Straight after the occupation we couldn't move for German patrols. I hope you don't mind me saying, but you smell of fish. Perhaps you'd like to take a bath?'

They left just before midnight, long after the curfew had begun, but Father Maes had dispensation, and he also had a sick parishioner in a farm on the border. They parked their bikes by a hedgerow and then Archie followed the priest through a wood, struggling to keep up with him. After they'd been walking for ten minutes or so they stopped, and Father Maes told him they were now in the Netherlands.

'Keep walking in that direction and after an hour or so you'll come to the road. Turn left and keep walking until you come to a junction. You'll see a bus stop there. The buses start running around six, six-thirty – until then, keep out of sight. You want a bus heading north, to Breda. You have a French Belgian identity on you, yes? Give it to me and take this. It's Dutch papers and Dutch money. If you speak no Dutch, try not to say anything.'

–

It had felt like a recipe for disaster, but to Archie's amazement, he arrived in Breda safely. And now he was on his own. MI6 had got him thus far, and he knew that from this moment it was for him to contact the agent Joop Brouwer had apparently told him about on his deathbed.

But the person he was about to contact was Ivan Morozov's agent. Or he hoped he was. He'd never entirely trusted the Russian, and now he was about to find out whether his instincts were correct. Behind the bus station in Breda, he found a telephone box and called the number in Dordrecht Morozov had given him.

'He's one of us,' Morozov had assured him. 'Dedicated party member. Went underground when they clamped down on communists in the docks years ago. Established links with our service in April. We trust him and so should you. His codename is Shark, and his real name is Marcus van Leeuwen. This is his number in Dordrecht. He lives on his own and works shifts, so if he's not in just try a few hours later. He speaks German. And you remember what to say?'

'Yes,' said Archie, 'I'm to ask if his cousin Petrus is still in Dordrecht.'

'Carry on please, Archie.'

'If he says no, that he's left town, then that means danger and I'm to make my way back to Belgium immediately. If he says yes, then he will say Petrus will be at his home at such and such a time, and that's when I should go there.'

'And you have the address?'

'Yes, on Hallincqlaan – is that how you pronounce it? – by Park Merwestein.'

–

'Holland's a bloody mess.'

It was the afternoon of Tuesday, 2 July, and Archie was sitting in a small office in the Broadway headquarters of MI6, which belonged to Piers Devereaux. It was the first time he'd been in Devereaux's office, and it was perhaps a bit smaller and less tidy than he'd expected, but it was on the fifth floor – just one floor above the executive offices – which reflected Devereaux's importance.

Piers Devereaux looked after Germany and – as far as Archie could tell – had recently taken on the Netherlands, but it was all slightly vague, and this was intentional. The Secret Intelligence Service was not one of those organisations which produced neatly typed lists of its personnel alongside their job titles and extension numbers. Devereaux was slim and elegant and had a reputation in the building for being bright, if sometimes difficult.

Within an hour – if that – of Archie producing his report on Joop Brouwer, he'd taken a call from Devereaux on the internal telephone: 'Would you be so good as to pop up to see me?'

And when Archie had asked if later in the afternoon was convenient, Devereaux replied that now was more what he had in mind.

As he climbed the stairs to the fifth floor Archie was full of trepidation. Devereaux was most probably taking a very dim view of his having gone to see the Dutchman without any prior reference to him; the first he'd have been aware of it was when he read the report. Archie knew he'd taken a risk, and now he was wondering whether he was about to regret it. If Devereaux was as thorough as people said he was, it was not impossible this could lead to him being unmasked.

The discovery through Special Branch that there was a Dutchman dying in St Christopher's Hospital had been too good an opportunity for Archie to risk. Of course, he ought to have cleared the contact with the senior desk officer looking after the Netherlands, but then they could have insisted on being present or sending along a Dutch Intelligence officer, of whom there seemed to be quite a few in London these days.

And there were too many hostages to fortune in the report... 'information received' – what if Devereaux insisted on knowing from who? And the reference to Brouwer supplying me 'in absolute confidence with the name of a contact in the Rotterdam docks who would be willing to assist us'? That was Morozov's idea: in fact, the contact would be one of their agents, the man who would take him to their spy in Rotterdam, the source he'd described as being 'as good as it gets'. But would Devereaux demand to know the name of the contact in Rotterdam docks?

'Come in, come in... Do sit down.'

Devereaux certainly didn't look annoyed, or even angry, and his demeanour was friendly enough, even if he appeared to have been weeping. He held out a scrunched-up handkerchief by way of explanation and said, 'Bloody hay fever,' and then picked up the report and glanced at it.

'I have to say, jolly well done. Good work. Very good work, in fact.'

Archie hadn't anticipated such a friendly reaction. For a split second he even wondered if Devereaux was being sarcastic, but he didn't appear to be. There was a pleasant smile on his face as he proclaimed, 'Holland's a bloody mess,' and Archie just nodded, unsure if he was meant to respond.

'You heard about Venlo, no doubt? Town on the Dutch side of their border with Germany. Two of our agents were captured there by the SS last November. A complete and utter disaster. Compromised all our operations in Holland, and they remain compromised. We've not been able to run agents there ever since. A complete coup for the Germans. We've no idea who to trust in Holland, or who's on our side and who's been turned. As it's not even two months since the Germans occupied the country it's still very early days, so any kind of resistance network is still very nascent. Certainly not established enough for us to tap into yet and know who we can trust. The country leaks like a sieve. Must be something to do with their dams.'

'Joop Brouwer did give me a very good contact, sir, and I hope that—'

'So I read in your report. Do you know this contact's name?'

'I know how to contact the contact, sir. All I know is his codename is Shark, and he lives in Dordrecht.'

'No other name?'

'No, sir. Brouwer was obviously being cautious.'

'Given the situation in Holland, I think we have to keep all the information – dates, places and the rest – absolutely tight. On the basis of who needs to know, I think the correct approach as far as Holland is concerned is that no one needs to know. That's the safest way.'

'I do understand, sir.'

'Am I to take it from your report that you're volunteering to undertake the mission you propose yourself?'

'I am, sir… I feel that with this contact in Dordrecht, I'm the best placed to—'

'Absolutely. Correct answer – was hoping you'd say yes. I think the Service has reached the point where we need to ask how productive it is to have so many officers stuck behind desks writing reports, as interesting as I dare say they are. Question is how soon we can get you out there. You'll need a full briefing, which will take at least two or three days, and then there's a crash course for agents in the field at a place in Yorkshire which you'll have to do. Ideally should be longer, but time is a luxury we do not possess. If what this poor chap told you is true, it is vital we check it out. That means…' Devereaux leant back to look at a calendar pinned to a board behind him. 'We're looking at something around the fourteenth to sixteenth of July. Leave it to me.'

–

Late in the afternoon of Tuesday, 16 July, Archie was in Marcus van Leeuwen's apartment on Hallincqlaan, the lounge overlooking the park and outside the sounds and smell of the nearby river Maas around them. Archie knew he shouldn't think like this, but the apartment didn't feel like that of a dockworker. It was neat and tidy, and the shelves were full with what looked like serious books.

Marcus van Leeuwen had been very proper: cautious at first, and then more relaxed, and finally quite open as he spoke about the occupation and how life was beginning to feel very difficult.

'Even for people who don't share my – our – politics, it is difficult. The restrictions, like rationing, and the curfew and the atmosphere of distrust, people one knows disappearing and others being arrested. The Nazis are everywhere, and the shame of the fact that too many of my fellow countrymen are only too happy to work with them. Collaborators.'

'And you manage to remain above suspicion?'

'I hope so. I have so far. It is a long time since I was openly active in politics. I was in a file at police headquarters, but happily a comrade managed to make that disappear just before the Nazis got here. I'm very, very careful. I'm thirty-four and one of my big regrets was that I'd never married. I'd hoped that by now I'd have a family. But as things stand, I'm very relieved not to be in that position. It's one thing to worry about myself, but if I had to worry about a family, too… that would be too much. As it is, I can get on with my job and concentrate on my work for the Soviet Union. Are you going to tell me how you came to work for the Soviet Union?'

Archie said he'd rather not, and the Dutchman said he understood and apologised for asking the question.

'You'll stay here tonight. Tomorrow, we meet the German at the port. I'll give you the correct clothes to wear and I have a dock pass for you.'

'What's he like, the German?'

'Important.'

Chapter 22

Korvettenkapitän Arthur Klein had been in Rotterdam for just over a month. In that time, he'd not had a single day off: he began work at the Kriegsmarine headquarters on Heemraadssingel at seven every morning. A couple of hours later he'd head to the docks and board the *Beatrix III* to inspect the barges and tugs which had recently arrived, and review the progress on those which were being converted.

The walk to the port was his main exercise of the day, the wind blowing fresh from the North Sea some twenty miles upstream helping to clear his head. If time allowed, he'd stop first at a cafe on Coolhaven, the dock where the barges would be loaded. A man of habit, he'd have a herring roll followed by a coffee, which he'd drink while smoking a cigarette and gazing proprietorially over the dock. The atmosphere in the cafe was not as hostile as when he'd first begun to use it. Then it had been very apparent that, as a German officer, he wasn't welcome. But he'd made a point of speaking Dutch and being friendly, and always left a decent tip, and now he was tolerated, though he could still sense disapproving looks. He'd have liked nothing more than to tell them he wasn't who he seemed to be; that really he was on their side.

Around midday it would be back to the office to write up reports on the situation in Rotterdam: updating the number of barges and tugs, and reporting on which ones were ready and on those in various stages of conversion. There'd be calls to Kriegsmarine officers in various ports and towns in northern Europe and beyond: gentle – at first – reminders about how the requisitioning of barges was an absolute priority for the Reich.

No, next week is too long to wait.

Perhaps if I call you the day after tomorrow, you'll have some definite news for me?

Let me repeat… The minimum length we're looking for is thirty-five metres: the minimum load is three hundred tonnes.

Somewhere between four and five there'd be a radio conference with Berlin for him to update them on progress, after which his 'to-do' list would have expanded to something approaching the unmanageable. At six o'clock he'd join the admiral in charge of the port for his senior officers' meeting. Occasionally a new vessel would have docked in Veerhaven, and he might be invited on board for dinner.

But that was maybe just once a week. Other nights, he'd eat at one of the officers' messes in the city, or on his own in his tiny but very comfortable apartment, which was also on Heemraadssingel, opposite the Kriegsmarine office and just a few doors from number 226, the Gestapo field office in the city.

His lounge overlooked the canal, which ran along the centre of Heemraadssingel, with neat sloping lawns on either bank and weeping willows touching its surface.

He'd begun to recognise quite how different the Netherlands was from Germany: it was a less ordered society and far more open, to the extent that people made a point about being seen to conceal nothing. One of his colleagues who was married to a Dutch woman explained that this was due to the country's Calvinist tradition, which saw openness as a virtue, even as an expectation. For example, when eating together Dutch people made a point of keeping their hands above the table, which was odd, but which bothered him far less than the fact that net curtains and shutters were frowned upon.

Every other evening he'd write to Frieda, replying to her letters to him. The tone of the letters had moved from friendly to romantic; they gave him every reason to think positively about the future.

It added a further complication to being a spy. Treason – and he was under no illusion that what he was participating in was treason – thrived in the dark.

Sometimes at night he'd hear car doors slamming on the next block, perhaps followed by a shout, and he knew someone was being dragged into the Gestapo building a few doors down. The thought that he was effectively on their side would keep him awake for hours, until he reminded himself that he wasn't really on the Gestapo's side. In fact, he was doing his best to undermine it. Twice a week – sometimes more – he'd write up a detailed report on the current situation with the barges, not just in Rotterdam but in the other ports, too: Ostend, Antwerp, Dunkirk, Calais and Boulogne. Numbers, types of barges and tugs, small, neatly sketched diagrams, maps of the English coast with possible landing spots and the routes of the invasion fleets marked. He'd write them all by hand on thin paper, which he'd then neatly fold and conceal in the cover of a well-used book containing navigation charts for the port of Rotterdam and the river Maas.

He'd hand the book over to Marcus when he boarded the *Beatrix III*.

The tall Dutchman with no small talk and eyes as jet-black as his hair was Ernst Schwarz's man in Rotterdam. Klein had no idea how Schwarz had found him and how the Dutchman got his reports back to Berlin or Moscow, but he never doubted that the reach of the NKVD was long and effective. It was best he knew as little as possible. That was the way the NKVD operated.

Van Leeuwen operated one of the dozens of tugs which moved around the harbour. His was one of the smaller ones, which had spent the last couple of years operating as a harbourmaster's vessel and as such was perfect for Klein, ideal for his daily inspections of the port and the various docks. Now van Leeuwen skippered the *Beatrix III*, which had been requisitioned by Klein. It meant his contact was always on hand. It really couldn't be simpler: once they were alone in the wheelhouse, Klein would remove his book of charts from his briefcase and hand it to the Dutchman, who'd hand him a duplicate in return.

Sometimes this would contain a message from Schwarz. The message could be as simple as him sending his good wishes and thanks, to asking detailed questions.

The last message he'd received from Berlin had puzzled him. It was neatly typed on flimsy paper; he'd read it three times before burning it and tossing the ashes overboard.

> Trusted agent from England will be brought to see you some time between 15–20 July. His mission essential to our cause and requires total co-operation. Security will be responsibility of SHARK.

Shark was van Leeuwen's codename. Klein had no idea what the trusted agent from England was called.

–

When Archie woke on the morning of Wednesday, 17 July, he had at first no idea where he was. He was on a sofa, the light streaming through the blinds, and as he sat up, he looked at his watch and realised it was six in the morning, which meant he'd slept for the best part of twelve hours.

Slowly, it all came back to him: he'd sailed from Harwich on the Sunday evening, arriving eventually in Zeebrugge early on the Monday morning, and he'd then travelled east across Flanders into the Netherlands, with no sleep, arriving in Dordrecht on the Tuesday – yesterday – afternoon. No wonder he'd been exhausted.

In fact, Archie now recalled how the Dutchman whose flat he was staying in had made him a meal. He'd found himself dropping off as he waited for it to be served. The man had made the sofa up for him and he'd fallen asleep immediately.

The Dutchman – Marcus – was in the tiny kitchen, and it was the noise he was making that must have woken Archie up. When he came through, Marcus put a large mug of coffee with no milk on the table and some clothes on the chair.

'Wear these. You'll blend in.' Hanging over the chair were some dirty dark blue overalls and a black reefer jacket. On the table was a dark grey woollen hat, and on the floor a pair of worn leather work boots and a pair of thick socks.

'This is the security pass for my colleague Willem. He's a comrade and often works with me on the tug. You're a similar height and build and could pass for him. In any case, as long as you're with me you'll be fine.'

'You said something about a tug?'

'I skipper a tug on the Maas, the *Beatrix III*. I usually take a Kriegsmarine officer around the docks. There's me, a deckhand and two engineers. Today you'll be the deckhand. The engineers are fine, we don't need to worry.'

'And you say you take a Kriegsmarine officer around the docks. Isn't that risky?'

'Not with this Kriegsmarine officer, no.'

–

They left Dordrecht just before seven o'clock that Wednesday morning, catching a tram and crossing the Maas into Zwijndrecht, through the south of the city and Feyenoord, eventually getting off just before Noordereiland, the island in the middle of the Maas.

'I have something to show you,' Marcus said. They crossed onto the island on a small footbridge and from there over the Willemsbrug to the northern part of Rotterdam. As they walked, Marcus explained what they were about to see.

'We must walk because no trams or cars can go this way any longer, even bicycles struggle. This is what the Germans did to our city.' They carried on walking into a rubble-strewn wasteland. The only buildings still standing on either side of the brick-strewn road were shells; whisps of grey smoke funnelled from the ruins and silent figures picked among the buildings, moving charred wood and bits of rubble.

'Two months ago, on the fourteenth of May, the Germans bombed the city. This area – from here and to the north – was the historic centre of Rotterdam. The bombing only lasted a quarter of an hour but in that time, they destroyed it – look around you. It took weeks for the fire to finally be extinguished, and it left nearly a thousand people dead and more than eighty thousand homeless. It's estimated that thirty thousand homes and other buildings have been destroyed. It burnt the heart out of the city. Look over there. You see those kids? There are dozens of them here each day, looking for their parents or their pets or toys... anything. German soldiers sometimes take pot-shots at them.

'Come, it's not such a good idea to hang around here too long. We'll head this way.' They headed west, eventually crossing the boundary of the bombing into roads untouched by it. To the south was the river and the port, and they walked through parkland and alongside docks. Half an hour later they came to a dock. Not far from a bridge with the Maas visible on the other side of it was the tug, the *Beatrix III*. A plume of thin black smoke was spiralling from the tall funnel reaching high above the wheelhouse.

'This is Coolhaven, and that's the boat. Johannes is our engineer and he's already on board. He's completely trustworthy, and in any case, he stays below deck. His grandson Paul is his assistant. Paul is deaf, and Johannes took him in when his parents tried to put him in a home when he was much younger. When we get aboard just try and look busy. Maybe tidy up the ropes on the deck, and while you're at it you can wipe the windows.'

Just after eight o'clock Archie noticed a tall navy officer striding along the path towards the boat. He was wearing a smart jacket with brass buttons and the distinctive Kriegsmarine hat, with its white top and gold eagle prominent at the front above the navy crest.

He hardly looked at Archie as he climbed aboard, calling out, '*Goedemorgen, Schipper,*' to Marcus as he greeted him from the wheelhouse.

Ten minutes later Marcus had edged the *Beatrix III* into Parkhaven and from there into the mighty Maas, which to Archie felt like the sea, a strong easterly wind buffeting the boat as it emerged into open water. Archie felt the speed cut, and then saw Marcus beckoning him into the wheelhouse. When he got there the German officer had the wheel. Marcus had to raise his voice above the noise of the engine and the wind.

'We'll head west into Eemhaven, where some barges arrived yesterday, and then come back into the river and head towards Waalhaven, where most of the barges are docked once they've been converted. Make sure you concentrate and remember what you see. I'll go down to the deck. You stay with him.'

The German said nothing once Archie shut the door and the two of them were alone. The British Secret Intelligence Service agent looked at the German Kriegsmarine officer, who glanced at him before returning his gaze to the river. It was difficult to know what to say, so awkward was the situation.

Archie felt nervous and conflicted, and was grateful that at least the tiny wheelhouse wasn't silent; the rhythmic thud–thud–thud of the engine was their backdrop. The German remained silent and hadn't even acknowledged him, but then they passed a freighter flying a Swedish flag. The freighter must have thought they were too close because it sounded a loud horn, and they turned swiftly to port. The German muttered something and then turned to Archie and smiled.

'You're English, aren't you?'

Archie nodded.

'You're English and I'm German and we're meant to be at war with each other, but in fact we're both working for the Soviet Union! What a strange world we live in, eh? Like in one of those children's stories where a character enters a forest and suddenly finds themselves in another land.'

'And a dangerous land, too.'

The German nodded.

'I imagine you know London well?'

Archie half-nodded because he was wary of giving away any personal information.

'I am assuming you are familiar with the British Library, where Karl Marx wrote *Das Kapital*? I've always wanted to visit that place, perhaps sit at the same desk as Marx. Maybe if this lot land in your country, I'll get to visit it. We can meet for lunch!'

They'd turned into the dock by now and the quaysides were full of barges moored alongside them. The German was smiling at the thought of lunch in London.

'But perhaps the idea of us being on the same side is not as crazy as it seems. Marx said nationalism is a bourgeois ideology, didn't he? He said that eventually the supremacy of the proletariat will lead to nations and states disappearing and being replaced by world communism. Is that not correct?'

Archie nodded, although he wasn't as well read on Marx as he ought to be, and he very much doubted that come the revolution he'd be treated as a member of the proletariat. But he liked the idea that his treachery could be justified by some kind of an ideology. It was one of the reasons Marxism appealed to him: it seemed to excuse a multitude of sins. When he'd been recruited all those years ago – nearly ten years now – he'd seen world peace as the answer to turmoil in the world and communism as the vehicle to achieve this. And he still believed that. He was glad the German did, too.

'You need to listen carefully, my friend. Yesterday Hitler issued an order instructing the armed forces to prepare for an invasion of Britain. It's all here... today's *Völkischer Beobachter.*' The German tapped a newspaper in front of him. 'Your country, Hitler says, "despite her hopeless military situation, still shows no signs of willingness to come to terms. I have decided to prepare, and if necessary to carry out, a landing operation against her." But in truth we've been preparing for this for months. That's why Rotterdam is full of barges. The plan is to invade your country with hundreds of thousands of men, plus tanks and artillery and supplies and... Well, you can imagine. And the main way of getting them across to your coast and land them is on these barges. We'll need hundreds of them, perhaps two thousand, if not more. And very few of them are self-propelling. Most of them will need to be towed across the North Sea and the English Channel by tugs and other boats, which is why you'll also see so many tugs in the docks here, moored three or four deep. I'm turning round now, back into the Maas, and then we'll go into Waalhaven, where you can't move for barges.'

The boat pitched and lurched as it caught the wash from a passing tanker and Archie gripped the side.

'We bring the barges here from all over Europe. This is the main base for them, but we also dock them in the French Channel ports and Antwerp and Ostend, too. The larger boats are the river barges, the small ones tend to be canal barges. This is a lot for you to take in, so I've written some information down for you here.' From his jacket pocket he took out a small leather-bound volume with *Die Bijbel* embossed in faded gold leaf on the well-worn front cover.

'There are five blank pages at the back. I've written on them in invisible ink. You know how that works? You simply subject the paper to heat, such as an iron on a low setting. The writing will then emerge. Obviously be careful not to burn the paper.

'I do this trip most days to see how my barges are doing, but I don't want to push it today... We're in Waalhaven now. Inside the rear cover of the Bible, I've inserted some very tiny strips of film which I took with a Minolta. They're photographs of the barges and other vessels. Can you see how many barges there are?'

'How many tanks can you get on a barge?'

'That's a good question, and the answer is more than you'd think. You see that barge over there? It's what we classify as an A2 barge, formerly a river barge. The canal barges are classified as A1, they're slightly smaller. I have a feeling that river barge is from the Rhine. It's fifty metres long and can carry a load of around three hundred and fifty tonnes. A Panzer tank is just under six metres long and weighs twenty-five tonnes. Plus, of course, you have to account for the crew of five, and fuel and ammunition and other supplies. If you look carefully at the bow you see on this barge here... let me slow down... you'll see that it's already been converted to allow for a ramp for the tanks and other vehicles to offload, and that accounts for some space. But it's not just tanks, of course.

'If you look on the quayside – over there – you'll spot some lorries. Those ones are Mercedes L3000s. They weigh four tonnes each and are slightly longer than a tank, at six metres. And the initial wave of troops we send ashore will be mainly the Panzer divisions, the Panzer grenadiers. Tens of thousands of them, maybe as many as one hundred thousand, I believe. They use the *Sonderkraftfahrzeug* troop carriers: twelve men including the crew. They weigh eight tonnes and are also six metres long. Don't worry, I know this is a lot of information I'm giving you. It's all written down in the Bible, so to speak. There are also diagrams of the barges, showing how they've been converted and will be loaded, and there are some photographs of them too. I've even added a diagram showing the possible invasion routes. Most of them start in Rotterdam and the convoys form up in the Channel.

'We're heading towards the Rotterdamsche Droogdok now, the dry dock where the actual conversion of the barges takes place. This is why Rotterdam is so useful. It's such an enormous port that we can do everything here.'

'The invasion...' Archie waved a hand in the direction of a row of barges. 'When will it take place?'

'It's the question everyone wants to know the answer to. I could give you a broad answer now – that we are not ready just yet, and that it will have to be before the end of September. But I think I will know soon. I've just heard that I must be in Berlin on Monday the twelfth of August for a very important meeting. I may have a clearer idea after that. I do know they're getting close to agreeing a date.'

'And is there a way of you letting me know?'

The German looked dead ahead and frowned. 'I can try to get a letter to your embassy in Stockholm, and then they could send it to London in their diplomatic bag. Give me a name for the letter to be sent to.'

Archie thought for a while.

'I don't know... How about you address it to "Mr Oscar Smith"?'

'That's all?'

'You can then say... how about, "Chairman, Oriel Engineering"?'

The German pushed a piece of paper and a pencil towards him. 'Please write that down.'

It was only when he handed the paper back that Archie began to wonder about his choice of wording, but by then it was deep in the German's pocket.

'Are you based here?'

The German looked firmly ahead as the boat turned back into the Maas and took a while to reply. 'I think it's probably best that we know as little about each other as possible, don't you? I have no idea of your name or what you do, it's safer that way. I think it's better that you suddenly appear in Rotterdam and then disappear. And if anyone asks, all I know is that this morning I had a different crew member on the boat. That happens. Do you know how you're going to get back?'

'Why do you ask?'

'Because I don't like the idea of you hanging around Rotterdam trying to think of a way of getting out. This is not a safe city.'

'You won't need to worry. I'm going to get out the same way as I came in.'

'That's all I need to know.'

Chapter 23

Hamburg
June 1940

'Welcome to Hamburg, Herr Visser. Have you been here before?'

Arnold Visser said he didn't think he had, though as soon as he said that he realised how stupid it sounded; either he had been to Hamburg, or he hadn't. It wasn't the kind of thing one was unsure of. In any case, from what he'd seen of it since he arrived the previous day, Hamburg was not the kind of city one easily forgets: Germany's second largest city, dominated by the North Sea, even though the coast was more than fifty miles up the Elbe.

The man in front of him seemed to be pleasant enough, quite unlike the more menacing Germans he'd encountered when he was arrested in Amsterdam, full of threats and lacking in any form of sophistication. He was intelligent and urbane and spoke in a quiet and even friendly tone, and although he wasn't tall by any means, he cut an imposing figure in his suit, which looked to be made of high-quality cloth and tailored to measure.

The man himself was smart, with a fine head of neat silver-grey hair and long fingers, which he moved around in an expressive manner and appeared to have been manicured.

All in all, not quite what Visser imagined a senior Abwehr official would look like.

'I trust my colleagues in Amsterdam told you what is required of you here?'

'Only to an extent, sir, yes – but if you were able to go over it again, I think I'd find that helpful.'

The man paused, as if he wasn't quite sure why Herr Visser was speaking in such a convoluted manner.

'But as I understand it, you did volunteer for this?'

'Only in the sense, sir, that it seemed preferable to the alternative.'

'Which was?'

'To be sent to a labour camp in Poland.'

'I see. But then, I understand you had committed a crime – the theft of a motor vehicle, belonging to a German official?'

'That's correct, sir. It belonged to a senior SS officer.'

The German raised his eyebrows and exhaled in an exaggerated manner, as if to emphasise to Visser quite how rash that had been.

'I do realise of course, sir, that I made a serious mistake, one which I deeply regret. I didn't feel that being sent to a labour camp in Poland was quite proportionate to the crime.'

'And you thought a few days in Hamburg felt altogether more agreeable?'

Visser found himself nodding, which he soon realised was probably a mistake, and was surprised at how easily the man had drawn him into it, which was probably a measure of how smart he was. Visser needed to be careful.

'In this building I am known as Herr Hamburg – it is an important part of our protocol that we refer to one another by codenames. Soon you will be given your very own codename. Now then, Visser, let me have a look...' He sat down in front of the Dutchman and crossed his legs, picking up a notebook.

'Arnold Hein Visser, born Zwolle in July 1913, studied at the Birmingham School of Art in England in 1934, and then in 1937 you moved to Amsterdam – is that correct?'

'Yes, sir.'

'How good is your English?'

'Very good, sir, though a little bit rusty, as the English would say.'

'And I see that in 1938 you joined the Dutch Nazi party. What led you to join the NSB?'

Visser shrugged. It was a good question; one he'd asked himself a number of times in recent months. 'I'm not too sure, sir. I think it was because I wanted to feel in control of my own destiny. Amsterdam was becoming full of Jews who'd moved there from Germany, including many who worked as artists, and I was struggling to get work. Like many people, I sensed that sooner or later the Netherlands could come under German control, and I think I must have felt that being a member of the NSB would...'

'Put you at an advantage?'

'Yes, I suppose so.'

'Let me assure you,' said Herr Hamburg, closing his notebook and uncrossing his legs, 'we are not an ideological organisation. We are not part of the National Socialist apparatus. The Abwehr is the intelligence arm of the German military. Some of our officers are Nazi party members, but many – including myself – are not. Our role is to provide the German armed forces with first-class intelligence. We specialise in telling our masters the facts, and we pride ourselves in obtaining those facts in a very skilled and objective manner. We avoid telling people what we think they may want to hear.

'The way military intelligence works is in many respects quite straightforward. We are required to build up a network of agents and establish a system for them to operate in, so that when our military masters come to us and say we require specific intelligence regarding Country X, for example, we are then in a position to gather that intelligence for them by using that network of agents. And this, Herr Visser, is where you come in.'

They were on the top floor of the west wing of the imposing building where the Abwehr was based on General-Knochenhauer-Strasse in the Rotherbaum district of Hamburg. The building was also the headquarters of the 10th Army Corps, and from early morning to late at night the corridors echoed to the sound of booted men hurrying along the tiled floors, all with a sense of urgency, orders being barked out from behind half-open doors, and officers gathered in small groups in front of the enormous windows, deep in hushed conversation. But the offices of the Abwehr were an altogether quieter place: the corridors were carpeted, and the muted conversations were always conducted behind closed doors. The atmosphere was almost that of an academic institution, and the man who had told Visser to call him 'Herr Hamburg' very much fitted that role as he explained matters in a clear and precise – sometimes over-precise – manner.

When Herr Hamburg told him that this was where he came in, Arnold Visser at first nodded as if he'd not quite understood what the other man was saying. Herr Hamburg seemed to sense this, because he repeated it and asked if he understood.

'Not entirely, actually. Perhaps if you could elaborate?'

The German said, 'Very well,' in a mildly exasperated tone, and said he'd spell it out more clearly, but that Herr Visser would do well to listen carefully.

'You'll recall that I said the Abwehr needs to build up a network of agents, and then be in a position to gather intelligence from places which are a priority for our military?'

Visser paused and nodded as he realised this had been a question.

'We are now required to provide our armed forces with intelligence related to the feasibility of our forces invading the British Isles. We have a very limited number of agents operating in Great Britain, but clearly, to provide the level and quality of intelligence that they require, we must increase the scale of our operation there. We are currently in the process of recruiting more agents. They need to meet certain criteria. They will have to be infiltrated by either sea or air, so will have to be physically fit. They must have a certain level of intellect and initiative, for obvious reasons. An ability to speak good English is also a requirement, for equally good reasons, and we need agents who we can trust. Although I did tell you that we are not an ideological organisation, we do nonetheless obviously need agents who are on Germany's side in this conflict.'

He paused and looked carefully at the Dutchman in an attempt to discern a reaction, and he seemed to pick something up because at that moment Arnold Visser, the twenty-seven-year-old graphic artist from Zwolle – the man who'd describe himself as an accidental Nazi – would have rather been anywhere else in the world. The well-mannered man in front of him had just been telling him he was to be a German spy in Britain. Frankly, if he was now given the choice of doing that or being transported to Poland to work fifteen gruelling hours a day, seven days a week, in a forced labour camp, he'd have very happily opted for that. In fact, he'd have been so grateful for the opportunity he'd have walked to Poland.

But there was no choice, that much was evident.

He told Herr Hamburg there might well have been an unfortunate misunderstanding, because he'd never volunteered for this and didn't think he was cut out for it.

'Nonsense, Visser!' The German slapped him on the shoulder in a reassuring manner and said that he clearly met all the requirements he'd outlined: he was young and fit, spoke excellent English, was clearly bright, and his loyalty to the Reich could not be questioned, given his membership of the Dutch Nazi party.

'You'll remain here in Hamburg for a few weeks while we train you for your mission. I can assure you that the training will be thorough. I can sense you're a bit unsettled at the moment, Herr Visser, and don't get me wrong, I do appreciate that being informed you're going to be a spy and sent on a clandestine mission into enemy territory is a lot to take in. I imagine you feel overwhelmed, but please be assured that the training is designed to ensure you have every chance of success and to keep you as safe as possible. Do you have any questions?'

Although he did have any number of questions, Arnold Visser now realised he was trapped and that his best option may be to play along with this. Maybe with some luck they'd realise he wasn't secret agent material, not a person in whom the future of the Reich could be entrusted.

Without appearing too wilful, he'd ensure he was below par on his training in the hope that Herr Hamburg or someone else with an equally ridiculous codename would take him aside one day and explain kindly that they'd reluctantly concluded that he wasn't the man for them, and he was being sent back to the Netherlands.

–

But it never turned out like that, though not for the want of trying. A constant refrain from his schooldays had been teachers telling him not to come across as being too clever, not to answer back quite so readily. 'Nobody likes a smart arse,' he'd been frequently told. So, during his training he was constantly ready to answer back, asking awkward questions, treating matters with a degree of inappropriate levity.

His approach clearly misfired. There were around half a dozen trainers for their small group of four agents, and to a man they seemed to find him charming and clever.

'You're just what we need,' one of them told him one day. 'Smart and friendly.' After that Visser adopted what he hoped was a surlier attitude, but at his weekly review session Herr Hamburg told him he'd observed he was quieter, and said this was undoubtedly due to nerves as his mission got closer, which was quite understandable.

The training was based on how his actual mission would unfold, starting with training on the nearby Außenalster as they paddled dinghies in pairs, then familiarisation with landmarks in the area where it was intended he'd land, map-reading – lots of map-reading – his cover story, how to travel to the next town to meet up with his fellow agent, and how from there they were to gather what intelligence they could on an important RAF base, and finally the journey to London to meet up with someone called Agent Lübeck and pass on all their intelligence to them.

'And then?'

'And then you wait. Agent Lübeck will give you your instructions. You will almost certainly be required to gather more intelligence. You won't be in London to go sight-seeing! Don't worry, though, you'll be in excellent hands. Lübeck is a well-regarded agent. As resourceful and intelligent as you'll find, everything someone in my position would wish for. Please make sure you do give them my regards!'

'What will we be waiting for?' It was Emil who'd asked that question, the agent with whom Visser had been paired. The two of them would land in England together, split up and then meet up before heading to London. Visser and Emil got on well; Emil was a draughtsman from Antwerp, married with two young children, and although Visser never quite gathered how he'd been recruited by the Abwehr, he got the impression he'd been press-ganged too.

'You'll be waiting for the arrival of our armed forces.' The trainer who said that was one whom he and Emil got on with especially well, because his mother was Dutch and was always happy to speak Dutch with him and Emil. 'And let me assure you...' He leant in close to them in his typically conspiratorial manner. 'You won't have too long to wait.'

'Meaning?'

'Meaning these things have yet to be decided, but the date I've heard...' He moved even closer to them. 'It is in September, but I didn't tell you that, though that's the gossip around this building.' The man with the Dutch mother leant back, rather proud of himself in the manner of someone important enough to have been in possession of such vital information. Later in the day he caught up with the two of them and said he had been franker with them than he ought to have been, and if they as much as whispered a word of what he'd said about the invasion date then there'd be serious repercussions.

And it wasn't as if they weren't aware of what these repercussions might be. In his second week in Hamburg, Visser had been called to a windowless room where Herr Hamburg was sitting alongside a shifty-looking man in an ill-fitting suit and the kind of complexion associated with someone who rarely ventures outside. At first the man said nothing, sitting alongside Herr Hamburg and smoking continually, carefully observing Visser through the spirals of smoke.

Herr Hamburg spent a while explaining Visser's new identity.

'For the purposes of this mission you will be Gerrit Hendriks, with the same date of birth as your own to make it simple for you to remember in case you're ever questioned. You are from Amsterdam, with an address of Kerkstraat by the Amstel canal. We understand you know that area?'

'Yes, I worked on Kerkstraat for a while.'

'Your story is that you worked for the Amsterdamsche Wisselbank on Damrak, close to the central station, so—'

'Yes, I know exactly where it is.'

'You dealt with foreign currency exchange there, mainly for tourists, hence your fluency in English. You decided to flee the country in April and managed to secure passage on a boat to England. Here are your Dutch papers and, in this envelope, here, your British identity card and a temporary residency permit. There's a further letter explaining you have permission to travel within a two-hour perimeter from London to look for work as an agricultural labourer. The envelope also explains your story in more detail. You are to memorise it, obviously.'

Arnold Visser picked up the papers and glanced through them. Although he was no expert, he was a graphic artist, and he had to say that although the Dutch identity card looked very authentic, the same could not be said of the British papers; they looked like poor copies, and the paper and card they were printed on didn't feel right. He was about to mention this when the other man spoke.

It was in a reedy Bavarian accent which Visser had always found tricky to follow. Before he'd said very much, Herr Hamburg stopped him and said he ought to have said that Herr Braun was from the *Geheime Staatspolizei*. He must have picked up that the term didn't register with Visser, and explained it was the Gestapo. If nothing else, he now certainly had Visser's attention.

Herr Braun explained that he wanted it to be very clear Herr Visser was not to entertain any notion that when he arrived in England he could surrender and opt for an easy life.

'We understand that one or two of our agents have done that. They've taken the coward's way out. But let me assure you that it is not an option for you. We'll know exactly what you're up to when you're in England, and if you surrender to the authorities, then we will soon know. And if you do take that unwise course, then the implications for your family will be most serious. We know exactly where they live in Zwolle, where they work.'

Visser said nothing could be further from his intentions; he had every hope that he'd carry out his mission to the best of his ability.

'And there's something else, Visser,' said Herr Hamburg. 'Your code-name. You are now Agent Tallinn. Your training has gone well, we have every confidence in you as an agent of the Reich. You depart next Thursday.'

–

The last few days of training were hectic. There were hours spent in a room where the walls were covered in maps and photographs of the area where he was due to land. Visser was meant to memorise the maps and the area in general. And then there were long sessions on what he was meant to look out for.

'Get as close as you can to the coast. We want to know what the defences are like, what artillery there is on the shore, how many troops are based there and where, what traps there are on the beach, if any, what military units there are in the town, what road signs and directions are there, and then – and this is very important – we need to know about the roads.

'When we invade, we will want to land our tanks and move them inland as quickly and as easily as possible. A Panzer tank is nine and a half feet wide. We must know if the roads from the town are wide enough. Sometimes the roads will become narrow country lanes, and that may be a struggle. Your feet are a foot long, you can measure the width of a road by pacing it – we need to know if you can manage ten paces across the road. Some British roads have weight restrictions, especially on bridges. Look out for those – a Panzer tank weighs twenty-five tonnes.'

–

Early on the morning of Thursday, 27th June, Agents Tallinn and Riga were woken and taken from the secure hostel on General-Knochenhauer-Strasse to the Abwehr headquarters for a final briefing by the man they'd come to know as Herr Hamburg.

There was a pot of coffee on the table in his office, and he invited them to sit down and drink. He complained it was already far too warm in his office, so he hung his jacket on the back of the chair and loosened his tie and was generally quite amiable, going over their mission once more and assuring them that their preparation had been detailed and thorough, and he really couldn't recall two better prepared agents and once the invasion had successfully taken place – not least, due to their efforts – then they'd be well rewarded.

Herr Hamburg explained what would happen next: they would be taken by train to Brussels and from there by road to Boulogne, where they'd be taken to the port to board their ship.

'Try and rest while you can – on the train, for instance. It's going to be a very long day. Wait here while I see if your escort is ready.'

When Herr Hamburg left the room, Visser stood up to pace. Emil seemed to be calm, but Visser was a bundle of nerves – in truth, he was terrified. It didn't help that he only had to look at a boat to become seasick. When he turned back from the window, he noticed something on the floor by the German's jacket. It was his wallet, and when he picked it up it flipped open to reveal his Abwehr identity card. Alongside his photograph was his name – Helmut Schröder – and his place of birth – Dresden.

It was strange to discover Herr Hamburg's real name. Up to now it was as if he'd believed he really was only known by his codename.

The journey to Brussels was uneventful, and at Midi station they were escorted to a car. Four hours later, after driving through the damaged landscape of recently conquered Belgium and northern France, they arrived in Boulogne-sur-Mer. They were driven through the port to Bassin Loubet at the northern end, close to where the Liane opened into the English Channel. It was now 10:30 and already dark when they were escorted on to a trawler called *La Mouette*.

They were taken to a cramped cabin under the wheelhouse, where the skipper was waiting along with two Kriegsmarine officers and the Abwehr officer who'd travelled with them from Hamburg.

Visser got the impression that the skipper had been press-ganged into the whole business, much in the same way he and Emil had. He seemed nervous and when he spoke, he kept his gaze on the floor. He explained that they'd travel at five knots, which was an inconspicuous speed for a trawler.

'It's twenty-five nautical miles to our destination, which will be about five miles off the English coast. When we stop, we'll put our nets out so as not to arouse suspicion. The tide will be in your favour, it shouldn't take you too long to reach land.'

Half an hour later, *La Mouette* slipped its moorings and eased out of Bassin Loubet and into the English Channel. Visser and Emil had been instructed to remain below deck until the boat was clear of the port, and when they were able to come on deck it was a fine night, with a full moon and little in the way of cloud. The two agents leant on the deck rail, smoking and wondering whether such a clear night was a good thing.

Meanwhile, the two Kriegsmarine officers were readying the dinghy on the deck. Just before two in the morning *La Mouette* dropped anchor with the bow facing west, so that the port side was the one closer to the English coast. The fishing nets were thrown to port while the dinghy was lowered into the water to starboard. A rope ladder was slung over the side, and with a notable lack of ceremony – not even a 'Good luck' – Visser and Emil were hurried into the dinghy.

It took them an hour to paddle to the coast, and although it was a calm night the waves were surprisingly choppy and they had to pause every few minutes to bail out. They'd been given a pair of binoculars and as far as they could tell, as they approached the coast there was no sign of life.

Their destination was a stretch of beach a few hundred metres south of St Mary's Bay. They allowed the dinghy to float onto the beach and then clambered out, crouching by the boat to catch their breath. Emil took out his knife and cut the side of the dinghy before pushing it back to sea, the air hissing out of it as he did so.

Ahead of them, the surprisingly narrow beach seemed to be clear apart from a few coils of barbed wire and behind that, a bank of sand dunes. Visser made a mental note of all this; it was exactly the information the Germans wanted. So far, so good. The two crawled along the beach and in between the barbed wire and then up the sand dunes, pausing at the top. There was no sign of life, possibly a couple of lights a long way to their left, and in front of them the coast road.

Here they were to go their separate ways: Emil would head north towards the town of Ashford and Visser west towards the nearby town of Lydd. The two men embraced briefly; the plan was for them to meet up again at Ashford railway station. Visser watched as Emil darted across the coast road and into a field opposite. Suddenly, he felt all alone in the world, and as if the weight of it were on his shoulders. He thought about just staying where he was, because if he was caught, he'd confess all, and after all, there was little compromising on him. It had been decided not to equip them with a radio transmitter or with weapons. The idea was that they'd be unencumbered as they picked up as much intelligence as possible.

But then he thought about his family in Zwolle and the threats the Gestapo man called Braun had made, and decided that what they'd asked him to do was maybe not that dangerous after all: just wander around for a few days and keep his eyes open and make a mental note of what he saw. Nothing incriminating.

He hurried across the road and into the field opposite. Ahead of him he could just make out Emil's figure before it disappeared against the hedgerow. Visser moved in the opposite direction.

His destination was Lydd, a small town five miles away, and his plan was to reach the outskirts just before dawn and to wait somewhere secluded before venturing into the town. His instructions were that Lydd would be an important destination for the Germans soon after they landed, a place where their forces would assemble before pressing on. Visser needed to find out quite how suitable it would be: were the roads wide enough? Were there enough open spaces where large numbers of troops and vehicles could gather?

He trudged slowly across the ploughed fields, feeling quite alone in the world. He was a German spy in an enemy country, and he couldn't quite believe how that had happened.

Nonetheless, he made it to the edge of the town in the expectant minutes before dawn, although there was little he could see in the way of cover. Eventually he came to a large house surrounded by a dense shrubbery, and he crawled into that, grateful for an opportunity to rest. He lay there until nine o'clock, drinking from his water flask and chewing on the spicy sausage he'd been given in his knapsack.

At nine o'clock he carefully hauled himself out of the shrubbery and headed into the town. He'd been told there was a station in the centre, and he was to find out what he could about it. On the way he remembered what he'd been told about the width of the roads, so when he was sure no one was watching he carefully paced out the road. Although it seemed to be narrow, it was actually fourteen paces wide, more than enough space for a Panzer tank to pass and a no doubt welcome part of his report, which he was already compiling in his head.

Lydd is a notably quiet place, perhaps more of a village than a town. However, the roads are not too narrow, at least fourteen feet wide. There would appear to be ample open spaces and the town is not overlooked. The main roads into the town seem to be easy to secure, and the town easy to attack and secure with little in the way of defences.

'Are you all right, sir?'

It was a policeman: friendly enough, inquisitive, studiedly polite and slightly overweight.

Visser hadn't spotted the man, who'd appeared out of a side street and was looking him up and down and seemed to be concentrating his gaze on his feet. When Visser looked down at them, he saw that his boots were coated with sand and mud and the bottom of his trousers were still damp.

Visser nodded and smiled, hoping he could get away without speaking.

'And where are you headed, sir?'

'To the station – I am in the area to find work – as a farm labourer. I wish to play my part!'

'And where might you be from, sir?'

'I am a refugee from the Netherlands.'

'And you have papers?'

Visser reached into his pocket and handed them to the policeman, who studied them carefully.

'I see that you're from Amsterdam, Mr Hendriks.'

'That is correct.'

The policeman frowned and turned the papers over and over in his hand, transferring them to his other hand and holding them at an angle to read them again.

'And where have you come to Lydd from?'

'A farm near Ashford.'

'And could you recall the name of the farm, or indeed of the farmer?'

'No, I'm very bad with English names, but I do recall it had many cows.'

'Farms do tend to, sir.' Visser felt mortified he'd managed such an inane response. The policeman had been busy making notes in his little pad but was looking up at him now, in the manner of a schoolteacher trying to work out whether a pupil was being sarcastic or just plain stupid.

'Can I ask you the colour of your eyes, sir?' He was holding up the Alien Registration card for Gerrit Hendriks, waving it as if helping to dry the ink.

'Blue.'

'And perhaps, sir, you could be so good as to tell me why the word "colour" on this card is misspelt?'

'Really?'

'Yes, really, sir. "Colour" is spelt with a "u" after the second "o", unless you're American, that is.'

Visser felt sick, and had a desire above all else to sit down and have a few minutes to gather his thoughts. When he'd first seen the forged documents, he'd thought they looked to be of poor quality, and sadly, it seemed he was right.

He thought about confessing all to the policeman there and then, but still hoped he could get away with it.

'And where did you sleep last night?'

'In a guest house.'

'Which one?'

'It was a house I passed and asked if they had a room for the night.'

'Where?'

'Towards the coast.'

'I think you'd better come with me, sir.'

Chapter 24

Hamburg and England
July 1940

It all happened so fast, to begin with, Manfred Hoffmann had no time to be afraid.

After that, he was terrified.

The hatch on the floor of the fuselage of the Heinkel had been pulled open and a rush of cold night air swept into the aircraft and then Reinhard, who'd been in charge of Manfred since he'd boarded the plane, grabbed him by the shoulder and yanked him towards the edge of the abyss.

Reinhard pointed at a pair of lights above him and was holding up his hand to indicate 'wait', and then Manfred remembered his instructions:

Red: don't jump.

Red and green: get ready.

Green: jump.

And when it finally turned green, Reinhard pushed him forward and now Manfred was tumbling through the black night sky, ten thousand or more fast-disappearing feet between him and what he'd been assured would be the Essex countryside, aware there was a chance that his parachute could fail to open or he could break something on impact, and he hoped that wouldn't be his neck.

—

When Manfred arrived back in Hamburg two months earlier – in May – it took Helmut Schröder until that weekend to come up with a plausible explanation as to why one of his agents had turned up in Hamburg three years after being dispatched to Britain… and not having been heard of since.

Until then, Schröder had taken the risk of Manfred Hoffmann staying in his apartment on Fehlandstrasse, but only because his land-lady, who lived on the floor below his, was away. As long as his visitor was careful and quiet and didn't go anywhere near the windows, then it was a risk just about worth taking.

And during this time, they concocted a story: one which, to be totally honest, Manfred knew was unlikely to withstand too much scrutiny, but he was counting on it not getting that far.

The story was that Manfred had feared being interned in one of the aliens' camps being set up by the British. Worried his links with the Abwehr would be discovered, he'd stowed away on a boat travelling from Dover to Calais.

'And from there, Manfred, you will have slowly made your way here to Hamburg.'

'Can't all this be checked? It all sounds a bit...' Manfred hesitated.

'A bit what?'

'A bit... unlikely?'

'Possibly, but there is so much confusion that anything is possible, and if I'm happy with the circumstances of your return then I don't think it will cause undue concern among others.'

On the Monday morning, Manfred Hoffmann left Schröder's apartment on Fehlandstrasse and caught an early morning bus to Bremen. Once there, he got off at the stop before the railway station and had breakfast at a cafe before walking to the station to buy a ticket to Hamburg.

Schröder had told him that when he arrived in Hamburg, Hoffmann was to present himself at the office of the railway police – the *Bahnschutzpolizei* – and ask for directions to the Abwehr headquarters, explaining he'd just arrived from Bremen.

The mention of the word 'Abwehr' raised an eyebrow or two, and a senior officer was called from a back office.

'What is your business with the Abwehr?'

'I worked there before the war. I am volunteering my services once more.'

The officer looked confused and asked Manfred if he could perhaps give him the name of anyone he'd worked for there.

'The man I knew best was a Herr Helmut Schröder. I've no idea if he's still there.'

The officer carefully wrote it down and said Manfred should wait where he was, and he'd make a phone call. He reappeared five minutes later and said yes, there was indeed a Herr Helmut Schröder there.

An alibi of sorts secured, Manfred took a series of trams across the city before arriving at General-Knochenhauer-Strasse, where he asked for Schröder.

Ten minutes later he was in Schröder's office.

'That all seemed to go according to plan, Manfred. Now the *Bahnschutzpolizei* have a record of you arriving at the railway station. I will put in a report explaining what happened to you and the circumstances of your arrival, and suggesting that after an extensive debrief, which I propose to carry out myself, we put you through a refresher training course prior to sending you back to Britain.'

'When would that be?'

'Perhaps one month, Manfred. Time is not on our side.'

'But I thought the war was going well?'

'Of course it's going well, Manfred, that is my point. Even my landlady's cat can tell it's going well! Look!' He turned round and pointed to a large map of Europe on the wall behind him. 'We control much of Europe already. Soon, we will control all of it! Come here, Manfred.' He beckoned the younger man to come closer, even though he wasn't far away to begin with. Manfred edged his chair closer to the desk and Schröder leant across it, so their heads were almost touching.

'It's now getting on for the end of May, Manfred. Before the end of September, there's a very good chance that not only will the Reich have conquered France, but Great Britain, too.'

'Great Britain – really?'

The older man nodded. 'Detailed preparations are underway to invade Great Britain, and these involve all the branches of the armed forces and our intelligence bodies, too – in fact, especially our intelligence bodies – and the role of the Abwehr here is paramount. If we are to mount a successful invasion – by which I mean something large-scale and permanent, rather than just a series of raids on the British coast – then our intelligence must be extensive and accurate. We are sending agents over to gather this intelligence, but we need more. With your knowledge of Great Britain and fluency in English, you'll be ideal. Which is why we need to get you back there as soon as possible.'

–

In the end, Manfred remained in Hamburg for five weeks. For the first fortnight he was in General-Knochenhauer-Strasse, undergoing an extensive debrief covering his three years in England. Much of the questioning was carried out by Schröder but others were involved, too, which meant that Manfred needed to always be on his guard as he remembered the golden rules: to stick to his story; to keep it simple; to give just enough detail to keep his questioners satisfied.

After two weeks Schröder called him into his office. He was pleased: it had all gone well, and although Manfred's story was an unusual one, it was plausible enough. Fortunately, no one had questioned it.

'Thankfully, my colleagues here believe you, Manfred. They think you're a credible agent, and we need to get you back to England as soon as possible. To that end, you'll be undergoing two or three weeks of field training, and that will take place at our training base at Polizeigefängnis Fuhlsbüttel. Part of this training will be how to jump out of a plane.'

'I beg your pardon?'

'Yes. Don't look so worried, Manfred. I've found the funds to equip you with a parachute! I'm joking. Look, it'll be perfectly safe. I'm told that dropping by parachute can even be a rather peaceful and serene experience – you float towards the earth and there's a perfect silence...'

'You've been told this?'

'Yes.'

'Have you ever tried it yourself?'

Schröder shook his head. 'I'm too old, Manfred, you'll appreciate that... and with my knees... but you'll get excellent training at Fuhls-büttel.'

Fuhlsbüttel turned out to be a strange experience. Away from his mentor's protection, Manfred was conscious that any small mistake would prove fatal. The training was divided into six broad areas: unarmed combat; how to behave during interrogation; advice on finding one's contacts in Britain and how to be sure they could still be trusted; what kind of intelligence to gather and how to report it; how to travel around Britain while avoiding suspicion; and last but most certainly not least, the parachute training.

The latter took place at the nearby Fuhlsbüttel airbase, and very soon Manfred formed the opinion that whoever had told Schröder that it was a serene experience was either seriously mistaken or was having a joke at his expense.

There were three of them on the course: Manfred himself, a tall Belgian, suspicious of everyone, and an overweight yet surprisingly agile Frenchman. It was explained that it wouldn't be possible to have a practice jump – all the training would be on technique: how to operate the parachute and how to land. They had to jump from varying heights onto different surfaces. The instructors taught them how to strap their ankles properly because they were the most vulnerable part of the body, and how to roll when you hit the ground and what to do when you did so. The instructor taking this session was also called Manfred.

'Roll naturally, for as long as your momentum takes you. When you stop, lie very still. Don't look up. Remain in that position for at least three or four minutes. It will take that long for your sight and hearing to acclimatise. Take out your compass and check where you are. Have a look around to see if you can spot any features in the landscape to help locate yourself. Remember the silk map sewn into the lining of your jacket. And when you're as sure as you can be it's safe, hide your parachute. There'll be a trowel in your knapsack. Use that and then get rid of it. It will take some explaining if you're ever searched.'

Manfred the instructor turned out to be a very friendly type and the two men got on especially well. Occasionally he'd stop by the Abwehr training camp by the police prison in the evening to join them for a meal or a drink after dinner, and this was how one evening the two Manfreds found themselves sitting together enjoying a cold beer on a warm June evening, looking out towards the prison.

They watched as two men walked by in the distance, close to the barbed wire fencing which surrounded the prison section of the complex.

'Two of your fellow agents there,' said Manfred the instructor. 'Do you know them?'

'I've never seen them before. Have you been training them, too?'

The instructor shook his head. 'No one is allowed to approach them or have anything to do with them, but you know, it's a small world. The instructors talk, we gossip... That's how it is, isn't it? The odd thing is, our agents travel to Britain in one of two ways: by dinghy or by parachute. But those two are different. They're having a U-boat take them all the way to Ireland. Would you believe that? They must be very important, that's all I know. Do you know anything about Ireland?'

'Not much, except that it's neutral in the war. Are those men Irish?'

'I wouldn't know – but from what I gather, they do speak English.'

–

For the last few days, Manfred Hoffmann was based back in the west wing at General-Knochenhauer-Strasse for his final briefing, which took place in a secure room on the top floor, the Alster visible through the large window.

Helmut Schröder carried out the briefing and he was accompanied most of the time by a woman called Edda – tall, blonde, with her pale features offset by bright red lipstick. Edda was quite possibly the most efficient person Manfred had ever encountered: she sat next to Schröder behind a long table, in front of her a series of files neatly arranged in what was quite possibly alphabetical order, each of them a different colour and the contents of the files separated by colour-coded stickers.

In fact, it was Edda who ran most of the sessions, though, at first, she did defer to Schröder. After a while he recognised how well informed she was and allowed her to take the lead.

On the first morning there was silence in the briefing room as Edda selected a dull orange folder and opened it carefully. Manfred was sitting on the other side of the table. Strong morning sunlight beamed into the room, picking out bouncing particles of dust.

'Your identity,' said Edda, removing a sheet from the folder. 'We're of the opinion that your English is good enough for you to pass as an Englishman and—'

'Are you sure? I know I'm fluent, but my accent... Surely...?'

'Any foreign identity immediately arouses suspicion,' said Schröder. 'The thinking here is to avoid that suspicion arising in the first place. We don't think your accent is that notable, but the key is to say as little as possible. There are plenty of people in this world who are of few words, who are reluctant to engage in conversation. You'll be one of them.'

'You'll be Albert Heath, same date of birth as your own, from Ipswich in Suffolk. You're making your way to London to find factory work. In Suffolk you were an agricultural labourer, which is a reserved occupation, meaning you were exempt from conscription. You're single, but there's a sweetheart, as I believe the English call their girl-friends. You support a football team called Ipswich Town. It's all here, Manfred – your back story.'

Edda picked up another file and pushed it towards Manfred.

'Don't open it just yet. There's more in there we need to discuss first. And in this envelope, here is your British registration card, wallet and other papers. Read them along with the folder. In three days' time you fly to Britain. Dropping someone by parachute at night is rarely a precise act, as I'm sure you were told during your training. There are so many variable factors, such as weather conditions, wind direction, navigational error and the height from which you jump. The best we can say is that we hope to get you down somewhere within a ten-mile radius, so for that reason we must drop you well away from built-up areas. This is the proposed landing zone.'

From a dark blue folder she removed a sheet of paper and unfolded it to reveal a large map. 'It's the Stour Valley, roughly ten miles north of Colchester, the town you'll be heading to. At this time of year, the farmland is quite dry and hard, but around the River Stour it's not too bad. The idea will be to drop you at night, and at first light for you to make your way to Colchester. You'll have a copy of this map with various features marked on it so you'll be able to work out where you are. Quite a lot to read in this folder.

'And when you get to Colchester, this folder tells you where to go and what to do when you're there. You need to read all this and memorise it before you leave Hamburg, because you won't be taking it with you. We'll meet again tomorrow and go through it once more and discuss any questions you have. By the time you leave Hamburg, everything should be clear.'

–

Everything was clear by the time Manfred arrived at Fuhlsbüttel airbase late on a Thursday afternoon in early July. They'd been due to fly on the Wednesday night, but the winds over the North Sea were too strong. They got the go-ahead at lunch when the Luftwaffe said the meteorological report was 'satisfactory'.

'Good westerly winds over the North Sea on your way over,' said Schröder. 'Not much of a moon at this time of the month and some low cloud, so that should help ensure you're not too visible. I don't usually accompany agents to the airport, you understand.'

The older man shook the younger one warmly by the hand and briefly clasped his shoulder and said, 'All the best,' and, 'You're very well prepared,' and then Edda knocked on the door and said the car was ready and they ought to get a move on.

At the Luftwaffe base at Fuhlsbüttel, Manfred was taken to a low brick-built building and down into a basement, with the distinctive feel of an air-raid shelter. There he met the five-man crew who'd be flying him over, though he was only introduced to two by name: Karl – the pilot and Hauptmann in charge of the flight – and an Oberleutnant called Reinhard, who'd oversee him.

Karl spread a map out on the table which took up much of the room. He was a short man with a friendly face and a strong Berlin accent.

'It's now seven o'clock. After this briefing we will eat, and my crew and I will check the aircraft is ready – we're flying in a Heinkel III. We will take off in four hours, at eleven o'clock. We will fly north-north-east over the Elbe to the North Sea. Over German Bight – here – we'll turn south-west towards Felixstowe, which is here. It's an important British port. We'll be part of a formation of six Heinkel bombers. It is important that as far as the British are concerned, we're thought to be taking part in a bombing mission. They know that if a plane such as ours flies across the mainland without dropping any bombs, then they may well be landing someone by parachute, and we don't want to alert them, do we? Tonight, we're only carrying one thousand pounds of bombs. Once we drop those, we'll carry on due west for twenty-five miles until we're over the drop zone. We'll fly at twenty thousand feet over the North Sea, dropping to fifteen thousand over Felixstowe, and drop you from ten thousand. I expect that will be around three to three-and-a-half hours after take-off. At all times you do what the Oberleutnant tells you. Do you have any questions?'

It was a lot to take in, and Manfred said he was fine thank you, he couldn't think of any questions. He asked if he could go for a walk, but Edda said he was to stay in the bunker until it was time to go to the plane, so he found himself a quiet corner and went through everything he'd had to memorise. He wasn't allowed to bring anything with him, and on top of all that, he had to plan very carefully what he'd do once he landed.

Cooper and the others had been quite clear about that.

'We're counting on you being sent back, Manfred. That's the whole purpose of your mission, please don't forget that. And don't forget that what happens when you arrive back in this country – however that may be – is absolutely critical, because you'll be given contacts and we need you to go along with that and it's imperative we know who these people are. Don't attempt to get in touch with us until it is safe to do so and until you believe you've exhausted your contact chain. Is that clear?'

Manfred had replied that he wasn't totally sure what they meant by a 'contact chain'. Cooper had explained that the Germans would most likely give him details of Contact A, who'd live near to where he arrived, and that person would pass him on to Contact B, and from there quite possibly to Contact C; the further along the line he got, the more important the contacts would be.

And Manfred had to remember all that, together with the telephone number for Cooper he'd memorised weeks ago before he left London, the address for his first contact, and then the further details of his mission, including what to do once he'd been passed through the contact chain. He was worried that everything was confused. He wasn't sure if someone asked him now where he was born, he'd know the correct answer.

–

Around midnight the pilot leant back from the cockpit and shouted that they were making better than expected progress. There was a strong tailwind, and it was quite possible that the drop would be closer to two in the morning.

'There's a very big air raid over London tonight,' he continued. 'With some luck, most of the RAF fighters will be diverted there.'

And that must have been the case, because they had a clear run into Felixstowe and encountered little anti-aircraft fire over it. Their Heinkel was only over the town for a minute at the most, dropping a couple of bombs before banking sharply away and gradually descending. It was at that point that Reinhard pulled Manfred over and opened the hatch, and they watched the lights.

Red…

Red and green…

Green

It was noisy at first as the sky rushed past him and Manfred felt his insides lurch up and then his body jolt as he opened the parachute, and he worried he'd pulled the cord a bit too late, but then everything went quiet, and without going as far as describing it as 'serene', it was certainly almost peaceful as he floated towards the unseen ground.

He seemed to accelerate as he got lower and he only saw the earth loom into view at the last moment, but thankfully it was soon enough to brace himself. Then, as his feet hit the ground, he remembered Manfred's instructions:

'Roll naturally, for as long as your momentum takes you. When you stop, lie very still. Don't look up. Remain in that position for at least three or four minutes.'

For most of those three or four minutes, Manfred Hoffmann was busy checking he was still intact. His legs and feet seemed fine and his arms, too, though one wrist was slightly sprained; apart from that, he was fine.

After five minutes he hauled himself up into a sitting position. He was in the middle of a ploughed field, probably fifty yards from a tall hedge and, behind him, a small wood. He looked around, carefully scanning the horizon. There were no distinguishing features, no landmarks that could give him a clue as to where he was. He took his compass out from his jacket pocket: south was in the direction of the tall hedge. Unless they'd got the drop completely wrong, then Colchester should be in that direction.

If not, he was in trouble.

He crawled over to the hedge and found a small dry ditch running next to it. He gathered up the parachute and placed it in the ditch, using the trowel to cover it with earth. And then he waited.

The sun came up just after five in the morning. When he peered over the hedge, Manfred could see a narrow road which led to a junction and one of the roads leading from that was, according to the compass, going south. He waited another quarter of an hour and headed in that direction.

He walked for the best part of an hour, with no sign of life, or of a bus stop. No vehicles on the road. Nothing.

When he heard a noisy engine approaching from behind, he assumed it was a bus, and he stepped to the side of the road and held out a hand to hail it. But it was an army truck. Edda had told him Colchester was a garrison town.

'Can we help you?'

'No, thank you.'

'But you put your hand out for us.'

Manfred laughed. 'Sorry. I thought you were a bus.'

There was laughter in the truck and someone said, 'Do we look like a bus?' and another person asked how much they should charge.

'Where are you heading, then?'

'Colchester.'

'Come on, we'll give you a lift. We're heading that way. Just don't tell anyone, eh?'

They dropped Manfred close to the station and he said he'd be fine from there, and once the army truck disappeared, he headed in the direction of North Hill.

He was exhausted by the time he came alongside the church. His back hurt from the jump – he thought he must have jarred it when the parachute opened – and his wrist was now painful, and he noticed his boots were covered in mud and was just grateful the soldiers hadn't appeared to notice that, too.

But he was nearing the end of his journey, or at least, this stage of it.

'Opposite the church – on the east side of the road – there's a narrow alley. Go down there and take the second left. You'll be in another alley, with the houses on either side backing on to it. On your right you'll see a blue door, which will be unlocked. The path will take you to the back door. There's a bell concealed inside the door frame, so no one need hear you knocking. Press it three times in quick succession, wait a few seconds and then press hard once more. Can you remember all that?'

Something else to remember. 'I'll have to, won't I?'

'You will. And you remember the lady's name?'

'Armstrong. Muriel Armstrong.'

Chapter 25

London
July 1940

When Archie returned, there was as close to a hero's welcome as could be expected of the usually restrained Service.

He'd expected his return journey from Rotterdam to be at least as hazardous as his journey there, but it proved to be anything but. Once he'd made it to Zeebrugge, a rendezvous in the North Sea was arranged within three days, and four days after that he was back in Broadway. People's reactions when they passed him in the corridor ranged from muted surprise to open congratulations.

It had all been rather overwhelming at first, with all the backslapping and the meetings. The Chief had insisted on seeing him within an hour of his return.

'An excellent job,' he said, rising from his desk and coming over to grip Archie's hand and shake it vigorously, showing little sign of letting go. 'Exactly what I want to see more of: senior officers getting out from behind their desks and actually venturing into enemy territory. We're an intelligence organisation, after all, not just a bunch of pen-pushers. You've been a trailblazer.'

Archie managed to pull his hand away from the Chief's grasp and muttered something about how he'd needed a fair degree of luck. The Chief said of course, and perhaps he'd like to write a report on how it was all done.

'You know… the training, how well prepared you need to be. How to prepare yourself… mentally, I think is the word I'm looking for. Think of it as a handbook for other officers we send out into the field.'

Phillips and Piers Devereaux were notably less effusive. Certainly, they were pleased with Archie and, indeed, at one point Phillips had said, 'Well done,' and patted him on the shoulder, but what they were most interested in was a thorough and measured report on the intelligence he'd gathered in Rotterdam.

Archie had rather hoped he'd have a couple of days off first, but he was given a small office on the top floor away from everyone else with a typewriter, with an adjoining bathroom and a camp bed in the corner, and told to get on with it.

It took him two long days, buoyed by the adrenaline of the mission and the dangers he'd faced down. When the report was complete, he handed it to Phillips and then took the weekend off. It was a pity he couldn't tell his wife a thing, because she'd have been impressed. All he was allowed to say was that he'd been away in Scotland, testing new radio equipment. 'In that case,' she'd replied, 'perhaps you could repair the wireless in the drawing room?'

And when he returned on the Monday morning, he was greeted by Phillips, who took him straight to the Chief's office, where they were joined by Devereaux.

The Chief was clearly delighted.

...a remarkable amount of detail... the different types of barges – two thousand of them! – and what they'll be carrying... can't say how useful this is... and the photographs and the drawings – the routes across the Channel – delighted...

'This –' he held the report up high, like a preacher displaying his Bible to the congregation – 'is of enormous significance. It confirms the German plans to invade this country are not just empty propaganda on their part, designed to scare us into holding peace talks with them. The threat is clearly very real and the danger to our shores is imminent. I've no doubt Winston will be most impressed. Absolutely vindicates him. I have to tell you that since your mission to Rotterdam the RAF reconnaissance chaps have been flying over the port, and the photos they've taken most certainly corroborate what you've told us. And you've managed to single-handedly raise the threat of a German invasion to a new level. It's all they're talking about across Whitehall. Quite a few very worried faces, I have to tell you.'

The Chief assured Archie his career in the Service would be a very bright one. By now they were in the doorway, when the Chief said to hang on because there was one more thing. 'The Invasion Warning Sub-Committee caught wind of what you've been up to, and one can't deny they have a certain claim on this, can one... "invasion" being the operative word, eh? Do me a favour and go and see them. Play a very straight bat and give them a very broad sense of what you found out. You don't even need to confirm it was you who went out there. Probably best to keep them guessing. And do try and keep it civil, eh? Winston disapproves of conflict, unless it involves the Germans.'

–

At the Invasion Warning Sub-Committee there'd been discussion about who should attend the meeting with the unnamed man from MI6. At one point Lieutenant Commander McConnell was going to be there along with Cooper and Pamela Clarke, but then they heard Cooper would be turning up alone. McConnell had decided it would be altogether more cordial if Cooper was there on his own.

'Get what you can out of him: sources, in particular. If we're to track down the German espionage operation in this country, this chap may be able to help us. He's bound to have a clue.'

The tension in the room was palpable and it was difficult for both participants – Archie and Cooper – to put their finger on quite what it was, because it remained unarticulated. For both men, it was an unease more than anything else: a sense.

A sense that one didn't trust the other.

A sense that each was not quite who they purported to be – or rather, that as well as being who they purported to be, they may also be someone or something else.

A sense that the other could reveal too much about them and as such represented a considerable threat.

Cooper was using his cover name of Malcolm Lyle. He wasn't sure how forthcoming the man from MI6 would be. Five minutes into the meeting he was even less sure. Archie had handed over a very abridged version of his report: a couple of drawings, no photographs, plenty on the barges and the tonnage of various German military vehicles. Cooper read it carefully and was left with the impression that while it was clearly important, it was of more use to military types than an intelligence operation.

'No questions I take it, Mr Lyle? I think you'll find it's a pretty thorough report.' Archie was leaning back in his chair, one leg crossed high over his thigh and his arms linked behind his head. His louche manner was designed to convey who was in charge, and that wasn't Lyle. The accent and manner descended from generations of people who were used to being in charge. Cooper replied that it was indeed a very thorough report, and he wondered if there was anything Archie had picked up in Rotterdam relating to how the invasion was being assisted in this country.

'Afraid you'll need to be a touch clearer.' A thin smile from Archie, one which couldn't have been less friendly. People like him were trained to imbue a smile with such menace.

'Was your source able to provide any intelligence on Nazi espionage operations in this country and the local support they may receive?'

'No.'

It was a warm day in late July, but Cooper felt the temperature in the room had dropped significantly. The other man looked as if he was ready to leave.

'Well, if that's all, Mr Lyle.'

'Your source... I understand how you'd obviously not wish to divulge their identity, and they're clearly very well placed, but it seems to me to be remarkably fortuitous that this source came to you via this chap Brouwer at St Christopher's Hospital, who you just happened to come across and managed to get to just a matter of days before he died, and he's able to give you a direct lead to such an excellent source.'

Archie unlinked his hands from behind his head and placed them on the table in front of him, the fingertips of each hand touching.

'And your point is... Mr Lyle?' He was staring hard at Cooper.

'Well... my point is that it's most fortuitous.'

'As you said, Mr Lyle. One finds that often hard work is rewarded thus.'

'And no leads at all on whatever contacts they have in this country?'

'No,' said the man still only known as D4 from MI6, who, with that, stood up and bid Cooper a good day before leaving the room.

—

Cooper remained in the room for a good while after the man from MI6 left. He was suspicious because the man had pointedly failed to answer his question about the lucky encounter with the Dutchman in the hospital.

And as he marched down Whitehall towards Parliament Square and from there back to St James's, Archie was suspicious, too. There was something about Malcolm Lyle which made him wonder whether he really was Malcolm Lyle. Throughout the meeting, he'd been mindful of Morozov's plea to help him track down the Englishman, Cooper. Could Lyle and Cooper be one and the same? He'd have to meet the Russian. A meeting was long overdue anyway.

Chapter 26

London
July 1940

At first, the woman looked at Manfred as if he was something the cat had brought home, so much so he momentarily forgot what he was meant to say. When he finally remembered, he spoke a bit too fast.

'I've travelled from Ipswich. Your cousin Henry said perhaps I could stay here.'

She was a large woman who looked as if she was coping very well with rationing, and she nodded as if she now understood and a smile crossed her face, revealing an uneven set of yellow teeth. 'Henry and his wife are so hospitable. How is she?'

She'd remembered her own response easily enough.

'Margaret? She seems very well. You must be Muriel.'

Muriel Armstrong nodded and said he'd better come in and would he like a cup of tea, and Manfred said yes please.

'You'd better get those boots off, dear. We'll have to get them cleaned. I'm not going to ask how you got here, but you're sure you weren't followed?'

Manfred said he was sure, as he watched in horror as she poured copious amounts of hot milk into the mug of already weak tea. The kitchen was cramped and stuffy, with oversized items of stained underwear hung from the ceiling to dry. A large greyish bra dangled inches from his head.

'You're my first guest, if you see what I mean... from The Group, that is. I've been told you'll stay here for a day or two while I contact the right people and then you'll be moved on. We all have to do our bit, don't we?'

'We certainly do.'

'Can't be having this lot leading the country astray, letting the Jews take over everything and the communists run the place. The sooner the Germans take over, the better!'

'Are you here on your own, dear?'

She nodded in a resigned manner. 'Afraid so, ever since that so-and-so of a husband left me for his fancy lady in Chelmsford and my Nigel joined the Merchant Navy. I keep myself to myself. I do what I can to help The Group.' She paused, looking at him through suspicious eyes. 'You're not English, are you?'

'I think the less you know about me the safer it is all round, don't you agree?'

'I was hoping for a German. When I said I wanted a German they said I had to take what I was given.'

–

He never did tell her, though it certainly wasn't for the want of trying on her part. In the three days Manfred spent with her she constantly pried: she'd always wanted to visit Germany; what was the best place there to visit; was German a difficult language; is it really true there are no Jews left in Germany?

And to every question, Manfred told her he had no idea. He was just Albert Heath from Ipswich.

He couldn't wait to leave. On the morning he'd arrived he was so exhausted he went to bed, and when he woke up in the afternoon he asked if he could take a bath and she reluctantly agreed. It was not a comfortable experience: although the door was closed, he suspected he was being watched. And that night, Muriel Armstrong tapped on his door at midnight and, without waiting for a response, entered the room and sat on the bed, closer than he was comfortable with, and said if he was 'lonely' at all he should let her know.

He said he was fine, thank you.

He'd arrived at her house early on the Friday morning and could have wept with joy when, on the Sunday evening, she announced he'd be moving on the following day. They were at the kitchen table, listening to a comedy programme on the radio, which was barely audible through the static, but that didn't stop her laughing noisily, tears streaming down her cheeks.

'Here's your train ticket, dear,' she said as she dabbed her face with a filthy handkerchief and passed an envelope to him. 'There's cash in it, too. I've been told to tell you that you're to leave here at ten tomorrow morning and walk down to the station. There's a train at 10:25 to London. When you get to Liverpool Street Station you're to head to Finsbury Circus.'

She leant back in her chair and folded her arms across her chest.

'And then what?'

'That's all I've been told. Head to Finsbury Circus. I've no idea if that's even a real circus! Looks like you're being passed up the chain. Who knows, you may even get to meet the big cheese!'

'Who is that?'

'That would be telling, wouldn't it? I've heard about them but never met them. They deal directly with Germans, I'm told. Not even sure I should have been told that. Best keep it to yourself, dear.'

–

Manfred did as he'd been told. He assumed he'd be watched as soon as his train arrived at Liverpool Street, and he'd just crossed Wilson Street towards Finsbury Circus when a tall man appeared alongside him.

He was dressed for the City and doffed his bowler hat. 'Please follow me.'

Manfred followed the man as they headed back towards Liverpool Street Station and onto Bishopsgate. As they approached the junction with Old Street, the man paused to allow Manfred to catch up with him.

'We'll catch a number 22 bus to Dalston. I'll sit on the upper deck, and you should do likewise, sit a few rows diagonally behind me. Follow me when I leave the bus.'

Manfred followed the man as instructed when the bus stopped close to Homerton Station, and they headed north onto Lower Clapton Road. The man turned right into a side street and then left before heading up the path of a semi-detached house. Once inside, he turned to face Manfred.

'English or German?'

'Pardon?'

'Would you prefer I speak in German or English? My German is pretty damn good, you know – *ich spreche sehr fliessend Deutsch!*'

'I think we ought to speak in English.'

'Very well, then.' The man looked disappointed at having been denied the opportunity to demonstrate his linguistic skills. 'You'll be here on your own. There's food in the kitchen. Under no circumstances whatsoever are you to leave the house, do you understand?'

'How long will this—'

'I've no idea. You're to be patient. Don't turn on any lights or appear by a window or make any noise. The house will be locked from the outside. Someone will come to see you, someone very important. But you're not to worry, you're in the system now.'

When the man left, Manfred heard the front door being locked from the outside. He remained in the hall for a while and then walked through the kitchen and tried the back door, which was also locked. There was a loaf of bread in the kitchen and some milk on the side, along with a large tin of broken biscuits and a few tins of Spam and soup next to a bag of potatoes and half a dozen shrivelled apples, but that was about it.

He was trapped in a house in Dalston and felt thoroughly miserable. He thought about what Cooper had told him before he'd left for Hamburg back in May.

'…you'll be given contacts, and we need you to go along with that and it's imperative we know who these people are. Don't attempt to get in touch with us until it is safe to do so and until you believe you've exhausted your contact chain.'

The contact chain. The man in the bowler hat had assured him he was 'in the system now' and that someone 'very important' would come to see him.

He'd just have to wait.

–

He waited for four days. The days themselves were not too bad, if one discounted the sheer boredom, relieved only by the fact that he found a few dusty volumes of Dickens on a bookshelf in the lounge. He'd sit in one corner of the lounge, the curtains drawn, reading by the little light which came in from the hall.

But the nights were terrifying: he'd lie on the bed, fully dressed, wide awake and waiting for the air-raid siren to pierce through the city, and when it did – every night he was there – he'd hurry to the cupboard under the stairs, which he'd cleared out so there was enough room for him.

And there he'd stay, for hours at a time, terrified by the tremors and crashing around him. It felt as if he were at the epicentre of the air raid, and he feared that if the house was hit no one would bother searching an empty property.

Around six o'clock on the Friday evening he was in the kitchen preparing himself a Spam sandwich when he froze. There was a noise from the hallway: a key turning in the lock, then the door slowly opening and slow footsteps in the hall.

Manfred grabbed the small table knife he'd been using to slice the Spam and watched the kitchen door. When it swung open, he found himself staring at a woman perhaps in her forties, with a short haircut and a figure you'd have to describe as thin rather than slim. She was wearing a coat despite the warm weather and carrying a shopping bag as well as a handbag. She looked at him and then at the knife, which he realised he was brandishing in her direction, so he put it down.

The woman pulled up a chair and sat opposite him. From her handbag she produced a packet of cigarettes and a lighter and began smoking, without offering.

'You're going by the name of Albert Heath?'

He nodded.

'From now on you'll be known as Agent Stettin. Let me see your papers.'

He passed them to her. 'That's good enough for the time being. After your first mission we'll find you another identity. Did Hamburg tell you where to go?'

'They said to Pevensey Bay, between Bexhill and Eastbourne.'

'As a landing beach, I guess?'

Manfred shrugged. 'They want me to check the defences and get what I can on the beaches.'

She smiled and said it was about time, too. 'When you've gathered your intelligence you're to return to London. By Homerton Station there are three telephone kiosks. Next to the telephone in the middle kiosk there's a small shelf. You'll find a small piece of chalk taped under it. Use that chalk to mark four "x"s' on the inside of the door. I'll check it every day, so I'll know you're back. Then come back here. I'll show you where the back door key is concealed.'

'That's all?'

'That's all. You'll hand over your intelligence to me and I'll get it passed back to Hamburg. At last, we're getting something done now. Hardly any of the agents who've been sent over make it as far as me. Heaven knows what's been happening to them. I dread to think. You're to know me as Agent Lübeck.'

Chapter 27

Hamburg, Ireland and London
July 1940

Within MI6 the phrase used to describe the process of bringing agents back from an operation was 'coming in from games', its origins inevitably being the public-school background which pervaded the organisation. The image of a perspiring agent returning to base muddy and exhausted was an apt one.

Sometimes it was the handler who decided when to bring the agent in at what they believed was the optimum time, when they'd got as much as they were going to get out of an operation. At other times it would be the agent's call: maybe they would decide it was too dangerous to carry on, or the intelligence they'd gathered was too important not to be passed on there and then.

And of course, there were times when an operation had come to an end, sometimes through failure, at other times through disaster, and in those circumstances it would be a matter of fortune or otherwise if an agent was able to return at all.

But if it was the agent making the call – literally to come in from games – then they'd make a telephone call with a prearranged code.

In Manfred's case, he decided the time had come following the visit of the woman who called herself Agent Lübeck to the house near Homerton Station. He'd left the house with her and had been supposed to head south, to gather intelligence around Pevensey Bay, and on his return to the house leave the mark in the middle telephone kiosk by Homerton Station.

But Manfred never did travel as far south as Pevensey Bay. Once he reached Victoria Station and was satisfied he'd not been followed, he headed for a telephone box and did what Cooper had told him when he left the safe house in May before his mission to Hamburg.

It was a woman who answered WHI 7492.

'I purchased a jacket from you in May and I wish to return it now.'

'Very well…' A slight pause and the rustling of paper. 'May I ask, is the jacket damaged?'

'No, it doesn't fit properly.'

'Very good, then.' The code assured her that Manfred wasn't in immediate danger. 'I'll have a word with the manager. If you'd be so good as to call back in a quarter of an hour.'

An hour and a half later Manfred was reunited with Cooper and Pamela. He repeated the description of the woman who'd come to the house and went over once again what she'd told him to do.

There was some discussion as to whether Manfred had brought himself in from games too early, but they gave him the benefit of the doubt. There wasn't much else they could do.

At that point Cooper contacted Superintendent Martin Docherty, his main contact at Special Branch. The two men got on well together. They did each other favours.

Docherty undertook to help trace the woman who'd called herself Agent Lübeck, but to no avail. They left a mark as instructed in the telephone kiosk outside Homerton Station and kept the area under observation, but no one matching her description approached the middle kiosk.

She must suspect something, they decided. Maybe Manfred had enjoyed a lucky escape.

–

There were few on the IRA Army Council who wouldn't concede that Operation Hamburg, as they'd rather grandly called it, had been ill conceived and poorly executed.

It had seemed like a good idea when it was first proposed, although no one would actually admit to being the person who came up with the idea in the first place.

The problems began on the two IRA men's journey back from Hamburg. Their Abwehr case officer in Hamburg, Günter König, had accompanied them to the submarine base in Wilhelmshaven and watched as the two Irishmen were led onto U-65, the submarine which would take them close to the Irish coast. Although he felt positive about the mission – Joey Gallagher was indeed a bright man and seemed to have fully grasped the details of his clandestine operation in England – König had his doubts about Sean Maguire, but didn't worry too much as it was unlikely he'd be travelling to England.

But König was concerned that Gallagher was clearly unwell. He had been when he arrived in Hamburg, and although he'd seen various doctors none of them could diagnose anything. They said it could be nerves, while Gallagher himself said maybe it was the German food.

Gallagher's health deteriorated on the voyage, much to the annoyance of Maguire. The two men didn't get on particularly well as it was, and Maguire found having to share a tiny cabin with someone who was continually throwing up was more than he could cope with.

About fifty miles off the west coast of Ireland, U-65 rendezvoused with a small Irish trawler. Joey Gallagher had to be carried onto the trawler and was barely conscious when the boat docked at Rossaveal in Connemara. He was treated by a local doctor and then taken to Dublin, where he was admitted under an assumed name to a hospital that had an understanding with the IRA.

The following day the doctor treating Gallagher met with MacBride and Duffy from the Army Council.

'Is there a possibility of his being able to travel, Doctor?'

'Travel where?'

'To the mainland, Doctor.'

The doctor had stared at them as if they were out of their minds. 'The only way your man will travel to the mainland is in a coffin, boys. When he arrived here yesterday there was a possibility he wouldn't make it through the night. He has a very serious liver condition. We've stabilised him and he has a chance of getting through it now, but he's out of action for the time being.'

'Weeks?'

'Months, boys.'

–

When the Army Council met the following day, they agreed that Operation Hamburg must continue. Although the Germans hadn't actually promised to send weapons in as many words, there was an understanding that these would be forthcoming if the IRA carried out espionage on their behalf on the mainland.

So, the mission would have to go ahead, despite Gallagher's unfortunate indisposition. And if this mission contributed in some way to a successful German invasion of the British mainland, then all the better. If that happened, then there was a possibility that within weeks the Republicans could be in control of the whole island of Ireland.

And notwithstanding some reservations about him, it was further agreed that Sean Maguire would take Gallagher's place. Sure, the Wexford man could be hot-headed and possibly even unreliable at times, but he had been through all the training in Hamburg and knew what to do. And although considerable doubts were raised about his suitability, these were soon dismissed.

First, they had to get him over there, which was no longer the simple matter it once was. When the war started the British authorities had passed an Emergency Powers Act. Travellers to Britain from Ireland needed to show they had employment arranged and a travel permit – a Travel Identity Card – issued by the Garda, the Irish police.

Sean Maguire was summoned back from County Wexford, where he'd gone to rest after the stay in Hamburg. In the space of one hour, he was presented with a new identity – Ciarán Byrne – and a letter from a builder in Wimbledon in south London offering him employment as a bricklayer. He was driven to the Garda station in Pearse Street to obtain his permit.

He spent the night in an IRA safe house in Tallaght where he was briefed on his mission: who to contact in London and what to do once he was there. It was obvious to all present that Maguire was not in a great state: he seemed nervous and had clearly been drinking a lot, and perhaps as a result of that had trouble grasping what he was meant to do. One or two people present felt that they ought to delay his mission until Maguire was better prepared.

But in the end, it was felt that the sooner he got over to the mainland, the sooner the Germans would start supplying weapons to the IRA, and the sooner Britain would fall to the Germans and the sooner there'd be a united Ireland.

So, Sean Maguire – now Ciarán Byrne – was woken at four in the morning and given one final briefing. He was then driven the short journey to the port at Dún Laoghaire, from where he was to catch the mail boat to Holyhead on Anglesey in North Wales.

Maguire first ever visit to the British mainland was taken aboard the London, Midland and Scottish Railway's TSS *Hibernia*. He spent the journey in a miserable state, still hungover from the night before and nervous about what lay ahead. Despite the wind and the rain, he spent much of the five-hour voyage pacing the decks, going over and over in his mind what he'd been told.

Ciarán Byrne was not in itself a difficult name to remember, but when you'd been Sean Maguire all your life it was another matter, especially when the name Ciarán Byrne was easily confused with Ciarán Kelly, his best friend from County Wexford.

And that would be his undoing when TSS *Hibernia* docked at Holyhead.

–

When Jack Brown was transferred to Special Branch and promoted to inspector, he had every expectation of great things. When he was posted to run the Special Branch operation at the port in Holyhead, he wondered how good a career move this was.

But that didn't stop him being utterly professional. It had been made clear to him that as the Dún Laoghaire mail boats were the main route from Ireland to Britain, then that was the most likely way the IRA would send people across. 'We may be at war with Germany, Brown, but they're not our only enemy!'

And so, when his sergeant took him aside on a wet Wednesday morning, Inspector Jack Brown took what he had to say very seriously.

'I'm slightly concerned about this passenger.' He showed Brown a Travel Identity Card in the name of Ciarán Byrne with an address in Dublin.

'What's the problem?'

'When he was asked to confirm his name, he said it was Ciarán Kelly, before quickly correcting it to Ciarán Byrne. And when I checked his case, I came across this.' He handed a card to Brown. It was an Irish driving permit in the name of Sean Maguire from Enniscorthy in County Wexford.

'I don't think he meant for us to see that, because it was inside a jacket.'

'So, we don't know if this chap is Ciarán Kelly or Ciarán Byrne or Sean Maguire?'

'There's more, sir. A Sean Maguire with the same address is on our IRA watch list.'

'Have you confronted him about this?'

'No, sir, I thought I'd best mention it to you first.'

'Well done, Sergeant. And his onward travel arrangements?'

'He has a ticket for the noon train to London Euston.'

'Single or return?'

'Single, sir.'

Inspector Brown glanced at his watch and closed his eyes for a moment in contemplation.

'Very well, Sergeant. Go back to the man and apologise for keeping him and assure him all his papers are in order and he's free to carry on. Don't forget to apologise. And make sure you smile.'

'Really, sir?'

'Really, Sergeant, yes. I shall follow him on the train, and you're to telephone London and pass on all the relevant details so that when he arrives at Euston he can be followed. If he is here on IRA business, then he's clearly up to no good and we need to know just what that no good is.'

–

Thanks to the very cordial relations that existed between the Invasion Warning Sub-Committee and Special Branch, Cooper was the first person outside the police to hear about the Irishman.

Superintendent Martin Docherty had contacted Cooper soon after the Irishman's arrest. Ciarán Byrne, he was told, had arrived at Euston Station on a train from Holyhead just before ten o'clock on the Wednesday night. The first place he went to was the Royal George, just round the corner from the station, where he ordered a pint of bitter with a whiskey chaser before using the pay phone close by the toilets.

According to the Special Branch men watching him, the Irishman left the pub soon after that, walking east along Euston Road, pausing a couple of times to ask people for directions. He walked past King's Cross Station and then turned left into Caledonian Road. In the pitch dark of the blackout, it was tricky for the men to follow him, but eventually they spotted him waiting at a bus stop, and five minutes later two of them followed him onto the number 659 bus in the direction of Walthamstow.

The bus passed through Islington and Tottenham and into Edmonton, where he got off at Silver Street Station.

At that point, he looked a very confused man. 'Like a lost boy,' one of those following him said later. He stood in the gloom, no light from anywhere to pick him out, a dark figure barely visible in the shadows. And then he went into a telephone kiosk, which was lit by the weakest of dim yellow lights.

Five minutes later a woman came into view, suddenly appearing out of the dark from an alley by the station. She knocked on the kiosk and the Irishman emerged. They appeared to be introducing themselves to each other – slight bows of the head and a handshake – and then they walked away together, up Victoria Road in the direction of Pymmes Park.

Once the pair had been followed to a house near the park, a decision had to be made by the senior Special Branch officer on duty at Scotland Yard.

Protocol stated that MI5 should be informed unless there were extenuating circumstances, but as far as Special Branch were concerned MI5 had not exactly been playing ball with them recently when it came to arrests. These, he decided, counted as extenuating circumstances. He ordered that the house should be raided at first light and the occupants arrested.

Special Branch could hardly believe their luck. The man and the woman who'd met at Silver Street Station the previous night were the only occupants of the house. During a search, Special Branch found a radio transmitter set in the attic, along with a concealed aerial and code books. When they confronted the woman with this, she said she'd only speak further if she could have a solicitor.

It was explained to her that under wartime regulations this would not be possible, and she was reminded that the maximum penalty under the Treachery Act was death.

At this point she broke down and admitted her real name was Bridget McKearney. She insisted that she'd been forced into spying for the Germans by the IRA, who had told her they'd harm her family in County Donegal if she didn't co-operate. The man who'd arrived last night was one of them.

All of which meant that by the time they got to Scotland Yard, Ciarán Byrne was in an awkward position. The two men interviewing him were Inspector Jack Brown, who'd followed him from Holyhead, and Superintendent Martin Docherty. Brown was able to confront him with the fact that he'd initially given his name as Ciarán Kelly at Holyhead and was carrying an Irish driving permit in the name of Sean Maguire from Enniscorthy in County Wexford, which they'd subsequently discovered in the house in Edmonton.

And would that, he was asked, be the very same Sean Maguire from Enniscorthy in County Wexford who was a member of the IRA.

Maguire had no idea how to cope with all this, especially when the workings of the Treachery Act and the death penalty it carried were carefully explained to him.

He was quite overwhelmed. It wasn't his fault he was in this position. It was typical of the high-ups in Dublin to throw someone like him into a situation like this. Hamburg had been bad enough – he'd never really known why he'd been sent there – but now it looked like this trip to London could end at the gallows.

'If I were to co-operate with you, would that make a death sentence less likely?'

Docherty said, 'Most probably, yes.' He was struggling to conceal his delight.

'Because there are quite a few things I could tell you about the Germans planning the invasion of your country. Surely that's worth sparing me, sir?'

–

It was at this point – the mention of the word 'invasion' – that Docherty had called in his friend Cooper from the Invasion Warning Sub-Committee, and Cooper joined the two Special Branch men in the interrogation room.

Maguire told them everything: the trip to Hamburg; Joe Gallagher; the Abwehr; where they were trained and Günter König; and the journey back to Ireland in a U-boat.

That was all fine, he was told, but what were they being trained to do in Hamburg?

'Help the Germans prepare for an invasion of your country, sir. There's something called "The Group", which this woman at whose house you found me runs. We were to work with them to gather information to be passed on to the Germans. And in return, the IRA would be sent weapons and munitions by the Germans, and we'd be in a favourable position when they invade your country.'

'Favourable in what respect, Maguire?'

'We'd get given the whole of Ireland, sir. At least, that's what we hoped.'

Cooper took over the questioning. 'You say "when they invade your country", Mr Maguire. Is that correct?'

'Indeed, sir.'

'You sound certain that they're going to invade. What makes you so sure?'

'Well, sir, you'll understand that I wasn't the main man in Hamburg, by any means. That would be Joe. If he was here, he'd be able to tell you everything. But I'm not quite the fool that people think I am. I kept my ears open, and I picked up plenty from Mr König and Joe and others like Mr Schröder. And I can tell you, sir, not only do they plan to invade but they even have a date!'

When Cooper described this moment to Pamela later, he said the atmosphere in the room became so charged it was as if the room was lifted high above the ground.

They waited for Maguire to volunteer the date, but he stayed silent with a grin of sorts across his face.

'And may I ask, do you know that date, by any chance?' Cooper did his best to sound matter-of-fact.

'Of course I do, sir!'

There was a stirring in the room. Cooper said later he worried Maguire was playing games with them.

'And perhaps you could share that date with us, Mr Maguire?'

'If I do so, sir, there'd be no more talk about a sentence of death, would there?'

Cooper heard one of the Special Branch men say, 'Absolutely.'

'Very well, then... It's the twelfth of September, sir, which I think you'll find is a Thursday. They call it *Donnerstag*, but I think it's the same thing.'

Chapter 28

During his journey back from Rotterdam in the fourth week of July, and certainly once he arrived back in London, Archie had come to realise how reckless he'd been with the German officer: using 'Oriel' in the name of the fake engineering company was a serious mistake. It was yet another example of him thinking he was being clever. By choosing the name of his former college at Oxford, he'd obligingly provided a link to him: a possible clue as to his identity should anyone bother to delve further.

He needed to find a way of stopping anyone connecting the letter with him. His solution was his colleague Gilbert Cavendish, an unassuming type, a bit older than him and someone often unkindly referred to as a 'late starter'. No one had a bad word to say about Cavendish, but few had much positive to say about him either; he was regarded as reliable and loyal, certainly, but perhaps a bit plodding. 'Lacking flair', someone had once said, and that had stuck in Archie's mind. He'd been surprised that Cavendish had been promoted along with the others.

During a break in writing his report for the Chief he'd sought Cavendish out and suggested a walk in St James's Park, and Cavendish was clearly thrilled to have been asked. Archie asked Cavendish how he was and congratulated him on the birth of his latest child. Noticing that the somewhat chubby man was out of breath – he'd once unwisely admitted to having been called 'Podge' at school – Archie suggested they sit down on a bench by the lake.

'I wonder if you'd be able to do me a huge favour, Gilbert?'

Cavendish said he was always happy to help.

'I'm afraid that for reasons which are far too boring to go into, I've ever so slightly queered the pitch with the Scandinavian Desk at the

Foreign Office. Nothing serious, and the Chief and Devereaux know all about it and they think the Foreign Office is overacting – as is their wont. However...'

He lowered his voice and leant forward, closer to Cavendish, who did likewise.

'It means, though, that... Well, let me put it like this. I'm expecting an important letter to be sent on by our embassy in Stockholm. Given the unfortunate frisson which exists between me and the Scandinavian desk, I'd prefer it if I wasn't the one they associated with the letter.'

Cavendish blinked rapidly as he stared at a family of ducks paddling by.

'So, I'd be forever grateful, Gilbert, if you were to contact the Scandinavian Desk and say if and when a letter arrives in the bag from Stockholm for a Mr Oscar Smith of Oriel Engineering, then it's for you.'

'That's all?' Cavendish looked at him, still blinking fast.

'And if you could contact them today, that would be much appreciated.'

Cavendish nodded. 'And there's no comeback on this for me?'

'Good heavens no, Gilbert! Quite the opposite, in fact. Lots of slaps on the back and a good dinner at my club, eh? Best not to let anyone know about this because of the sensitivity, but I'll make sure the Chief knows quite how helpful you've been.'

–

It had rained pretty much non-stop over the weekend, and when Archie arrived in Broadway on the morning of Monday, 2 September, he was drenched. He'd not yet dried out when there was a tentative tap on his door and the smiling rounded face of Gilbert Cavendish appeared.

'I took a call from Wells at the Foreign Office.'

Archie asked who Wells from the Foreign Office was.

'You know – Scandinavian Desk! You asked me the other week to contact them about a letter arriving from Stockholm.'

'Ah, yes. And...?'

'And it's arrived! I feel like the postman at Christmas!'

With a broad smile on his face, Cavendish presented an envelope to Archie.

c/o British Embassy Stockholm

Mr Oscar Smith

Chairman, Oriel Engineering

London

Archie held the envelope in both hands and was effusive in his thanks, and told Cavendish to let him know when a good evening for dinner would be.

Once Cavendish had left, Archie opened the envelope.

All it contained was a sheet of paper: the month of September torn out of what was clearly a German calendar. A circle was drawn around a *Donnerstag*: 12 September.

Archie sat very still, oblivious now to the heaviness of his soaking wet suit and the greasy sheen on his body from the rain and the perspiration. He was almost afraid. He glanced out of the window across the streets of St James's and Victoria and pictured German columns marching down them.

Ten days until the invasion: Thursday, 12 September.

The irony for Captain Gustaf Lindström was that his smuggling operation had begun as a favour for someone. It wasn't as if he needed the money. Or the trouble, for that matter.

He'd taken over as master of MT *Greta Bengtsson* in December 1939 and it was a steady, well-paid job. Not exactly one which tested his skills as a master mariner or took him to the exotic parts of the world he'd had in mind when he'd joined the merchant navy. Once a week the *Greta Bengtsson* would depart Stockholm with its cargo of fuel and head through the Baltic into the North Sea and dock three days later in Rotterdam and deliver its load.

There'd be one night in Rotterdam, and then they'd begin the return voyage at first tide the following morning.

Until the German invasion, Rotterdam had been a pleasant port in which to spend a night, but that all changed after the Nazis occupied the city in May 1940. The movements of foreign crew were restricted and the air of menace which had fallen over the city made trips ashore less pleasant. But there was a bar on Parkhaven which remained friendly enough.

And that was where his problems began.

The bar on Parkhaven was run by a large Dutchman called Cornelis, who always greeted Lindström as a long-lost friend. The Swede smoked Gauloises cigarettes, which were popular in Sweden and easily obtained. Cornelis enjoyed Gauloises, too, but they were less easy to get hold of in Rotterdam and, after the Nazi occupation, almost impossible to buy.

One evening Lindström left what remained of his packet with Cornelis and on his next trip he brought a packet for him. Cornelis suggested that if his good friend Gustaf could bring a few more packets, then he'd happily exchange them for alcohol. By the end of June Gustaf Lindström was bringing twenty packets at a time, and in return Cornelis would give him two or three bottles of spirits, which he had a good supply of. Sometimes it was vodka, other times whisky – all of which he could sell in Stockholm.

On a pleasant Wednesday evening in August – the 21st – he was walking back to the *Greta Bengtsson* from the bar on Parkhaven with two bottles of Polish vodka in his knapsack when he was stopped by a tall German in Kriegsmarine uniform.

'Papers, please.'

Lindström showed his papers, including his shore pass, and asked if there was a problem, and the German asked to see inside his knapsack.

'Do you have a permit for these, Captain?'

'I didn't realise I needed a permit.'

'But you have a receipt, then?'

'I'm sorry, sir, there's clearly been a misunderstanding. Had I realised I needed such documents, then of course—'

'This is a very serious matter. Do you realise that?'

Lindström said he hadn't realised it was such a serious matter. From his wallet he produced a high-denomination Swedish krona note and offered it to the German.

'Are you attempting to bribe a German officer? That is an even more serious matter. I could have your vessel impounded!'

The Swede knew what a serious matter that would be: if the *Greta Bengtsson* was even a day late back into Stockholm, the owners would be furious. He'd almost certainly lose his job and his master's licence. He apologised profusely and said if there was anything he could do

– anything – to clear up this misunderstanding, then he'd be more than happy to oblige.

'Come with me.'

The German officer led him into an empty office close to the quay where his ship was docked. He locked the door and closed the blinds.

'I am prepared to overlook these matters if you do me a favour.'

'Of course, sir, of course...'

'Do you know where the British embassy is in Stockholm?'

'Yes, it's in Diplomatstaden. I had to go there for a visa once.'

'When you return to Stockholm, I want you to go there and hand this letter over to someone senior. Do you understand?'

Lindström took the envelope. It was addressed:

c/o British Embassy Stockholm

Mr Oscar Smith

Chairman, Oriel Engineering

London

'That's all?'

'That's all: but I shall know whether you've given them the letter. If not, when you return to Rotterdam there'll be very serious repercussions.'

–

Korvettenkapitän Arthur Klein watched as the Swedish captain hurried along the quay towards MT *Greta Bengtsson*. He was pleased with a job well done. Of course, he'd have no way of knowing if the letter was handed in to the British Embassy in Stockholm, but the Swede didn't know that. Klein had no doubt he'd deliver the letter.

There was a definite spring to his step as he headed back to his apartment.

As he passed Coolhaven and crossed the road towards Heemraadssingel he became aware of a man some twenty yards in front of him who kept glancing round, and two more at a similar distance behind him. He was certain no one had been following him when he left the docks. He stopped to put a foot onto a low railing and adjust a shoelace. The pair behind him also stopped.

Klein wondered about turning round and heading away from Heemraadssingel, but where could he go? In any case, it may just be his imagination that he was being followed – he had been living off his nerves recently. But as he approached the building where he lived, two men got out of one of the long black Mercedes parked there and approached him.

He should keep walking to the next block, they said, and Klein knew what that meant, because the Gestapo headquarters for Rotterdam was on the next block, and now he had no idea what to think.

–

The previous week had been a busy one back in Berlin for Arthur Klein. He'd arrived on the Saturday and spent most of Sunday with Frieda.

They'd arranged to have lunch because Frieda was due to spend the afternoon at her aunt's house in Grunewald, but halfway through the meal they found themselves holding hands, reluctant to let go. Frieda said, just for once, her aunt would have to hold her Sunday afternoon *salon* without her niece present.

They left the cafe on the Unter den Linden and strolled down to the Tiergarten, where they walked arm in arm for nearly two hours. Klein made sure that at one point they passed the row of three benches where Ernst Schwarz would leave a chalk mark on one of the legs. But there was none there, and instead they sat on one of the benches and Frieda said that she would quite understand if Arthur felt she was being at all… presumptuous, if that was the right word, but both of her flatmates would be away for the weekend and would he like to come back to her apartment?

He replied, no, he didn't think she was being at all presumptuous, and they burst out laughing at the same moment.

When they arrived at her apartment on Budapester Strasse it was clear she'd prepared for this. The flat was neat and tidy, with vases of fresh flowers in the lounge and her bedroom, and she lit candles in both rooms and produced a cake, which she just happened to have baked that morning.

'Would you like some, Arthur? It's a *Marmorkuchen* — my grand-mother's recipe. And there's a schnapps, too. They go well together!'

'That sounds like a good idea, thank you!'

She hesitated. 'In fact, Arthur, I have an even better idea. Maybe we have our cake and schnapps afterwards!'

It was two hours before they got round to the cake and schnapps. He'd been nervous at first, but that quickly disappeared because it seemed so natural and so perfect, and Frieda was so beautiful and not at all shy.

When they lay in her bed afterwards, covered in the crumbs from the *Marmorkuchen* and giggling from the schnapps, Arthur felt life was about as perfect as it could get. He thought about when a good time would be to ask Frieda if she'd like to come with him to Aachen to meet his family.

It was slightly awkward when he reported for duty at eight o'clock the next morning at the Shell-Haus. Frieda arrived an hour later, and they made a point of avoiding any eye contact with each other, even when Rear Admiral Kurt Fricke asked Klein if he remembered Frieda.

Most of that day was spent in deep discussion with Fricke and Vice Admiral Otto Schniewind: Klein briefing them, the two admirals asking him a series of searching questions. During the day different officers and other officials would be brought in, but they spent the time going through the details of the barges in considerable detail. The table was covered with charts and diagrams, and the walls hung with lists of different types of barges and what they could carry. An enormous map was produced, showing the routes from various ports across the North Sea and the Channel and potential landing zones in Britain.

It was nine o'clock when Fricke said they would call it a day.

'Tomorrow all this information will be presented to Grand Admiral Raeder, and on Wednesday we all gather for a conference on the invasion.'

'I thought the Führer had already decided it is happening, sir?'

'But not the date, Klein, that has yet to be announced. I expect we will be told on Wednesday. Make sure you're around tomorrow, we will need you to check everything once more.'

—

Klein spent the Tuesday at the Kriegsmarine headquarters, still avoiding any contact with Frieda. He was due to return to Rotterdam on the Thursday and he and Freida had agreed to have dinner on the Wednesday night, and she promised to spend that night with him in Charlottenburg.

He left the Shell-Haus at lunchtime on the Tuesday and headed for the grocery shop on the corner of Lutzowstrasse and Woyrschstrasse. The woman behind the counter – the one who always reminded him of a character from a Wagner opera – was the only person in the shop. She glared suspiciously at him as he entered, and glanced through the window in case he'd been followed.

'Please can you tell him I'm in Berlin until Thursday? I need to see him before then.'

He knew he'd broken protocol. He should have gone through the nonsense of buying honey and arranging a meeting that way.

'Maybe you can suggest to him that we meet here tomorrow evening? The shop has a back entrance, doesn't it?'

Given the invidious position he'd put her in, she looked surprisingly calm.

'What time tomorrow evening?'

'Let's say seven?'

'I'll see what he says. If the meeting's on, then I'll place this large jar of pickled cucumbers in the window – this one, here. There's an alleyway just past the shop. You enter the back entrance from there. I'll leave the door unlocked.'

Klein was relieved. Meetings with Schwarz rarely lasted more than half an hour. He'd arrange to meet Frieda for dinner at eight o'clock.

–

The conference with Grand Admiral Raeder on the Wednesday had been held in a large stuffy basement of the Shell-Haus with nearly fifty officers present, all of whom were involved in different aspects of the planning of the invasion of Great Britain.

The head of the Kriegsmarine even singled Klein out for a special mention – 'excellent work by Korvettenkapitän Klein in Rotterdam, most thorough. Who knew there were so many barges in Europe?'

– and just before they broke for lunch, Raeder asked everyone to pay attention.

'Although the aerial assault of Britain is not going as well as the Luftwaffe expected, we have reached the point where the Führer believes we need to fix a firm date to work to for the invasion of Great Britain. If we do not, then we simply cannot plan properly.'

The grand admiral looked around the room.

'I can tell you that Thursday the twelfth of September – exactly one month from now – has been chosen for the invasion of Great Britain, which will be known as Operation Sea Lion. I've never pretended that a large-scale invasion of this nature is going to be anything other than highly dangerous and complex. But if it succeeds, then it will be the greatest military operation of all time.

'And the war, gentlemen, will be over.'

–

The meeting finished mid-afternoon, which gave Klein time to tell Frieda he'd meet her in Café Kanzler on Kurfürstendamm at eight.

When he approached the shop on Woyrschstrasse the large jar of pickled cucumbers was in the window, meaning the meeting was on. He turned into the alley and pushed open the back door of the shop. It was a small room with boxes piled high and a door leading into a darkened hallway. Ahead of him there, he saw a figure standing motionless in the shadows. It was silent for a moment before he heard Ernst Schwarz's voice say, 'In here.'

There were two chairs in the centre of a storeroom.

'I'd no idea you were returning to Berlin.'

'I thought it best to wait to contact you until I got here. Is everything all right with you, Ernst?'

Schwarz shook his head. 'Berlin gets worse by the day. People one thought one could trust… Either it transpires that trust was misplaced or they disappear. I'm not sure how much longer I can carry on here. What do you have to tell me?'

Klein told him about the conference and the date of 12 September for the planned invasion.

'Moscow will be pleased. And the Englishman who came to Rotterdam… You were able to help him?'

'I hope so.'

'Does he know the date of the invasion?'

'I only found it out today, I just told you.'

'Very well.'

Klein didn't mention his plan to let the Englishman know through Sweden.

'We may not meet for a few more weeks, if not longer. Continue to communicate through Marcus. I'm planning to leave the city. They're looking for people to work on farms in Schleswig-Holstein. That may be safer.'

–

When Klein left the shop and turned into Woyrschstrasse he didn't spot the shabby van parked a few yards from the entrance to the alley. But the people inside it spotted him. They recognised him as the same man who'd entered the alley some twenty minutes earlier, shortly after Schwarz.

There was a hurried discussion as to whether one of them should follow the tall man, but just then they saw Schwarz emerge and they concentrated on him as he was their priority. No doubt, he'd soon oblige them with the name of the other man.

–

An hour after his arrest in Rotterdam, Arthur Klein was taken to the main Gestapo headquarters at Scheveningseweg in The Hague.

No one said a word to him. He acted outraged and said this was no way to treat an officer of the Kriegsmarine and demanded to see a senior officer.

But he was told to shut up, and then pushed into a dark cell with nothing to eat and a stinking bucket in the corner, and a narrow bench to sleep on with a thin blanket reeking of sweat and urine.

The following morning – the Thursday – he was flown to Berlin. His interrogation took place at Prinz-Albrecht-Strasse, the headquarters of the Gestapo. It was very quickly apparent they knew everything. They told him Ernst Schwarz had been arrested the previous Wednesday, soon after the two of them had met.

'We'd seen you leaving the shop on Woyrschstrasse on the Wednesday, but it was only yesterday that Schwarz finally revealed your name, shortly before he died of his injuries. We know he was a senior Soviet agent, and if he resisted for so long giving us your name then you must be especially important. He also told us about the Dutchman, van Leeuwen. He has now been dealt with. The easiest course of action for you would be to tell us everything.'

Over the course of the next three days, Arthur Klein found himself in an increasingly impossible situation. All he could do was deny he'd ever met Ernst Schwarz. But it was hopeless. He was beaten up and tortured, and at one point was convinced he was about to die.

–

He was taken to Plötzensee Prison on the Saturday, by when he had a good idea of his fate. His only consolation was that Frieda's name had never been mentioned. That, and the letter to the Englishman. They'd obviously not seen him hand over the letter to the Swedish captain the night he was arrested.

On the Monday he was dragged into a hearing of the People's Court held in the prison. Within minutes he'd been found guilty of espionage and 'aiding the enemy' and was sentenced to death.

Two days later – the Wednesday – the public prosecutor entered Klein's cell on the ground floor of House Three, which was next to the execution block. Klein was to be beheaded the following morning. He would be given paper and a pencil to write to his family, who would also be sent an invoice of four hundred Reichsmarks to cover the cost of his detention and execution.

'Am I not able to appeal?'

'That has been dealt with.'

–

They came for Klein early on the morning of Thursday, 29 August. He'd read about people showing courage and calm acceptance at times like this, but he was terrified. He'd not slept for one minute the previous night as he struggled to write to his family left-handed, as they had broken most of the fingers on his right hand when he was tortured.

Tears flowed freely down his face as he was marched across the small courtyard. He felt so weak that he stumbled more than once, and by the time they reached the execution shed he had to be dragged in.

He wasn't listening as the public prosecutor read out his death sentence.

All he could think of was Frieda and 12 September.

At least I told them.

That was a victory, of sorts. But as he stared at the guillotine, it felt more like a defeat.

Chapter 29

The atmosphere in the basement offices of the Invasion Warning Sub-Committee in the Old War Office Building had been frayed for the past fortnight, partially due to the air raids, which meant few people were getting a decent night's sleep and were living on their nerves, and also because of a staff meeting the previous week, when Lieutenant Commander McConnell had been considerably franker than many of those present thought wise.

People have their eyes on us, he'd announced. The wolves are at the door, he told his now confused staff. Rather than being a free-standing subcommittee of some other obscure body, there was now talk of them becoming part of the Combined Intelligence Committee, and in the process losing the autonomy they'd hitherto enjoyed. And worse still were the rumours that MI6 was seeking to take over the organisation.

He wanted to reassure them he was doing all he could to defend their interests.

After the meeting he called in some of his staff individually. When he met Cooper, he told him how grateful he was.

'You're doing an excellent job, Cooper. You have an ability to get on with people. That's most important. The Invasion Warning Sub-Committee needs all the friends it can get if it is to survive as a discrete entity. Each and every one of us needs to get out there and cultivate our allies and supporters in and around Whitehall. I sense the Foreign Office may well be sympathetic to us. You reported a meeting recently with a senior chap there, did you not?'

Cooper thought for a moment. 'Ah yes... Robert Wells. We were at the same meeting and walked back to Whitehall together. It was a hot day and we stopped for a drink by the river and got on terribly well.'

'And his job?'

'Runs the Scandinavian Desk. Used to be number two or three in Oslo. Speaks Norwegian – I didn't think anyone spoke Norwegian, apart from Norwegians, of course.'

'Take him out for supper, Cooper, somewhere nice. I'll pick up the bill. Butter him up, get him on our side. Make sure he appreciates just what a good job we do.'

–

They dined at a restaurant in Jermyn Street, and Robert Wells kept repeating, 'Well, this is a real treat!' and nodded in clear agreement when Cooper spoke of the invaluable work done by the Invasion Warning Sub-Committee.

Wells promised to do all he could to put in a good word at the Foreign Office.

'Would you mind terribly if I bent your ear about something now?'

'Of course not, Robert.'

'I don't know how much you chaps in all the different intelligence bodies dotted around London know one another?'

'I'm not too sure what you mean, Robert?'

'Well, there must be hundreds of you. Is it the kind of community, if that's the right word, where everyone knows each other?'

'Far from it… Because of the nature of what we do there's inevitably a lot of secrecy. Often names aren't used, and if they are, they may not be one's actual name.'

'So, you may not be Malcolm Lyle?'

Cooper managed a laugh and said something about not being important enough to be known by anything other than his real name.

'Let me try a name on you, Lyle. Gilbert Cavendish. MI6?'

Cooper shook his head. He'd never come across a Gilbert Cavendish at MI6 and, as far as he was aware, they were now known somewhat ridiculously by a letter and a number, like D4 who'd been to Rotterdam.

'Why do you ask?'

'Slightly awkward this, Lyle, and in normal circumstances I wouldn't raise it, but then you and I are chums now, aren't we, and, well… Well,

I had an odd encounter with Cavendish the other day. Wouldn't mind getting it off my chest.

'Last weekend a letter arrived in the diplomatic bag from our embassy in Stockholm. They put it on a flight to Scone in Scotland and then the bag comes down on the train from Dundee, I think it is. The letter was accompanied by a note from our naval attaché, man called Rice. Evidently, a Swedish tanker skipper by the name of Gustaf Lindström brought the letter to the embassy. As it was a walk-in, as I believe you chaps call it, the man would normally have been seen by George Weston, the MI6 Head of Station there, but he was out of town. The skipper told Rice the letter was very important and had been given to him by a German navy officer in Rotterdam.

'Rice told me he wasn't sure whether he hadn't broken a rule or two, but once the Swede had mentioned a German navy officer, he took it on himself to open the envelope and photograph the contents.'

'So, the envelope had been opened?'

'Rice thought of that. He rewrote the name and address on a new envelope so no one would suspect. I'd already been approached by Gilbert Cavendish at MI6 to look out for a letter to a Mr Oscar Smith of Oriel Engineering, London, which he was expecting in the bag. I gave the letter to Cavendish two days ago – on Monday.'

'I'm puzzled why you're raising this with me, Robert?'

'The letter contained a page torn out of a German calendar with one date highlighted: the twelfth of September. Any idea of the significance of that?'

Cooper felt a shudder run through his body. He shook his head and reached for his glass of wine, gripping the stem so tightly he worried it may snap.

'Seems odd to go to all that trouble and subterfuge just to send a page from a German calendar. Anyway, it's been on my mind a bit so thought I'd share it with you. You never know, do you?'

Cooper said, 'No, you certainly don't,' and, 'Good heavens… If that's the time we ought to get a move on before the bombing starts.'

–

Except that, unlike Wells, Cooper didn't head home. He waited at the end of Jermyn Street and bid farewell to Wells as he turned left towards Piccadilly Circus and then turned right into Haymarket.

Instead, Cooper returned to the office and explained to the duty officer that he needed to write up a report.

His mind went back to July and the interrogation of the IRA man, Sean Maguire: the man who'd tried to buy his way out of a death sentence by offering the date of the invasion. And the date Maguire had given?

Thursday, 12 September.

The same date that Wells had just told him was in the envelope from Stockholm. This new intelligence corroborated that.

Thursday, 12 September.

Today was Wednesday, the fourth.

Eight days to the invasion.

—

'Moscow is aware.'

It was the previous day – Tuesday, 3 September – and it was Archie's first visit to a new safe house in Islington: an end of terrace in the shadow of the Whittington Hospital. Archie felt uncomfortable: the house was filthy, with dirt covering the surfaces and mould on the wall. An unpleasant odour seemed to be coming up through the drains. All that Archie knew of this area – not one he'd normally frequent – was that the hospital had originally been built to treat smallpox, and he worried – irrationally, he knew – he'd catch something.

But Ivan Alexandrovich Morozov had made himself at home. He was in the back room with his shoes on the floor and his stockinged feet on the sofa and a large ashtray on a chair next to him. Archie sat on the edge of a chair opposite the Russian. He was too tense to relax and sit back.

'So, tell me, comrade, what news do you have that it's so urgent you see me?' Morozov had asked even before he'd sat down.

Archie told him about a communication he'd received from the German navy officer in Rotterdam, how it had come through the British embassy in Stockholm, and no, of course no one had suspected, and just in case people asked awkward questions he'd set up one of his colleagues to be the apparent recipient of the letter.

'And this is what was in the letter.'

'And what is this, comrade?'

'A page from a German calendar.'

'I can see that.'

'I asked the German in Rotterdam to let me know when he became aware of the date of the German invasion of this country. He agreed to let me know through a letter to be passed on through the British Embassy in Stockholm. It looks like the invasion will be on Thursday the twelfth of September.'

Morozov nodded and didn't look especially impressed or surprised. 'Moscow is aware.'

No 'thank you' or 'well done' or a reference to how important this intelligence was.

'How is Moscow aware?'

'You're not our only agent, comrade!'

Archie felt deflated. He'd expected a more positive reaction, and a bit of gratitude certainly wouldn't have gone amiss. In fact, he'd hoped they'd be so pleased with him that they'd agree to the request he'd been planning to make, to ask to lie low for a while. He needed a break from the pressure of serving two masters. If they'd asked him for how long, he was going to ask for six months but wasn't sure if that was pushing things.

'We gather intelligence from around Europe and then put it all together and analyse it. That is how our business works. When two, three four... who knows... sources of intelligence corroborate one another, then we know to believe that and act upon it.'

'So, others have identified the twelfth of September?'

The Russian didn't reply. Archie wondered about the other Englishman: the one called Cooper, or maybe Shaw, whom he'd been asked to look out for – the one who was also supposed to be working for the NKVD, but who they rather carelessly seemed to have lost track of. In May Morozov had shown him an unhelpfully blurred photo of this man, such poor quality that it was impossible to identify him. But in July he'd had his meeting at the Invasion Warning Sub-Committee and there'd been something about Malcolm Lyle which left him uneasy.

Archie had not been able to put his finger on what it was about Lyle that made him feel uneasy, and he didn't look like the man in the blurred photo, but then, no one looked like the man in the blurred photo. It was such poor quality. He decided to mention him anyway.

'Does the name Malcolm Lyle mean anything to you?'

Morozov frowned and shook his head. 'Who is he?'

'He works for something called the Invasion Warning Sub-Committee, which is based in the Old War Office Building in White-hall. I had to meet him when I returned from Rotterdam and there was something about him that made me wonder...'

'Made you wonder what, comrade?'

'Whether he could be this man Cooper.'

'And what made you think that?'

'Hard to say. Intuition, maybe?'

'And did he look like the man in that photograph I showed you?'

'No one looks like the man in that photograph.'

'Maybe you should try to meet him again. Arrange to meet and give him the date of the invasion. Find a way of dropping the names Charles Cooper or Christopher Shaw into the conversation. See how he reacts. But you'd better get a move on.'

'Why is that?'

Morozov held up the page from the calendar. 'Because if this is true, there are just nine days to the invasion.'

—

When he left the safe house, Archie walked up Archway Road past the smallpox hospital towards Highgate. It was a pleasant evening, and it would allow him plenty of time to be sure he wasn't being followed.

And to think.

And he thought about what he'd told Morozov: about how it was nothing more than intuition that had led him to suspect Malcolm Lyle.

And as he trudged up the hill and then into the more agreeable streets of Highgate, he thought more about what had caused this intuition.

If Lyle was indeed Cooper, and a Soviet agent – albeit a non-functioning one – then he, too, was a traitor.

Like him.

And like him, there'd be almost impossible to detect traits in his behaviour and demeanour. Almost impossible, but they'd be there: almost imperceptible tics, unexpected glances, an air of disguised unease.

Unseen perhaps to the human eye, but not to that of a fellow traitor. After all, it takes one to know one.

–

After his dinner with Wells from the Foreign Office on Wednesday, 4 September, Cooper had typed up his report on the meeting and the information he'd divulged about Gilbert Cavendish from MI6 and the invasion date.

He'd placed the main copy on Lieutenant Commander McConnell's desk and a duplicate copy on Pamela Clarke's, and decided it was too late and too risky to try and return home. He put up a camp bed in his office and tried to sleep.

But it wasn't just the discomfort that prevented him sleeping. There was something about what Wells had told him that didn't feel right. It felt unresolved, and it wasn't until the following afternoon – the Thursday – that he realised what it was. This was after he'd received considerable praise for his report and assurance it had been passed into the system, though without mention of the Cavendish connection. McConnell felt the situation was too sensitive to draw MI6 into it.

Cooper was on the bus home and was going down Baker Street, and as they passed the junction with George Street – no more than two or three hundred yards from his old office in Bryanston Square – he thought of Percy Burton. His mind went back to a particular meeting with Burton in what must have been September 1938.

Burton had confided in Cooper about a traitor – a well-placed Englishman working for the Soviets. At first, Cooper was worried Burton may be talking about him, but it was clear from the details Burton gave that it was another person and, in any case, they had a codename: Archie.

Burton's purpose in confiding in Cooper was that there was a frantic search on for Archie, and he was telling him because 'you may pick up some hint or clue about him'.

Archie, Burton said, had almost certainly been seen in Moscow in May 1937, and the same person who'd seen him then had come across him fleetingly in London in August 1938. They were reasonably certain, based on information from a Soviet contact, that he'd been in Paris in May 1938. The man who'd seen him in Moscow and then London thought he'd recognised him from Oxford, from a chess tournament in 1930 at Merton College.

Other colleges had taken part, including Oriel.

Oriel Engineering.

Cooper thought the name on the letter sent to Cavendish would provide the clue: Mr Oscar Smith. But he'd not been able to trace any Oscar Smith. Nor, for that matter, any company called Oriel Engineering.

But that appeared to be the connection: Oriel. The Oxford college connected to the traitor called Archie and, it would appear, the name he'd so foolishly given for the letter.

This pointed to Gilbert Cavendish being Archie.

Cooper couldn't decide on what to do with the information.

Of course, his most obvious course of action was to report the matter to McConnell first thing in the morning.

But as he relaxed in the bath that evening, he thought that if Gilbert Cavendish was indeed Archie, then that meant Cavendish was a Soviet agent. And Cooper's abiding fear was that the Soviets would discover him and get him working for them again. And if that happened, then he'd need to have some secrets up his sleeve.

Secrets like the identity of Archie.

You never know when you may need secrets like that.

He resolved to sleep on it and make his mind up in the morning.

But then in the morning, he got a phone call.

–

'Perhaps we should meet up.'

The voice on the other end of the line didn't introduce itself at first, but Cooper recognised the patrician tone and the confident upper-class drawl, and sure enough it was the man from MI6 who'd come to meet him in July after his mission to Rotterdam: the one somewhat ridiculously known as 'D4'.

He suggested they meet on the north side of Lambeth Bridge, on the strip of green alongside the Palace of Westminster. Cooper arrived five minutes early, but the man from MI6 was already waiting and shook his hand and seemed far more friendly than when they'd met a few weeks before.

They headed along the north bank of the river in the direction of Chelsea. A smattering of small talk, and Cooper said he hoped he wasn't being out of order, but was he really meant to call him by a letter and a number; D4 laughed and said, yes, it was all rather silly, wasn't it, and why not call me… John.

Cooper realised that whatever this man's name was, it certainly wasn't John, but then they were all playing a game, weren't they, so may as well go along with it.

So he asked John what this was all about, and John turned round to check no one was close.

'I thought you chaps ought to know that we've become aware of a date for the start of the German invasion. It's the twelfth of September.'

'Six days' time?'

John said yes and Cooper did his best to look shocked. It was the same date given to them by the Irishman and in the letter to Cavendish.

'A colleague of mine at the Service by the name of Gilbert Cavendish found this out from a good source of his.'

Cooper immediately thought how odd this was, because the man walking alongside him had hitherto been only known by a letter and a number, yet somehow he was able to bandy his colleague's real name about. It felt as if he was going out of his way to tell him the name.

'May I ask you, Lyle, whether the name "Charles Cooper" means anything to you?'

At that moment a double-decker bus passed them, allowing Cooper a moment or two to compose himself.

'Sorry, I didn't catch what you said.'

'I asked if the name "Charles Cooper" means anything to you.'

Cooper's heart was beating so fast he felt unsteady, but he managed a frown and the appearance of thinking carefully, and then shook his head.

'No, I'm afraid it doesn't. May I ask in what context?'

'Just generally… You know… someone possibly of interest to us. That's all. They may use another name: Christopher Shaw. Ring any bells?'

'Would that be Shaw with "a-w" or "o-r-e"?'

'I believe it's spelt "s-h-a-w".'

'I can check on our list of collaborators, if you like. Would that help?'

The man from MI6 looked disappointed and impatient to change the subject. The two of them stepped aside as a large man barrelled past them.

'You can do, but I doubt that's the kind of list he'd be on, to be honest. Anyway, it was just something of a long shot. Forget it.'

They walked on in silence as far as Vauxhall Bridge, when the man from MI6 announced he really must get a move on and it had been nice chatting and they really ought to do it again soon. And with that, he crossed Millbank and headed into Pimlico.

Cooper was unsure what to make of the whole business. He was shaken to the core by the mention of his name and his alter ego Christopher Shaw.

He sat on a bench, staring at the surprisingly fast-moving river as its colour changed from dirty blue to dirty green, and he tried to gather his thoughts. He'd certainly have to write up this encounter and would focus on the date, and on Gilbert Cavendish, but would obviously not mention Charles Cooper or Christopher Shaw.

He crossed the road and caught the 77 bus back to work.

He took a seat on the upper deck and enjoyed the view. As they passed the Morpeth Arms pub, he was convinced he spotted the man calling himself John from MI6 enter it. And he wasn't alone. Alongside him was a larger man, not unlike the one who'd hurried past them as they'd walked along the river.

–

'Do you think it was him?'

Ivan Alexandrovich Morozov pulled a face. 'It could be – it's hard to say. Remember, I've only seen a poor-quality photograph of him and read the descriptions of people who knew him.'

'Perhaps if you'd not been walking so fast.'

The Russian shrugged. 'But what it is about him that made you suspect he could be our agent, the man Cooper?'

'I told you, intuition.'

'And you gave him the date?'

'Yes.'

'That's something, at least. Now there's no excuse for the British not knowing the date.'

'And acting on it.'

'Hopefully. And you attributed this to Cavendish?'

'Of course. Hopefully any connection with me will be a tenuous one, if at all.'

'Why did you choose this place, comrade? We ought to have met further away from where you'd met him.'

'Convenience. It's haunted, you know? Used to be the site of a prison from where they transported convicts to Australia. There are still some of the cells in the basement.'

The Russian laughed loudly. The mention of prison cells appeared to have cheered him up.

Chapter 30

He spotted the Englishman and what he assumed was his wife in the park on a warm Sunday afternoon at the end of August, when he was enjoying a pleasant stroll with his own wife and children.

Nikolai Vasilyevich Zaslavsky was convinced he recognised him, and as he got closer, he was more certain. The one thing an NKVD officer based in the Foreign Intelligence Unit at the Lubyanka knew like the back of his hand was the names and faces of the intelligence officers among the foreign diplomats based in the city, and it was well known that George Banks was the MI6 Head of Station in Moscow.

Zaslavsky's first thought was that this was no chance encounter – that the Englishman had arranged to be there at the same time as him – but that seemed highly unlikely. It was the first time in a while that Zaslavsky had taken his family to this park, and Banks hadn't so much as glanced in his direction. And it was highly unlikely Banks would bring his wife with him on a clandestine assignment; it simply was too much of a risk if something went wrong.

It was, he quickly concluded, a coincidence.

Nevertheless, it was a coincidence that would need to be reported. Zaslavsky made a note of the time and of the direction George Banks had come from, and at the fountain he told his wife they'd turn round and head for the small lake, which enabled him to follow the Englishman from a safe distance and observe what he was up to. He memorised what Banks was wearing and what his wife looked like, just in case it wasn't his wife, because if that was the case then the NKVD would be absolutely delighted: that would open Banks up to all kinds of possibilities for blackmail. But Zaslavsky concluded that the woman with him was his wife, if for no other reason than the fact that they barely spoke.

Zaslavsky watched as they paused by a bench and the woman sat down. Banks walked over to the nearby ice cream stand, and he decided to follow.

This was how he found himself no more than a few feet from the Englishman, just one person between the two of them. And this was how he managed to fall into conversation with the Englishman.

He couldn't help but hear Banks struggle to order two ice creams in distinctively accented Russian, so he stepped forward and asked in English if he could help. Banks looked surprised and not a little suspicious, but told Zaslavsky what he wanted – one large strawberry ice cream and one small plain one – and they agreed it was a pleasant day and Zaslavsky translated the order.

And he left it at that. He broke all protocol by failing to submit a written report on the encounter within twenty-four hours and didn't even mention it to his senior officer in the Foreign Intelligence Unit. Instead, he hatched a plan.

It was one that had been forming in his head over the past eighteen months. Up until March of the previous year, Zaslavsky had been a senior officer in the OMS: the International Liaison Department of the Comintern, the Communist International. The OMS was the most secret department of the Comintern; its job: to carry out illegal and clandestine activities abroad. Then in March of 1939 the OMS had been disbanded. Many of its officers were purged, most of them killed.

Zaslavsky had been one of the lucky ones. He'd been transferred to the NKVD and for a short while he believed all was well. But it didn't take long to realise that was an illusion.

In fact, it became apparent that officers who'd joined the NKVD from other intelligence agencies were never entirely trusted. They were the ones regarded as expendable, useful scapegoats for any mistakes made by the organisation or for any operations that went wrong. Over time, Zaslavsky witnessed the overnight disappearance of many colleagues from within the NKVD.

He was beginning to doubt he'd survive much longer.

He needed a way out.

He did have a possible physical route out: he'd been attached for a few weeks to the NKVD bureau in Odessa and hoped to arrange a transfer there. Moscow never quite trusted Ukrainians and preferred to staff the bureau with native Russians. And from Odessa he could arrange a clandestine passage across the Black Sea to Istanbul. But that would require hard currency for the bribes – both to get him across the Black Sea and once he was in Istanbul, and for wherever he headed after that.

But getting that amount of hard currency was quite another matter.

And that was where his plan came in.

The following Sunday was 1 September, and he told his wife he had to go into work. At lunchtime he headed to the same park where he'd encountered the Englishman the week before. He was counting on George Banks being a man of habit. He'd heard that the British were a people set in their ways. And sure enough, at more or less the same time as the previous week, the Englishman and his wife appeared from the same direction and made their way to the same bench. There the lady sat down, then Banks joined the queue for ice cream.

Zaslavsky slipped in behind him. There were four people in front of him. He leant close to the Englishman and spoke quietly: it didn't do to be overheard conversing in a foreign language.

'Good afternoon, Mr Banks.'

George Banks turned around, looking shocked.

'May I speak with you, Mr Banks?'

Zaslavsky stepped away from the queue and the Englishman followed him.

'I have some information for you.'

'I don't know what you—'

'Information for the British government, Mr Banks.'

The Englishman blinked and wiped his forehead.

'In exchange for… funds… I can supply the British government with the names of two British traitors.'

Zaslavsky could tell Banks was a professional because he now looked calm, as if he was just having a chat with an acquaintance. 'What traitors?'

'British men who are in important positions in London and are working for the Soviet Union.'

'Go on.'

'Obviously, anything substantial I tell you will have to be in exchange for cash. I'll want Swiss francs.'

'That is something we would be interested in but would take some time to arrange. Maybe if we meet here this time next week – the eighth of September?'

'Very well.'

'But I'd need something more to go on.'

'Their codenames are Archie and Bertie.'

Zaslavsky could have sworn he spotted a flicker of recognition on Banks's face when he said 'Archie'. He hoped Banks didn't ask him too many questions, especially about Bertie, the young man called Charles Cooper he'd personally recruited as a Soviet agent, though the Englishman hadn't realised at the time he'd become a Soviet agent. As far as Zaslavsky knew, Bertie had long ceased contact with the NKVD station in London.

'And you can supply their full names and other details?'

'In exchange for the Swiss francs, yes.'

'Very well, I shall see you here next Sunday.'

–

The admirals of the Kriegsmarine gathered in a private room above a bar in an alley just off Hildebrandstrasse on the evening of Thursday, 5 September. The impending invasion of England, just seven days away, was the only topic of conversation. The consensus among the admirals was that, despite its imminence, it still felt improbable. But much of the planning was complete, and by and large the barges and other vessels that would cross the Channel and the North Sea were in place. The weather forecast was good and the landing places had been identified.

There was little sense of anticipation, though. If anything, the mood was one of foreboding. None of those present could quite believe that Operation Sea Lion would end in anything other than disaster. The fact that they'd warned of this was of little consolation.

'It can't be too late, can it?' one of the admirals asked, and someone asked him what he meant.

'Too late to stop it.'

'On what basis, Klaus? We've given our advice and provided caveats and warnings until we're blue in the face. If the meteorological reports changed and forecast storms, maybe... but that's not the case now, is it?'

'There's a possibility, you know.' It was Vice Admiral Otto Schniewind. 'If it was known that the British are aware of the date of the invasion and are expecting us, then maybe the Führer would have second thoughts.'

'And how on earth would they know that?'

'Are you all aware of the situation regarding Korvettenkapitän Arthur Klein?'

Most of those around the table nodded, but one or two shook their heads.

'Klein was a highly regarded officer: an engineer and a very smart man. We transferred him to Rotterdam to co-ordinate the acquisition and conversion of the barges – nearly two thousand of them – for the invasion. We believed he was doing an excellent job, but it transpires he'd been a communist for many years, and a spy for the Soviet Union. In the middle of August, he was back here for a series of meetings relating to Operation Sea Lion, and on the fourteenth of August – a Wednesday – he was present when Grand Admiral Erich Raeder announced that the invasion was to be on the twelfth of September. Early that evening, Klein was observed entering the rear of a shop on Woyrschstrasse, where we now know he was meeting a man called Ernst Schwarz, another KPD member and a Soviet agent.

'Schwarz had been running Klein for a number of years. He was the man who passed on intelligence from him to Moscow. Schwarz had come under suspicion and was being watched. After that meeting on the fourteenth of August, Schwarz was arrested and Klein returned to Rotterdam. It wasn't until the following Wednesday – the twenty-first – that Schwarz finally revealed Klein's identity, and we arrested him that evening in Rotterdam. He was brought back to Berlin to be interrogated by the Gestapo and was executed last Thursday, on the twenty-ninth. A stain on the loyal and patriotic reputation of the Kriegsmarine, gentlemen.'

'That is indeed shocking, Schniewind, but I don't follow how that means the British can be aware of the invasion date?' Rear Admiral Kurt Fricke looked as surprised as everyone else present.

'Klein met with Schwarz a few hours after the grand admiral announced the date of the invasion, so we have to assume he gave the date to Schwarz, but as Schwarz was arrested immediately, he wouldn't have been able to pass this on to Moscow. But we also know that

Schwarz revealed the name of another communist agent in Rotterdam, a Dutchman called Marcus van Leeuwen. This man was held by the Gestapo in The Hague, where he was interrogated and then executed. We're told that during his interrogation, van Leeuwen said something about Klein meeting a British agent who travelled to Rotterdam in the middle of July.'

'So, he was in contact with the British?'

'So it would appear. We've only just become aware of this.'

'And what date did you say this was, Otto?' asked Rear Admiral Kurt Fricke.

'I understand it was on or around the seventeenth of July.'

'But he wouldn't have known the invasion date then, would he?'

'No, but we do know he was in contact with the British, as well as the Soviets. Between his finding out the date of the invasion and his arrest he had a full week to pass on the date of the invasion to the British before we caught up with him. There must be a very good chance they're aware of it.'

'But we don't know that for certain, do we?'

'Maybe not, but it's a reasonable assumption nonetheless,' said Schniewind. 'If we were to let it be known we believe the British know the date, there's a possibility this will lead to the postponement of Sea Lion.

'And we'll be saved the humiliation of defeat. After all, we're now just seven days from the invasion. This is urgent.'

There was a muttering of agreement around the table.

'And all thanks to Klein's treachery,' said someone.

'Indeed… Naturally, one does not condone treason in any shape or form,' said Schniewind. 'But one would be foolish to disregard the fact that Klein's act of treason may well have served a purpose.'

–

On Monday, 9 September Admiral Wilhelm Canaris gathered the Abwehr senior officers based in Hamburg in a secure room in the basement of the west wing of their headquarters on General-Knochenhauer-Strasse.

As if to emphasise the importance of the meeting. he was joined by his deputy, General Hans Oster.

The admiral spoke at length and in quiet, measured tones. He wanted to express, he said, his gratitude and appreciation for *all* the hard work put in by *all* the officers here in Hamburg, and *no one* should think for even one minute that their efforts went unnoticed.

'And now, my dear colleagues, we have reached a crossroads.'

He paused and looked around the room, looking more of an academic than a distinguished former U-boat commander.

'You are all aware by now, of course, that the invasion of Great Britain is scheduled to commence on Thursday, in three days' time. We'll have to see what happens on the day and thereafter, but whatever the outcome, your efforts in getting us to this point are not insignificant.'

Helmut Schröder glanced around the room. He doubted he was the only person there who thought that Canaris was being particularly enigmatic and choosing his words with extreme care. It was noticeable that he was hardly brimming with enthusiasm when he spoke of Operation Sea Lion.

There was a reception of sorts after the meeting: nothing too grand, drinks and a selection of cold meats and cheese. Schröder was about to leave when Günter König stopped him in the corridor.

'Can we talk, Schröder?'

Schröder stopped and turned round as König came alongside him.

'Of course, Günter.'

'I didn't mean here, obviously. Perhaps in your office?'

As soon as they entered it, König shut the door.

'What kind of game are you playing, Schröder?'

'I beg your pardon?'

'You know full well what I mean. I've suspected for a while that you were up to no good, but I couldn't put my finger on it. But then with Canaris' performance today, announcing the date of the invasion as if he were announcing a funeral, and all the caveats he used... that clarified my thoughts. To be blunt, Schröder, I suspect you've been playing some kind of double game all along, and have probably been encouraged in it by Canaris and Oster. Everyone knows they're hardly enthusiastic supporters of the Führer. They don't want Sea Lion to succeed, and you've been helping them by jeopardising our so-called espionage operation in Great Britain.'

Schröder managed a noisy laugh. 'And how on earth do you imagine I've done that, König?'

'By sending over such an incompetent and hopeless bunch of so-called agents who were bound to fail. Tell me, how much intelligence are we getting from them? My sense is that those who didn't get caught almost upon arrival just gave up. Did you ever see any Marx Brothers films? They'd have made better spies!'

'I'm very surprised to hear you watched films with Jews in them, König! I hope you've reported that.' Schröder managed to sound pompous and for a moment the other man looked worried.

'Shut up, Schröder, you know what I mean. I believe you knowingly selected, trained and sent over a bunch of clowns. You've been undermining Sea Lion all along.'

'You've definitely been watching too many films, Günter. You have what my mother used to call a fertile imagination. If you're going to make such outrageous claims, then my advice would be to have a shred or two of evidence to base it on. If you can't manage that, then I suggest you shut up.'

König looked furious.

'It's treason, Schröder. That's what you're up to – treason. Don't worry, I'll find proof.'

Schröder sat quietly at his desk as König stormed out, and then walked over to the window and watched as he hurried to his car and drove away.

Only then did he leave his office and walk along the corridor to the office being used by Admiral Canaris. Canaris told him to come in and sit down.

'You look a bit flustered, Schröder. What is it?'

'I think we may have a problem, sir.'

—

They either came for you at your home very late at night or in the early hours of the morning, or they picked you up as you arrived at work, siphoning you off from the queue at the entrance or with a firm hand on yours as you opened your office door.

In Nikolai Vasilyevich Zaslavsky's case, it happened as he left the lift on the third floor of the Lubyanka. A large man blocked the doors as they opened, and when Zaslavsky said, 'Excuse me,' the man pushed him back in and another man pushed the button to take them to the lower basement, which was ominous in itself.

It was Monday, 2 September, the day after his second meeting with George Banks in the park, and so he assumed he'd been spotted and tried to think up a plausible explanation.

But an hour into his interrogation it was clear this was nothing to do with the Englishman. It turned out a contact of his in Paris from his OMS days had handed a list of Communist Party members in the city to the Nazis, and now they were looking for someone to blame.

The fact that he'd had no contact with this man for three years and minimal contact before that counted for nothing.

He was a former OMS officer now in the NKVD.

Never trusted.

His days always numbered.

A matter of time before they came for him.

It would be wrong to say that Zaslavsky was resigned to his fate, because he was distressed beyond words. He may never see his family again, and no doubt they'd be evicted from the comfortable apartment near the Kirov metro station.

All he could do was concentrate on being compliant and not argue too much, and hope against hope that he'd be treated leniently and sent to a gulag. If they caught even an inkling of his meeting with the Englishman, then there was no question he'd get a bullet in the head in this very building.

–

When the Russian didn't turn up as arranged at the park on the following Sunday afternoon – 8 September – George Banks went straight to the British Embassy on Sofiyskaya Naberezhnaya, close to the Moskva River.

In normal circumstances he wouldn't have taken what the Russian had said too seriously, but the very fact that he'd mentioned Archie was of enormous importance. Banks was only too aware of a British traitor known as 'Archie' who'd been in Moscow in March 1937, and the fact that the Russian had used his codename meant the intelligence he was offering was probably genuine.

And that, in more or less the same breath, he'd spoken of another traitor called 'Bertie' made this an even more pressing matter.

Banks encrypted an urgent telegram to London:

FURTHER CONFIRMATION OF EXISTENCE OF ARCHIE STOP BE AWARE OF ANOTHER SOVIET AGENT CALLED BERTIE OPERATING IN LONDON STOP REPEAT, ALERT TO TRAITOR CODENAME BERTIE STOP PERHAPS IN TANDEM WITH ARCHIE STOP REGRET UNABLE TO PURSUE CONTACT WITH INFORMANT STOP

And that was that. He returned the envelope bulging with Swiss francs to the safe in the ambassador's office and found himself resigned to what would have to be chalked up as another near miss.

–

It would be fair to say that all hell broke loose at MI6 headquarters on the morning of Monday, 9 September when the telegram from Moscow was decrypted.

Within minutes it was on the desk of the Chief. Within minutes of that, Sir Stewart Menzies had called in his senior officers and shared with them the news that they were now searching for two traitors.

'Archie would appear to have a pal: Bertie. It goes without saying that finding this Bertie must now be an absolute priority. How's Phillips these days, Piers?'

'Still looking for Archie, sir.'

'You'd better break the news to him that he's now looking for a Bertie too.'

Phillips had taken the news calmly. Piers Devereaux had explained they had very little to go on. But the fact that someone who knew about Archie had revealed there was also a Bertie, and the two were apparently connected, was quite shocking.

'The Chief wants all stops pulled out. Ask around, Phillips. See if any of your chums in the other services have ever come across a Bertie.'

Phillips had gone to see Simpkin at MI5 straight away and shared the shocking news. Simpkin said he'd never come across a Bertie, but promised to check all the files and share the name with other colleagues.

And then he'd taken a taxi to Whitehall to see Lieutenant Commander McConnell at the Invasion Warning Sub-Committee.

'Never come across the name, Phillips,' he'd said, shaking his head. 'Wife's brother's a Bertie, but he's as far removed from a Soviet agent as could be imagined... races pigeons.'

'It's a codename.'

'Yes, of course I realised that. Are you all right for me to share this, put the word out among my chaps?'

Phillips replied that he saw no harm in that, so McConnell decided to brief his staff in small groups. Pamela Clarke and Charles Cooper were among the first.

Cooper was so shocked to hear his own Soviet codename – Bertie – that it took him a moment or two to realise they were talking about him. During that moment or two he managed to just about compose himself.

'And there're no further details on this Bertie?'

'I've told you all we know, Cooper. His existence has been alerted to us and he's linked with that other Soviet agent, Archie.'

'So, no name, no clues, no—'

'As I said... no.'

'So, another traitor, sir?'

'It would appear so, Pamela, yes.'

She shook her head and Cooper quickly joined in and said, 'Shocking.'

'They seem to be everywhere, sir. Archie, the Nazi collaborators... this other traitor... "whilst bloody treason flourish'd over us".'

'I beg your pardon, Pamela?'

'Shakespeare, sir. *Julius Caesar*, Act Three, Scene Two, if I remember correctly.

'"O, what a fall there was, my countrymen!
Then I, and you, and all of us fell down,
Whilst bloody treason flourish'd over us".'

Epilogue

The exact date on which Hitler agreed to the postponement of the invasion scheduled for 12 September remained unclear. It may well have been that he had taken on board the doubts of his advisors in the army, air force and navy in early September. or maybe he'd even waited until a day or two before the planned invasion date. The confusion over exactly when it was abandoned summed up the uncertain nature of it.

As far as those in London were concerned, Sea Lion wasn't so much postponed as just never happened. And in the way of these things, there was no shortage of people in and around Whitehall and the higher echelons of the armed services and the intelligence agencies prepared to take credit for their part in Sea Lion never happening.

And when it became clear that the threat of invasion was over, there was likewise no shortage of people with an opinion as to the reason for this. Many attributed it to a serious strategic error made by the Luftwaffe in the conduct of the Battle of Britain. In their effort to destroy the RAF and thus protect the skies during the invasion, the German air force had been attacking RAF Fighter Command bases throughout the south of England with considerable success. Victory was in their sights. But on 25 August there was an RAF bomber raid on Berlin and an incandescent Hitler demanded revenge: he ordered the Luftwaffe to switch their attacks to London, which began on the night of 7 September. And although the heavy bombing of London cost upwards of 40,000 lives and caused an enormous amount of destruction, it did have the unintended consequence of relieving pressure on Fighter Command, allowing the RAF to regroup and ultimately able to claim victory in the Battle of Britain.

On 17 September Hitler officially authorised the postponement of Sea Lion, and a few weeks later – on 12 October – he agreed to the redeployment of the forces gathered for the invasion. As the Soviet Union had always feared, he now began to turn his attention eastward. If he couldn't conquer the United Kingdom, the Soviet Union would take its place. On 18 December 1940, Hitler Directive 21 was issued in great secrecy, outlining Operation Barbarossa, the invasion of the Soviet Union.

In Germany the consensus was that the Führer had taken his time, but had finally come round to accepting the folly of Operation Sea Lion: that the notion of transporting tens of thousands of men across the English Channel and the North Sea was too fraught with risks, especially after their failure to eliminate the RAF.

In the Kriegsmarine headquarters in the Shell-Haus, near the Bendlerblock in Berlin, there was an enormous sense of relief. The admirals had never been confident they could safely transport that many men and that much equipment while the Royal Navy still controlled the waves.

In Hamburg, Helmut Schröder was confident he'd played his part, too. He was clear in his mind that helping to deliberately sabotage the German intelligence operation in Britain had emphatically not been an act of disloyalty, or even treason. On the contrary, he had no doubt that in doing so – by selecting sub-standard agents and sending them over so ill prepared – he'd ultimately most probably saved many thousands of German lives and helped ensure the war didn't come to a sudden and ignominious end.

As far as he was concerned, he'd helped save Germany from a humiliating defeat.

There had been the problem of Günter König, of course. After Canaris' meeting with his officers in Hamburg, Schröder's disagreeable Abwehr colleague had confronted him, convinced that Schröder had been playing a double game, as he described it.

When he told Canaris what König had said. the admiral was clearly worried – so worried, in fact, that he instructed Schröder to deal with the problem 'as a matter of urgency'. When Schröder asked precisely what he meant, Canaris replied in an uncharacteristically blunt manner.

'Get rid of him.'

General Oster had also been in the room, and he took Schröder aside.

'We cannot afford any delays, Helmut. König is clearly a great danger to us. He drinks, I understand?'

'Schnapps, sir.'

'Take this.' Oster handed him a small brown glass bottle containing what appeared to be a coarse white powder.

'It's strychnine, Helmut. I suggest you buy a bottle of *geist* schnapps, one made from rowan berries. That has a particularly sour taste, so hopefully he won't spot the added ingredient. There're two hundred milligrams in here. Half of it should be enough to kill him. When he's gone, telephone this number and the matter will be dealt with.'

'And you just happened to have this on you, Herr General?'

Oster allowed the thinnest of smiles. 'I find that in my position, carrying it is a wise precaution.'

Helmut Schröder telephoned König at his office in the Polizeige-fängnis Fuhlsbüttel. He wanted to apologise for any... misunder-standing, he said. He'd been put under the most intolerable pressure by the admiral, and he'd appreciate the opportunity to... confide in him?

'Come up now, Schröder.'

'I'd really appreciate your advice, Günter. I shall bring a good schnapps with me – a bottle I've been saving for a special occasion.'

–

König seemed so distracted – excited, even – that Schröder was about to confess all, he hardly noticed as Schröder poured the schnapps with his back turned. Schröder's hand shook as he stirred the strychnine into the large measure and handed it to König, who downed it in one go and held out the glass for a refill.

'Strong stuff, Helmut. It's been a while since I had a rowan berry *geist*. Where did you say you got it from?'

'An old friend, Günter.'

Oster had told him that the poison could take up to a quarter of an hour to work, so Schröder spoke slowly and in unnecessary detail of how the admiral had suggested the type of agents he recruited, and what type of training, and of how by the time he suspected something was wrong it was too late and he realised he'd been incriminated and... König had been enthusiastically making notes, but now he'd stopped writing and was blinking as if his vision was affected. He was sweating profusely and his complexion had quickly turned from pale to almost a crimson red.

He looked even more like Hitler now. Manic and disturbed.

'I feel… somewhat sick, Helmut… Perhaps I should…'

He loosened his tie and struggled to breathe, then closed his eyes and his face creased in pain and then he slumped face down on his desk, his body convulsing as he appeared to choke. Schröder waited two or three agonising minutes until Günter stopped moving and then checked his pulse. He was dead.

Schröder locked the door and then telephoned the number Oster had given him.

Stay where you are. Only open the door when someone knocks three times and says they've come to repair the light.

They arrived within half an hour. Three men in blue-grey overalls pushing a large crate on a trolley.

Leave now. Everything is in hand.

–

A similar fate befell Bridget McKearney.

Since her arrest in July, she'd been interrogated at length by various people. She knew that some of them were from Special Branch, but they were from other agencies, too, and never introduced themselves properly.

She'd been told early on that the more she co-operated, the more that would count in her favour at her trial. When she asked what trial that might be, a man who said he was a solicitor was brought in to explain that she'd be tried under the new Treachery Act. She'd replied that surely that wouldn't apply to her as she was Irish, but the man assured her it did and furthermore, if found guilty under the said Act then the only penalty was death.

By hanging.

So, McKearney told them all she could about The Group: names and the various contacts she had, and how she communicated with Germany – though most of what she told them they already appeared to know.

Then she was sent to a prison apparently on an army camp somewhere in the Midlands, where she was kept in a basement cell and told nothing.

The consensus in London was that they weren't going to get much more out of McKearney. She'd served her purpose. Special Branch were of the view that she should be put on trial, but MI5 and the Invasion Warning Sub-Committee thought even a trial *in camera* could compromise national security.

So, on a blisteringly hot afternoon towards the end of September, Bridget McKearney was given a mug of strong tea. Soon after finishing it she noticed she felt sleepy and relaxed, and when she was led from her cell, she was in a compliant mood. She was still compliant when she was led into another cell, and it was only when she was in it that she noticed a noose fashioned out of sheets attached to a ceiling fitting, and by then it was too late, and she stopped being compliant.

Suicide, such reports as there were, said.

–

Sean Maguire worried he'd told the British too much. He knew he shouldn't really have told them anything at all, but the trouble was, once they'd mentioned the possibility – more a probability, if he was honest – of a death sentence... well, that certainly concentrated the mind.

The problem was that they were most persuasive and at times quite friendly, and he found it hard to know when to stop. He told them the date of the German invasion of Britain, which he soon regretted because that seemed to be what they really wanted to know, and he worried he may have revealed it too soon.

And then the superintendent from Special Branch called Docherty – a good Irish name, as it happened; he'd said he knew of a few Dochertys back home in County Wexford – told Maguire they weren't pressing charges, and he was being sent back to Ireland.

He thought that was the end of it. When he arrived in Dublin, he told them he just wanted to go home and they said he'd be able to, but would first need to stay in the safe house in Tallaght where he'd stayed before travelling to Britain. They had to debrief him.

Charles Cooper had been instructed to sort Maguire out. He could see why – they could hardly have him wandering around Ireland broadcasting the date of the German invasion to all and sundry – but what he was being asked to do seemed quite extreme.

Yet he did as instructed. Special Branch had an IRA informer in Dublin called Ronan, and Cooper travelled to Northern Ireland on an RAF flight and was driven to meet Ronan at a safe house near the border in County Tyrone. Ronan understood what he was to do and was grateful for the generous expenses given him to cover the cost of his trip north 'and a bit extra'.

Back in Dublin, Ronan let it be known in all the right places that he'd heard that Sean Maguire had been very helpful to the Brits, and this backed up what the IRA was also hearing from trusted sources in London.

On his second night in Tallaght, Maguire was told everything was fine now and he was going back to County Wexford. When he expressed surprise that he was travelling there so late, it was explained that there was a car waiting, so unless he wanted to go by bus the next day then he ought to get a move on.

They headed south out of Dublin in the direction of County Wexford, but somewhere south of Wicklow they came off the main road and when Maguire asked why, one of the men sitting a bit too close to him in the back said it was to get petrol, even though they'd just passed a petrol station.

This was the point at which Sean Maguire began to worry. It didn't feel right. Perhaps he shouldn't have told the Brits anything. Perhaps he should have asked not to be sent to Hamburg. Perhaps…

Then he spotted a sign for Magheramore, which he knew was a long beach, and he asked why on earth they there were, but the other man – also sitting too close to him on the other side – said to shut up, and when the car stopped soon after that Maguire was dragged out and down to the beach, and when they ordered him to kneel down he felt his knees sink into the wet sand, and when he looked up the moonlight picked out the slow movement of the waves in the distance, and he thought about the Germans invading Britain in these rough seas, and then he felt the revolver being held against his head and someone grabbing his hair, and when he screamed, the crashing of the waves drowned it out, along with the shot that followed.

–

Charles Cooper was not the only person at the Invasion Warning Sub-Committee who felt that the other members of The Group – those whom they could identify and track down – ended up being treated too leniently.

The feeling in Whitehall was that with the threat of a German invasion over, the danger of a Fifth Column was less acute. Certainly, having a group of people who were collaborators was distasteful, to say the least, and they'd need an eye to be kept upon them, but they were no longer a priority.

Cooper and Pamela spent much of September and early October compiling a definitive list of members of The Group based on the existing list and what Bridget McKearney had told them. Quite a number of those on the list were subsequently arrested and detained under the Wartime Regulations, some of them, indeed, for the duration.

As satisfying as that was, Cooper couldn't help thinking that had the German invasion been successful, these would have been the very people who'd have helped the Nazis run Britain.

A couple of years in prison seemed hardly to fit the crime.

–

Ivan Alexandrovich Morozov had devised a plan, and when he carefully outlined it to Archie at the end of September, it was clear he regarded it as an inspired plan, quite possibly the work of a genius.

This was not an opinion shared by Archie, who listened to it with mounting horror.

'So, to summarise, comrade… We will identify a suitable flat, one we have never used before, and which suits our rather specific purposes. We will search for a place with a room where we can place a two-way mirror and have space to observe the lounge through it. The place will be rented in your name. You will invite Malcom Lyle to it and tell him it is where you stay when you're in London.

'Once in the flat, we will photograph Lyle from behind the two-way mirror. We will then be able to show good-quality photographs to people in Moscow who knew Charles Cooper and will be able to confirm whether it is him. Or not, as the case may be.'

'And what do I do with him when he's in the flat?'

'Chat with him, Archie.'

'About what?'

'You'll find something to talk about, I'm sure. Maybe indicate you're looking for a move and are looking for his advice… I don't know. Just make it plausible so he doesn't suspect anything.'

Archie thought it was a ridiculous plan, flawed in more than one respect.

But then Morozov discovered there was no one left in Moscow who actually remembered Charles Cooper well enough to identify him from a photograph.

Nikolai Vasilyevich Zaslavsky, the OMS officer who'd recruited Cooper in Moscow in the summer of 1937, had been the victim of a most untimely purge of former OMS officers in the NKVD and had been executed in early September.

Ernst and Ida Maurer, the couple who'd spotted Cooper in Switzerland in the spring of 1937, had last been heard of in Berlin when the war began but had since disappeared.

And then there was Eduard, the man who'd originally assessed Cooper in Berlin and arranged for him to visit Moscow. He was a highly experienced agent and would certainly have been able to identify Cooper. But Moscow told him that approaching Eduard Vladimirovich was quite out of the question. He was 'somewhere in southern Europe… operating in the most clandestine of circumstances', whatever that meant.

Wasn't everyone operating in the most clandestine of circumstances?

As for Osip, the OMS *rezident* in London… Annoyingly, Morozov had himself killed Osip in a flat in Acton in London the previous March. He had to say that, at the time, he had thought Osip would be of more use back in Moscow where he could be properly interrogated. But he doubted that even if that had been the case, he'd still be alive now.

There was another possibility which for a while he was hopeful of – Misha, the publisher at Goslitizdat Moscow who'd been the 'front' for Cooper's recruitment. But Misha, it turned out, had been purged in the winter of 1938 and sent to a camp in Siberia where, most annoyingly, he'd died the following winter.

Eventually Morozov concluded it was both too risky and pointless to entice this Malcolm Lyle to the apartment and possibly alert him to something being up on the off chance that he may be Agent Bertie, especially as no one would then be able to confirm his identity. He called Archie to a meeting at the safe house in Archway to give him the news. But there was another matter to raise first.

'What news do you have on the German invasion, Archie?'

'Oh, there'll definitely be a German invasion.'

'Really?'

'But where the invasion is of, that's another matter. I'd say that there's now far less of a chance of them invading this country, but a greater chance of them invading yours.'

'What makes you say that? You have specific intelligence?'

'Every indication we have is that the invasion of this country has been postponed.'

'Postponed or abandoned?'

'I couldn't tell you, I'm afraid. As far as we can tell at the moment, all the mechanics for the invasion are still in place – the troops, the ships and the barges. Our aerial reconnaissance confirms that. But who knows? Certainly, they're missing the ideal conditions for crossing over. Next week we're into October and only a fool would attempt such a large-scale crossing in the winter.'

'And what makes you say that they'll invade the Soviet Union?'

'You. You told me that the Soviet Union was concerned that if Germany didn't invade this country, then they'd turn their attention to you. The more one thinks about that, the more one takes the view that is true.'

In fact, Archie had recently written a very well-received paper on this, the thesis being that Hitler was, above all else, an imperialist intent on expanding the borders of the Reich. If he couldn't do that to the west then he'd do it to the east.

Morozov gazed out of the window, clearly in a reflective mood.

'And what about Malcolm Lyle, this plan of yours...? Have you found the right apartment yet?'

Morozov shook his head. 'Do you hunt, Archie?'

'Of course.'

'You probably hunt on a horse. When I was taught to hunt it was in the freezing forests, and my grandfather always said that the most successful hunter waits for the prey to come to them rather than the other way round. You need to be intuitive and, above all, patient. Now is not the right time, but sooner or later Bertie will come to us, whether he's this Malcolm Lyle or someone else. Then we'll have him.'

'And that's it?'

'For the time being, yes. That's it.'

–

Rather like Operation Sea Lion, the Invasion Warning Sub-Committee faded away: there one day, gone a couple of weeks later.

It had been evident through the summer of 1940 that its days were numbered; more than one intelligence agency and branch of the armed forces had their eyes on this slightly anachronistic but surprisingly efficient outfit operating out of a basement of the Old War Office Building in Whitehall.

In fact, it was a touch more complicated than that: there were those who felt that, with the prospect of an invasion now apparently gone, the Invasion Warning Sub-Committee had served its purpose. It could now be dissolved.

The administrative staff – the secretaries, the clerks – along with the draughtsmen who compiled the maps and the people who developed and analysed photographs, were easily absorbed elsewhere.

Most of the intelligence officers had been with the Invasion Warning Sub-Committee on attachment from the armed forces, which is where they returned.

That left a small number of officers, including Pamela Clarke and Charles Cooper, and one afternoon late in September the two of them were called into McConnell's office.

'You are, of course, aware of our fate.'

They could hardly have been more aware because even as the lieutenant commander spoke, the noise of offices being dismantled and furniture being moved along the corridors was all too apparent.

'I'm to be head of Royal Naval Intelligence in Scotland. It gives me a good deal of satisfaction to say that there has been much interest from various agencies for your services. I am pleased to say that you will both be joining the Ministry of Economic Warfare.'

McConnell leant back and smiled and Cooper was just grateful that he was apparently not under suspicion and wasn't being linked with

Bertie, but he couldn't help thinking that he knew nothing about economics and couldn't be less suitable for such a transfer.

Pamela clearly thought the same.

'Seriously, sir? Whatever my strengths are, economics isn't one of them. What are we meant to be doing there, sir – look after the distribution of ration cards?'

McConnell laughed loudly and said they'd soon realise it was nothing of the sort.

'In July, very much at the instigation of Churchill, various bodies involved in combatting the Nazis in Occupied Europe were brought together – from the Foreign Office, the War Office and MI6. The new organisation is known as the Special Operations Executive, and its role is to liaise with resistance groups in Europe and conduct its own sabotage and espionage operations. It's organised through different sections, each relating to a different country or part of Europe. The SOE comes under the aegis of the Ministry of Economic Warfare, hence your transfer there.

'Up until now they've been operating out of St Ermin's Hotel, but I'm told they're moving to their own premises at 64 Baker Street in a couple of weeks.

'You'll both be based there. Your full duties will be explained to you in due course, but I can tell you that you'll both be working for Maurice Morgan. He's a very bright chap and quite personable, too. An academic, I understand, speaks half a dozen languages.

'Maurice wants you two for a unit he's setting up to be based in the SOE headquarters, which will support the different country sections as and when they need such support. Sounds jolly interesting. You're to meet Maurice tomorrow morning and start next week, once everything's done here.'

McConnell said that was all and as they left, he asked Cooper to remain behind.

'There is the question of your name. When you joined us Murray was on your trail, which is why you became Malcolm Lyle and have remained so. You now have the choice of continuing to be known as Malcolm Lyle or reverting to Charles Cooper. Any thoughts?'

Cooper certainly did have thoughts. What he couldn't tell McConnell, of course, was that the Soviets knew both of his previous identities: Charles Cooper and Christopher Shaw. It would be too dangerous to go back to one of those identities, and now seemed a good time to dispose of Malcolm Lyle. A new identity would put more distance between himself and the past.

'Possibly a new identity altogether would be a good idea, sir?'

'Glad you mentioned that. Maurice suggested it. How does Simon Draper sound to you?'

'Sounds rather like a cricketer, sir!'

'And, one very much hopes, like a first-class spy, too.'

–

Now that British intelligence services were aware of the existence of a second traitor, the hunt for Bertie and Archie intensified.

Both Phillips and Harvey from MI5 suspected Archie worked for MI6, possibly even one of the seven MI6 officers promoted at the beginning of 1940.

Not just these seven, but eight when one included Charles Whittaker, who'd been unsuccessful in the interviews when his affair with an older woman who was involved with the Liberal Party was discovered. This and his failure to get promotion made him a suspect.

Then there was Tommy Browning, who'd not been successful initially in applying for promotion because Harvey from MI5 had raised concerns about his homosexuality, which was seen as making him vulnerable. But Browning was well connected: his father had been killed at Cambrai, and the old boy network intervened successfully to have him reinstated.

But in Phillips' mind, the doubts remained. Another suspect.

There was, of course, Timothy Kerr-Walters, who'd committed suicide in May, days after his suspicious financial affairs had been brought to the attention of MI6. There were all kinds of unusual and unexplained deposits in his bank account, along with a link to a Dutch communist on the run in London for whom he'd obtained a false identity card.

There were those who were convinced that Kerr-Walters was Archie, but Phillips wasn't so sure; in any case, the Chief wasn't minded to have a dead man labelled as a traitor.

But that didn't prevent him remaining a suspect.

Edward Slater – the *Honourable* Edward Slater, indeed – wasn't a suspect as such, but it had become apparent that he was a biddable type and notably insecure, the kind of person always keen – perhaps too keen – to be friends, the type always picked last at games. Phillips sensed this insecurity came from the fact that Slater was the second son of an earl, so had to make do without the title and other privileges enjoyed by his older brother. And as such, he'd inherit a bit of farmland maybe, perhaps with a house if he was lucky, and possibly a painting or two, but when it came down to it, being the second son of an earl was worse than second best and certainly not worth the paper it was written on.

It gave Slater a chip on his shoulder and a sense of resentment against society that he deemed had dealt him a rough hand. But none of this had shown in his work.

Gilbert Cavendish was perhaps the most inoffensive and indeed inconspicuous of all those appointed, and in many ways the least likely candidate for a traitor; that was until he'd been identified by a chap called Lyle at the Invasion Warning Sub-Committee as the conduit for intelligence from a German source identifying the date for the invasion. It had never been clear how Cavendish had established this link and that made him a suspect.

And then there were the remaining three: Rex Larkin, Anthony Stokes and Walter Morley.

None of them had given any obvious cause for suspicion. On the contrary, all had been described variously as 'solid', 'resourceful', 'clued-up' and 'first-class'. Hardly words one associated with treason.

But the more Phillips thought about the situation, the more he thought that if this Archie had managed to operate so successfully yet clandestinely as a Soviet agent for so long, then by definition, he was clever, cunning and above all, careful – unlikely to be the kind of person to make mistakes.

In truth, he told Harvey from MI5 over a drink at his club one evening, they were no closer to identifying Archie.

'And it's not just Archie, is it, Phillips? The whole business is now compounded by the second traitor – this Bertie – being thrown into the mix.'

To his regret, Phillips replied a touch too sharply. 'Yes, one is well aware of that, thank you very much, Harvey.'

He apologised and Harvey said not to worry, he quite understood what a difficult business this all must be – a strain, even – and would he like another drink?

'Do you think these two chaps know about each other?'

'Which two chaps?'

'Archie and Bertie, Phillips. Could they be acting in tandem?'

'I honestly don't know, Harvey. They may not even be aware of the other's existence. I doubt it, though, because Moscow prefers to isolate its agents. Keep them in their own little world. They're not keen on the idea of their agents palling up, if you know what I mean. They could even turn out to be rivals, who knows?'

Both men fell silent and contemplated their drinks and the enormity – and indeed, gravity – of the task ahead of them: hunting for two traitors.

'But at least we appear to have seen off the invasion, eh?'

'True – and wouldn't it be ironic if one of those traitors helped us in that?'

Author's Note

The Second Traitor is a work of fiction, and therefore any similarities between the characters in the book and real people are unintended and should be regarded as purely coincidental.

Having said that, there are some exceptions, which I'd hope would be obvious, including historical figures such as Churchill and Stalin and others who are referred to in the text, though not appearing as characters themselves. We do meet a collection of German Kriegsmarine (Navy) admirals: Admiral Wilhelm Canaris; Grand Admiral Erich Raeder; Vice Admiral Otto Schniewind; and Rear Admiral Kurt Fricke. All these actually existed in the roles as described in the book, but I've used them here for fictional purposes. Likewise, with the head of MI6 (the British Secret Intelligence Service), Sir Stewart Menzies. It seemed to me that if I didn't name him then I'd have to have a fictional head of MI6, which would have lacked credibility given how well known he is. All other named MI6 officers are fictional, including any of them who may or may not be Archie. Another real character who we meet in the book is Ivan Maisky, the Soviet ambassador to London during the war. Regarding the Kriegsmarine: the restrictions placed on the German navy after World War I by the Treaty of Versailles are as described in the book, and the Kriegsmarine did indeed attempt (with considerable success) to circumvent this by using front organisations such as NV Ingenieurskantoor voor Scheepsbouw in The Hague (as described in Chapter 7).

At the heart of *The Second Traitor* is Operation Sea Lion, the German plan to invade the British mainland. Operation Sea Lion is absolutely genuine. As mentioned in the book, Sea Lion was announced in Hitler's Directive 16 in July 1940, although planning had been underway for months prior to that. What was never clear was the exact date (if one existed) for the invasion – I've seen perhaps a dozen dates in September

305

1940 which were believed to have been the chosen date. Therefore, I chose Thursday, 12 September as the date in the plot. Likewise, it is unclear exactly when the invasion was postponed. That seems to have happened somewhere between late September and 18 December 1940, when Hitler's secret plans for the invasion of the Soviet Union were announced. All the planning for Sea Lion – details such as the ports to be used, their routes, the proposed landing areas and the procurement and conversion of barges – is, I hope, accurately reflected in the book. I've also tried to put Sea Lion in the context of what else was happening in connection with it: the Battle of Britain; the tensions in Berlin; the replacement of Neville Chamberlain by Winston Churchill; and the fact that there was a British 'peace camp' in which the Duke of Windsor certainly played a role.

If you'd like to read more about Operation Sea Lion I can recommend three non-fiction books on the subject: *Operation Sea Lion* by Leo McKinstry (John Murray, 2014); *Invasion 1940* by Peter Fleming (first published 1956, various publishers); and *Invasion of England 1940* by Peter Schenk (Conway Maritime Press, 1990).

Other than The Annexe (which featured prominently in my previous novel, *Every Spy a Traitor*), all the organisations featured in the book are genuine – including the little-known Invasion Warning Sub-Committee, which actually did exist until some point in 1940 and was located in a basement of the Old War Office Building in Whitehall, which is now a luxury hotel. I was able to visit the hotel in early 2024 and look around the basement to get a sense of where the Invasion Warning Sub-Committee was based.

Most of the locations in the book – such as towns and street names – correspond to how they were during that period. One fictional place is Flockham, the village in Oxfordshire featured in Chapter 2.

The links between the IRA (the Irish Republican Army) and the Nazi regime which feature in the book are reasonably well documented. At the centre of this is Seán Russell, who was the IRA Chief of Staff up to 1939. The following year he visited Berlin to discuss the IRA's co-operation with prominent Nazis. He travelled from Berlin to Hamburg, where he and another IRA member were trained by the Abwehr. Russell boarded a German submarine – U-65 – at Wilhelmshaven in August 1940 but died (apparently of natural causes) before they reached the Irish coast. Extraordinarily, a statue of Russell stands in a Dublin

£4,650 in 2024 ($5,800 or €5,415). As far as I can tell, the UK interest rate during the Second World War was around 2%.

People often ask me about the research process for a book like this. I do try, where possible, to visit as many of the locations as I can. In the case of *The Second Traitor* I spent some time in Hamburg, and I'm very grateful to my guide there, Evan Ladd from Tours By Locals. In Hamburg I managed to get into the building which was the HQ of the Abwehr but is now luxury flats – we were soon asked to leave! I also visited the site of the Stadthaus, which was the base of the Gestapo in the city, and where there's now a disappointingly small memorial museum squeezed in between the luxury shops. They do, however, publish *The Stadthaus and the Hamburg Police during the Nazi Era* (Metropol Verlag, 2021).

I also visited Rotterdam, and would like to express my thanks to Ron Brand and his colleagues at the impressive Maritime Museum in the city, and to the historian Jac Baart for generously sharing his expertise on the city's involvement in Operation Sea Lion.

I'd especially like to thank my agent, Gordon Wise, and his colleagues at Curtis Brown. Gordon has been enormously supportive and encouraging for many years now, and I'm delighted to be able to express my appreciation. Likewise, my sincere thanks to my publishers, Canelo, who couldn't have been more supportive and professional with the manner in which they've handled all three of my series published by them – eleven novels – prior to this one. In particular, I'm most grateful to my editor at Canelo, Craig Lye, and his colleagues, including Iain Millar.

I'd like to thank Steve O'Gorman for his skilful copy-edit. Steve managed the not inconsiderable feat of producing a copy edit with a sense of humour. It is very rare for an author to smile while reviewing a copy-edit.

And thanks, too, to everyone who helped me with aspects of the book and answered seemingly odd questions as I was writing it.

And, finally, to my family – especially my wife, Sonia, my daughters and sons-in-law, and my grandsons – for their encouragement, understanding and love.

Alex Gerlis
London, December 2024

park – almost certainly the only statue to a Nazi collaborator in a Western European city.

And on the subject of the Abwehr... The plot in the book that German military intelligence may have deliberately sent over incompetent agents to the UK is one put forward by some German historians in recent years, who believe that this was a deliberate act of sabotage by Abwehr officers based in Hamburg. At the heart of this group was Herbert Wichmann, on whom the character Helmut Schröder is loosely based.

Arnold Visser – the Nazi spy in the book captured in Lydd – is loosely based on a real German spy called Karl Heinrich Meier, who's a good example of the incompetent agents sent over by the normally highly efficient and careful Abwehr. Meier landed on the Kent coast in early September 1940 and was arrested after he knocked on the door of a pub in Lydd early in the morning, asking for a pint of champagne cider. This, along with his wet trousers and shoes, foreign accent and lack of familiarity with British currency, alerted the landlady. Meier was hanged at Pentonville by Cross and Pierrepoint, the same men who execute Visser early in *The Second Traitor*.

And talking of executions: Arthur Klein is executed at Plötzensee Prison in Chapter 28. Plötzensee was a dreadful place, where countless atrocities were carried out. I recommend this website if you wish to find out more: The Bloody Nights of Plötzensee – Gedenkstätte Plötzensee (gedenkstaette-ploetzensee.de).

The Group is a fictional organisation, although the existence of British fascists and pro-Nazis is not. They would have been eager collaborators had the Germans invaded this country. The Regional Commissioners described in Chapter 8 did exist. If you want to read further on this subject, I can recommend *Nazi Spies and Collaborators in Britain 1939–1945* by Neil Storey (Pen & Sword, 2023) and *Hitler's British Traitors* by Tim Tate (Icon Books, 2018).

The Venlo incident referred to in Chapter 21 was responsible for the undermining of British Intelligence in the Netherlands throughout the war. HMS *Codrington* in Chapter 18, which takes Manfred to the Netherlands, was indeed one of the two Royal Navy ships sent over in May 1940 to evacuate the Dutch royal family.

At various points in the book Timothy Kerr-Walters visits moneylenders. When he borrows £100, that would equate to around